DEATH LIKE ME

Translated from the Italian by Peter Burnett

Copyright © 2016 by Rita Monaldi and Francesco Sorti
Translation copyright © 2016 by Rita Monaldi and Francesco Sorti

All rights reserved.
No part of this publication may reproduced, stored, or transmitted in any form, or by any means, electronic, mechanical or photo copying, recording or otherwise, without the express written permission of the authors.
ISBN: 978-17-9026-177-2

Cover designer: Studio Jan De Boer
Cover picture: Cecil Beaton, Portrait of Mona Williams at Capri © Sotheby's

IP *for* AMAZON Direct Publishing
https://tinyurl.com/ycuj6h7w

MONALDI & SORTI

DEATH LIKE ME

A Novel

ILLUSTRATED EDITION

JP

for AMAZON Direct Publishing

TO THE READER

The contents of this book are 100% pure fiction. While the characters correspond in part to the names of men and women who really lived, they do not represent real entities, just the bare historical and esthetic memory those men and women left to successive generations. What *they* really were and did remains explicitly outside the purview of this novel – as should be the case with every genuine piece of storytelling.

CONTENTS

SETTINGS — 9

CAST OF CHARACTERS — 9

APPETIZER — 11

CAPRI, SUMMER 1939
The Filly from Kentucky — 15
The Nature Prophet — 24
Recognition — 33
Woman like Me — 41

ROME, SUMMER 1957
SANATRIX CLINIC, ROOM 32
A Splendid Woman — 49

CAPRI, SUMMER 1939
Dog like Me — 63
House like Me — 70

CAPRI, SPRING 1935
The Englishman in Paradise — 79

BLIGNY, JULY 1918
War like Me — 99

CAPRI, SPRING 1935
Accursed Tuscans   113
Captains Outrageous   118

CAPRI, SUMMER 1939
Malaparte's skin   127
Indifference   132
The Black Prince   134
The Good Man Lenin   137
The Black Wind   145
Night like Me   157

ROME, SUMMER 1957
SANATRIX CLINIC, ROOM 32
The Eyes of Death   165

CAPRI, SUMMER 1939
God Shave the King   171
Du Côté de chez Carmine   179
Roses of Flesh   187

ROME, JUNE 1924
The Technique of Revolution   199

CAPRI, SUMMER 1939
Of their Sweet Deaths   211
Prison Escapes   226

ROME, SUMMER 1957
SANATRIX CLINIC, ROOM 32
Once More, a Splendid Woman   231

CAPRI, SUMMER 1939
Blood like Me   237
Naked Men   249
Adolf Kaputt   267

BLIGNY, JULY 1918
SAARBURG, AUGUST 1914
The Blind Sun   281

CAPRI, SUMMER 1939
Warm Beds   293
Almost a Crime   299
Damp Fire   310

PRATO, 1912
Earth like Me   317

CAPRI, SUMMER 1939
Awakening   325
Quisisana Chaos   326
Human Meat   336
The Traveling Companion   345
Tomorrow's History   349
The Amazons   358

ROME, SUMMER 1957
SANATRIX CLINIC, ROOM 32
¡Viva la Muerte! 375

CAPRI, SUMMER 1939
Cricket in Capri 383
The Guardian of Disorder 403
The Great Imbecile 409
Don Chameleon 414

CAPRI, AUGUST 31ST, 1939
The Defense of Freedom Never Comes Free 443

CAPRI, SEPTEMBER 1ST, 1939
Moussolini 463

ROME, SUMMER 1957
SANATRIX CLINIC, ROOM 32
Death like Me 467

AUTHORS' NOTE 475

PHOTOGALLERY 483

SETTINGS

The island of Capri
A room in a Rome clinic
Battlefields at Bligny and Saarburg, France
The city of Prato, Italy, and surroundings

CAST OF CHARACTERS

LEADING MAN

Curzio Malaparte (1898-1957), *Italian writer, collector of women and trouble.*

BEHIND THE SCENES

Benito Mussolini (1883-1945)
Adolf Hitler (1889-1945)
Stalin (1878-1953)
Lenin (1870-1924)
Warren G. Harding (1865-1923), *US President 1921-1923*
Harry F. Sinclair (1876-1956), *American oilman*
Maksim Gorky (1868-1936), *Russian writer and revolutionary, a refugee in Capri*
Aleksandr Bogdanov (1873-1928), *Russian writer and politician, rival to Lenin*
Hermann Goering (1893-1946), *Commander-in-Chief of the Luftwaffe and Hitler's designated successor*
Doctor Edmund Forster (1878-1933), *military psychiatrist. He treated the young Corporal Adolf Hitler in 1918.*

SUPPORTING CHARACTERS

Febo (?-1942), *Malaparte's dearest buddy*
Pamela Reynolds (1915-1935), *young English poetess*
Richard Reynolds (1868-1947), *father of Pamela, member of the Fabian Society*
Percy Winner (1899-1974), *American journalist, old friend of Malaparte, official in the Office of War Intelligence (OWI)*
Mona Williams (1897-1983), *American millionairess, star of illustrated magazines*
Count Eddie von Bismarck (1903-1970), *Mona Williams´ lover*
Prince Francesco Caravita di Sirignano (1908-1998), *womanizer and spendthrift*
Axel Munthe (1857-1949), *Swedish doctor and novelist*
Chantecler (1905-1981) *Jeweler and dandy, hero of Capri nightlife*
Edwin Cerio (1875-1960), *former mayor of Capri*
Edda Mussolini Ciano (1910-1995), *Mussolini´s daughter*
Prince Philipp von Hessen (1896-1980), *Hitler´s intimate*

ALSO FEATURING

Galeazzo Ciano (1903-1944), *Italian Foreign Minister and Mussolini's son-in-law*
Noël Coward (1899-1973*), composer of musicals and writer of comedies*
Gracie Fields (1898-1979), *English singer and actress*
Barbara Hutton (1912-1979), *American heiress*
Giacomo Matteotti (1885-1924), *martyr of anti-Fascism*
Amerigo Dumini (1894-1967), *Italo-American hit man, killer of Matteotti.*

And others...

Appetizer

"We've been looking for you all day, Signor Malaparte," said Marelli, the tall bald one. "We need to talk to you. Criminal proceedings have been instituted against you, and the charge is homicide."

The two guys from the OVRA kept staring at their shoes. They looked so ill at ease, you'd have thought the bad news was for them, not me. It's not every day that Mussolini's secret police get to gatecrash parties of the rich and famous, with the band belting out Cole Porter, waiters serving Chablis by the gallon and everywhere, dishes overloaded with canapés.

Like all low-ranking snoopers they must have been paid peanuts, and there they stood, frothing at the mouth and wide-eyed at all that was going on around them.

"So I'm accused of murder. And who is it I'm supposed to have killed?"

"Signor Malaparte, this isn't the time or the place for such matters. Be so good as to make yourself available for a talk with us tomorrow. Would 2 o'clock suit you?"

"I've never harmed anyone. Except during the war, when I was at the front."

"Of course, of course, as you say… But we'll talk about that tomorrow. You're a writer, aren't you?"

"You know that already."

Once they'd got over their initial unease, the two men from the OVRA grabbed handfuls of tiny vol-au-vents garnished with Mozzarella, olives and capers and gobbled them down in unison.

"So you'll have nothing to worry about. You won't be short on imagination!"

And they disappeared into the crowd, guffawing, with their mouths still half full.

CAPRI, SUMMER 1939

The Filly from Kentucky

"You're cruel, Malaparte. I've invited you a thousand times, but tonight's the first time you've deigned to come."

While Mona Williams was greeting me in the driveway of her Capri villa, my eyes kept switching from her marvelous aquamarine eyes to the enormous Cartier sapphire pendant straining at her diamond necklace.

This was Mona's favorite visiting card when receiving guests: a reminder that she had married Harrison Williams, a man worth 600 million dollars.

Her collection of ex-husbands included Henry James Schlesinger, the most eligible bachelor in Kentucky, and James Irving Bush, the handsomest man in America. Yet for Mona happiness had never come from love, but from Chanel, Lanvin, Balenciaga and those other deities who three years before had elected her "the world's best-dressed woman." Whatever Mona did, the papers went crazy about it, whether it was taking tea in bedroom slippers in her Paris residence, throwing a party in her enormous mansion on Fifth Avenue, or galloping across the meadows of her immense Oak Point estate at Bayville, Long Island. To crown her dreams, in other words to give the Europeans a lesson in elegance (she, the daughter of a Kentucky groom), Mona had bought herself the most beautiful and luxurious home that a human mind, or at least Mona's mind, could conceive of.

With Harrison's death (although this, no one could yet foresee) she was to attain her apotheosis, marrying her private interior decorator, Count Eddie von Bismarck, and thus becoming the Countess Mona Travis Strader Schlesinger Bush Williams von Bismarck. Not bad for the daughter of a Kentucky groom. And here they were now, she and her famous Cartier sapphire, welcoming me at the entrance of her Capri villa.

"Mona, tesoro, you're quite right," I said, excusing myself and kissing her hand, "You've invited me a thousand times. But you know perfectly well that I accept invitations only from the thousandth one onwards."

"So it's quite true what they say about you, Malaparte. You're insolent and presumptuous."

"Only when I'm facing a woman who's too irresistible. Please, please, tell me your husband's far away in America."

"Yes, but he's on his way here to beat you up," retorted Mona, giggling with some embarrassment, since she regularly cheated on her beloved Harrison, who never came to Capri and got his own back with Coco Chanel. For a fleeting moment she'd mislaid the fake English accent with which she disguised her vernacular. Meanwhile she had forgotten me and was waving to someone else: behind me, down the long pergola-covered drive, came the much-loved singer Gracie Fields and her husband Monty Banks, escorted by a throng of friends.

Mona, Gracie and Monty exchanged kisses, embraces and little squeals as though they'd not seen each other for years (while in fact they'd lunched together only three days before). Without so much as a glance for the friends who surrounded them, all three disappeared laughing up one of the innumerable leafy paths that wound their way across the park.

Il Fortino, as Mona's residence was called, was one of the most exclusive corners of Capri, and its foundations stood on no less than the ruins of a villa that had belonged to the Roman Emperor Augustus. Over the centuries, these walls had sheltered the cream of the planet's bipeds: monarchs, heads of state, bankers and artists of unsurpassed fame. The lady of the house liked to remark casually that this had been Bizet's home, and that the composer had been inspired when writing one scene from *Carmen* by the sound of the waves breaking on the private beach below the villa.

More than a villa, Il Fortino was in truth a ranch, but a ranch with no cattle, just one magnificent filly from Kentucky. Spread over a great terraced area sloping down to the bay between Capri and Naples, Il Fortino consisted of three separate buildings and a luxuriant park of some twenty-five thousand square meters. Giving onto the northeast coast of Capri, it enjoyed an immense view over the entire Bay of Naples, all the way to Vesuvius; and, looking inland, as far as the eye could see, a panorama of the sinuous hills of Capri and their constellation of little white houses with domed roofs, all designed in that unmistakable style peculiar to the island, which I have always found so adorably boring.

Mona had made the Fortino her own little personal empire. Walled like a fortress, impossible to photograph from outside, the property included a stretch of coastline where its owner could land without setting foot in the rest of the island and having to mingle with the common people. She did not even depend on others for water, since Mona stored rainwater in enormous cisterns in which she would bathe, and she claimed that the secret of her beauty lay in those rainwater baths and nothing else. Mrs. Harrison Williams, as Mona was called in *Vogue*, had caught the gardening virus and had filled the park with so many plant varieties that you might at times have thought you'd wandered into the Amazon rainforest.

If you really want to understand what I am writing, you must have set foot at least once in some great Capri villa, with its garden, its flowerbeds and shady groves. On Capri every plant species grows to twice the regulation size, like prehistoric monsters, and the aroma of the plants and flowers is so absurdly intense that there's a risk of becoming drugged and falling stunned to the ground. When you first land in Capri, if you're sensitive to perfumes, you'd do well to wear a plug on your nose, or something of the sort. That evening, the effluvia of the wisteria, the roses, the magnolias and the newly mowed lawns of the Fortino, mixed with gusts of salt and seaweed-laden sea air, came close to suffocating me. The wind blew through the crests of the trees like an orchestra of flutes, emitting the gentlest sigh, almost a whisper, a secret murmuring of women's voices.

"D'you see that guy? It's Malaparte!" Sudden whispering spread through a little group of American girls as I passed.

"Malaparte? Who's that?"

I sheltered from the wind behind a tree to light a cigarette while the girls gossiped on.

"The handsome guy in a tux, the one with the brilliantine and spats. Haven't you heard of him? Why, he's a phenomenon."

"And what's so special about him?"

"He's a writer. And completely nuts. Ran away from home at sixteen to join up during the Great War. After the Armistice he became a radical Fascist, but then he had the nerve to make fun of Hitler and Mussolini. They say the Nazis burned his books in Germany. He ran away to France, but the Italians arrested him. Now Mussolini's leaving him free only because he's too well-known a writer. When he started, no publisher would touch him, he had to pay to get his books printed. But now he's a star, women are crazy about him. If he's mad at somebody, he challenges them to a duel, with sabers. And he always wins."

I walked along the driveway, lit by two great rows of torches. The asky, where a little sunlight broke through, was furrowed with dense, glutinous yellow-to-amber clouds. The stream of guests arriving seemed unstoppable, the chattering and laughter were like the buzzing of a swarm of giant wasps. The torchlight, stirred by the evening breeze, deformed the lineaments of the faces transforming them into oblong masks: blackish African masks, Javanese masks, Dyak headhunters' masks from Borneo.

"Ciao, Malaparte! Bernard Grasset sends his greetings from Paris."

I returned the greeting automatically, waving my hand in the vague direction of those grotesque faces, without managing to recognize them; maybe it was the Duke Diaz, or the Marchese Medici del Vascello, or one of the innumerable cousins and nephews of the King of Italy who liked treating themselves to an outing to Capri from time to time: the Duke of Pistoia, the Duke of Ancona, the Duke of Bergamo or the Duke of Spoleto, all of them so very distinguished yet indistinguishable, like the eggs of Capri's famous quails.

Drawn onward by the flood of guests, I caught a passing glimpse of Virginio Gayda, the all-powerful, all-Fascist and ultra-racist editor of the *Giornale d'Italia*, who was laughing with a glass of wine in his hand, and proclaiming in a loud voice that England was finished; he didn't know that he had barely five more years to live, for soon war would break out and one day a bomb would blow him to smithereens in his own house in Rome, just as he was taking an English lesson.

Clearing a gangway for myself with my elbows, I made it first to the entrance of the main reception room, then to the library. This was a huge oval room with enormous picture windows giving onto the garden, furnished with a mix that veered from Louis XV towards the Rococo. Count Eddie von Bismarck, Mona's officially accredited lover, passed by, greeting me with a polite wave of the hand. He had been taken on by Mona's husband as decorator and master of ceremonies because he was a genuine European aristocrat, and also because he was homosexual, so that with Mona, who loved her villa, her jewels and her garden far more than she loved men, he'd not be getting up to much.

I liked Eddie von Bismarck. He hated Hitler, Nazism, the stupidity of Nazism and the stupidity that had in those years triumphed in Germany. There's only one thing worse than a cruel people and that is a people both cruel and stupid. Eddie was the grandson of the great German Chancellor Bismarck, who may have had many defects but was not stupid. Count Eddie von Bismarck may have been a penniless nobleman, but he was one of the rare German aristocrats, generals and civil servants who realized that Hitler was mad, and could already foresee war, defeat and the collapse of their old world.

"Hello Eddie, what news from the old country?"

"Bad news, Malaparte, nothing but bad news. It's like living in a nightmare, everyone's terrified. Sometimes people disappear from circulation without explanation and never return home. But no one breathes a word, they're all complicit. No one dares speak out."

"Here too in Italy, there are plenty of things that can't be written or said."

"Yes, but you're human. Nazism is inhuman, while Fascism is still human," said Eddie, sipping his Bloody Mary. "Mussolini is a human being. He has a feeling for music. He plays the violin."

"I don't know whether Fascism is human. And Mussolini's a dreadful violinist. His playing sounds like the death throes of a cat. Don't drink too much, Eddie."

"You can count on me. Malaparte, d'you think there'll be war?"

"Surely not, Eddie."

A little further off, a piano could be heard. At the keyboard, that charming rascal Noël Coward, a great chum of our hostess, was crooning *I went to a Marvelous Party*. Four or five splendid young girls in search of Prince Charming were disporting themselves around the piano, the sort of girls who are always to be found at the Acquasanta golf club in Rome. They kept filling Noël's glass, passing him the ashtray and flirting outrageously, in the hope that he would carry them off that very evening and soon they'd be on a plane to Broadway, to Hollywood, to making their fortune in America. Quite indifferent to these graceful creatures (he was more interested in men) Noël went on tinkling away distractedly at the keyboard and chatting with anyone who came within range.

"Stop, Malaparte! I've news for you: the Duke of Kent's mad about your books."

"Really? I wonder how he can possibly like them."

"To tell the truth, so do I. Maybe it's because he's not yet read them."

"Splendid, if that's the case, tell him to keep it up."

"What did you make of Mussolini's speech yesterday?"

"I didn't hear it, Noël. So what interesting things did the Duce have to say?"

"Nothing. As usual, he had nothing interesting to say. I simply adore Mussolini, there's no one quite like him when it comes to coherence."

"You're right, Noël, he's a champion of coherence."

"Listen to this song, Malaparte, it came to me here in Capri. Tell me if you like it."

> *Why must the show go on?*
> *It can't be all that indispensable.*
> *To me, it really isn't sensible*
> *On the whole,*
> *To play a leading role,*
> *While fighting those tears you can't control.*

Then he suddenly stopped, fumbling for the next words, and grimacing in embarrassment as though to excuse himself, with an indefinably comic overtone, and the girls around the piano all burst out laughing. Noël Coward really was a charming rascal.

"You've a splendid refrain there – you really must build it up into a complete song though. Toodle-oo, Noël."

"Wait a moment, Malaparte! D'you think there's going to be war?"

"That's for sure, Noël. There'll be war and Hitler will conquer Europe."

Noël Coward smiled rather weakly, he couldn't see whether I was joking or not. He was launching into his next song, while a liveried waiter served me a glass of white wine, when I felt something hot and viscous sticking to my back, between the shoulder blades. It was hot violet breath, the breath from the look of someone staring at me from behind. I turned.

"Good evening, Malaparte. Glad to see you back in Capri."

It was Axel Munthe, good old Axel, the famous Swedish doctor, who had become a worldwide celebrity thanks to his tacky book of memoirs, which had sold by the million. Munthe had been on the island so long that he'd become a walking, talking lump of Capri, a Capri rock that went around with a beard, a large mustache, dark glasses, a hat and a walking stick.

"Good evening, Doctor Munthe, the pleasure is all mine."

He was sitting in an armchair, leaning on his stick and wearing a pair of blind man's dark glasses. In Capri he had built himself an enormous sun-kissed villa with panoramic views, but he preferred living in the dark in an antique stone tower, surrounded by the wind, his dogs and his birds. Munthe did not care for human beings; he liked only Capri's birds. He became animated only when he heard one of them twittering, and then he'd point his nose upward, towards the treetops, like a gun dog. Spending a fortune, he had bought an enormous stretch of the Anacapri hillside, high up, in the most mountainous part of the island, in order to create there a refuge for passing migratory birds, safe from Capri hunters. He was a true gentleman, the epitome of generosity.

"Never would I have expected, Doctor Munthe, to find a man of science like yourself at an event as frivolous as a party at Mona Williams' place."

"My dear friend, you must not forget that I'm a solitary fellow, and from time to time I must get away from my prison and habituate myself to human company all over again. After which I return to the shadows, to my birds and my dogs. You must come and visit me sometime."

"I shall, I promise", I said, melting into the crowd, "meanwhile remember me to your birds."

Munthe and I had spoken to one another in French; he spoke only broken Italian, he'd never managed to learn it properly. Half the inhabitants of Capri spend a lifetime on the island without speaking a word of Italian: the English and the Americans, because they mix only with one another, the French, out of laziness, the Germans because they're quite incapable of learning. In Axel Munthe's case, the affectation was for theatrical effect. He spoke French and feigned blindness to give himself an air of suffering and mystery, in keeping with his self-bestowed role as the romantic and impenetrable Nordic genius. I was, I think, the only one to have understood that he could see perfectly well. That evening I had turned towards him precisely because I'd felt him staring between my shoulder blades. His was the look of a man with eagle eyes, a look that bored right into objects, one that could even see through bodies.

Yet there was no reason to be scared, I thought, for Capri is a wonderful place, where so many people care for me.

More and more guests kept squeezing into the rooms of the villa in search of drinks and canapés. No time to draw breath between one greeting and the next, and I was beginning to feel ill at ease. People are always accusing me of being an exhibitionist, and perhaps they're right, but they don't know that I prefer to exhibit myself before no more than four or five persons at a time.

Suddenly, an impatient rumble rose in unison from the milling crowd at the Fortino: darkness had enveloped the party. It was the usual blackout that struck Capri unfailingly in the early hours of the evening, and would go on until the Fascist government made its mind up to provide better electric and telephone lines from the mainland. The blackout lasted a couple of minutes, during which nothing could be seen in the reception rooms of the Fortino but the orange embers of cigarettes and dark silhouettes bumping into one another and laughing; then the light returned.

A hand gave me a friendly pat on the shoulder.

"Malaparte, now what a surprise! I thought you were in Eritrea. I read your war correspondent's reports in the *Corriere della Sera*. Yet here you are in Capri!"

"I was in Eritrea a while ago. My way is to experience things first, Arturo, and only afterwards to write about them."

"I'd say a *long* time afterwards. Your Eritreans will have had time to fade since then."

Arturo Assante, Neapolitan lawyer and journalist, was a wide-awake fellow who always knew everything about everyone. That evening he was insinuating, in the friendliest manner possible, that I was writing my reports from the front at home, without ever having gone there. Obviously, there was some truth in this, but only some. I did indeed go to war, but I continued writing my articles in the months that followed, so that readers had the impression that I was still at the front. What's more, at war I took part in the fighting, shooting and risking my skin, while the other Italian journalists lay low well behind the rearguard.

"Have some champagne, Malaparte!" said Assante pointing out a waiter bearing a trayfull of coupes.

"Champagne? No thanks. Reminds me too much of when I was an officer on war service."

"You drank champagne during the war?"

"Champagne's a region in France. In 1918 my soldiers died there, at Bligny," I answered drily, and moved away, taking advantage of the arrival of my friend Edwin Cerio.

The German machine guns cut us down one by one, with a steady stream of bullets. Then the blast of a caliber 50, the hill blown in two, the sky darkened by a tidal wave of mud. Half the battalion buried alive, screams, wailing. Dig in, at once. My shovel hits a strange ball. Pull the severed head out from the helmet and drop it in the waiting sack, along with the other bits of flesh.

Bligny 1918. As I approached Edwin Cerio, memories were tormenting me like old bullets lodged in my skull.

✑ ✑ ✑

The Nature Prophet

Cerio was one of the few Italians on the island I truly respected. He was cultured, witty, at ease in society, and generally we got on very well. Precisely for that reason, I felt a little peeved when he too greeted me with a joke.

"Good evening, Signor Massullo," said he, miming a bow, with that ultra-serious expression he took on when jesting. Only a slight tremor of his little white goatee betrayed his amusement. He had spoken in a loud voice, so as to be overheard by as many people as possible.

"Signor Malaparte, I beg your pardon," I replied.

"But they tell me here in Capri that you're building a house at Cape Malaparte."

"I'm building a house at Cape Massullo and I've decided to call it Cape Malaparte. D'you think that's forbidden?"

"Well, then I'll call you Massullo. D'you think that's forbidden?"

"I'm entitled to my name."

"And we Capresi are entitled to keep our place names. If we can't keep the old name of the rock where you're building your palace, we'll label *you* with it."

"My house is no palace. It is... like me. Hard. Severe. But free. And stop calling yourself Caprese, you with your English mother, your Argentine wife and your American sister-in-law!"

Cerio ended up smiling, and after toasting one another we embraced like brothers, just as we did whenever we met on the streets of Capri. Many guests had been present at our little performance, and they greeted our final reconciliation with applause.

Cerio was something of a Nature prophet. He had been Mayor of Capri for three years and had tried hard to protect the island's coasts and hills from the big contractors and hoteliers who were getting their hands on Capri in those days and starting to cover it with bricks. At that moment we were joined by Giorgio Cerio, Edwin's brother, and Mabel, his splendid American wife. For Mabel, Giorgio had dumped Jenny, his former wife, likewise American, and likewise beautiful and frightfully rich. It had been such a scandal in Capri, but it all calmed down after Jenny committed suicide.

"Come outside!" called Giorgio and Mabel, "Barbara Hutton's arriving."

"All right," I said "let's go and meet her."

We went out into the park. The orchestra had been ordered by Mona Williams to play only Cole Porter, because he was a good friend of hers. Yet the dance floor had suddenly emptied: in little groups, everyone was walking down the slope that led to the sea, amidst the perfume of the pines, the myrtles and the broom. By now, it was dark, and in the distance, a sort of luminous whale had appeared in the sea, an enormous fish full of chandeliers, phosphorescent eyes and gilded filaments. This was the *Warrior*, Barbara Hutton's yacht, the world's largest. Mona had sold it to her not long before and now its new owner was gaily sailing the world's oceans. Babsie Hutton, America's youngest and wealthiest heiress, had a crew of 45 sailors and this enabled her calmly to dedicate herself to her favorite sports: having fun, throwing money to the wind and marrying the wrong men.

I went down the slope that led to the beach chatting with Mabel Norman. Like all women who are too rich, Giorgio Cerio's wife was worth nothing as an artist, and yet she was a fascinating woman.

"Malaparte, how long will you be staying in Capri? It's been ages since we've seen you around here."

"I'm off tomorrow."

"Tomorrow! Why, what's the rush?"

"I've got heaps of work to be doing in Rome, it's all been building up during those months I spent in Eritrea. I just came to check that work on the house at Cape Massullo is going according to plan. I'll be seeing the master builder tomorrow."

"What are you going to call your house? Don't tell me you'll be giving it some silly little name like *Villa delle Rose*."

"I'm calling it House like Me."

"Now, there's a fine name for you."

"I know. It's a fine name because that's its true name."

No sooner had we gotten to the rocks than we heard applause and loud greetings. The *Warrior's* launch was about to land. Standing in the boat, between two rows of muscular sailors, wrapped from head to foot in a blanket, was the gorgeous Babsie Hutton.

The moment the launch beached, Mona Williams, surrounded by four torchbearers, advanced on Babsie with a squeal of jubilation. A cheer went up from the multitude, as though George Washington had just landed on the banks of the Delaware.

After Barbara Hutton, the launch disgorged a motley group of her English and American friends, producers, directors and actors. Only Lady Milbanke had remained on board the *Warrior*, Barbara explained thoughtfully, because Lady Milbanke had a headache, and Lady Milbanke had such dreadful headaches.

"Malaparte, have you met Babsie Hutton? If you like, I'll introduce you. She's a darling," said the Prince of Sirignano.

"Babsie Hutton? No thanks, I'm not interested," I replied, "I'm getting married."

"You? Married?" exclaimed Sirignano, wide-eyed, "With your beautiful widow, your Virginia Agnelli? Are you joking? Don't tell me her family have given you their blessing…"

"No, old man, it's not her I'm marrying. I'm marrying my house on Cape Massullo. As soon as it's finished, I'll go and live there with Febo."

"To Hell with you, Malaparte. You, your jokes and your mongrel."

"Febo's no mongrel. He's an Etna Cirneco. It's a most noble and ancient breed."

"If I'm not indiscreet, how are things with Virginia?"

"That's all over and done with. Come on, Sirignano, let's get back to the party. I feel like a Martini."

Back at the Fortino, where the orchestra had just launched into *In the Still of the Night*, Chantecler came to meet us.

"Folks, this is *the* big night. Even Edda and Galeazzo are coming!"

Chantecler had grown up wanting to be a poet, but his father, who was a well-known jeweler and purveyor to the King of Italy, had compelled him to go into the family business. Chantecler had taken his revenge by becoming the craziest dandy on the island. Armed with a meticulously cultivated mustache, by night he moved from one party to the next, disguised as a woman, a friar, an ancient Roman. By day, he wore mauve, yellow, pea green clothes, and never put his nose outside the house without his famous shoes, of the very finest leather, with even the soles spit-and-polished. In his splendid villa at Tragara Point, giving onto the sea of Capri like a theatre stage, he owned a wardrobe of over two hundred items, all kept on show in an enormous salon. It was he who had launched the fashion for red trousers, at first despised then copied by all. And Chantecler had an almost exaggerated success with women. First, he'd get them thoroughly worn out with wild partying; then he'd fleece them, selling them his extravagant and dreadfully expensive jewels. Three years previously, a Swedish millionairess, madly in love with him, had him seized and brought to her yacht, meaning to carry him off to Sweden by force. Chantecler had had to fight it out with the crew, jumping into the sea and swimming back to Capri.

"Chantecler, once again you're seeing double," said the Prince of Sirignano adopting his best paternal tone, "Edda Mussolini and Galeazzo aren't in Capri. With all that's going on in the world, do you really imagine the Duce's daughter and her husband the Foreign Minister are coming to waste their time here?"

Sirignano was right. At the age of 31, Count Galeazzo Ciano, Mussolini's son-in-law, had become the youngest foreign minister in Europe, so that he must at that moment have had very different matters on his mind. Hitler was gobbling up Europe piece by piece and Italy, which had just set foot in Eritrea and Albania, was doing its damnedest to imitate him.

"And yet I'm telling you they'll soon be here," insisted Chantecler, "They were seen landing two hours ago from the hydrofoil. They've come for Mona's party."

"You're mad, Chantecler," said Sirignano. War could break out any day. D'you really think our Foreign Minister's got nothing better to do than dillydally at Mona Williams' place with people like you?"

"You're the mad one, you think you're descended from San Gennaro," retorted Chantecler, who was disporting himself in a strange electric blue suit.

A little group had gathered around us, shepherded by the young Prince Rospigliosi, a tall, handsome fair-haired Oxford graduate. Rospigliosi had managed to gather together the three queens of the evening: Mona Williams, Babsie Hutton and Gracie Fields. One seated next to the other on the divan before me, their sheer concentration of beauty left my head spinning.

Of Mona, her eyes, her class, her matchless elegance there's nothing more to be said – anyone who ever picked up a copy of *Vogue* or *Harpers' Bazaar* in those days will know what I'm talking about. There she sat smoking, her legs crossed in a pose that was at one and the same time elegant and audacious, something that only she could bring off. In the air made opaque by cigars and candles, sheathed in the simplest little black dress that set off the Cartier sapphire, Mona seemed to have stepped straight out from a painting by Sargent. There was something of that young Capri peasant girl with her look of mysterious malice whom Sargent, an artist so pure, so tenacious, so American, had gotten to pose for hours on end on the island's hills under the beating sun, straining to winkle out her dark secret.

Babsie Hutton wore a backless green Mainbocher creation. Her skin was airy; it shone with silvery light, the same silvery light Babsie had as a child gone hunting after on the top floor of the Woolworth Building, the family skyscraper, on clear days in New York. With her eyes scintillating like gems, her perfect complexion, both pearly and transparent, her diamond tiara and her necklace with its two rows of enormous emeralds, she had us all bedazzled.

Gracie Fields' appearance was not as sensational as that of her two millionaire friends; she had just undergone a nasty operation in

London, yet she still had extraordinary charm and, above all, nothing could take away that look of hers, overflowing with carefree humanity, not even success as one of the world's best loved singers. Too much wealth had crushed that quality in the two other women.

Rivers of champagne and Black Velvet flowed, and by now conversation in the group had degenerated into a rowdy mix of English, Italian and Neapolitan dialect.

"Stop annoying the ladies," said Rospigliosi to Chantecler, who had lifted up Mona Williams bodily and seated her on his lap.

"It's not my fault if they all want to be annoyed by me!" replied Chantecler while Mona blushed and giggled excitedly.

The group burst out laughing. Mona was delighted with her Italian friends, those charming Italian savages who treated her just like any old auntie, caring nothing for her sapphire, her aquamarine eyes, her white gloves, her fake British accent or her photos in *Vogue*.

Babsie Hutton too was in great form. No one was asking her the whereabouts of her latest husband, a Danish prince with an unpronounceable name, or their three-year old child. Babsie was already into her third Alexander, which she claimed was a digestive. She was complaining about Cholly Knickerbocker, his lying articles and William Randolph Hearst's papers that published them. Instead of showing some fellow-feeling, Sirignano guffawed and whispered some sea-dog's obscenities in her ear. Sirignano's strategy of conquest was infallible: treat every shopgirl like a millionairess, and every millionairess like a shopgirl.

Babsie blushed and laughed, and kept on laughing, she couldn't stop laughing. No one could imagine that one day all her men would leave her broken-hearted, that she'd be cheated by her lawyers, that she'd leave Cary Grant despite the fact that he alone loved her, that her son would die young, that drugs and alcohol would reduce her to a skeleton, that she'd die in a hotel room, abandoned by everyone, with barely three thousand dollars in the bank. Little Babsie was happy that evening, and she laughed and laughed, she just couldn't stop laughing.

Mona rose from Chantecler's lap with a sigh. "What a pity Cecil couldn't be with us this evening. He could have taken some nice photos," said she, alluding to her personal photographer, her beloved Cecil Beaton. Beaton's *Portrait of New York* had only just come out. No one had read it in Rome, and yet they were all praising it to high heaven. I'd ask: have you read Cecil Beaton's *Portrait of New York*? And they'd reply: yes, but not in person.

"Prince, is it really true that you're descended from San Gennaro?" I asked Sirignano.

The speaker, now standing beside me, was Prince Francesco Caravita di Sirignano, one of the most amiable men with whom God has endowed the earth. Like Edwin and Giorgio Cerio, Sirignano had an English mother and spoke impeccable mid-Atlantic English, which went well with his extraordinary propensity to collect young women on the London-New York line: he was as unstoppable in the act of conquest as in that of abandoning his conquests. His sense of humor made him, in private, utterly impervious to Fascism: so olympically indifferent was he to Mussolini and his thugs that he kept a whole collection of anti-Fascist hymns and songs in his house – in those days more dangerous than stockpiling explosives – and yet he accumulated them as though it was just like collecting butterflies or postage stamps. To the good manners of old England, he added the good-humored wantonness of a Neapolitan gentleman, for he was descended from San Gennaro, the Patron Saint of Naples.

"Three centuries ago, my family married into the de Gennaro family, the heirs of the saint. Since then, we've all had a mark on the back of our necks in just the same place where, in the year 309 A.D., San Gennaro was martyred by beheading with a sword. My grandfather had that mark, then my father, and now I have it too," and he bared his neck. We all stretched out our necks to look.

"But there isn't any mark!" exclaimed Gracie Fields.

"Of course not. It only appears on San Gennaro's feast day, then it disappears again."

"It's true, I've seen it with my own eyes," I confirmed.

"Is that so, Malaparte? How extraordinary!" said Babsie.

At that moment, through one of the windows giving onto the garden, we caught sight of Count Germano Ripandelli, the Mayor of Capri, who was conversing with Mafalda of Savoy, the daughter of the King of Italy, and with her German husband, Prince Philipp von Hessen, the only man in the world who had access, at any hour of day or night, to Adolf Hitler's private apartments.

The Prince of Hesse was looking around, visibly bored, paying much attention to the panorama and precious little to the guests who were being introduced to him. Every now and then, he'd look into the villa, scrutinizing Mona's furniture, her pictures and her carpets. The Prince acquired works of art on behalf of the Führer, who trusted him blindly. The Prince of Hesse, the King of Italy's son-in-law, was an exemplary husband (he'd turned out three children with Mafalda) and a true aristocrat. He had started out as a penniless good-for-nothing, had set up as an interior decorator, and had prospered thanks to his acquaintances. Perhaps that, too, is why the Führer trusted him blindly. No one, not even Mafalda, could understand what lay behind his occasional explosions of blind rage, unstoppable outbursts of fury all too like Hitler's famous temper tantrums.

Philipp von Hessen turned to bestow a brotherly greeting on Eddie von Bismarck. They were great friends. Eddie called Philipp «Phli». That was quite normal. In the Hessen family they called one another Fischy, Ri, Mossy, Chri, Bogie and Doggie. Even Hitler was given a delightful nickname: in the Hessen household they called him "Ini". Who knows whether, in private, Hitler and the Prince of Hesse called one another Ini and Phli?

"Don't you see I was right?" commented Chantecler victoriously, "The Prince of Hesse has just arrived. If Mafalda and her German husband are here, surely Edda will be…"

"Look, if you keep on buzzing around his daughter Edda, Mussolini will have you exiled to Sardinia by express mail," I warned him.

"My dear Malaparte, so far you're the only one here to have been relegated by Mussolini," retorted Chantecler.

"Is it true that you were sent into internal exile, Malaparte?" asked Babsie Hutton with her delicious little voice.

"Yes, it's true. But for a serious reason. And not because I was trying to bed his daughter, like Chantecler."

"But it's Edda who wants to go to bed with me!" protested Chantecler, "while all I want to do is sell her a ring or perhaps a pair of earrings..."

"Is it true that Edda too is coming this evening? I'd so love to see her," said Barbara Hutton.

"Of course it's true," said Chantecler.

"But why does Mussolini get so mad at you, Malaparte?" asked Gracie Fields.

"It's nothing to do with me. It's the Duce who's always putting his foot in it, then complaining when anyone talks about it. Once, for example, he was going through a difficult period. It was 1924, Matteotti had just been killed and Fascism was in trouble. The government was on the point of falling and the Duce couldn't keep the situation under control. I said publicly that if Mussolini could not guarantee order in the country, it would be best if he resigned. Then he summoned me to Palazzo Venezia. When he received me, I greeted him with the words: "At your orders and disorders, Excellency."

Once more, the group sniggered in unison.

"Who was killed that year?" whispered Babsie Hutton.

"Matteotti, darling," Prince Rospigliosi murmured in her ear, "an Italian politician, a Socialist."

"Mussolini had him killed," added Mona in a loud voice. She, with her steely character, did not fear Fascism and, unlike her friend, she was always well informed.

"Matteotti's death will bring Mussolini bad luck."

"Please don't let anyone say such things. The Duce's as superstitious as a child," I said.

"Mussolini...superstitious?" exclaimed Babsie Hutton incredulously.

"At the head of the State, he relegates dozens of truly valid collaborators to outer darkness," I explained. "He keeps them away from official business simply and solely because they have a reputation for bringing bad luck.

"But aren't you afraid of criticizing Mussolini publicly?" asked Barbara Hutton, looking more and more amazed and more and more immaculate in her blissfully angelic innocence.

"I've already been sent into internal exile, and served my sentence. The next stage is the death penalty. Or a heavy jail sentence. But Mussolini knows I've a big reputation outside Italy. It's not in his interest to execute a writer. D'you know what he does to keep culture under control? He gets them to give him the latest book by some young author, then he browses through it, and if he doesn't like it he writes on the frontispiece "starve him". After that, he passes the book to the Minculpop, our Ministry of Culture, so that they can isolate and impoverish the offending author. But it doesn't always work. Those in power are afraid of us writers, because we're above and beyond power."

"And how do you manage to resist, Malaparte?" asked Gracie Fields.

"Mussolini has me arrested from time to time, when the big Nazi bosses like Goering or Himmler come to Rome. The police knock on my door at dawn. They keep me inside for one or two days. Then they release me when the Nazis leave Rome."

"How awful," commented Mona Williams, checking with a lightning glance in a big mirror that her make-up was still in order.

"That's why Malaparte is building himself a wonderful house in Capri: to get himself placed under house arrest," said Chantecler.

All the Italians present started laughing, while struggling to conceal their laughter, some burying their noses in their glasses, some coughing, some turning away.

🖋 🖋 🖋

Recognition

"No question about that – he'll get himself arrested soon enough!"

This was a new voice, but one that I recognized. The voice of a German military man speaking English. No doubt his English was learned in horribly boring private lessons, by dint of stubbornness, a painful chore.

He was an SS major, in uniform, perfectly turned out, his face covered with a film of sweat because of his over-heavy and close fitting attire, with freshly polished jackboots; he looked like a bottle of Riesling just out of the ice bucket. For a moment we stared at one another, neither of us showing any sign of surprise. There are memories that get lodged in you like bullets.

My soldier is staggering slowly forward, holding the red and white guts spilling out from his belly with one hand. With the other, he's holding his rifle and firing, once, twice, three times. His face is yellow, black and violet, his eyes are empty, unseeing, dead. He's been hit in the shoulder and the hip, yet he keeps moving on and on, with that tremendous strength that only dead men have.

"You're quite right," I replied, "I'll manage that. Getting arrested comes naturally to me – just like cowardice comes naturally to some others I could think of. Quite naturally."

The murmur around me increased, growing louder and rolling forward like a wave. Other guests had drawn closer to our table, the better to listen. Outside, the orchestra went on playing Cole Porter. I adore Cole Porter, in certain circumstances his music becomes an absolute must. Well sung, a Cole Porter song is like a pink cloud. That's how you can tell if the band's playing properly – Cole Porter's music should sound like a pink cloud.

"Our dear friend Malaparte does tend to exaggerate. And he's forgetting his duty of hospitality towards the friends of Italy."

Someone now had stepped in. It was Filippo Anfuso, Personal Private Secretary to Foreign Minister Galeazzo Ciano, Mussolini's son-in-law.

Anfuso too was a fixture in Capri. He kissed Mona Williams' hand, as she looked on, already bored with the skirmish between me and the SS officer. Outside, the orchestra had begun playing a swing number.

"Herr Sturmbannführer," said Anfuso, "I'd like to remind you that we, on this island, played host last year to Marshal Goering... So, our exemplary relations with the German people..."

I laughed.

"That is enough!" hissed the Nazi officer, who turned on his heels and, pushing through the crowd that had gathered round our table, headed for the door. Mona Williams stood up to calm him, following him as would any good hostess, but without undue haste.

In the room, silence fell. The only sound came from Noël Coward at the piano, still joking with the gaggle of girls crowding in on him, dreaming of Broadway and swinging their hips in time to the music:

> *Why kick up your legs*
> *When draining the dregs*
> *Of sorrow's bitter cup?*
> *Because you have read*
> *Some idiot has said*
> *'The curtain must stay up`*

"What did that German officer say? Why did he go away?" asked Babsie Hutton.

"He was offended because I just couldn't help laughing when I heard the name of Marshal Goering," I replied with affected compunction.

As though by magic, the group of guests that had closed in on us vanished. Only Sirignano, Chantecler and Rospigliosi, upset though they were, had stayed put. Anfuso rushed towards me, took me by the arm and dragged me out into the garden.

"Will you stop playing the fool once and for all, Malaparte? This evening you're really looking for trouble."

"You know perfectly well that I need trouble, a writer always needs trouble. Or else, what could he write?"

"Stop being a fool. Do you know who that officer is?"

"You tell me."

"He's an officer in Himmler's SS. In Germany they've hated you ever since you wrote *The Technique of Revolution*, because in it you called Hitler a fool. Didn't you see that the Prince of Hesse is here tonight? Do you want the Führer to ask Mussolini to relegate you?"

"They've done that already. They stuck me in Lipari for quite a while."

"And they'll do it again if you don't pull yourself together. But this time they won't keep you in Italy: they'll send you to our colonies in Libya, among the Bedouin."

Filippo Anfuso liked me. The Prince of Sirignano liked me too. In Capri, many people liked me. What's nice about a place like Capri (and there aren't many such places in this world) is that life's so good there that you end up making friends with a whole lot of people who, anywhere else, would spit in your eye. And that's the truth.

"Malaparte, please, please listen to me, I beg of you. *Prospettive* is a fine magazine. One of the best I've ever read. You've earned a fortune, thanks to all the orders that Ciano got for you. Forty thousand copies in a single run, for the number on the Spanish civil war. That was quite an achievement, wasn't it? But you mustn't exaggerate. You are not invulnerable. Ciano's gotten you out of trouble more than once. Next time, he might not be able to."

"Stop it, Anfuso. I know how to behave."

"No, you don't. And you've already clashed with that SS major once before, a few years ago. Isn't that so?"

"I see that you too have your spies."

"Stop talking nonsense. We're on an island with an area of ten square kilometers. If you sneeze in your house on Cape Massullo, they'll call out *God bless you!* from the far corner of the island."

Anfuso squeezed my arm hard, looking me straight in the eyes. Then, a long moment later, he relaxed his grip.

"Malaparte, I know you. But there are many who don't want to know you. They detest you and that's all there is to it. Never forget that."

Anfuso turned sharply on his heels and went back to the party. Princess Mafalda of Savoy and the Prince of Hesse had drawn near. Anfuso wanted to pay his respects to the two royals. The Prince of Hesse was yawning, and with some reason, for his ancestors had been princes of the blood for four centuries, while their hostess was the daughter of a Kentucky groom. All the guests were wondering what Hitler would get up to in the next few days or the next few weeks. The Prince had sometimes been seen coming out of the Führer's room, or so they said, at six in the morning. His yawn became a smile with the approach of his dear Eddie von Bismarck, who was scared of the Nazis but not of his friend Phli.

It was dark. Down below, on the beach where Babsie Hutton had landed, the sea was casting tentacles of salty foam and briny black saliva on the rocks. It was a black sea. It looked like motor oil, crude petroleum, black shoe polish. It made me think of the Americans' oil, the oil that had killed Matteotti, but I dismissed the thought, I couldn't face it. I looked into the distance. The luminous silhouette of the *Warrior* had shrunk with her return to deeper waters.

The more I tried to get rid of that thought, the more it tormented me.

On the back seat of the car, two men are beating the life out of Matteotti. His face is covered in blood, but he's resisting, screaming and kicking. The car's skidding and swerving. Keep him still, damn you! A flash of steel, a flick-knife blade emerges and disappears into Matteotti's guts, between his fine black jacket and his tie. It's quiet now, the car's driving straight once more. Inside it, the air is warm and soft, but there's something hard there, a cold core of death.

Enough of that, I said to myself, gritting my teeth.

I yelled to Filippo Anfuso, before he was engulfed by the flood of visitors: "They say there'll be war, in September, and that Hitler's on the point of invading Poland. Is that true?"

Anfuso turned briefly, before disappearing:

"No it's not true. There will be no war."

I looked behind Anfuso and caught sight of a sad, noble face in the crowd, that of Mafalda of Savoy. The princess was on the arm of her husband the Prince of Hesse, alias "Phli". She was looking out to sea. Mafalda saw me in the dark, and smiled. Her smile was at once beautiful and severe, full of sadness and humanity. She could not yet know that she had few more years to live, for war would come and the Germans would carry her off to die in a concentration camp, at Buchenwald, alone and forgotten by all, even by her father, the King of Italy, and never again would they let her see her children. She could not imagine that she'd die in Buchenwald, she who regarded herself as a German princess, she who loved Germany and felt herself to be faithful to Hitler.

I stopped for a few minutes and listened to the sound of the sea. The sea was black and it was bellowing, it was bleating, it was lamenting. That's not a good sign, I said to myself; when the sea laments like that. I must get back home, I thought, Febo will be waiting for me, he too will feel how the sea's whining. Febo senses these things at once.

Meanwhile, perhaps to distract attention from my row with the Sturmbannführer, which would certainly be circulating among the guests, Mona had ordered that the fireworks were to begin. A green phosphorescent rose opened above our heads with a velvety swish, followed by a bang. Salvo upon salvo followed, accompanied by enormous red, blue and green orchids, spreading in a rain of white, yellow and violet sparks above the park of the Fortino. Just as well, I thought; the rockets and the bangers will keep them all from hearing how the sea's lamenting, so they'll not get worried. The sea's lament portended nothing good – anyone could see that.

A lament for old memories, death-filled memories.

Matteotti's body lies stretched out on the ground. Four men are trampling on it, they're kicking it and jumping up and down on it like mad, as though it were a mattress. There's a black, sticky drool running from Matteotti's mouth. It looks like blood, but it's oil. Black rivulets are oozing from his nose, his ears, his eyes, his torn belly. Matteotti's no longer a man, he's a dummy swollen with crude oil.

Enough, I said. That's quite enough.

Now the orchestra was playing at full volume, people were dancing, the temperature was delightful. On the dance floor I saw Princess Nadejda of Braganza moving with gay abandon, so young, so lovely, so happy after her snap divorce at Reno and so hungry for men. Who could ever have imagined that she too had not long to live, and she'd take her own life in London barely seven years later?

I looked at the moon, the Capri moon, the moon of southern Italy, so different from the moon everywhere else in the world. It is a warm moon dripping honey, a moon which you could just about lick, standing on tiptoe on Mount Solaro, and if no one does that, it's because they don't know that little secret, they don't know that on Mount Solaro in Capri you need only stand on tiptoe and, hey presto, you can lick the moon, a bittersweet moon tasting of white wine, seawater, bay leaves, pineapple and honey.

Not far off, I overhear two voices, a man's and a woman's, a brief altercation. They're under a tree, he shakes her by the arm and snarls some words I can't catch in Neapolitan dialect, then goes away. She stays leaning against the tree and covers her face, perhaps she's crying. Then she pulls herself together and starts to run, she wants to go indoors and rejoin the party, but she doesn't see me and runs straight into me.

A brief exchange of banal apologies, excuse me, I didn't mean to, no, not at all, the fault is mine, are you all right? Just the time to catch a vague glimpse of her profile in the shade, her curly hair, and to smell her perfume (*Shocking* by Schiaparelli, in those days one would smell that everywhere in Paris) and then to watch her disappear, running, into Mona's villa.

I went back in. I felt like being on my own for a while. This time, I went to the library where in the midst of the crush I noticed a fine 18th century Venetian cabinet, and in it, a number of antique books. A few guests were seated around it, and a pair of them were browsing through the volumes. I too drew near, and read on the spine of one volume a most curious title:

BESTIE DELINQUENTI

"Delinquent Beasts..." I was on the point of taking the book down from the shelf, when I was interrupted by Princess Maria Anna Pignatelli Aragona Cortès (nicknamed Mananà), a somewhat overexcited noblewoman who'd fallen on hard times and had been invited because she was descended from a Spanish Viceroy, from a Pope and even from the conquistador Hernán Cortés. Mananà's face was caked in white powder that made her look like a ghost, with her eyes outlined in black and a little fringe falling across her forehead. She was a painter and in her house she used only black silk sheets.

"Stop it, Malaparte! They tell me you're quarreling with German officers. Be careful, those people are very dangerous," she said in her rather strident voice.

She took my hand in hers and caressed it.

"You are very kind, princess. But you really mustn't worry about me."

Every princess adores having a gentleman tell her that she's kind, and treating her like a mother. The princess sat down on an armchair and I kneeled down beside her. All around us, people were drinking, laughing and smoking.

I turned towards the library cabinet and looked for the book that had caught my attention. But in its place, I found a gap. Someone had taken it.

I looked all around me and saw the Sturmbannführer leaving the library with a book in his hand. I could not hold back a grimace of surprise.

"Is something wrong?" asked Mananà.

"Oh, nothing important. I wanted to take a look at something, but someone else took it away. What were we saying?"

"I'm worried about you, Malaparte! You were overheard insulting an SS officer!"

"Forget it. That's nothing."

It was at that moment that I felt my last words take on a life of their own, travelling far from me, wending their way between the guests' heads like magic projectiles and striking at last the face, the neck, the eyes and lips of a woman whose voice and odor I knew, whom I'd already even touched, but whom my eyes still did not know.

She too seemed to be sniffing me out in the same way, blindly, like a bloodhound. She moved gracefully among backs, arms and bellies, dodging the immense backside of Baroness Soldatenkov. I dropped Princess Pignatelli and in a few moments the woman and I were facing one another, smiling, in the midst of the crowd, without knowing what to say to one another.

"May I apologize once more?" said she, rather awkwardly, "a moment ago in the garden I fell on top of you."

"Don't try getting some dubious rejoinder out of me. If you know me, you know that I've a long tongue."

"You're right. It's a wonderful coincidence. I love your books. But I wasn't expecting to meet you here. And above all, I could never have imagined literally bumping into you..." said she, laughing, "but you're right, let's avoid dubious repartee. It's hot in here, shall we go outside?"

🖋 🖋 🖋

Woman like Me

We spent half an hour in the park of the Fortino, without telling one another anything special or really interesting, as one does when one wants to keep the best in reserve for later. We spoke strolling among the trees, looking straight in front of us, only from time to time studying the other's face, to catch the effect of a certain word, a sentence, a silence. I didn't need to look at her; I already knew how she was made, because I had always wanted her to be just so: a woman to be proud of, a woman to love as I could love myself, if I were a woman. I'd always wanted her to be like this, a Woman like Me. Slim and soft, hips full and slender, a small statuesque head, a fine mouth, her voice deep and sweet. Her hair soft and curly, as soft as the down of some birds; her eyes so clear that they were almost white, the iris speckled with tiny brown dots. Her forehead clear and white, where day and night came gently together, where perhaps one day, I'd find my landscape, my setting sun, my destiny.

"We could go on talking like this all night," I said after a while.

"That's true, all night," she replied.

"What is your name?"

"Lucia. I'm called Lucia."

"A lovely name. It means 'luminous'. Perhaps it's the most beautiful Italian name a woman could have."

"Actually I'm German. But only by birth."

"That's why your eyes are so clear, They're almost white. So, you're German. Then it must be Hitler sending you to me. To get me to shut up."

She laughed. "Not even Hitler could shut Malaparte up."

"Please Lucia, call me Curzio."

"All right. Or should I call you Kurt Suckert? Or Curtino?" said she, laughing again.

I stopped, brushing my arm against hers. "How do you know what I was called when I was a boy?"

She told me things that everybody knew: "You're one of the best known and best paid writers in Italy. And also the most intelligent, the most cultivated, the most original. You're not afraid of taking risks. You even stand up to Mussolini. You have all the women you want. All the clothes you wear look the same on you: they all look good. You're tall, slim and well built. You used to be Kurt Suckert, Kurt Erich Suckert, the son of a German weaver who settled in Tuscany. Extremely early literary talent, almost a child prodigy. The war in France, winning the Medal of Valor for bravery at the Bligny massacre, a diplomatic career, abandoned later in favor of a literary one, a few years spent starving in Rome, while you looked for the right connections. Then, the first books, published at your own expense, and at long last, success. You started off as Kurt Suckert, Kurt Erich Suckert, almost a child of Germany. Now you're Curzio Malaparte, a great writer, one of the best scions of Italy. And you're the talk of the town."

"For someone who's never met me in person, you know an awful lot about me," I said.

"You're a great writer, I'm a great admirer. And anyway, all this is in the public domain."

She was quite right. How could I imagine that people didn't remember, that they didn't know? That my father was German, that my real name was Kurt Suckert, that Curzio Malaparte had for years been my pseudonym, legalized by ministerial decree, none of this was secret. Nor was the fact that in Prato, my birthplace, the family called me Curtino – why, there must have been at least five hundred people who knew all that.

"And what about you?" I asked.

Lucia yawned.

"My story's less interesting than yours. My mother was a Neapolitan aristocrat who'd fallen on hard times; my father, a German artillery officer. They met when he was on vacation at Sorrento, a short engagement, then they got married in Germany and soon divorced on grounds of incompatibility. Mama came back home and died young. Little Lucia was raised by two aunts, got a degree and began work as a schoolteacher. As you can see, it all fits into a telegram. Shall we go in and have a drink?"

A schoolteacher. Adorable, I thought as we went in, but just a schoolteacher...

"I've no one to accompany me back to the hotel," she said in the end.

Just then, we saw three men coming towards us. The first was Ripandelli, the Fascist mayor of Capri. The two others I didn't know: a squat, fat guy wearing a lightweight overcoat and a tall thin one with a hooked nose, who was almost completely bald.

"Signor Malaparte, these two persons are looking for you," said Ripandelli with a certain embarrassment, having found me with a lady. Lucia looked shocked, moved aside at once and returned to the party.

"Yer Honor, Signor Malaparte. My name is Bianchi," said the small guy, shaking my hand, "and this is my colleague Marelli. We're from the OVRA."

Ripandelli walked away, leaving us to ourselves.

"Good, so what do you want to check on? Would you like me to take you to see my house?" I said calmly.

I was used to seeing people of that kind; for various reasons I had, in the last few years, met with plenty of them. The most interesting thing about the OVRA was that no one really knew what it was or how it worked. People didn't even know what the initials stood for; there were all sorts of interpretations, but no official one. The name

OVRA rhymed with *"piovra"*, meaning a "giant octopus", and maybe that's why Mussolini had coined it, to spread the vague, menacing idea of a slimy beast that moves underwater and surfaces everywhere.

The OVRA could exile you to some wretched islet or get you sacked from your job or make you sleep atop a concrete pole, all on the basis of rules as confused and haphazard as the militia they hired: civilians and military men, barmen and Deputies, hotel doormen and journalists, housewives and prostitutes. It guaranteed that no one in Italy could sleep in peace, because every conversation could be overheard, every lack of Fascist zeal noted down, every expression of mistrust for the regime placed on an enormous file with your name and surname, and so much the better if the reports were pure calumny and the sentences unjust, because the exercise of real power is not based on justice but the whims of the powerful. There were quiet ladies living in retirement, paid by the police to move around Italy by train and make friends with their travelling companions, inciting them to speak ill of the Duce, after which they'd take down their names and inform on them. There were girls who got their ex-fiancé arrested, youngsters who told on their brother, fathers who sold their sons down the river, businessmen who used a well-targeted calumny to get rid of a partner, an employee, a competitor. There were kids paid by the Balilla and other Fascist youth organizations to report what their parents thought of Fascism, Mussolini and the regime. And I knew that every single day, someone was reading my mail, listening to my telephone, checking on my friends, because by now even I, a veteran Fascist from the very beginning, was among those who could no longer be trusted.

"We've been looking for you all day, Signor Malaparte," said Marelli, the tall bald one; "We need to talk to you. Criminal proceedings have been instituted against you, and the charge is homicide."

After arranging an appointment with me at my house the next day, the pair from the OVRA went off with their mouths full of *vols-au-vent*, and I was left alone staring at the moon. It was no longer dripping with honey, it was no longer warm and bittersweet: I saw it cold and flaccid as a jellyfish. A gelatinous, dead moon, that made me think of the OVRA interrogation at two tomorrow, the questions they wanted to put to me, which I could in part imagine yet couldn't guess at, like flies buzzing in a dark room.

I could hear the orchestra still playing inside Mona's villa. I could return to the party, find Lucia and that very night make myself at home on her white schoolmarm's belly. Or go home to my place to sleep, and to meditate on how to face the next day's interrogation.

I needed to think hard before acting. Every single step I took would remain black on white, indelibly recorded by my own pen.

That evening, I was not living real life but (like every writer) just telling a tale. They'd obliged me to do that. Once I'd written, there could be no turning back. What was written was written. I'd not have been able to change a thing.

Do you want to know why?

Because I was dead.

ROME, SUMMER 1957
SANATRIX CLINIC, ROOM 32

A Splendid Woman

The most important meeting in my life took place shortly before I died, in room 32 of the Sanatrix Clinic in Rome, under the oxygen tent.

One June morning towards 11:00 I was lying on a steel bed, wearing my black-bordered white pajamas in my white hospital room, surrounded by steel trolleys, and steel cupboards, immersed in the clinic's good stink of formaldehyde, the stink you find in all hospitals, a cold, white stink, cold as steel. It was a fine sunny day, Sister Carmelita had opened the window for me and the air carried the perfume of resin from the trees in front of the clinic.

I had a terrible pain in my chest, and my legs were cold and yellowish like butter. My neck was covered with livid patches, the veins on the back of my hands were punctuated by blackish coagulated blood. I was all swollen around the eyes, and as pale as a marble statue.

Sister Carmelita was helping me to sit up in bed (for some time now I'd not been able to do it on my own). At some point I had let my head fall back. With that slight movement of the neck, my heart collapsed.

My lung cancer had been discovered months earlier, during a trip to China. But as no one was willing to tell me the truth, I pretended I'd not understood and told everyone that I had TB. That cancer was the final effect of the mustard gas I'd breathed in as a youngster, when I was commanding a flame-thrower assault unit and the Germans had attacked with gas, at Bligny. That was in September 1918 and the First World War was just coming to an end.

Sister Carmelita understood at once that the crisis was serious and rang the bell. In a flash, the other sisters rushed in, then the doctors. At the close of their visit, the consultant, Professor Pozzi, proclaimed:

"Pericarditis. Gentlemen, I fear we are coming to the end. There's not much time left, maybe only a few hours."

He thought I was unconscious, because I had my eyes closed. But I was perfectly conscious: I had heard my death sentence.

The sisters brought in the oxygen tent and set it up quickly. My heart was performing some kind of African dance. More than once in the next five days, it stopped, hurling me into a dark abyss. But the pericarditis did not deprive me of my senses. I could hear quite clearly the comings and goings of the medical staff, the door of my room opening and closing, the sisters' murmurings, the noise of the medicine trolley. Outside, in the corridor, the concerned voices of people asking to see me, to bring me presents, to interview me, to get their photo taken by my bedside. Curzio Malaparte had reached the end of the line and nothing in the world would make them miss the show! They'd come to see him kick the bucket, the author of *Kaputt* and *The Skin*, the writer who'd sold books by the million, the rebel, the maverick. They wanted to enjoy the death throes of that insolent lover of liberty who boasted that he'd never really sold himself to anyone: neither to the Fascists, to the Communists nor to the priests.

Politicians, journalists, actors, former comrades in arms, former colleagues, former friends, former lovers, an entire seraglio of monkeys, peacocks, serpents, parrots and leeches: they all wanted to have their photo taken with me in hospital and then to tell something sensational about my last days alive. It was a siege; from readers I received more than a hundred letters a day. Through my room filed processions of high State officials, ministers, even the President of the Republic. Not even for a war hero had I ever seen such a mobilization. I was brought talismans, blessings and charms by the dozen; an anonymous lady reader had sent me a relic: the leaves of a wreath that had been placed on the corpse of Pope Pius X. This would bring instant healing, the lady assured me, provided one had blind faith in it. The most unctuous guests were the representatives of the atheist church and the regular one, the Communists and the priests. They left me not one moment's peace. Both congregations dreamed that, once my casket had been sealed, they'd be making a grand announcement: "Malaparte was one of us."

I understood them. In hospital, I'd confessed myself to Father Rotondi, the intelligent Jesuit who'd been assigned to me for the salvation of my soul, and in the end I'd even taken the sacraments. The Pope in person had sent me his blessing. This, despite the fact that he'd banned one of my masterpieces, *The Skin*. He'd placed it on the Index. This had displeased me, but I'd pardoned the Pope, because I respected him greatly.

On the other hand, I'd just taken out membership of the Communist Party. The Communists were the only party that had treated me well after the war. I had great respect for Togliatti, their leader. He'd done his calculations and decided he wanted me on their side. He wasn't bothered by the fact that I'd been a Fascist, or that I was not ashamed to repeat it. From the moment of the American landings in Sicily in 1943, all the rest of Italy had been pretending there had never been any such thing as Fascism, nor could they remember who Mussolini had been, and they pretended they'd forgotten that we'd made war on Hitler's side and that when Nazis came to Italy, we applauded them. They all feigned ignorance, pretending they didn't know that Europe had turned into a rotting, putrefying mother, a body that had brought living children into the world when she was already dead: like the dying woman I'd seen giving birth among the smoking ruins of Monte Cassino in 1944, when I was advancing on Rome with the US Fifth Army of General Mark Clark.

One day in my hospital room Monsignor Rotondi, the Jesuit, had crossed Comrade Pietro Secchia, a high Communist official. I had cordially introduced them, obliging them to greet one another. Deeply embarrassed, Rotondi and Secchia had shaken hands, then swiftly returned their hands to their pockets, as though to clean them.

It was quite clear how things would work out: after my funeral, priests and Communists would go on squabbling over the booty. The first would claim that, before I died, I had torn up my Communist Party card, the second would swear that my conversion was an invention of Catholic propaganda.

And so, in order to keep everybody happy, on my bedside table I had placed all the objects and presents I had received, forgetting none. Behind bottles, telegrams, packaging, boxes cans, boxes of candy and chocolates (so many that even if I could have lived another thirty years, I'd never have been able to ingurgitate them all), there stood, in full view, a photo of the Pope; a little coffee cup bearing the arms of Prato, my native town, a present from the Communist mayor; a statuette of Saint Rita; two porcelain lions donated by the comrades of the Chinese Communist Party; a reproduction of a medieval Madonna, and so on and so forth.

Next to the Sanatrix Clinic there was a private villa with a big garden, where a dog would bark from time to time. On that June night the dog's barking awoke me.

I had heard it said that at the point of death we have visions of the dead, of parents and friends who have already gone over to the other side; but I'd never believed that. That's why I was taken aback when my brother Sandro appeared to me. He'd died a few years before, likewise of cancer, likewise in a clean, white, well-kept hospital like the Sanatrix Clinic. I'd gone to stand by him during his last hours, but when I'd arrived at the door of his room in the clinic, I hadn't knocked. I'd stopped in front of the door and then I'd gone away, not to see him die. Not because I didn't love him. Simply, I was afraid to see him die.

Sandro was handsome; he'd always been gentler and more handsome than me. Now he was sitting on the bed, near me, and looking at me. The sisters heard me talking to him and thought I was delirious.

I said to him: "Come Sandro, come nearer! Get me out of here, Sandro, let's go away. Even you can't free me. Why do I have to put up with so much?"

He replied: "It's the blood, Curzio, it's Matteotti's blood."

I answered him: "No, Sandro, please. I don't want to talk about Matteotti's assassination."

I spent the days that followed between life and death. Every now and then I'd weep. Not out of fear, but rage; and I preferred to do it alone. I was not afraid of dying. Simply, I did not want to. I'd always had the impression that I'd not make it to old age. But I did not want to leave the great theater of the world where, although I'd met with plenty of trouble, I'd been so much at ease. I was famous, I had a marvelous house in Capri, not yet sixty and still so many fine projects running through my head. Why did I have to leave all this so soon?

My brother Sandro was by my side almost every day. I saw him as a white light, pure spirit. He'd busy himself massaging me and unknotting the muscles on my side, where the enlarged liver was pressing against the abdominal wall and the pain was tremendous. Then he'd take out a pack of cards and, while we played, we'd talk of Bligny. I said to him: "Do you remember the dead at Bligny?"

"Yes, Curzio, I remember them. There were so many of them, there were thousands. They covered the whole earth."

"What happened to all those dead, Sandro?"

"They're cured, Curzio. I too was so sick, don't you remember? Now I'm cured. Look at me."

"Why am I not yet dead, Sandro? Is it because of the blood of those dead?"

"No, Curzio. It's because of Matteotti's blood. And the tears of your women. And American crude. And the Spanish dead in Malaga".

"Please, Sandro, don't tell me these things. I don't want to hear them."

By now, my last moments had come. Oriana Fallaci, the journalist, came to see me. She wanted to help me write my last book: I had all the notes ready under my bed. "Let me handle it, Malaparte. I have to go to New York tomorrow, but in two weeks I'll be back here with you." "Forget it, Oriana. Stay on in New York." "Come off it, Malaparte. Don't you want me to help you?" "Don't come back, Oriana. In two weeks I'll be dead."

From France came Lichtwitz, General De Gaulle's personal physician, with whom I'd made friends in Paris. He gave me his *bains de jouvence*, which he expected to lessen my pain: but they didn't do a damn thing for me.

My novelist colleagues were the most ungrateful. Céline, whom I'd done so much to help, even with money, didn't so much as send me a get-well card. Cendrars, who'd been so friendly, simply disappeared. Henry Miller, who'd written me such kind words, failed to show up.

Dogs are far nobler than writers. Only they truly suffer after the death of a man. Zita, my last little dachshund, died a few hours after me.

At last, that afternoon came. It was hot; I was with Sister Carmelita, who was reading me a few well-wishers' cards that had just arrived. In the end the good sister fell asleep on the chair at my bedside, worn out by the heat and fatigue. I too closed my eyes, suspended between sleep and waking.

I saw Sandro coming towards my bed. There was a feminine figure behind him. The woman was wearing a fine pearl grey tailleur, perhaps a Pierre Cardin, sun glasses, kid gloves, and on her head a silk scarf.

This time my brother remained silent. No war, no memories, no Bligny: Sandro smiled at me, stepping to one side, and then he disappeared. Then I could see the woman's face. I had to make an effort to recognize her, because her attire, and above all the dark glasses, came as a surprise to me. She put her gloves and sunglasses in her handbag, she took off the headscarf and let her hair fall loose. A splendid woman, slim and proud with greenish blue eyes and a face as clear and shining as that of a *biscuit* porcelain doll. At last I recognized her face: it was Mona Williams. But it could not be her. Mona was in Capri, in her villa by the shore.

She looked at me with a calm, serious expression, overflowing with tender kindness.

"Hi Curzio. I am Death."

That's not possible, I thought, Death can't have such a beautiful face, a face like Mona Williams', the world's most fascinating and elegant woman. Death is a walking skeleton, everyone knows that, Death comes with a scythe and a sack for our bones.

"I've taken on the appearance of a familiar face," said the woman, reading my thoughts, "because I knew it would reassure you and give you pleasure."

I said nothing, dazed by the blinding beauty of Death, by her *biscuit* porcelain features, those of the splendid millionairess Mona Williams, the world's most elegant woman.

"Know, dear Curzio, that my heart overflows with motherly tenderness for all those I come to take on earth."

"So you've come to take me?"

"I waited a long time, to see if your brother Sandro could get you to change your mind," she said without answering my question, "It's I who sent him to you because you loved him. But it was no use. Your heart grew no softer. That's why I've come now to offer you another chance. Your last chance."

"So, what am I supposed to do? Call a press conference and publicly confess my sins?" I asked in exasperation.

Her eyes were full of apprehension. The tender lady with the white skin, so dignified, so tall and erect, feared I might turn down her offer. She had in her look that purity, that dignity, that perfection only some American women possess. The same purity, the same perfection, the same morality as American soldiers, the dignity of the soldiers of the US Fifth Army, the soldiers of General Mark Clark who, in 1944, died uselessly in their thousands to liberate Europe.

Two burning blades of anguish and hope wove themselves together in my throat. In a few seconds, there passed before me my life, my errors, my terrors. I saw all the missed opportunities, my bad faith, my arrogance, my presumptuousness, my self-centeredness, my mean thoughts and deeds. I saw all the harm I'd done and all the good I could have done.

I gathered up my strength and wheezed forth: "O sweet Death, the only thing I've known how to do in my life is to write. The only I can expiate is by writing. But just look at me: in this state, what can I do? I'm a breathing cadaver. I can't even hold a pen in my hand!"

"That does not matter," said Death with a smile full of understanding, like Mona Williams' smile, one replete with gentle superiority, the smile of the New World supplanting the rotten old one. "All that you men cannot do, I can. You desire to write. If you are not up to it, I shall do the necessary."

I may have been half dead, yet some sense of reality still remained to me. And I thought: that's enough; it's too much. Why should all this happen to me, just to me? I wanted to stammer some clumsy thanks; but even before I could open my mouth, the splendid lady answered my hesitations.

"You have nothing to thank me for, Curzio Malaparte, for all I deny or grant is according to the Justice of Heaven."

"But then God exists."

"Of course He exists."

"And Hell, and Paradise…"

"They exist too. And over them all reigns the Justice of Heaven."

The Justice of Heaven: and I'd just taken out a Communist Party membership card! "Malaparte you're an idiot," I said to myself. The lady tried to conceal the smile which my thoughts had provoked in her.

"So, Curzio Malaparte, we shall write the book of your expiation. But take care! You have chosen to redeem yourself by telling a story. So you'll dictate the book, you'll be its only begetter, and at the end you'll sign it. What you'll have written, you will have written. If your repentance is sincere, if you've not lied – writers always lie – your soul will be safe."

I remembered that I'd already said goodbye to my pen. I'd handed it to a journalist friend: "John, take it away and bury it. I'll not be needing it anymore." I know that he buried it right there, in front of the clinic. If someone digs there, maybe they'll find it.

"How many days do I have?" I asked.

"Since it's in my power to do so, I suspend Time for you. Despite what you men believe, Time does not really exist. It is just the breathing of the Creation. Do you understand me?"

"More or less. I'm no philosopher."

"This suspension of Time, during which you can do all that you wish to, will last until you've completed the book. After that, Heaven will decide whether or not there's goodwill enough in you and you're really prepared to cleanse yourself of the old Malaparte."

"And after that… you'll take me with you, won't you?"

"Yes. But it depends on you, Curzio Malaparte, whether I take you to Heaven or Hell."

She sat on the edge of my bed, as so many of my visitors had done, crossing her legs with the ease of a mannequin, the self-assurance of

Mona Williams when she sat on the damasked divans of her Capri villa.

Inexplicably, I found the strength to raise myself a little and sit up on my own, without anyone's help. That hadn't happened for weeks. I was thirsty. The girl rose, took a bottle from the table, filled a glass with water and handed it to me. As I gulped it down, I realized that I had completely forgotten Carmelita. I turned towards the sister: she was immersed in a deep lethargo, immobile as a wax statue. Then I looked at my face in the little mirror I kept on the bedside table, and gave a start. I no longer looked like a dying man. The swelling around my eyes had gone. The long beard was scarcely visible, my complexion had turned rosy again, the blue patches on my neck had disappeared. I looked at my arms: the blackish coagulated blood that punctuated the veins on the back of my hand had vanished. My chest no longer tormented me and my legs were no longer cold but alive, and longing to stretch.

Death called me to order with a delicate tap on the knee.

"May I introduce two good friends?" she asked.

I heard someone knock gently at the door. Two immensely tall and lanky young men wearing grey pinstriped suits and ties entered the room. They were good-looking and wore rather solemn, shy expressions. One was holding a parcel under his arm and the other, a small suitcase. Their boss made a sign and the pair sat down on two chairs. After gesturing discreetly to request my permission, they laid the parcel down on my bed. They opened it. It contained a thick pile of paper. The case, however, contained a typewriter, a brand new Remington.

"These are two of my angels," said the lady, "two Angels of Death. They've come to help us. One will type your book from dictation. The other will make sure you're free from hunger, thirst and fatigue. With my help, the book will come to you easily, for I have always been queen over mortal things on earth. But take care: the book will be typed in the same indelible ink I use to record my sentences, against which there is no appeal. This is because the redemption of a soul must be complete, there can be no uncertainties. No deletions. No second thoughts."

"And... am I to start at once?"

"Yes, that you must. For all the time during which you'll be writing, you'll be cured – as you've seen in the mirror."

In my life I'd never managed to do anything good, apart from writing. I was born for that. And now I was measuring up to something absolutely new: now, I must write not to live well, but to die well.

"One moment," I said, "there's something important I need to know. Once this book's been written, who's going to read it?"

"All those who want to know your heart's secret. They'll read this conversation of ours, too, but they'll think it's an invention. Well then, what literary genre will you opt for to redeem your soul? A treatise, a poem, a fable… Or perhaps a news report, like those you wrote from the Russian front, from Eritrea or from Romania…"

"A novel", I replied, "It will be a novel."

"Fine. Have you already a title in mind?"

From her handbag she drew forth a gold lighter and a cigarette holder. She lit up and blew a large violet cloud. She was smoking just like the real Mona Williams, with the same eyes lost in the void, the same unmistakable way of holding the cigarette between her fingers, as though it was a highly precious object, one of her diamond and platinum diadems.

Then she turned, almost embarrassed: "I was forgetting: for as long as you keep writing, you can do many things which were out of the question till now: you can eat, smoke, get up… Nothing can hurt you. Until the book's finished."

I stared at her in fascination, while the curtain of smoke from the cigarette, made incandescent by the summer sun streaming in through the window, almost hid her from my eyes. It was an enchanting vision. I adore looking at a woman who knows how to smoke with class, above all when she's very special, like the one who stood before me.

She offered me a cigarette, and I accepted. It was centuries since I'd last taken a few puffs, six months – maybe more. I'd always had to cut down on smoking, because of my bad lungs, but the hankering had never left me. One of the two youngsters in grey pinstripes brought me a glass with my usual liquor, a bit less watered down than usual. I could take a few liberties; after all, I had Death's guarantee.

"Are you ready?" she asked.

"Well... yes, I think I've come up with a good idea for the beginning. For the location I've chosen Capri, where I built a house, as that was the thing I cared for most."

The two young men in grey pinstripe suits sat down and made themselves comfortable. One crossed his legs and started quietly reading the paper. The other dragged the table I used for my meals across the room, set up the Remington and fed in the first sheet of paper.

Mona Williams' double put one hand on her heart and closed her eyes, as though to concentrate. Then she opened her eyes again, those marvelous greenish blue eyes, and looked into mine, and I back into hers.

I took one last hesitant glance at Sister Carmelita and saw she was still snoring. I began my dictation.

"The novel begins just before the start of the Second World War. The scene: a great party in a Capri villa. Chapter 1: *Capri, summer 1939. The filly from Kentucky.*"

The Angel of Death began tapping away at full speed on the Remington.

Although I had often managed to keep up a steady flow when writing, I'm not the kind of writer to whom words come easily; I've always struggled to turn my sentences well and find the right turn of phrase. When I was dictating a letter to my secretary, I'd sometimes even get stuck. This time, the tale unfolded perfectly and without a break, as never before. Nor was that the only strange thing about those moments.

When I came to the point where the narrator has just spoken with the men from the OVRA, and I wasn't sure whether to go home and sleep or to return to the party and look for the beautiful woman with the curly hair, I stopped.

"Now the scene shifts to Capri village, in front of a café. It's still night. The title of the chapter is *Dog Like Me*. And that of the chapter that follows is *House like Me*. What d'you say to that?" I asked Death.

"I like it. Go on, Malaparte. Heaven and Hell are listening."

CAPRI, SUMMER 1939

Dog like Me

In the end, I'd decided to leave Mona's party and return home alone. I didn't want to have anyone in the way, while I was inwardly rehearsing the hesitation waltz of questions and answers I'd be dancing next day with the men from the OVRA. Night was almost done, it was not long before dawn. I'd walked by moonlight along the dark silent roads that led from the Fortino to the inhabited center of Capri, all the way to the now deserted town square.

"Look! There's Malaparte."

I'd just passed in front of the one and only place that was still open and – Hell! – someone had recognized me.

It was Zum, the oldest café in Capri. It used to be called Zum Kater Hiddigeigei (an allusion to an old German poem that by now everyone had forgotten), and for several years now it had been renamed Caffè Morgano, but people still called it Zum. It had been set up when Capri tourists came mostly from Germany: whole squads of frigid pianists, archeologists wearing pince-nez, bearded painters and moody poets. The same Germans who still, mixing with American, English and French tourists, frequented that smoke-filled place because only there could they find a five or six day old copy of the *Berliner Zeitung*.

"Who goes there? Friend or foe?" I answered gaily, hoping that some late-night meeting could distract me a little from my worries.

Behind the door, I caught sight of the prickly beard of Willy Kluck, the philosopher sculptor. Behind him stood Julius Spiegel, the mute dancer, nicknamed "Gratis". They were looking at me wide-eyed, astonished to see me there at that unearthly hour. Willy Kluck came out.

"Did you come here looking for me, Malaparte?"

"Willy, what are you doing at Zum at this hour? You should have been in your bed hours ago."

Kluck did not answer. He fixed me with those little grey-blue eyes of his, the color of his Berlin sky, always a little scared and uncertain, as though he were a ghost. Willy Kluck had been a great sculptor, and he'd given up his career in Germany to live in poverty in Capri. He seemed to me a little crazy, and if he was up at that hour he'd probably had too much to drink. I'd usually meet him in the early morning, lost in his abstruse meditations. He wrote a lot, entire philosophical treatises, in which he explained how to attain universal peace and cancel out the frontiers between nations, how to make all men good, and so on. But no one could read his masterpieces: he scribbled them all on tiny strips of paper, then threw piles of them into the sea from the Migliera, the highest viewpoint on the island.

"You came looking for me, is that not so?" he repeated.

"No, I didn't come looking for you. Go home, Kluck."

By the whitish light of the moon his hollowed-out face looked like marble, one of those blocks of Carrara marble he once used to carve and which he'd abandoned in Germany twenty years earlier, together with the woman he loved. They say that he kept drawing her face secretly, obsessively, in a sketchbook, still young and beautiful (the Germans are specialists in unhappy love affairs). Kluck lived only on eggs, milk and the weeds he picked on the hills of Capri. He was always saying: "Capri is a sky blue madhouse where everyone can become himself." No one knew what he meant, but everyone assented because they knew he was a philosopher.

Standing behind him was Julius Spiegel, the deaf-mute dancer who swore he knew seven languages, and earned his living performing strange dances he claimed he'd learnt in Java. To survive, he scrounged cappuccinos in the cafés and sandwiches in the bars. He could say only "gratis", holding out his hand, and no one could refuse him. On his head he wore his usual wide straw hat, while his fingers were covered in rings and a necklace of amulets hung from his neck, together with a woman's handbag, which confirmed his ill-concealed sexual preferences.

Those were the Germans who really loved Capri, like the painter-prophet Diefenbach with his long beard, bare feet and preacher's tunic, who'd painted some of his best pictures in Capri. These were the crazy Germans who'd die rather than ever leave the island. The others, the frigid pianists, the archeologists with pince-nez and the moody poets like Brecht and Rilke had never understood a thing about Capri and had soon gone away.

"If you didn't come looking for me, what are you doing here?" asked Kluck. It seemed he couldn't think of anything else. He must have had plenty to drink, good old Willy.

"I was just passing, on my way back from a party. Go to bed, Kluck."

Even Spiegel the dancer seemed rather taken aback by his friend's insistence. Zum was closing at last, a group of four or five American tourists, all arm in arm in a shapeless human knot, emerged gaily, bearing glasses and a flask of wine, then stumbled into an alleyway like an immense drunken millipede, murdering the latest popular song at the top of their voices.

I turned towards the two Germans. Poor Spiegel and Kluck looked like two characters from the *commedia dell'arte*, two sad pulcinellos, two puppets hanging from a nail.

"Gratis," implored Spiegel in his strident voice, holding out his hand to me. I dropped a few coins into his palm. I don't understand why people say I'm mean. When I find myself facing an unfortunate like Gratis I don't need to be asked twice, I always give them something. What I can't abide is to have to spend a fortune on household items. I always tell Maria, my housekeeper: you look after the food, I've got other things on my mind. But it's just as though I'd said nothing, and on she goes, day after day, complaining "Signor Malaparte, the pantry's empty again today," and so she comes asking me for money for meat, bread and vegetables – in other words it's a real pain. Why can't people learn to leave their fellow human beings in peace?

"Kluck, stop your boozing now and go get some sleep," I said.

"But aren't you going home?" asked Kluck, and I felt a note of apprehension in his voice.

"No, I'll take a stroll. It'll soon be dawn. I want to see the sun rise. In Capri dawn's beautiful."

Kluck and Spiegel saluted me with a wave of the hand and made their way unsteadily towards the little square. Kluck turned to stare at me one last time, tripped and almost dragged his friend down in his fall. Wherever they lived, it would take them quite a while to get home.

I was alone again. I had almost no desire to sleep. The first light of dawn was emerging and I decided to wait for the sun to come up and to take a coffee the moment they opened the shutters of the cafés on the square. But instead of enjoying solitude and silence, I heard footsteps draw near, and then a voice.

"What happened to you, Malaparte? At the party they were looking for you everywhere, even among the rocks."

It was the voice of Ambassador Ottavio de Peppo, a bigwig at the Foreign Ministry.

"I was very tired and left without saying goodbye," I said.

"Mona was asking all over the place where you'd gotten to, also because of the theft."

"What theft?"

"The theft of the book, for heaven's sake! Didn't you hear? They were all talking about it at the party."

"What book was it?"

"The book's not the problem. The fact is that inside the book there was something that Mona cared for very much. At least, that's my impression, because she was in one hell of a state. But she didn't want to say what it was."

I'd seen the Sturmbannführer take away a volume from Mona Williams' bookcase. But it would be too dangerous to accuse an SS officer openly, without cast-iron evidence. That could cause a serious diplomatic incident and, seeing the charges that the OVRA was waving in front of my nose it really was no time to get myself in even more trouble.

"And then, d'you know what? It seems there were two men from the OVRA at the party. Only the mayor knew what they'd come for, and he wouldn't tell anyone."

"The OVRA's everywhere," I said.

"The OVRA's everywhere," repeated De Peppo, "'Bye, Malaparte."

The sun was coming up, Capri's narrow streets were slowly filling with insomniac old men, fair, rosy-cheeked bathers, and shop assistants and waiters out on their first errands. The rest of the island would be coping with hangovers from the ten or twenty parties that had taken place the night before. The meeting with De Peppo had revived for me everything that had gone wrong at the party, in particular the encounter with the two inquisitors from the OVRA. I didn't want people around me, I longed for the solitude of House like Me. And I wanted to see my Febo.

I left behind the Grand Hotel Quisisana with its cargo of American millionaires, Russian ex-countesses and Swedish nannies and moved away from the built-up area, eventually reaching the road that led home.

To get to House like Me, even today, you need to have muscles in good order. If you don't, you'd do better not to venture out from your hotel. To get an idea of what it's like, you need first to understand that it's built on an enormous prow that juts out to sea from the cliffs. When the wind blows hard, foam gets into the open windows, just as it gets into a ship caught in a storm, and I'm not joking. At House like Me you can land by boat (and in my plans I in fact designed a stairway excavated from the cliff face), but it's a terribly awkward climb. So it's far better to come on foot. Once you'd gotten away from the built-up area, you'd have to walk for about half an hour through the scrub, taking care not to trip up on protruding rocks, not to get lost, and not to scratch yourself on the bushes. Once you come in sight of the sea, you have to go down slowly towards the cliff, and that's not easy, so that even here I've had to build a long, steep stairway to get to the house, altogether about a hundred steps. But then in the end you get there: to the left and the right stand the high verdant cliffs of Capri; a little further off, that quirk of Nature, the Faraglioni, three little Himalayan peaks rising from the waters; and before you, the sea of Homer and Virgil. House like Me rests on the Massullo promontory, the enormous cliff that rides in triumph in the midst of this peerless vision, and let no one take offense if I say what I think of it.

The first time they brought me to Cape Massullo, I was overcome by too much beauty, and I wept. The second time, I decided that cliff must be mine, and I bought it. In principle, you couldn't even build a kennel there for Febo, because of the restrictions linked to the landscape. But I was friends with Count Galeazzo Ciano, Mussolini's son-in-law, and with plenty of influential people; knocking at a few doors I found a way to obtain planning permission. Exploiting one's friendships was doubtless a rogue's gambit, but I'd have been a fool not to take advantage of them. And it's worse to be a fool than a rogue. Besides, I have, I believe, done something for Capri: a shapeless cliff, Cape Massullo, now bears the most original, the most modern, the strongest and the freest house in all Italy.

By now I was almost home, and I decided to announce my arrival to Febo, even if obviously, thanks to the divine premonition of animals, he already knew where I was. I barked long, loud and joyfully into the wind, then waited. Myself, I simply adore barking, it's one of Nature's loveliest and most satisfying gifts to mankind.

In seconds, there was Febo in the middle of the path, just a few yards off, among the mastic trees and myrtles, his tail vibrant with joy. He held back for a moment, then sprang forward and rushed at me so incredibly fast that he almost knocked me to the ground. We knotted together like one great big ball of fur, arms, paws and legs, and rolled on the ground in a whirl of kisses and licking, growls and somersaults. I'd left him alone so long, and we really had to celebrate to make up for that.

"Tarapoonchilanchi," said I, holding his head in my hands and speaking the secret language that only he understood, "Tarapoonchilanchi tarapoonchilah". When I pronounced those magic words, Febo understood instantly whatever I commanded, and would carry out even the most arduous tasks.

Febo became very, very serious, and looked me intensely in the eyes, to show that he'd understood my greeting, my declaration of love. He understood everything I said, but if I said "Tarapoonchilanchi" with the right tone, he understood even better, because that was Febo's secret language.

When I say this, no one believes me, but I've always talked with dogs. When I was going round Europe as a war correspondent, in the evening I'd bark from hotel windows, from balconies, from roofs, to see if there were any dogs around. If I found one, we'd have a long-distance chat, after which I could sleep easy.

That way, I got to know African, Finnish, Romanian, French, German and Russian dogs. And both before and after Febo, I've had other dogs. But none could ever give me such joy as he did. In my books I've written it clearly: if I'd not been a man, if I'd not been the man I am, I'd have wanted to be a dog, to be like Febo. I've never loved a woman, a brother, a friend as I loved Febo. He was a Dog like Me, a noble being, the noblest being I've ever met. At night, keeping him near me was like having a light, an innocent moonlike light illuminating the whole room with the glow of his blue eyes. He was my mirror, my shadow, my secret ego. Every writer, every actor, every musician finds his image in a dog, the dog lays bare his unconscious and enables him to become himself. I'd even say that a dog's real job is to heal his master's unconscious. Freud could only live with his Jo-Fi at his side, and he never got over her death. Byron had Boatswain, and when he died he dedicated him an epitaph that still today knots one's throat. Steinbeck had Toby, who tore to bits the one and only manuscript of *Of Mice and Men*, but he laughed and pardoned him. Billie Holliday had Mister, her faithful boxer with whom she shared everything: concerts, rehearsals, studio recordings, maybe even drugs. That madman Errol Flynn had Arno, and loved him so much that he beat to a pulp the journalist who wrote that he hadn't really loved him. Buster Keaton had Elmer, and when his wife divorced him for infidelity and took the dog with her, he became as sad as the characters he played.

Everyone has the dog he needs to become himself. Mine was the luck and the honor to have Febo. We met when he was still a puppy, and I was sad and lonely, confined to Lipari. It was he who chose me: first he inspected me from afar, then he followed me, and in the end, he courted me. He'd understood perfectly that I was on that godforsaken island because I'd been deprived of my liberty. He could see I was unhappy, alone, humiliated and in poor health. When I suffered bouts of night fever he stayed beside me in silence, caring and discreet, trying to hide his anxiety. I'd read him aloud letters from my mother, he'd stare at me with his azure eyes full of mute understanding, and I felt that he understood all that there was to be understood about me.

I stood up, looked seaward, and on the terrace of House like Me caught sight of the slim figure of Adolfo Amitrano, my masterbuilder. He was on time, as ever, and was waiting for me. In his hand he held a piece of paper and he was sniggering under his breath. It was the postcard I'd sent from Rome to Febo in Capri. I always did that when we were apart for a long time. I'd keep a postcard on me for a few days so that it would be well impregnated with my smell. Then, I'd write: *For Febo Malaparte - Capri*. And I'd send it like that. The Capri postman knew that he could find Febo at House like Me. When he received it, Febo would make a fuss of it as though it were me in person. He'd lick it and bite it, and when he slept, he'd keep it beside him until my return. We'd sleep together, one beside the other. Sooner or later he'd return to the Paradise of Bones, where all dead dogs end up, and I didn't want to waste one single moment of his presence. We'd celebrate good news together: I'd buy two fine steaks, I'd grill them rare, then I'd lie naked on the floor beside him and we'd eat side by side, like two brothers, sinking our teeth into the steaks in our dog's bowls, without plates or implements. If you've a dog, I say, you must treat him properly. What the deuce is the point of keeping him if you don't do what he likes?

When he died, I buried him just there, beside the path that leads to House like Me, and every time I passed that way, I'd bark in the usual way as though Febo could still come to meet me, and jump on me for joy. I know he could hear me.

House like Me

For those unfortunates who've never even seen a photo of my house in Capri, there are a couple of things you must know. First of all, it has no roof: it's covered by an immense rectangular terrace, with absolutely no parapet. You get up there from the garden by a gigantic stairway, which widens in a V as it goes upwards. I'd built it like this in memory of Lipari, where Mussolini had sent me into internal exile, because in Lipari there was a beautiful, sad church with a V-shaped staircase. From the terrace of House like Me, the sea spreads out in all its power, space and time no longer exist. I'd go running round the terrace, I'd even go up there on a bicycle: but whoever goes onto that terrace had better take good care, because if you fall to the rocks from up there, you're a goner. The terrace is separated from the entrance only by a low, sloping comma-shaped white wall, a sort of sail, the only curve in the whole house, which is hard, severe, essential, all corners and angles.

When work started, I'd taken on a fashionable architect, with an elegant office and many, many young secretaries. As soon as I understood how much money he wanted to get out of me, I employed a good Capri builder. He and I decided everything, step by step, as the project advanced, without even any plan. Acting as my own architect, I managed pretty well, spending only half. Wouldn't any sensible person have done as much?

Indoors, on the upper floor, I wanted an enormous living room with great rectangular picture windows giving onto the sea, onto the cliffs of Capri and the Faraglioni, which are like vast Rembrandts made of light, sea and sunshine. When the house was at last ready, years later, I'd brought it off just as I'd imagined it at the outset: with no concessions, no hypocritical smiles, with sparse furniture, few simple, well chosen pieces, and a fireplace backed by a Jena crystal wall, so that you can admire the blue of the sea through the flames. On the floor below, besides the services and the kitchen, there are four guests' bedrooms; and these are plain, Spartan, truly beautiful. Overlooking the sea, like the prow of a ship, my study, with my work things: books, typewriter, art and papers. Only my personal bathroom is rich, in Pompeian-style, with green marble facings. Six can eat in the dining room; eight, if you squeeze them in. This is no pleasure villa, built to impress guests. I never wanted guests and snoopers, except for the few women worthy to share my bed, the only double bed in the whole house. I built House like Me to work, to meditate, to be at peace with myself, in silence. Gramophone records and music, I had, but never listened to. I never even wanted the telephone (there was one, but it was always kept off the hook). I wanted House like Me just for the two of us, Febo and Malaparte. That's all.

Nowadays, people wonder what was going on in Malaparte's head when he'd shut himself up there to write for months on end, without a wife and without friends, all alone on top of a cliff, in the interminable winter evenings. Forget it. What I was, what I thought, what I did in House like Me, that's my own business. Every man truly finds himself when he's alone, naked, in the toilet, before the mirror with shaving soap on his chin and a razor in his hand, face to face with his own damn thoughts.

I climbed the great stairway, with Febo following joyfully on my heels, and joined Amitrano on the terrace.

"Good morning, Signor Malaparte."

Adolfo Amitrano was one of those modest, reserved, timid men, yet full of pride, to be found among the people of Capri. He'd accepted the challenge of building a house in an impossible place. I wanted a house on that cliff beaten by the sea and the winds, and Adolfo had said yes to that at once; yes he'd build it.

"Did you find everything in order?" I asked.

"More or less. But I've got to bring more bricks. And I'm afraid we'll need plenty of water for the plaster."

We made a rapid tour, taking notes in Adolfo's note pad.

Then we sat down again on the terrace, with our legs hanging over the edge. Amitrano took a pack of cigarettes from his pocket and offered me one.

Febo nestled by my side, proud of being part of our trio of males; if he'd been able to, he'd have smoked too. He sat looking at the sea with us. Febo just loved looking at the sea by my side. He remained ever vigilant, with his ears pointing straight up, observing in the salt-filled air the sea phantoms that only he could sense, the blind forces that move the waves, the winds, the black whirlpools of the Mediterranean, and he protected me.

"Adolfo, d'you remember what happened here in Capri in May four years ago?"

"That's a long time ago, Signor Malaparte. Pardon me, but I don't remember."

Adolfo was someone thoroughly correct, and he had great respect for me. I was a writer, someone who lives by words. Something mysterious for a person like him, a master-builder, the son and grandson of other master-builders, accustomed to thinking of concrete things, to a world made of square meters, bricks, wooden poles, shovels and pickaxes.

"Then I'll help you. Four years ago someone died on the island, up on the heights at Anacapri. An English girl."

"Ah, that I remember. She was one of the English girls who lived at Villa Monticello with their father."

"You remember, of course? That was not a good death."

"No, it was not a good death, Signor Malaparte."

"Did they find out afterwards what had happened?"

"No, Signor Malaparte, we never found out. Some said it was an accident. Others said that maybe someone had killed her. And others said it had been a suicide, and the family didn't want that to be known."

"It's always been like that in Italy."

"Yes, it's always been like that."

"And… who said it could have been a murder? The police?"

"No, that was all just gossip in the days after the funeral."

"Did some say I had something to do with her death?"

"Yes, Signor Malaparte, some said that."

"And did you believe them?"

"No, Signor Malaparte, I never believed that."

We fell silent for a few moments, letting our gaze wander to the horizon. A seagull passed screaming above us, gliding towards the cliff face behind us. Amitrano would surely have liked to ask me why I was asking him now about that old story; but he did not do so. That would not have been him.

"How long will you be staying in Capri, Signor Malaparte?"

"I don't know. A few days, I think. Maybe a few weeks, maybe months. I want to be here to see with my own eyes when the last stone of this house is laid."

Adolfo knew perfectly well that I'd be leaving the next day, but he asked for no explanations. He put out his cigarette, crushing it on the bricks of the terrace, then put the butt in his pocket, rather than leave rubbish lying around. Adolfo Amitrano was someone thoroughly correct, someone who doesn't ask too many questions.

"Three new workmen will soon be arriving at the port of Marina Grande. I've brought them in from Naples. If you don't need me now…"

"Go ahead, Adolfo. I'll stay here awhile."

I needed to think, to put some order in my memories. Pamela, or rather, Pam. Pam Reynolds, that was her name.

It had happened in the spring of 1935. Barely four years ago, but it felt like a century. How the world had changed! Hitler hadn't yet begun to gobble up Europe bit by bit. Gorky, Pirandello, García Lorca and Chesterton were still living. So were Jean Harlow and Ravel, Edith Wharton and D'Annunzio. George V was still on the British throne, Franklin Delano Roosevelt was still serving his first term in office, Gershwin had just written *Summertime*, and I'd been arrested.

They'd taken me in Rome, just back from a trip to France, towards midnight, in my hotel bedroom. I told everyone I'd been arrested for anti-Fascism, but that wasn't true. I'd simply quarreled with one of the most powerful Party bosses: Italo Balbo, the famous pilot, the hero of the transatlantic flight from Tuscany to New York. Balbo had become Minister of Aeronautics, and he was immensely popular. Even the Americans had erected a monument to him in Chicago. By quarreling with him, I thought I was doing a favor to Mussolini, who feared Balbo's competition.

Mussolini preferred to keep on the right side of Balbo, so he sacrificed me. He had me arrested and sent into internal exile in Lipari, off the coast of Sicily. Without books, without a radio, buried among prison guards, convicts, fishermen and Carabinieri, plagued by the damp that penetrated even the stones, I'd been left there to rot. I had no one, and from six in the evening I had to stay shut in the house on my own. It was then that I met and tamed Febo. Meanwhile the bouts of fever had begun. Soon they found TB in both lungs, after-effects of the German gas at Bligny. Lipari was set to become my tomb.

"You're the one good thing I found in Lipari, aren't you?"

Febo looked me in the eyes and licked one of my hands. He'd understood.

The doctors were not in any doubt, I had to get away from that damp, windy island, which could not have been worse for my suffering lungs. I was transferred to Ischia, which had a far milder climate and was above all nearer the mainland. The surveillance regime was also somewhat less rigid, yet my health did not improve; it was at that point that I wrote to Ciano and asked him to plead my cause with Mussolini. Mussolini was his father-in-law and would surely lend an ear to him; and so it was.

They then sent me to the Tuscan coast, to Forte dei Marmi, the smartest seaside resort in all Italy. The beach was frequented by the families of wealthy people, industrialists and artists. They drank whisky and gin & tonic, they listened to the blues (which had been banned by Mussolini), they smoked American cigarettes instead of our Nazionali, made from the evil-smelling tobacco from our African colonies, and they spoke English, German and French. I felt safe: it was no place for Mussolini, who remained a proletarian under the skin. His wife Rachele had herself built a chicken pen at their Rome villa, the wonderful villa of Prince Torlonia.

At Forte dei Marmi I was assigned a little house in the middle of a pine wood. I was still under surveillance, but discreetly, without any exaggeration. I could receive visits from abroad, I could receive my publishers, I could dine out, I could even write and publish articles. On one condition: that I should not leave Forte dei Marmi for as long as one hour.

One day in May 1935 I received a message from Ciano. He wanted me with him in Capri, and it was most urgent.

CAPRI, SPRING 1935

The Englishman in Paradise

Mussolini's son-in-law wanted at last to meet me in person, and he'd found the perfect occasion for such a meeting. He was on the point of buying a plot of land to build himself a villa in Capri and he wanted my opinion. "This will be the best possible time to get to know one another," he had written, bearing in mind that hitherto we had been in touch only through intermediaries, or by letter. Forte dei Marmi or Rome were too indiscreet, he had added.

It was clear that there was something else behind his request. Ciano admired me and wanted to get to know me. As a young man, he'd wanted to become a novelist. He had written and produced a number of comedies for the theatre, but he had failed. He admired me because I had succeeded in one of the few areas that remained closed to him, for all his great power. But above all, he hoped that one day, thanks to my contacts and my capacities, I might be useful to him. And he wanted to recruit me. With his usual easy-going outlook, Ciano failed to take account of the fact that Capri too was full of people, many of whom would be able to recognize me. But there was no changing his mind.

On the next day at dawn, a car driven by a chauffeur from the Ministry of Foreign Affairs came to fetch me, and drive me south at full speed, to Naples, and there, to the port, where the boat for Capri was moored. I was accompanied by two policemen; I had been authorized to bring Febo with me on the trip and even to have contacts with strangers, so long as I took pains not to be recognized by them.

In the previous few months Mussolini had grown tired of having Balbo constantly in the way. He had become far too popular, so he'd appointed him governor of the Italian colony of Libya. My principal enemy was far away, and that was a good thing. Yet if rumors were to get around that I, who had been condemned to internal exile, was taking a quiet break in Capri, there would have been a scandal. Balbo and his friends would have had a word to say and Mussolini would have had to send me to some insalubrious place where I'd again have risked dying.

My two escorts were plain-clothes police, no longer young and both somewhat overweight, in other words, two pen-pushers from police headquarters who couldn't wait to retire and look after their grandchildren.

As soon as we moored in Capri, at the Marina Grande pier, I hid myself behind a straw hat and a fine pair of sunglasses. It was the end of May, an extraordinarily hot May, and the weather was enchanting. A uniformed policeman came to meet us with a message from Ciano: the Minister of Foreign Affairs apologized profusely, but urgent government business had kept him in Rome. I was, however, to wait for him. In the next 24 or 48 hours he would take the hydrofoil and come with all speed to meet me.

My two guardian angels were appalled. Instead of going straight back home to Forte dei Marmi, they had to stay and wait on that island in circumstances utterly intolerable to their cops' mentality; they could not leave me free, but neither could they keep me in handcuffs. Ciano, thoughtless as ever, had left no instructions as to how we were to behave, where we were to wait for him, where to seek hospitality. What is more, I knew Capri well, the two policemen did not, and they didn't know where to turn.

As we were to avoid anyone recognizing me, I proposed that we should find refuge on the higher, less tourist-frequented part of the island, among the hills of Anacapri. There was in fact one inhabitant of Anacapri who knew me well, namely that old rascal Axel Munthe, the famous Swedish doctor. In case we should meet, it should be enough to keep well away from him: Munthe, who loved to pretend he was blind, would never have dared greet me from a distance of thirty meters.

We took a taxi to Anacapri and drove along the panoramic highway excavated from the cliff face high above the sea, from which the two cops took in open-mouthed the immense view over the Bay of Naples, to the Sorrento Peninsula and the heights of Capri dotted with villas, the island's grandiose cliffs; and even those two bored, lazy cops understood the beauty of the place.

The sun had already gone down when we arrived and took up lodgings in a modest little *pensione*. The news came to me on rising the next morning: Ciano had telegraphed via police headquarters that he could not yet move from Rome. The wait would be longer. I had brought nothing with me but the necessary changes of clothes; so I could neither read nor work. After breakfast, I decided to take a walk.

Always discreetly followed by my two guardian angels, I crossed the sunlit districts of Caprile, Pagliaro and Le Boffe. These names will mean nothing to outsiders, yet they remain forever carved in the mind of whoever has set foot there. If you don't go there at least once in a lifetime you'll be missing one of the loveliest sites that the Lord has given us on this earth, and for that you'll have only yourself to blame.

I walked along the Damecuta road between rows of enormous agaves, amidst perfumes of rosemary and wild fennel, while the faraway sea flashed at me with its reflections, yellow, green and violet. Febo trotted along behind me, hanging back only from time to time, to follow a hen or flush out a cicada. I regaled myself with the thought that perhaps Ciano had already arrived in the island with a free pardon, perhaps my internal exile was almost at an end, perhaps I'd soon be returning home to Rome.

At one point, I became tired of the quiet alleyways of Anacapri.

"I want to climb Mount Solaro," I announced to the two cops, who were already tired and panting, as I pointed out the peak jutting up into the sky before us. It was the highest mountain in the island, the magic mountain from which one could lick the moon and taste it, just by standing a little higher on tiptoe.

"Signor Malaparte, that is not possible."

"And why not?"

The two looked at one another, thoroughly embarrassed.

"Too far. Too steep. It would be exhausting."

"Not for me," I replied, and kept on walking.

We left the asphalt road and went ahead, struggling against the stony terrain, the bushes and the heat that was growing with every passing moment. The two cops, soaked with perspiration trudged nervously behind me and Febo, but did not feel like commenting on our choice of route. They were in any case counting on me not to attempt to escape: I'd surely be recaptured and that would be to throw away any chance of an early pardon.

The distance between me and my two watchers was constantly growing longer. I had comfortable lightweight summer shoes, while the two policemen wore coarse leather loafers, perhaps good for crossing a meadow, but not for the rocks of Anacapri.

"Malaparte, wait for us!" they yelled.

"Hurry up," I replied, "I want to reach the top of Mount Solaro before lunch."

Turning, I saw in the distance that one of the pair had taken off one shoe and was trying to bind his bare foot with a handkerchief.

I stopped for a few moments. But the heat was so suffocating, and the gestures of the cops were so clumsy that I soon lost patience and set off climbing again.

"Malaparte, stop at once!"

I turned back. One of the two cops had hurt his ankle. The cut was not too big, but he was losing a lot of blood.

"We'll have to find a doctor," I observed, "So you'll have to draw up a report and explain this to your superiors. Perhaps the doctor will recognize me," I added.

The two cops looked at one another sullenly, imagining the trouble ahead, and the risk that I might complain about them to Ciano.

"Let's not complicate our lives," I said. "I propose a pact. You go and take a rest in some tavern, there are good ones in Anacapri. Go to the doctor alone, without me. The injury's not bad, I know these things, I've seen plenty of war wounds. Meanwhile, I'll go walking with Febo and we'll meet again this evening at the *pensione*. Is that agreed?"

I had a little money with me, which Ciano had provided for small expenses. With a handshake, I slipped a few bank notes into the hand of one of the pair, who rapidly pocketed it.

They were good guys. But just to be able to walk a bit alone with my Febo, without them, was a blessing I wasn't prepared to forego.

I started walking again and soon met with a pleasant surprise: Febo and I came to the Migliera trail. To our right, far away we saw the blackish stain of the isle of Ischia. To our left, the peak of Mount Solaro.

Febo looked in turn at the summit, burning under that early summer sun, and barked loud.

"You're right, it's too hot. We'll climb Mount Solaro some other time," I said, and we took the Migliera to the right.

A walk along the Migliera is a fine way of exploring Anacapri without tiring yourself much. There's a slight climb which takes you from the center of the village towards the south-west of the island. It wanders gently through the countryside between banks of gorse, low stone walls, old gates that lead to white peasants' houses, farms, small fields and vineyards. On every wall, every hut, in every corner exposed to a little sunshine, there rise triumphantly violet bougainvilleas, rosy wisterias, purple oleanders and amber yellow broom.

You walk along the Migliera for a few kilometers, lulled by this friendly rural landscape, but just when you think your walk is coming to an end and there's nothing more worth seeing, you realize that you're on the top of an immense windswept cliff.

On the cliff's edge there's a viewing platform, but it's as well not to lean over unless you want to miss a few heartbeats. You realize that you're on an overhang plunging directly into the sea, over three hundred meters below. Not even the most perfect photo could give you any idea of it. From up there, your gaze ranges 180 degrees right along the whole south coast of the island: from the lighthouse at Punta del Faro meeting the sea to the far right, to the Faraglioni rocks, upright and proud, at the opposite cape. The vertiginous height gives you the impression of having come to roost in an eagle's nest – no, far higher, above the clouds. When you tire of all that dizzying beauty and look down, you'll see the waves striving to leap upwards just to see how far they can reach.

"Keep back, Febo. Don't go too close," I commanded.

Febo obeyed. Yet I myself felt drawn by the abyss of the Migliera, by its three-hundred-meter plunge to death. I approached the precipice and sat on the edge, with my legs dangling over the void. Febo came to my side. I took a pebble and threw it down. It disappeared silently, swallowed up by the abyss. Febo barked, as though to take the measure of the chasm with his bark. I picked up other, bigger pebbles and threw them down one after the other into space. Some bounced off the rocky walls of the great precipice; others fell directly into the green and blue waters of the bay below. I searched around myself and at length found a fine stone, as big as a loaf of bread. I was on the point of casting it down when Febo barked.

"Don't do that. It's dangerous."

Someone had come up behind us. It was a young woman and she had spoken in English. I turned. Before me stood a graceful young girl dressed in white and blue; she looked like a well-bred young lady. She must have been eighteen or twenty. She was standing a few paces behind us.

"You're right," I said, putting the stone down, "I could hit some boat down below."

"No, that's not what I meant."

"What, then?"

"You'd better get up. The place where you're sitting is too loose and unstable."

I obeyed. After rising to my feet, I gently toed the piece of ground on which I'd been sitting. A big lump of earth gave way and fell. I followed it for a few moments in silence. Febo barked fiercely.

"It seems you've saved my life," I said at last.

The girl smiled rather hesitantly; she couldn't understand whether I was joking.

"I'm quite serious, you saved me. I could have fallen."

"That would have been terrible," she replied; "But it's not your fault. A few weeks ago, they took away the parapet in order to put up a new one. Only, they've not yet done anything."

If I'd fallen into the Migliera chasm, I thought, laughing inwardly, no one would have been able to get it out of Mussolini's head that I'd committed suicide. I could just hear the Duce's voice: that Malaparte wanted to play the tough guy, but a couple of years internal exile was enough to break him.

"I don't know how to thank you," I said to the young girl dressed in white and blue. She had a sad, serious face, and her eyes were not affable, but they were good. She was a delicious little girl, sad and very graceful.

"I'm glad nothing happened to you."

"I'm glad too."

She bent over, prodding one knee delicately.

"Does it hurt?"

"Oh, nothing serious. A little sprain when I went swimming from the rocks at Torre Saracena beach."

"Can you walk all right?"

"Obviously not," said the girl with a little smile.

"Where do you live?" I asked.

"At the Villa Monticello, near the road to the Blue Grotto. Do you know the place?"

"Maybe I do. Permit me to accompany you."

"Oh, that's most courteous of you, but I'd not wish to disturb you. Coming up here, I walked without too much difficulty, but just now the pain in the knee has been getting worse."

Febo moved forward, wagging his tail, to receive a few caresses, which the young woman willingly gave him. I offered her my arm and we walked along the Migliera.

"Are you here on vacation?" she asked, "I've never had the pleasure of meeting you here in Capri."

"I'm here on an outing with two friends. But they stayed behind and there's no need for me to wait for them."

"I feel guilty. You're dumping them because of me."

"Don't worry, they're the kind of friends it's always a pleasure to dump."

The young woman laughed.

"And now may I ask what so young a girl was doing near such a dangerous precipice?"

"I wanted to be alone. To think. And to write."

"To write? And what do you write, if I may ask?"

"Nothing much. Thoughts. Sensations. Various silly little things."

"I've understood. You write poetry."

"Do I have to confess to that? Well yes, I do sometimes write poems."

"Interesting. And are your poems well received?"

"The others like them. I don't. I throw almost all of them away. I only keep the best ones."

"I imagine the others come to a dramatic end, thrown from the Migliera viewpoint."

"Of course," she said with a smile.

"I'd like to read some of your poems, if you'll allow me."

"I didn't mean to spare you that torture," said she, laughing.

She was a sad girl, but she knew how to laugh, and she'd laugh just when I hoped she would. She was an adorable young English poetess dressed in white and blue, and perhaps she'd saved my life.

"Tell me about yourself," I said, "What are you doing at Anacapri?"

"Oh, there's not much to tell. My father, Richard Reynolds, used to teach Classics, English and History at King Edward's School in Birmingham. Then he left in 1922 for Egypt, and then Capri, on account of my mother's health. Two years later, my mother died, leaving me and my two sisters orphans. Despite all the difficulties, my father decided to stay on here. He even remarried, but unfortunately three years ago he was again bereaved. As you can see, a good deal of bad luck. But don't worry, it's not catching."

"It must be terrible to lose one's mother so young. How did your father manage to see to the education of three girls, all on his own?"

"He always had a good housekeeper, and there were friends who helped us. We were never short of food to eat. And then, thank God, my father's a teacher, so we've received all the education we needed."

"So misfortune did not win every round."

"No. But it's always there, lying in wait for us. Two months ago my sister Diana died. She'd not been married long, and she'd given birth a month earlier. I'm sorry, I shouldn't be boring you with these tales."

"Please, don't say such things. And pardon my indiscretion."

We wandered among the white houses of Anacapri while the sun beat down on our necks with its burning fingers. Every now and then we'd cross an old woman dressed in black, a group of boys running barefoot, a farm hand pushing a handcart full of vegetables, a stonemason with white blotches on his vest and trousers, almost like camouflage for hiding in the clouds, hastening to the property of some well-to-do outsider, a Malaparte, a Ciano, a Mona Williams, to beautify their lives.

Suddenly I saw him on the other side of the road: Doctor Axel Munthe. He wore his regular outfit: beard and moustache, hat, dark glasses, and an unseasonable dark woolen suit. He stood under a tree, feeding a little flock of birds. In his hand he held a loaf of bread and he smiled as the birds crowded round his feet, flapping their wings and fighting to conquer the crumbs that the Swedish doctor was scattering on the ground. Oh, Professor Munthe, how many wars mankind would have been spared if they'd been capable of feeling even a tenth of your extravagant love for birds!

"Come, let's go this way," I said to the young woman, drawing her sharply into an alley.

In the sudden change of direction our hands had brushed against one another, then almost unintentionally, they had joined. She accepted my hand, without showing either pleasure or annoyance.

"This isn't the way to the Villa Monticello," she remarked with a touch of irony.

"I know; how's your knee?" I asked.

"It'll get by."

We strolled around a delicious little house that seemed to have come out of a fairy tale. The front door was all surrounded by flower pots; from within there issued a sweet smell, the odor of some hot pie, an almond pie, dusted with candied sugar.

I couldn't make up my mind what to do; if I were to turn back, there was a risk that I'd end up face to face with Axel Munthe. If I kept going, this was not the way to the Villa Monticello, who knows where it led? I felt that the young girl was leaving me free to choose. I decided to go on unhurriedly exploring the alleyways of Anacapri, in search of an idea. Febo trotted happily down those little roads full of pleasant cottages, washing lines and crooked little windows. By now the streets were empty, it must be almost lunchtime. From the houses came the clinking of plates, the voices of children crying and parents scolding them, doors slamming and occasional laughter. The people of Anacapri were eating their ravioli, their vegetable soup, their *cianfotta* stuffed with artichokes, aubergines, potatoes and tomatoes, all sitting at table in their bare rooms, surrounded by worm-eaten old furniture repainted blue, green and white. I and the English girl dressed in white and blue kept holding hands, without looking one another in the face, without talking, just like that.

"How long do I have to wait?" She asked suddenly.

"To wait for what?"

"For you to tell me about yourself."

"You wouldn't like it."

"Let me be the judge of that."

"Very well. I'm a convict. I'm out from prison on parole, but I'm under guard. To get free, I had to rid myself of the two cops keeping an eye on me on the slopes of Mount Solaro, but if I don't return to my lodgings this evening, they'll be out hunting for me all over Capri."

The young girl dressed in white and blue laughed blissfully.

"I just adore your jokes."

"You don't understand. I'm quite serious. You're risking trouble walking with me. I'm not in good odor with the Duce. You, your father and your sister could be expelled from Italy. Mussolini detests the English."

"That's true," she said, becoming serious again, "but Mussolini isn't all Italy. Here in Capri no one has ever troubled us."

At last, I found a path to the Villa Monticello. I persuaded my companion to clamber over a little wall, to cross a little field and then an orchard. It was not ideal for her knee, but I did all I could not to tire her.

"I'm beginning to believe your escape story," she said, with a hint of amusement, as we advanced painfully across the rough terrain of the orchard.

"You must excuse this ordeal, but a fake blind man was on the point of catching sight of me, and I had to bypass him."

She laughed again: "I want to introduce you to my sister Mynie. She has a surreal sense of humor, just like you."

We had just completed our awkward crossing of the fields, at last rejoining the road to our destination, when I exclaimed:

"You're certainly going to hate me, I've made you jump and crawl all over the place. Let me take a look at that knee."

I leaned over to examine the joint. As I gently touched it, a certain thought came to my mind, which I repressed with some difficulty. In the end, I stood up again.

"It looks all right to me. But it would be better if you leaned on me again."

She produced half a bar of chocolate from goodness knows where.

"Would you like a bit? My father's giving a little reception at Villa Monticello, but I just didn't feel up to it. I grabbed this before leaving. Have a taste, it's very good."

I accepted. She broke a piece off and, gesturing that I was to let her, popped it in my mouth.

Moments later we were kissing. We spent a good quarter of an hour, maybe more, sitting under an apple tree, not far from the roadside, exchanging chocolate kisses. From the olive groves of Anacapri the wind bore a perfume of sea, salt, olives and broom, blending it with the odor of chocolate; and it was so good. Sometimes chocolate and olives can make a perfect match. I've tried to explain that to many people, but no one believes me.

Then, without a word, we set off again for Villa Monticello.

"How am I to introduce you to my Dad? As a passing convict?"

"Certainly. In such cases it's always best to tell the truth."

"And what name should I give for you? Al Capone?"

"Announce Mr. Suckert. Kurt Erich Suckert."

"Ah! So you're German?"

"Only on my father's side."

I didn't want to introduce myself under a pseudonym; but the name Curzio Malaparte was too well known to risk it, while Kurt Suckert had been in disuse for years now, and a young English girl would probably not know that.

"I'm Pamela. But you may call me Pam. Till today I'd never kissed a convict."

"That I can imagine. In the prison visiting room, there's a grate in the way, and when we escape we don't set aside much time for kisses. Now, show me one of your poems. One of the ones you've not thrown off the cliff."

"Are you sure? Very well. But you don't have my permission to say you didn't like it," she said, taking the notepad and extracting a page folded into four, with a brief text typed on it:

SHADOWS

Do not put out your hand to touch the shadows.

> *They are so beautiful, the shadows, crimson, vermilion, violet, azure and green.*
> *But it is terrible, terrible, to find out that they are intangible and without life.*

"It's beautiful. Sad, but beautiful."

"Thanks. Now that you've pleased me, you can say what you really think," said she, laughing.

"It's a beautiful poem. Sad but beautiful," I said.

She returned the page to the notepad. I saw the trembling that shook the breast of that strange sad girl, her expectations in life, her hunger for light and warmth, but there was something else, too. She was young and full of life, even attractive, and yet, within, I felt she was already disappointed, wounded, wilted.

"How do you manage to understand English so well?" she asked, "It's not your mother tongue."

"I sometimes translate poetry."

"From English? And why?"

"To pass the time on the long winter evenings, when the wind was howling in the fireplace," I intoned with exaggerated rhetorical accents, "and I was a prisoner on an island in the middle of nowhere."

"And what was it called, this island of yours in the middle of nowhere?"

"Lipari. It was called Lipari."

Pamela smiled, this time rather more weakly. Perhaps she was beginning to suspect that there might be some truth behind the prison joke.

We heard a sort of cheep, a defenseless, desperate squeaking. We searched behind a shrub and found a tiny naked trembling fledgling. It must have fallen from its nest and was struggling desperately among the pebbles and calling for its mother. We looked up and saw her anxiously circling above our heads. Searching above, among the fronds of a flowering wild cherry tree, we discovered the little refuge of interwoven twigs and leaves. Fortunately, it was not too high. I picked the little thing up gingerly, climbed onto a wall under the tree and thence, into the branches; then, stretching out, I managed to return it to the nest. Climbing quickly down, I took Pam's arm and hurried off so that the mother bird could return home and complete the happy end.

"Perhaps Nature had decided to let it die. Why did you save it?"

"I don't know. Because I could, I suppose. *If I can stop one Heart from breaking…*" I said.

"*… I shall not live in vain. If I can ease one life the aching or cool one pain, or help one fainting robin unto his nest again, I shall not live in vain.* You shouldn't quote the great Emily Dickinson to an aspiring poetess. It's humiliating."

"You're right, it was clumsy of me. But she's the writer I most enjoyed translating on Lipari. On Lipari I learned that men and animals are allies."

"Did you save other birds?"

"No. It's I who was saved. By this dog."

Out of modesty, Febo pretended he'd not heard. He just trotted along more quickly, on the tip of his paws, lightly, almost as though he were dancing. These are things you come to notice when you've really gotten to know your dog, things that no one else can understand, and if someone doesn't believe this, it's his problem.

A few minutes later we entered the gate of Villa Monticello. The feeling in my skin told me that Pam would a thousand times rather have stayed alone with me, and to hell with the party, but by now we'd arrived. Gay voices could be heard, noises of pots and pans, laughter, a violin tortured by inexpert hands. Febo began to growl quietly, there was something he didn't like.

We entered the garden. Under a pergola pierced by sunlight, it was full of people. In the middle of the space there was a large table spread with a splendid display of fruit, teapots, plates and decorated porcelain cups, a dish containing cheeses and cold cuts, a couple of tarts, bread, butter, jams and a mass of other things to eat covered with cloths and lids. Pam took a piece of cheese and some raisins from a dish and stuffed them into my mouth laughing, as she'd done with the chocolate.

Mynie, Pam's sister, came to meet us. She was a graceful young woman with chestnut colored hair, clear eyes and a warm smile, but less provocative than her poetess sister. I was introduced simply as her friend Kurt; Mynie looked hard at me, exchanged an imperceptible glance of complicity with my companion and led me to the table.

I drew near. All around, there was a motley group, among them a string of elderly English and American ladies with whom I exchanged greetings and smiles from a distance, and a little group of Capri children playing ball; inside the villa, a gentleman of mature years was making his violin whine, accompanied by an out-of-tune piano. Febo kept growling quietly, I told him not to, but it didn't work.

"Is there another dog here?" I asked.

"Yes. A friend's dog," replied Pamela. "It's the first time we've had guests since Diana died."

I saw her move round the table and approach a small group, among whom two unexpected figures stood out: two German SS soldiers. Judging by his decorations and his insignia, one of them must have been quite a high-ranking officer. Behind him, a fellow soldier lower in rank, perhaps his adjutant. They were smart and wearing dress uniform, complete with sabers, like every fine officer when he's on public display. In the last few years, especially since Hitler and Mussolini had formed the Rome-Berlin Axis, tourists from other countries had melted away while the Germans, both civilians and military men, sprang up like mushrooms. Strange, however, to find two of them, and of that kind, in a little party for old aunties. Then I saw what was worrying Febo: behind the two soldiers sat an enormous Doberman. He was sniffing at the air, he'd noticed Febo's presence.

Pam and the young German officer murmured a few rapid phrases, to which he responded with brusque gestures, casting an exploratory glance in my direction. From the few syllables exchanged between the two, one could guess at an intimacy, which I had disturbed. Perhaps I'd do well to stand aside, I thought. Pamela, however, came towards me flushed and nervous, took me by the arm and led me toward the group with the two SS men.

People I'd never seen before greeted me cordially, the children were running in all directions, screaming and treading on feet and skirts, and no one was complaining; but on Capri, that's normal, it's all quite natural. On Capri you must always walk down the street wearing a pair of loafers and a fine pair of bathing trunks and thinking you're poor but happy, otherwise you've come to the wrong place.

"May I introduce you? Kurt, this is my father, Richard Reynolds," said Pam leading me to a gentleman with a fine white moustache, a rosy complexion and a veiled expression. Around his melancholy eyes he had a fan of wrinkles typical of one who has tasted suffering in many forms. He wore an impeccable colonial outfit like those often to be seen in Cairo and Libya in those days. I would have liked to tell him that I had heard of the recent death of his daughter Diana, Pam's sister, but then I thought that was hardly appropriate; I had only just arrived in that house of misfortunes, so I let be. Reynolds scrutinized me somewhat suspiciously, then decided to get by with a joke.

"It's a pleasure, Kurt. Good to meet people who've the nerve to frequent my daughter."

"Daddy, don't be silly. Kurt, this is Helmut... I mean Sturmbannführer Helmut Aichinger," said Pam looking at the officer with a certain tenderness but also a very slight hint of irony. Then she hurried to the table, to serve herself.

"I didn't quite catch your name," said Pam's father.

"Suckert, Mr. Reynolds. Kurt Erich Suckert. Thanks for your hospitality, Mr. Reynolds, but I think I really must be on my way. I did not mean to intrude. I just helped Pamela to return home because of her knee."

"What knee?" asked Mr. Reynolds.

"Her knee. Pamela's sprained knee, of course," I said, discountenanced by the question, but Reynolds and the two SS men looked at one another hesitantly.

At that moment the Doberman began to move in Febo's direction, by my side. He had sad, nasty eyes. He was a very unhappy dog, one could see clearly that no one had ever sent him postcards and no one had lain on the ground beside him to sink his teeth with him into a fine bleeding steak. Febo did not move, he stiffened, becoming as hard as a stone dog, but he did not move. If the Doberman were to leap at his throat he could kill him with one bite. The Doberman's ears and tail had been cropped, to intensify its aggressiveness. A dog that can't wag its tail or protect its eardrums from noises that are too loud will become crazy, as crazy and cruel as its master.

"This dog's intentions aren't good," I said in a loud voice, "call him back."

"Oh, don't worry, he's a good boy," replied the Sturmbannführer.

"You say so?"

"There's no such thing as bad dogs, just bad masters," said the Sturmbannführer, laughing.

The two dogs faced one another for a long time, both baring their canines. A fight would break out any moment.

"Sturmbannführer, call off your dog!" I yelled.

Instead of acting, the SS officer was exchanging a few amused comments with his adjutant.

Febo kept growling and stood his ground, motionless on his noble Etna Cirneco paws, his fine, agile paws inherited from Cretan, Turkish, Syrian and Lebanese dogs, dogs of great antiquity painted on Greek vases from the time of Homer, Callimachus and Lucian.

The Doberman did not attack. The mental fight between the two dogs was over. Febo had not yielded. The Doberman had perhaps convinced himself that Febo's meat was poisonous, that it would bring bad luck to tear a dog like that to pieces, that the deities who rule over dogs would not approve. I felt my gentle friend lie down by my side, worn out by the tension, and lick one of his paws, to regain his composure. I gave him a caress to let him know how pleased I was with him.

"Don't take it badly, Signor Suckert," said the Sturmbannführer with a jovial expression, while the Doberman returned unwillingly to him, looking gloomy.

"I was only afraid your dog might get hurt," I said.

The Sturmbannführer guffawed, followed by his attendant.

"The name Suckert says something to me," he said, "are you German?"

"My father is. But when he was still young he moved to Tuscany, and there he met my mother."

"I see. Then I must have heard your name on some other occasion."

As I feared, someone still remembered my old name. Or the Devil had brought off one of his masterpieces. I looked more closely at the Sturmbannführer's face, at his blue eyes, hard, yet shifty, the eyes of one who loves war, but does not love fighting in person.

"French front, 1918", I said, "I was at Bligny, on the Marne, under the orders of General Berthelot."

"Then we were on opposing sides," said the Sturmbannführer, with a conciliatory smile.

"Yes, we were on opposing sides," said I, without returning his smile, as the torrent of memories suddenly overwhelmed me. Memories of the summer of 1918, and I, a young rain-soaked officer struggling to save my men from a massacre. Memories. A story of men, poor lads, a poor boy of nineteen who did not want to die, and a few companions who could do nothing for him.

BLIGNY, JULY 1918

War like Me

The rain was coming down hard on the woods at Bligny, it kept hammering at the muddied ground. It had begun at 10 in the morning as a fine, transparent drizzle, the kind of rain that falls in France – at Reims, in Champagne, on summer afternoons.

In the spring, the Germans under General Ludendorff had launched a horrendous offensive: the ensuing casualties, more than two hundred thousand dead and wounded and the destruction of the British Fifth Army. They had advanced to within 50 kilometers of Paris and were preparing a new attack, in Picardy and along the Aisne-Oise front. In the summer of 1918, my regiment was stationed among the woods at Bligny in the Ardre valley just outside Reims. There we awaited their attack.

Marshal von Hindenburg, the German Chief-of-Staff, had decided to test new offensive tactics. First, a massive bombardment with gas bombs. Then a surprise attack by troops brought to the front in total secrecy. These would infiltrate our lines with small assault units armed with light cannon and automatic weapons, making their movements agile and unforeseeable. Lastly, a massed attack with enormous reserves of infantry and tanks.

I, a young officer of barely twenty, promoted in the field, commanded the 94th Section Flame Throwers. To make myself quite clear, flame throwers are not stuff for young ladies. My men had to force their way on foot into the enemy lines and flush out their infantry, house after house, trench after trench, roasting them alive. And as flame throwers were the terror of any infantry, if those using them were captured, a terrible revenge was exacted: they were tortured and killed.

We were first out. We had to advance to where the Germans held a strategic position on top of a little hill behind a wood which everyone called the Bligny mountain. I asked my superiors to provide us with field gun cover, but they gave us none.

We went onto the attack at two in the morning, by moonlight. We had covered barely a hundred meters when the German machine guns began to cut us down. I heard my men advance screaming among the bullets. Exploding thighs and knees sprayed splinters of bone and rags of flesh, then they fell face down in the mud. Yet on we went, on and again on, through the dreadful firestorm. After running a few minutes I threw myself, filthy and panting, into a ditch. By now I had barely a hundred men, but we were a few paces from our objective: the German bunker on top of the Bligny mountain.

To my right, I could still hear the machine guns, ra-ta-ta-ta-ta, confused complaints and harrowing screams of pain. I saw a few soldiers staggering like drunken, crippled or blinded cows. At first I thought that our men of the 51st Infantry had been fighting Germans hand-to-hand; then I understood. They were my men who, in the blind heat of the advance had crossed a vineyard. They had gotten bogged down in mud and entangled with the stakes and wiring that propped up the vines; as they struggled to free themselves from the trap, the German machine guns had time to take careful aim and pick them off one by one. They were screaming, screaming, my boys, as the burning clusters of bullets tore right through them, shattering skulls, smashing hip bones, piercing shoulders and thighs. I shut my eyes tightly not to see, crying out in turn so as not to hear the cries of my boys, then blocking my ears, then again my eyes which would open again of their own accord, and wishing I had four, ten, twenty hands, not to see and not to hear.

In the end, silence. I drew my fingers away from my face furrowed with tears and took my binoculars. Not a man was left standing in the vineyard, save for one soldier hanging from a stake like a puppet, a poor dead Pinocchio. The German machine guns had torn their chests open, but they'd not managed to unhook him from that stake.

Every now and then I heard a shot come whistling over my head. I saw some of my men coming towards me, trying to rejoin the main group. The machine guns started singing again, ra-ta-ta-ta, and again I saw my boys fall one by one, under the hail of bullets from the German machine guns. Only one of them, a very young lad from Palermo, had almost succeeded in reaching my ditch, but a burst of gunfire opened up a row of black daisies in his chest, and he too fell, a few meters from me, when he'd very nearly made it.

It was raining. It was not cold, but the rain was falling, thin, pallid, insistent. Time to move on. Crawling diagonally in relation to the top of the mountain, we managed to worm our way, as silently as serpents, into the little wood beside the fort. We stood up only once we had entered the wood, and then we crossed it until we could see the grey wall of the bunker. Within the fortification, we could see the Germans' little flag.

We could take no prisoners, and we took none. We attacked screaming like madmen, like primitive men assaulting a mammoth. First, we shot at the sentries, then we lit our flame throwers and in unison we reached out their infernal tongues onto those poor German boys. We saw them scream and leap like maddened devils, and there spread in the air that smell of burnt insects, of burnt-out moths, that tremendous smell released by every fingernail, every hair, every human bone consumed by fire. The flames blew up their ammunition, their pistols, the cartridge belts of their machine guns, burning their clothes, their uniforms, their hair. There was a bigger explosion and one of our boys fell, hit by a shrapnel splinter that set fire to the petrol tank around his neck. The boy was surrounded by a white, yellow and red flash and became an enormous walking flame. He began to scream and thrash about, calling his mother, he seemed a soul in Hell, but we could do nothing for him. Moments later, he crashed to the ground and kept on burning in the mud. Another was hit by a rifle bullet and his tank exploded, so violently that he was blown many meters, while some of us collapsed, deafened by the shock wave, hands and faces torn by the shrapnel that flew in all directions; but at once we started firing again and spraying the inside of the bunker with flames. To give ourselves the courage again to roast those poor German boys from the Ruhr, from Hesse, from Franconia, we screamed too, we screamed like wild beasts, thinking with rage of our companions who had just died in the vineyard, and as I fired I said to myself that one day I'd tell this tale too, only I'd warn everyone that this was not a war story, because men's history is never one of war, men's history is one of beasts who kill, beasts who are killed, assassins lighting a cigarette with trembling fingers, poor lads staring in the eyes the assassin who's about to kill them.

We stopped only when we thought all the Germans were dead, all burned, blackened and stinking like toasted moths. Our breathing was heavy, our faces soot-blackened, acid sweat drenched out skin, our trousers were soaked with urine.

We were down to twenty. I'd lost four fifths of my men, but we had taken the bunker, I'd carried out my orders. That was what counted: to have carried out orders.

We were counting the bodies when we heard a bellowing, something like a donkey complaining, or a wild boar. It came from the woods.

I went to look for the source of that noise. Could there be a wild boar going for a walk in the woods in the midst of all that pandemonium? Following the sound, I found the answer. It was one of my boys, Michele Santoni. He was a lad from the class of '99: kids of seventeen, eighteen or nineteen born in 1899 and sent straight to the front because the others, the older ones, were all dead. Santoni was nineteen, a baker by trade, a giant almost two meters high and as broad as a barn door, all muscle, with a great big head, two hands as wide as frying pans and a mop of black hair like a wire brush. He was a lad of the class of '99 and he'd been at the front for less than a year; every day he wrote a letter to his mama. We all loved Santoni in my regiment, because he was good, stubborn and as patient as a mule. I myself was fond of Santoni, because he was a good guy, a good old fathead, a fat-headed baker, and Santoni must have understood that, for he liked me too, even when I ill-treated him. He was a lad of the class of '99 and he didn't always understand my orders, poor old Santoni, because he was just a baker and a fathead, but when he'd understood, he obeyed thoroughly, to the letter. Because of his qualities, which are so rare nowadays, I'd always entrust him with the heaviest duties, jobs too hard for anyone else.

Now Santoni was sitting with his back to a tree and his belly ripped open.

His white and red guts had spilled out onto his lap, onto his knees, and he'd gathered them up and was holding them together with his huge hands. The rain was falling hard.

"Captain, it's a nasty wound, isn't it?" he asked me.

"No Santoni, it's not so terrible. The best thing for you to do is rest. Let's wait for reinforcements. As soon as things have calmed down, we'll get you away from here on a stretcher."

The others rushed up at once and covered him with a blanket. In less than half an hour Santoni would be dead. No, he didn't want to die, he was young and healthy and as strong as an ox, but he'd die none the less.

"Captain, Sir, can Santoni make it?" murmured one of the others.

"No, haven't you seen his guts? I've seen so many end up that way. If we shift him, he'll die at once. If we leave him in peace, he'll last a little longer."

We sat by Santoni, at his colossal feet, the biggest feet in the regiment, and tried to keep up his morale.

"C'm on Santoni, when you get back from your next furlough, you'll bring us one of your very own loaves, won't you?" said Masseroli, who kept an inn near Bologna.

"Of course I'll bring you one," said Santoni, grown deathly pale.

"Bravo, but make sure you get a good, long furlough, eh? You can even get them to give you ours, and in exchange you'll bring us back the loaf," said Agnello, a little Sicilian waiter with eyebrows as thick as a bush, and the group forced a laugh, just to cheer Santoni up a little.

Santoni laughed too, then he said: "Captain, the wound's hurting me too much, I can't take it."

"Keep it up Santoni, as soon as we get reinforcements we'll have you taken off by stretcher," I told him.

The rain stopped. Light shone through the branches; the moon emerged from behind the clouds, while the dark sky began to give way to the first bluish glimmers heralding dawn. How lovely the moon is at Bligny, when the night's warm and the air is clean, as it was after that rain! The sun had not yet come up and the moon was still shining, it was sunrise and the moon was still there, an ivory and mother-of-pearl moon, an enormous ivory and mother-of-pearl flatbread I'd have liked to get my teeth into, so ravenous was my hunger.

"Look," I said, "the moon's like a focaccia, don't you think so too? That moon makes me feel hungry."

"Yes Captain, it really does look like a focaccia. It makes us feel hungry too, Captain," said the others.

"Captain, I'm hungry too," said Santoni, "I'd like something hot. I'm so cold. It's very cold here, isn't it?"

"Yes, Santoni, it's very cold," I lied, "but you'd best wait till you get to hospital before eating."

"Captain, have I been a good soldier?"

"Yes, Santoni, you really have been a good soldier. I'll recommend you for a medal."

On hearing that, he raised his eyes to heaven, and for a moment he seemed relieved. Perhaps he was thinking of his mama, and the letter he'd write her with the news of the medal. Then he looked at me with a very serious expression:

"Captain, I can't make it. I'm in too much pain. Please kill me, I beg of you."

The group fell silent.

I'd liked to have said: don't worry, Santoni, the reinforcements will be here in a moment, there'll be a stretcher; but I no longer had the courage.

The other boys looked at me. The moon was blossoming now like a flower, it had turned orange and violet, it looked like a focaccia with apricot and plum jam, I'd have liked to pull it down and get my teeth into it, but I couldn't because Santoni was dying.

"Don't be silly, Santoni. Hold on, like a man."

"You heard me, Captain? Kill me. Don't let me suffer. Anyway, I know I'm going to die."

I shut up and looked at the others. They looked back at me.

"We can't, Santoni," I said.

"Yes you can, Captain," he replied.

His face was as round and white as a moon, he'd taken on the moon's colors, while the moon had taken on the colors of apricot and plum jam. Instead of the grey blotches on the moon, Santoni's face had holes, eyes, nose and mouth. It's a miracle, I thought, Santoni has a face the color of the moon, a real white moon, and the same form as a white full moon, I'd never seen anything like it. It had happened because Santoni was going to die and the moon felt for him, I thought, that must surely be why.

One of the men came up and murmured in my ear.

"What shall we do, Captain? Will you do it or will you leave it to one of us?"

"None of us will do it," I whispered, "It's not allowed. Besides, he'll die without any help from us, so there's no need."

"But he's suffering?"

"Everyone suffers at war."

Santoni weakly raised one hand, one of those hands as broad as frying pans, and pointed at the rifle beside him: "Captain, kill me. Please."

"Hell, let's at least say a prayer for Santoni!" I yelled, "People pray for the sick, don't they?"

"That's true, we should pray," said all the others.

"What's the best prayer for times like this?" I asked.

"The Our Father is perfect, Captain" blurted out Cipriani, who'd wanted to be a priest since he was a kid and had studied at the seminary, in Venice. "And you, Santoni, offer your pain to the Madonna, to save all the others. So when you go to Heaven, Jesus will put you next to her, d'you understand?"

Santoni nodded to Cipriani and smiled, aiming a pale look at the heavens. Maybe he was thinking it would be good to stay near the Madonna forever, and his mother would be pleased with him.

"You start, Cipriani, with the Our Father. We'll follow. Let's say it ten times."

Cipriani was a good lad. Now, as he began the Our Father, he joined his hands before his face, and we all imitated him because the wind was wafting over from the bunker the stink of burnt moths, the stink of burnt hair, burnt faces, burnt eyes. Only Santoni did not raise his hands before his face because he was using them to hold in his guts.

Just then we heard the German machine guns singing again. Ra-ta-ta-ta-ta. They were coming to retake the bunker.

At once, some grabbed their flame-throwers, some their rifles. Those of us who were on guard began firing.

"Captain, don't leave me here," said Santoni, his face whiter than ever, while the other men scattered.

"You've a nasty wound, you'd better not move. We'll let the Germans know there's nothing for them here, then we'll come back and get you."

I went off, glancing back at him one last time. Cipriani made a sign of the cross, without letting Santoni see him. We were leaving him to die alone, but there was no choice. Poor Santoni, I thought, you've been at war for barely a year and now I have to send bad news to your mother.

The bursts of gunfire were getting nearer. A German battalion was advancing on the Bligny mountain, and they were clearing their way with machine gun fire.

We crouched down and began to return the fire. The skirmish dragged on, while the moon gradually grew dim and the daylight grew stronger. More of our units came up under the mountain, catching the Germans between two fires. The combat was violent, but we managed to hold the position. We used hand grenades and they worked very well. The Germans must have lost their C.O. Their screams and the disorderly way in which they were moving gave us the impression that they weren't getting any orders.

Cipriani came crawling to my foxhole.

"Captain, the Germans are retreating."

"Are you sure?"

"From my position you can see it quite clearly. They have at least six dead and lots of wounded. They're in a state of total confusion."

A few moments later we heard shooting from far lower down. The Germans really had gone. We breathed a sigh of relief and cautiously emerged from our hiding places.

I wanted to know if Santoni was still alive. I went to see, while the others, as pale as death by the bluish light of dawn, looked to our dead.

Despite the short stretch of woodland between us and Santoni, I was worn out and I lost my way. I got to the place where I could have sworn I left the poor dying man, but I'd gotten it wrong. For a few minutes I wandered among the trees, trying to find my way. Not far off, I could still hear a few isolated shots from time to time.

I was just on the point of calling my men when I stopped, petrified: before me was a German soldier.

He was staggering painfully through the wood like a wounded beast, he must have lost contact with his men. Perhaps the last order he'd received was to open up the way to the bunker on top of the mountain. He had obeyed, but alone.

Suddenly he saw me too, and stopped. We stood motionless, about twenty meters from one another, each holding a rifle. Neither of us moved, almost as though each was hypnotized by the presence of the other. I've seen stags behave like this, when they come upon a hunter with his rifle pointing at them. They stand immobile, staring at their butcher with their utterly pure stare, astounded that death should have crept up so silently.

It was clear that neither of us wanted a duel. He, because he feared I might be quicker on the draw. I, because I had no more ammunition in my magazine.

"*Se ne vada!*" I said to him – go away! – hoping that he'd understand me.

"*No, se ne vada lei!*" – no, you go away! – he replied.

I was left open-mouthed. He'd spoken in perfect Italian. A German who spoke Italian.

"We've won. You Germans have withdrawn."

He stared at me fixedly with his blue eyes, a little dazed.

"That's not possible!" he replied.

"But that's how it is. Go away, or I'll call my men."

"If you call your men, I'll fire," said he, shouldering his rifle. I shouldered mine, as though it were loaded.

The German did not move. He just stood there with his rifle like a fool, and did not move. But if I moved, he'd shoot. I had to think up something.

"Why did you speak to me in Italian?" I asked.

"My mother was Italian, from Sorrento."

We both fell silent for a few moments.

It was surreal. I absolutely had to find a way of getting rid of this stupid German, who was almost a compatriot, before he worked up the courage to fire.

"Captain."

Hearing that voice both I and my adversary gave a start and looked all around us: no one.

"Captain."

It was a dead, colorless voice, like a breath of wind. The German took aim with his rifle. I did likewise.

"Captain Suckert!" said the voice, more clearly this time. The German began turning his gun around him, to the right and the left, looking for a target.

"Who is it?" I asked in a dull voice.

"It's me, I've come to save you from the Germans."

I heard a rustling of twigs and saw him emerge from behind a big bush, swaying like a scarecrow, like a puppet on a string. He looked like a vision from beyond the grave, one of those monsters that people Hieronymus Bosch's Hell. His face was torn by suffering, his eyes bulging, his nose sharp as a blade, the white skin of his face below his cheekbones streaked by deep yellow, violet and black furrows, the marks of one dying in agony. But most striking of all were his eyes, because they were empty, they were eyes like those of Brueghel's blind men, eyes that looked but saw nothing, seeking only me, to come and save me. With his left hand, he held the intestines hanging from his belly, with his right he grasped his rifle pointing it in front of him. He was going to force the German to fire.

The German must have thought he was having hallucinations and seeing a dead man walk, with that great cadaver advancing on him.

"Stop, Santoni!" I ordered.

Santoni obeyed and stopped. He'd never have dared disobey me, not even if I'd ordered him to jump into the sea with a writing desk tied to his neck.

"Halt!" cried the German, now that there was no longer any need. And he fired.

"Nooo!" I cried.

The shot hit Santoni in one thigh. Santoni fired too, but his shot went wide of the target. He began then to walk towards the German soldier, swaying like a drunkard, head lowered, holding his white and red guts in his left hand.

"Halt!" repeated the German, and fired again, twice, three times. Two shots went wide, the third hit Santoni in the shoulder, but that too was useless because Santoni was alive, yet he was already dead, a dead man making war. He fired back, and this time he aimed better. The bullet grazed the German's head. The latter tried again to fire, but his magazine was empty.

By now, Santoni was on top of him, with his guts, with his huge hands, his great head, his hair like a wire brush, his mighty mass of flesh. He charged the German soldier, knocking him to the ground and literally burying him. The moment Santoni sagged, I approached, but the German made a supreme effort and broke free from under the colossal body of my soldier. He dropped his rifle, then grabbed Santoni's, which was loaded, and aimed it at me. In the distance I could hear my men calling out as they searched for me.

For the first time I could look the German clearly in the face. His eyes expressed rage, fear and shame. He was the only one of our trio not to be either wounded or without a functioning weapon, yet he'd managed to do nothing. First, he'd gotten himself conned with my chatter, then he'd been knocked down by a dying man. He'd shown himself to be good for nothing, rage burned in his eyes, he was hungry for revenge.

He advanced and pointed Santoni's rifle at me. I backed off, seeking some refuge with the corner of my eyes. But I was out of luck. His hands were trembling, his rifle was swaying. He wasn't used to shooting at point blank and looking in his victim's eyes. My soldiers' cries were drawing nearer and nearer. I needed to gain time, to invent something.

"Don't shoot. My name is Suckert, Kurt Erich Suckert. My father is German like yours."

"My father's not German. He's Austrian," and pulled the trigger.

I dived to the right, the bullet whistled a few centimeters from my skull.

Again he pulled the trigger. Nothing! Now Santoni's magazine was empty too. I tried to jump on him, but he used his rifle like a club and hit me in the face, then on the head, after which he gave me a great kick in the chest that knocked me to the ground. Then he escaped into the woods, running downhill.

My men still hadn't come. Now I understood why they were finding it so hard to find me. The place where we'd left the dying Santoni was a long way off and my boys just couldn't make head or tail of the situation. They simply couldn't imagine that our good Santoni should have found the strength to stand up and come looking for me.

I rose to my feet. Santoni lay on the ground. I could see his enormous chest heaving up and down, his breathing was still strong. It seemed that nothing could give him peace, lasting peace. Now I understood. He was too big, too strong, too good to die quickly. Any other lad of the class of '99 would have been dead long since, yet he'd been able to walk with his guts spilling out, to shoot and even to engage in hand-to-hand combat. He had a new wound in his shoulder and was lying on his side, gasping. I smoothed his sweat-soaked hair away and stroked his great broad forehead.

"Captain Suckert," he said.

"Yes, Santoni."

"Captain Suckert, was I good?"

"You were great. You saved my life."

"Cipriani's idea was good, Captain Suckert."

I said nothing. I closed my eyes and recited the Lord's Prayer, as we'd been advised to by Cipriani, who'd wanted to be a priest since he was a kid and had been in the seminary, then I opened them again. Santoni was wheezing. I took his rifle and reloaded it, pointed at his temple, again closed my eyes and pulled the trigger. There was a big bang.

Then everything went black.

CAPRI, SPRING 1935

Accursed Tuscans

"So you're half Tuscan and half German," said Sturmbannführer Helmut Aichinger while my memories, like a colossal wrestler, at last relaxed their grip and I could breathe again.

"In fact, my mother wasn't Tuscan, she came from Northern Italy, from Lombardy. But I was born and raised in Prato, not far from Florence, in Tuscany. So I'm Tuscan."

"Are you proud of that?" asked Aichinger, with a challenging half-smile, "To me an Italian is an Italian. Tuscan or Roman, Venetian or Neapolitan, it's all the same thing."

Out of the corner of my eye I saw Pam's worried look moving from me to the Sturmbannführer and back, as though she were watching a tennis match.

"You see, Herr Sturmbannführer, it's hard to be Italian. But even harder to be Tuscan. We're an accursed race. No one despises us, but no one loves us either, and everyone's suspicious of us. Perhaps that's because where and when others weep, we laugh. And where others laugh, we just stand there and look at them laughing, silently, without batting an eyelid. Until the laughter freezes on their lips."

And the ironic little smile on Aichinger's lips did indeed freeze at that moment. He'd felt very sure of himself: Italy and Germany had been enemies in the Great War, now they were friends and allies. For a good Italian, for a good Fascist, it was simply not done to quarrel publicly with an officer from a friendly country. But I was not a good Fascist, at least not the kind he thought.

"In any case, you're not German," I added, "You're Austrian."

"My father was Austrian, but I am a citizen of the Third Reich. I am German to all intents and purposes."

"You're contradicting yourself. You're a hypocrite."

I heard the breath of everyone around us stop in unison, as though blocked by a pump.

The Sturmbannführer seemed to gasp. He blushed, then drew back slightly. He was tempted to dodge the provocation, but he was afraid to pass for a coward.

"Friends, here is our neighbor's specialty," interrupted Pam, hurriedly placing two plates with a piece of almond cake with cream before me and Aichinger.

"Yes, do take a piece of cake," said Richard Reynolds.

"Kurt, taste the cake," insisted Pam, purple in the face.

"No thanks. Now I'm making a nuisance of myself. I'd better be on my way now."

"Please, do eat the cake."

I accepted the dish, took a first bite and looked straight in the Sturmbannführer's eyes. There he still sat before me, with his well-polished boots, his well ironed uniform and his well-combed hair. Only the perspiration on his face and his shifty eyes showed up his agitation. But if I had stood up and gone, he'd not have batted an eyelid. The incident could have come to an end there.

It was Richard Reynolds, poor Richard Reynolds, who ruined everything.

"Come on now, we're happy, we're all friends here. Signor Suckert, how did you guess that our friend, Sturmbannführer Helmut Aichinger, is Austrian?"

"I didn't guess. It's he who told me," I answered with my mouth half full.

"Really? Then you've already met? What a nice coincidence."

Aichinger stopped eating his cake. I, however, continued, for I found it quite delicious, it really was an excellent almond cake with cream.

"No, it was not a nice coincidence," I said calmly, and went on eating, "We were at war on the French front, at Bligny, and he was on the point of shooting me. He meant to kill me. I was unarmed and I put it to him that, getting back to basics, my father was German just as his was. He said his father was not German but Austrian. Then he shot. So you see, Mr. Reynolds, the Sturmbannführer is a hypocrite. At Bligny, when it came down to showing mercy to an unarmed man, he didn't feel German. But today, he does. The cake's excellent, may I have another piece? And a little cream too, please."

Instinctively, the other guests backed away from me, a few centimeters, making a void around us. That's how things worked during the Fascist period in Italy, it was an animal reflex, something that had gotten under our skins and into all our hearts, even into the hearts of foreigners. Whoever created a scandal, whoever showed the slightest sign of rebellion, whoever didn't behave like a fine happy Fascist was shunned. Moments earlier I had been almost squashed in amidst little boys and smiling old ladies. Now I was alone, among scared, mistrustful people.

The Sturmbannführer did not know what to say. His reflexes were slow, as he'd shown at Bligny, seventeen years earlier. The thought came to my mind that his mother was from Sorrento, as he's said at Bligny, in other words from the tongue of mainland nearest to Capri. That's why he was in those parts, he was almost at home there. He too asked for a second slice of cake.

How strange, I thought, that Pamela should have been walking along the Migliera while a party was taking place at her home, however modest it may have been. And strange that her father should have known nothing about her injured knee.

Pam held in her hand a plate with a generous portion, and on it, a fine dollop of cream. She looked at me and at the Sturmbannführer, then at the Sturmbannführer and me, pale in the face, and did not know to which of us to give the cake. The Sturmbannführer meanwhile explored Pam's face, then mine, then again that of the young poetess dressed in white and blue, and her opaque, bewildered eyes, uncertain whether to offer a piece of cake to me or to the man who seventeen years before had tried to kill me. Richard Reynolds was looking at all three of us, perhaps he was thinking again about the tale of the sprained knee invented by his daughter, perhaps he'd understood everything about me and her.

The Sturmbannführer was muttering something in a low voice to his adjutant and sniggering up his sleeve with a superior air. In the end Pam served me the plate with the slice of cake, well garnished with cream. Febo wagged his tail and scratched at my legs with his paws, asking if he could have a taste. He loved cakes, especially cream cakes.

"Suckert, your memory's betraying you," said the Sturmbannführer at last, "I know what you're talking about. There was a skirmish between us Germans and you Italians. It was a ferocious battle. Our men held the bunker on the Bligny mountain. The Italian flame-throwers went to work, but my unit arrived in time to drive back their attack. Our troops showed exceptional courage and suffered severe losses, but they came out on top. If you'll permit me, Suckert, my memory's better than yours, because it was on that occasion that I won my first medal for valor."

"Sturmbannführer, you're a liar."

Some of the guests drew even further away from us, almost as though they feared a brawl or, who knows, a gunfight. Richard Reynolds did not know where to turn.

"Take care, Suckert. You are insulting me and my country."

"And you, Herr Sturmbannführer, are offending Santoni's memory".

"Santoni? And who's that?"

The Sturmbannführer's breath was short. Now it was his turn to feel his chest in the grip of that mighty wrestler, in the grip of war memories.

"He was one of my men. A nineteen-year-old baker, a lad of the class of '99. A hero."

"A baker hero? How interesting... More likely, one of those recruits who wets himself the first time he hears a cannon shot. Anyway, if he was a hero, he'll have had his satisfactions, his medals," said the Sturmbannführer, with a provocative expression.

"He won no medals. But unarmed, he knocked to the ground a coward who was serving in your army."

The old ladies and youngsters were slipping away, around us there remained only Richard Reynolds, Pam and Mynie. They'd all disappeared into the villa, where the whining violin and the ill-tuned piano were punishing the brave listeners with a drunken Mozart. The Doberman was growling again. Aichinger's adjutant, who was holding him now by the leash, gave him a buffet on the skull, to shut him up.

"Signor Suckert, that's quite enough I beg you..." said Reynolds, and then whispered something in Pam's ear. The young girl pulled me gently by the arm, while her sister Mynie did the same with my adversary, trying to draw him away.

"Suckert, if you don't withdraw your insults at once..."

"I do not withdraw them. And you will give me satisfaction for the offence to the memory of Private Michele Santoni."

I took the piece of cake in my plate and threw it at him, with all the cream. Before that uniform would look new again, it would need thirty washes and as many ironings by the famous Berlin pressers, to whom the Italian aristocracy sent their shirts by post. The cream dripped down from his uniform onto his jackboots.

The Sturmbannführer opened his eyes wide, more shocked than enraged. He made as though to rush at me, but his comrade (who had foreseen the danger) held him back with some difficulty, yelling some insult in German. Richard Reynolds interposed himself between me and the two squawking SS men and their Doberman. Pam ran to get help from Mynie.

"You have the choice of arms," I said while the Sturmbannführer, purple in the face, roared insults, "I have no sword with me, but your sabers will do perfectly, if your comrade-in-arms is prepared to lend me his. I am not superstitious."

The Sturmbannführer mastered his rage at last, the matter had become serious. The military code of honor was valid for all armies. His adjutant was cleaning the cream off his uniform and his boots.

"You'll pay for this, Suckert!" said he, shaking his fist.

"We shall meet tomorrow, at six in the morning, at the Migliera viewpoint, and there you must defend your honor. If you fail to appear, I shall shame you in all Capri. I shall publish an article in the Naples paper *Il Mattino* and buy up a thousand copies which I shall have sent all over Germany. Even to Hitler and to your boss, Reichsführer Heinrich Himmler."

I turned on my heels and left. Febo followed me, trotting proudly. As we crossed the garden, under the fine pergola pierced through and through by sunlight, he barked in the direction of the Sturmbannführer, as though to challenge him.

Captains Outrageous

Of one thing I was certain: the Sturmbannführer had never faced a duel in his life. One could see that from his soft, white hands, from his slow reflexes, from his shifty, uncertain look. I, however, had fought a dozen to date, and I'd lost none. Not even once. I'd beaten Fascists, Socialists, Communists, atheists, believers, civilians, military men, even that Uhlan lieutenant in Warsaw, who was thirty centimeters taller than me. These were duels to the first blood, in defense of honor, not life, but the wounds remained and they hurt forever. In the evening, I reported to my two police officers right on time. They were astounded that I hadn't tried to make a break, so that there'd be no need to sound the alarm. They informed me that, owing to urgent government business Ciano would not be arriving either on the next day or on the day after that. He apologized profusely and would be getting in touch with me at the earliest possible opportunity.

After a rather frugal evening meal I settled down in my modest little second-class tourist bedroom, which communicated with that of the two police officers.

"Sorry, Signor Malaparte, but we can't let you sleep in a completely separate room. Orders are orders."

"Please, gentlemen, no need to excuse yourselves. And goodnight," I said, before snuggling up in bed. "Just one favor: tomorrow morning, I'd like to get up early, at five, and take a walk on my own. I want to enjoy the sunrise. I've shown you that you can trust me. Agreed?"

The two police officers looked at one another thoughtfully.

"All right, Signor Malaparte."

That night I dreamed I was under a flowering apple tree. Pam was giving me her chocolate kisses and the breeze smelled of Anacapri olives. Then Pam's soft face became distorted, turning all dark and furry, and baring its gums with a ferocious sneer, it changed into the two SS men's Doberman, enormous and truculent. Now, I and Febo were in the Reynolds' garden, the sun was filtering through the pergola and the Doberman wanted to gobble us up in a single mouthful. Febo, stop that lousy dog, that Doberman's a killer, stop him!

I woke up.

I spent the rest of the night between waking and sleep, thinking I was crazy, irresponsible, suicidal. Putting myself in a predicament like that while I was still in internal exile, risking getting recognized by everyone, risking my very life...

On my way out, I explained to Febo that he couldn't come with me and he'd have to stay there and wait for me, but there was no need to worry. He whined with pain, he knew perfectly well I was lying, an Etna Cirneco knows when his master's lying.

I arrived at the appointed place a little in advance. The sun had yet to come up behind the Sorrento peninsula, where the Sturmbannführer's mama had been born. Some early gulls were screaming in the fresh morning air and sweeping with grey wings across the abyss of the Migliera viewpoint. There, on that cliff, I'd met Pamela, and just look at all the trouble that had come of it. Damn Ciano, I thought, you've made me travel six hundred kilometers and now look at the mess I'm in.

The Sturmbannführer was late. I was met by Reynolds.

"Suckert, please don't fight, I beg of you. I've come only to say this. It would be a scandal for me too, and for my name."

"Where are Pam and Mynie?"

"At home. They too say this is a ridiculous business."

"D'you have a trustworthy friend, Reynolds?"

"My farmer, the man who looks after our orchard and our garden. Why?"

"Go and call him. I need a second for the duel."

"But you shouldn't even..."

"Please do what I say, and don't argue."

I said that I absolutely needed a second so as not to be outnumbered, in case the two SS men tried some dirty trick. Reynolds obeyed.

The Sturmbannführer arrived almost half an hour late. His face was swollen and showing signs of fatigue, he must have spent a sleepless night, writing his will. He'd had the good sense not to bring his Doberman. He was wrapped in a magnificent grey cloak which matched his tragic pallor and his limpid blue eyes, all of which conferred on him the irresistible aura of a romantic hero. I however was still wearing the crumpled and dirty city clothes I'd worn during the car trip from Forte dei Marmi, and I'd not even shaved. When all was said and done, it was just as well that Pam hadn't come, I said to myself. My second, a good Anacapri peasant, was terrified. I calmed him down, saying that nothing bad would happen, after all a duel was nothing but a game between boys who'd not grown up properly.

"I leave you the choice," said the Sturmbannführer, and got his adjutant to lay the two sabers before me. They were two splendid items, with decorated hilts terminating in a lion's head with red glass eyes and handles in black. Both were perfectly balanced, identical in form, weight and dimensions, and I chose one at random.

Taking the saber in my hand, I noticed that where the hilt joined the blade there was a strange symbol. It looked like a letter of the Etruscan alphabet or that of some strange Oriental language, and it was incised in a little oval.

"What are you doing, Suckert? Doesn't the arm suit you?" asked my adversary's second.

"On the contrary. It suits me perfectly."

Reynolds made one last attempt to restore the peace. "I beg you, gentlemen, I appeal to your sense of reason..." But no one paid any attention to him.

We took our distances and exchanged military salutes.

Then began the encounter.

I squared up to him with three successive advance-lunges, each of which was well parried. The Sturmbannführer did not fight as badly as I had expected. His leg movements were good, as was his posture, his cuts were well calculated, but in his lunges he lacked courage. In *moulinets*, too, I was better than him, because the saber calls for a certain fantasy, a degree of inner freedom that a major in the SS could not possess.

There was no in-fighting in the first three or four minutes; only a couple of times did I manage to graze my adversary, but without wounding him. Soon, fatigue would come into play. I tried a diversion; with a couple of leaps I moved behind him and drew him towards the viewing platform. Aichinger's adjudant yelled hoarsely in protest at this feint. However, he quietened down when he saw that I had placed myself with my back to the abyss at the edge of the belvedere, in a position of weakness. Reynolds and my improvised second watched the spectacle in fascinated horror.

Emboldened by the desire to push me over the edge, the Sturmbannführer recovered both strength and fantasy. He performed a couple of well executed advance-lunges, and was on the point of getting the better of me, when overconfidence caused him to expose a flank and, with a side thrust I caught him between the forearm and the ribcage. He groaned with pain and surprise, but he did not stop: to save his honor he had to risk everything in an attempt to wound me in the same lunge, as though we had struck one another at the same time. He lowered his head and charged at me as poor Santoni had charged him seventeen years before, Santoni with his huge hands and feet, his hair like a wire brush and his white and red guts spilling out from his belly.

"No!" I heard Reynolds and his factor cry out, as I parried the Sturmbannführer's enraged and disorderly blows and backed towards the abyss.

My heels were just thirty, twenty, ten centimeters from the edge. Suddenly, I dropped to the ground and rolled over on myself like a wineskin, sliding sideways.

The Sturmbannführer badly miscalculated his onrush: no longer having his adversary in front of him, he stopped sharply, but his boots kept skidding forward. He fell on his backside and the saber slipped from his grasp over the edge and down, down into the sea. He found himself sitting on the brink, with his legs dangling comically over the void.

His adjutant ran to assist him, and I too rushed forward to help him from that perilous and humiliating posture.

"I can manage," he said, brusquely rejecting my hand. And he rose to his feet, trying to look as dignified as possible.

"I'm glad it didn't end up worse," I said.

"Worse? I never thought that could happen."

"Then I'll show you what Pam showed me."

I drew near to the edge of the viewing platform and dug my heel into the lump of earth where the Sturmbannführer had landed on his bottom. The clod broke away and fell silently into the void.

The Sturmbannführer's eyes switched from the Migliera Leap to the outstretched hand with which I offered him reconciliation.

I always did that when I'd won. Even with that odious Uhlan lieutenant I'd beaten in Warsaw, and to celebrate we got drunk together for three days in succession. Only after a duel can one become true friends.

The Sturmbannführer remained rigid, trembling with injured pride. With a harsh croak he ordered his adjutant not to dress his wound in our presence. The blood ran down his side and stained his uniform breeches. I returned my saber.

"That belongs to my adjutant. The one that fell was mine," said the Sturmbannführer, "and you, Suckert, owe me what it cost."

He turned and left. The adjutant followed him. Turning before he disappeared behind a tree, he looked at me and spat on the ground.

"My compliments, Suckert," said Reynolds, drawing near; "tell me the truth: are you a professional swordsman?"

"No. I'm just an officer on leave."

I'd won two victories, I thought, but both must remain secret: I'd won a duel, and no one knew who I was.

The day after the duel, I had to leave Capri. The two cops had received orders from Rome: as was to be expected, Ciano had cancelled his trip.

Before making my way to the port, I made a brief visit to Villa Monticello. I owed the people there apologies, and farewell greetings.

Reynolds was not at home, a friendly housekeeper received me on the doorstep.

"Mr. Reynolds and the two young ladies are out shopping, they'll be back soon. You'll be the person for whom Pam left an envelope, I'm sure."

"I don't know."

The woman scrutinized me from head to foot.

"Yes, it is you," she concluded happily, with a broad smile.

She ran into the house and emerged waving the envelope.

"If you like, you can sit down and read here, in the garden," she said with just a hint of roguishness, before returning indoors.

I sat down on a chaise longue in that fine garden, now empty, under the sun-pierced pergola.

I opened. Inside the envelope I found another envelope. Losing patience, I tore it open and found the message:

SEHNSUCHT

When those I love have gone away from me I am hungry.
I eat up all there is in the house
And then put on my shoes and go out into the street.
I go from shop to shop gathering together golden brown crescent rolls,
Thick, dark bars of chocolate and clusters of smooth,
Translucent grapes, pieces of cheese.
The rolls are dry, the grapes are sour, the chocolate tastes of earth.
Little by little I finish them all; I loosen my belt and light a cigarette,
But I am still hungry.

Sehnsucht: my father never managed to teach me German, his own mother tongue. But when he spoke to me of his past, of those fine lost years of his youth, had explained to me the meaning of Sehnsucht, one of the few words in German that cannot be translated into other languages. A mixture of heartache, nostalgia and yearning for impossible future joys.

I rolled the page between my hands, then folded it and looked elsewhere, into the distance. The air smelled of myrtle, rosemary and figs. From the chaise longue in the garden of Villa Monticello my gaze wandered across the road and over the silvery flutter of the olive trees of Anacapri, their foliage moving in the wind like seaweed driven by the current, the deep sea current.

The sky was deep blue, clean and transparent. I put the paper and the two envelopes in my pocket. It's incredible how deep and dazzling the blue of the sky can be in Capri, like an alabaster surface, a luminescent screen.

A few moments later, I got up and knocked once more, to say thank you.

"Would you like me to give a message to Miss Pamela?"

"No, just tell her I'm leaving today. But if she goes back in a little while, she'll find me in the place where we met."

"I'll give her the message. Is there anything else I can do for you?"

"No, thanks. That's all fine."

As I walked past the villa gates, I realized that there was something written on the second envelope, the one that contained Pam's lovely, sad poem, but I'd been in such a rush to open it that I'd not stopped to read it. I rummaged in my pocket and took out the envelope:

For Curzio Malaparte

I smiled and lengthened my stride. When I reached the viewpoint, I glanced down at the bottom of the abyss into which both I and the Sturmbannführer had come within a hairsbreadth of falling. The saber must be down there, I thought, three hundred meters below, buried forever among the blue and green rocks of the cove below. I sat down on a little mound, reread Pam's poem and got ready to wait. Perhaps she'd come.

A week later, at Forte dei Marmi, a friend brought me news: the very day of my departure from Capri, a young English poetess had died at Anacapri, falling from a cliff.

I returned to the island only three years later. I went to visit Pamela's grave. But I did not return to Villa Monticello, nor did I look for Richard Reynolds.

CAPRI, SUMMER 1939

Malaparte's skin

Only a few hours remained before my interrogation by the men from OVRA. There was no point in moving from Cape Massullo. I went into the house, or rather, into the building site of what was to become the most beautiful house in the entire Mediterranean; at least that's how I see it.

I wandered around the living room, lazily I explored the guest bedroom, the kitchen, the studio with its three windows giving onto the endless sea. At the same time, I was mentally rehearsing the questions that would soon be put to me, and the answers I could give. Febo was following my movements from afar, studying them and my face like a child who wants to learn from adults.

I felt a need for air and wind, I had to return to the terrace. I was just on the point of leaving the living room when I caught sight of a wooden object, on the floor, perhaps a picture that both Amitrano and I had missed: it had been buried under a pile of cardboard packaging which the wind had driven on top of it.

I picked it up: it was a chessboard. Someone had left it there, and it could have been just about anybody, because the path leading to *House like Me* was unfenced and there was no gate, so anyone could get in.

Behind, on the side used for playing backgammon, there was a sentence, scratched onto the wood:

WHO IS LIKE GOD?

And to one side, a little lower:

PAM

At that moment, I heard a voice: "May we come in, Signor Malaparte?"

The men from OVRA had arrived. They came in.

I sat them down on two old stools. They looked all around, stunned by so much beauty. From one of the great windows giving onto the sea there was a matchless view over the Faraglioni, and the steep verdant cliffs of Capri. The sea, which had grown a little rough now, raised explosions of effervescent spray, foaming like Cartizze Prosecco.

"You've a fine house, Signor Malaparte."

"I know. Thanks."

"Perhaps a bit too isolated," said one of the pair.

"That's how I like it. Hard to get at."

"Let's get down to business, Signor Malaparte. Does the name Pamela Reynolds mean something to you?"

"I knew Pamela. Ours was the briefest of acquaintances. I met her only once, a couple of days before she died."

"You must explain where you were at the time of Miss Reynolds' death."

"I'd already gone down to the port at Marina Grande in the late afternoon, and then I took the ferry to Naples. I was accompanied by two police officers, we had to return to Forte dei Marmi. At that time, I was still in internal exile."

"That, we knew. We have already retraced the two officers in question. They say that perhaps you did not leave in the morning, but in the afternoon."

"Perhaps?"

"Perhaps."

"Don't they remember?"

"They don't remember well," said Bianchi, the squat, fat one, looking almost pained.

"I did not see Pamela Reynolds die. Nor had I any motivation for killing her. I've never harmed a hair on anyone's head, except in wartime."

"We know about that, Signor Malaparte. You were awarded decorations for valor. Did you have an affair with Miss Reynolds?"

"No. We'd only just met. Two days before she died."

"That means nothing. In a couple of days, a notorious seducer like you, Signor Malaparte, can work miracles," said Marelli with a snigger, while his companion joined in the laughter.

Febo, snuggling by my side, was following the dialogue word by word, without missing a syllable. The two men from the OVRA were empty-handed, not a note-pad, an exercise book or a pen between them.

"Aren't you going to draw up a report on this interrogation?" I asked.

"That won't be necessary. This is not an interrogation. It's just a chat, to gain information."

"What do you mean? I thought I was charged with homicide."

"There are well-founded suspicions against you, and a file has been opened. Beyond that, we can tell you nothing."

"How are you going to remember what I've said if you don't take it down in writing?"

"We've a good memory, don't worry about that. We'll be putting in a service report. But that's none of your business."

It was just as I feared. Instead of a formal statement setting out my replies, which I'd be able to read and sign, the two men from the OVRA would give their superiors a vague report containing whatever they wanted to put in it.

"Malaparte, do you know Sturmbannführer Helmut Aichinger?"

"Yes, I know him. Was it he who initiated proceedings against me?"

"No, it was not him. Did you ever have words with Signor Aichinger?"

"We had a confrontation during the war. Later, we fought a duel. And we met again yesterday evening, at Mona Williams' house. On all three occasions, I came out on top."

"Do you know what the relations were between the Sturmbannführer and Miss Reynolds?"

"Ask the Sturmbannführer."

"But it's you we're asking."

"You're beating up the wrong track. I and the Sturmbannführer were not rivals in love. Crimes of passion aren't my thing."

"Leave that up to us to decide. Do you want to answer our question?"

"I think they had a relationship."

"Good. That's what we wanted to hear. Do you have an alibi for the time of Miss Reynolds' death?"

"I've already told you. I was with the two police officers who'd escorted me from Forte dei Marmi."

"But they don't confirm that. You must understand that your answer is not enough. We need to understand how the young lady died."

"It could have been suicide. Pam was very sad."

"Did you and Miss Reynolds ever have, how shall I put it, moments of particular intimacy?"

"Ours was only a friendship."

"And how would you define a friendship between a beautiful unattached young woman of twenty and a handsome man of nearly forty who is notorious for having, how should I put it, many female admirers?"

"How could I describe it? A sky-blue friendship."

"Sky-blue?"

"It was sky-blue like all sincere, loyal friendships, too swift to be born and to die. Had it been self-interested or impure, it would have been yellow, perhaps with an orange streak. Every sentiment, every sensation has its special color. That's true even of bad smells. Tolstoy said so too. Every feeling has a color, and sometimes even a form. *A white and red, square horror...* That's a phrase of Tolstoy's. D'you see? I didn't invent this."

"Enough of that, Malaparte. We aren't poets."

"Nor am I. I'm a gravedigger."

"A gravedigger?" asked Marelli, exchanging a confused glance with his colleague.

"Yes, a gravedigger. I dig graves for dead ideas. I bury them under new, fresh, live, victorious ones. I do this with my books and my articles."

"And do you kill these ideas, too, before you bury them?" asked Marelli, winking.

"No. I kill nothing and no one. Gravediggers handle other people's dead."

They sprayed me with another burst of stupid, fussy questions about Aichinger's adjutant, the party I'd attended, and the duel. The two guys from the OVRA knew perfectly well that duels were forbidden by law, but I was a reserve officer, who could be called up at any moment, so I was morally subject to the military code of honor, as was Aichinger. If it were to become known that I'd fought and won my nth duel against a German officer, that would only have won me further publicity, and many people's sympathy. They were less nosy about the reasons for my presence on Capri at the time of Pam's death because they knew it was Ciano who'd brought me to the island. All that those two, and whoever was giving them their orders, wanted was to be able to hang my skin, Malaparte's skin up publicly, stained by dreadful suspicions. Before they could do that, they probably needed me to contradict myself or make some other false move.

"You are not to leave Capri," they concluded, "until matters have been made clear."

"And how are they to be made clear? You can't start a trial for homicide without any statements."

"It's not for you to weigh that up. For the time being, you are to remain at our disposal. We need an address where we can find you at any moment. Where will you be staying?"

"Here. In my house."

The two guys from the OVRA looked all around, speechless.

"But this house isn't yet fit to live in."

"Yes it is. It suits me fine just as it is."

There couldn't be a worse place to arrest someone: they'd have to come on foot, after half an hour's walk through rocks and vegetation.

"But excuse me, Malaparte, how are you to cook and prepare yourself something…"

"You don't write charge sheets. And I don't live in a normal house."

Febo barked, meaning that no answers were allowed.

While the two men from the OVRA were making their way up the path from *House like Me*, I thought quickly. They'd said the case against me hadn't been brought by the Sturmbannführer. So, who was behind it then? I took the chessboard, slipped it into an envelope and walked with Febo towards the center of Capri.

🪶 🪶 🪶

Indifference

"Agreed, we writers are always rather up in the clouds. But how is it possible that you'd never thought of this?" said Moravia.

The chessboard with the mysterious inscription was lying on the kitchen table among breadcrumbs, cups and table napkins. Alberto Moravia was sitting with Elsa Morante, his companion, a writer like himself, in the kitchen of the Anacapri house where they were guests. He was in his pajama, she was in her dressing gown, because I'd come without warning, and they were drinking coffee. Moravia had his usual bored, tired look, with his eyelids half closed. A man indifferent to everything, or at least that's how he tried to look. It was clear that he was not pleased at my visit, but I'd explained that the matter was urgent.

"In Hebrew, the phrase *Who is like God* reads Mi-ka-El," Moravia continued, "in other words, Michael. That's where Saint Michael gets his name. He's the Archangel who fights and triumphs over the fallen angels led by Lucifer who, out of pride, had proclaimed himself God's equal."

"I couldn't think of that. You're a Jew. I'm not," I said.

"And what's that got to do with it? Christians know these things too, my friend. Saint Michael is mentioned in the Old Testament, in the book of Daniel, but also in John's Apocalypse."

Alberto and Elsa had married in church a few years earlier. Father Tacchi Venturi, Mussolini's confessor, had officiated. They'd married because he was fed up with going to fetch her and bring her home in the evening, when it was cold. Now they lived together, so Moravia didn't need to stick his nose outdoors and could stay ensconced in his armchair.

"Are you all right, Curzio?"

Moravia seemed troubled by my sudden arrival and my strange questions.

"I'm fine. And you?"

"I'm bored. I'm forever bored. I can't get away from boredom."

Moravia was pale, gaunt, his eyes kept shifting. Two years before the Fascists had assassinated his cousins the brothers Rosselli. It had been done by the *cagoulards*, the French Fascists, but everyone knew the order came from the Italians, from Mussolini. Like every Jewish writer then, Moravia was having a hard time: the Italian government's new race laws made it impossible for him to sign books or articles. To help him earn a little money, I gave him work on the magazine I'd founded, *Prospettive*, under a pseudonym, of course. I sometimes thought Moravia was a better writer than me. He'd written *The Time of Indifference*, a great novel. As for me, I'd not yet written *The Skin* or *Kaputt*.

He took the chessboard from the table and turned it round in his hands.

"Have you got it then? Whoever sent you this chessboard meant: Saint Michael. You could have thought that one out for yourself, Malaparte."

"You're right, I could have thought it out for myself."

"How long will you be staying in Capri?"

"I don't know. I've got to watch over the work on my house."

"But that's going to take quite a while still."

"Yes. Sorry, but I've just realized I'm wanted somewhere. Ciao Moravia, see you in Rome."

I took the chessboard from his hands somewhat abruptly and made my way to the front door, where I'd left Febo waiting for me.

I left Moravia and his Elsa taken rather aback, in their kitchen smelling of coffee.

The moment he saw me appear outside in the garden, Febo looked at me with eyes full of curiosity. "Tarapoonchilanchi tarapoonchilah," I said to him. "Sorry to have kept you waiting. Writers are strange people, they're full of complexes."

Febo agreed, with an affectionate little growl.

Saint Michael... San Michele, Moravia had said: then the message could hardly have been more commonplace! In Capri, San Michele is a specific place: one of the island's best-known villas, belonging to Axel Munthe. I walked towards the Materita Tower, the Swedish doctor's usual lair.

It must have been a coincidence, but as I made my way to Munthe's dull residence, the sky clouded over.

The Black Prince

When I arrived it was late afternoon. I didn't like going to the Materita Tower; it felt, not like a Capri house but some obscure Nordic dwelling, as cold and taciturn as I imagined Munthe's Sweden to be. It was an old sixteenth century watchtower, where Munthe had written those memoirs of his, which had brought him fame and earned him a fortune, one for which he had no use now. It was a massive square tower and somewhat obtuse; to make it less unfriendly, Munthe had pierced Medieval double lancet windows in its walls and had added crenellations that gave the tower a fake-archaic and delightfully kitsch appearance, like those ancient Germans in a Wagnerian melodrama, with their blond tresses, tin hatchets and horned helmets.

The sky was streaked with white and pink clouds, as fresh and innocent as a child's cheeks. The crenels of the Materita Tower rose in the midst of odorous cypresses, Aleppo pines and holm oaks. I stopped at the gate, which was framed by two pilasters in the form of crenellated towers, as in a Gothic novel. I was on the point of pulling the chain that rang the bell, hanging to one side, when I tried pushing and saw that the gate was open. I heard a frenetic scrabbling, the sound of gravel disturbed, and then I saw charging towards me at full speed a happy gang of five or six dogs, all of different breeds, a Maremma sheepdog, an Irish terrier, a Kaninchen dachshund, a Braque from Auvergne and a pair of American Foxhounds; God alone knows how Munthe had amassed that collection. Febo stiffened.

"Mopsie! Gaul! Popette! Leave the visitors in peace!" cried a voice from inside the tower.

Munthe's dogs stopped as though by magic, hesitated briefly, then backed off, disappearing into the park surrounding the tower. They were good dogs, as gentle and well-educated as their master. A dear old Swedish doctor could, I thought, only have dogs like that, good, well-trained dogs. Febo calmed down at once.

"What a surprise, Malaparte! I wasn't expecting you so soon," said Munthe welcoming me into the main sitting room of the tower, on the ground floor. It was a vast, dull room, with windows framed by great brown curtains, and it was darker than Munthe's dark glasses, so dark that it was hard to distinguish the thousand objects with which Munthe had filled it. The Swedish doctor was wearing his usual heavy woolen suit, a white shirt and bow tie, a green cape and a nondescript hat pulled down over his ruffled hair. We sat down on two enormous antique armchairs of wood and studded leather and Febo curled up near me, disconcerted by all that pointless darkness.

"You must excuse all this darkness, Malaparte, but you know... my blindness..."

"I can imagine. It must be terrible."

"It is indeed, my dear friend. When sight abandons us, we feel alone. Alone like the few decent Germans who remain in Hitler's Germany. Alone in the midst of a wolf pack. It's dreadful what's happening in Germany. The Germans are a *krankes Volk*, a sick people."

"Yes," I said, "they are a *krankes Volk*."

"It is because of my blindness that I had to abandon the Villa San Michele, which was too exposed to the sun. That brilliant light dazzled me. I needed some rest for my poor eyes."

"I understand."

I was beginning to adjust to the absence of light. At last I could pick out in the penumbra the incredible mass of antiques, reproductions and junk that Munthe had accumulated year in year out in the tower: fake baroque furnishings with fake wormholes, Italian Quattrocento Madonnas carved in the legs of some office desk, Persian carpets, Art Deco lamps, Renaissance broadswords, marble Roman columns, an Empire-style clock, a medieval bas-relief. There was even a thirteenth-century rose window placed in one wall, stolen from some country church or, perhaps, commissioned from some Naples stonemason. This was the arsenal Munthe kept ready for use against well-padded and ingenuous visitors: after being ill-treated and intimidated (Munthe had even kept Greta Garbo waiting outside the door of Torre Materita), some rusty ring or fragment of a Roman coin, which Munthe swore had been found on his estate, was palmed off on the wealthy visitor, obviously for a stratospheric price. Well displayed on an octagonal marble table lay some books, covered in dust. These were the innumerable translations (into French, English, Russian, Portuguese...) of the memoirs of the master of the house.

A maid traversed the darkness, left Febo a bowl of water and served us tea in a fine porcelain service, silvery with touches of blue, in the style of the Tsarina Catherine, and perhaps authentic. After serving us, the maid disappeared at great speed, silently, impeccably. The master of the house was notorious for the extreme harshness with which he reprimanded his servants, often reducing them to tears. Closed in that black tower, Munthe was like a black prince, a sad black prince barricaded in the pitch dark of his fake blindness.

Inside the tower, everything, even Munthe himself, gave off a sweet greasy smell, the smell of antique furniture and Swedish castles, the smell of Drottningholm, the same sweet greasy smell I was to rediscover years later, when I was a refugee in Sweden, during the war. In Anacapri Munthe was known as "the ram", because he rarely washed so that the smell never left him, but also because even at an advanced age he had an irrepressible sexual appetite, so that he'd sown his bastards all round the island. Whenever some serving girl produced a child with a rather pronounced chin, Munthe's distinguishing mark, people would at once round on her "Congratulations, here's another kid for the ram!"

"Now tell me, Malaparte. What can I do for you?"

"A few years ago a young English girl, Pam Reynolds, died here in Anacapri. It seems she committed suicide, jumping from a precipice."

"I remember. That was very sad. They say she threw herself from the Òrrico cliff."

"Now I must confide something very delicate in you, Doctor Munthe. May I have your word that you will mention it to no one?"

"You have my word, Malaparte. Don't forget that I am a physician. I am used to keeping secrets."

"Well, someone is trying to frame me. They are saying that I have something to do with Pam's death. Perhaps even that I killed her."

"Don't tell me... But that's horrible. How can I help you?"

I picked up one of the dusty books from the octagonal table. It was the English translation of Munthe's memoirs, called *The Story of San Michele*, because it told the tale of how Villa San Michele came to be built.

"This is just what I wanted to talk to you about. Villa San Michele".

"Villa San Michele... What do you want to know? It's a piece of my life. I built it with my own hands; but I don't live there anymore. Now I even get the servants to sleep here. I just go there from time to time."

I showed him the chessboard with the scratched inscription which I had until that moment kept wrapped up in the Manila envelope. I explained to him the shared meaning of *Who is like God* and *San Michele*.

"I don't understand who can have wanted to leave me this strange message," I concluded. "What do you think? Could Pam Reynolds' death perhaps have something to do with the Villa San Michele?"

Munthe fell briefly silent. I noticed he was shivering slightly, as though holding back a sneeze. Then I realized that he was laughing. We were both seated in the dark, talking of a murder of which I'd been accused, yet Munthe was laughing. He was laughing kindly, quietly, as only a dear old Swedish doctor could laugh.

"My poor Malaparte, but don't you understand! The allusion on that chessboard is crystal clear, and it has nothing to do with the Villa San Michele".

"Well, what has it to do with, then?"

"Do you know what god-building is?"

🖋 🖋 🖋

The Good Man Lenin

Without waiting for a reply, he led me outside.

"This is the time when the birds sing. My birds," said Munthe, his voice as ecstatic as that of a prophet.

We emerged from the tower into Munthe's property. The daylight hurt my eyes. Munthe, however, passed unhesitatingly from darkness to light; he was inured to spending entire afternoons in the dark, to receiving guests in the dark, to perceiving drafts and vibrations like a bat, and then suddenly issuing forth with his dogs and his birds. The perfume of the sea and of pine resin freed my nostrils of the sweet, greasy smell of the Swedish doctor and his pseudo-museum. We strolled a few yards among the bushes and the pines, with Munthe leaning on his walking stick. Febo followed us, wagging his tail.

"Malaparte, you are young. You don't know Capri like the old man who stands before you. Anyone my age who was living between 1908 and 1910, when you were still a small child, will recall how all Europe was once full of Russians. They were clandestine wanderers; they'd been living in hiding for years, having fled their mother country because the 1905 revolution, when they'd hoped to overthrow the Tsar, had been a failure. They were trying from abroad to pull the strings for a new revolution, which was to come off only ten or twelve years later. One of their spiritual leaders, if one may put it that way, was the great writer Maksim Gorky. And Gorky, as you know, lived here in Capri."

At that time, Naples and all Italy were crawling with Russian exiles, said Munthe, as well as more or less subversive Italian Socialists. The Italian police kept a check on them all, but couldn't always come down on them with a heavy hand, because the Socialists had a considerable following in Parliament and in the press. When Gorky arrived in Capri in November 1906, hundreds of Neapolitans and Capresi gathered on the quayside to applaud him.

"I met Gorky. Seven years ago in Moscow."

"Then perhaps he'll have spoken to you about the School of Capri. Or maybe not…"

"No, that was never mentioned."

"These are things, dear Malaparte, that, when you get down to it, everyone knows, but no one's willing to chatter about. And one day they'll be clean forgotten. It's no accident that Stalin had Gorky killed, along with so many others."

In Capri, Munthe went on, Gorky and other exiles had founded a real revolutionary school. Their intention was to train the party leadership to organize the revolution, the final one, which was after all to break out in 1917. The island was to serve as a strategic base for the selection of political personnel as well as providing a school for ideological training. It was indeed called the School of Capri.

"You really must excuse me, dear Malaparte, if I'm telling you things that you may already know, but one memory leads to another... After all, what's left to a poor old blind fellow like me? Memories, nothing but memories."

The School of Capri was more than a mere organizational reference. Gorky's goal was to create a new culture, a new proletarian knowledge base, a world view, a view of art, literature and music tailor-made for workers, peasants, the poor and the exploited. Not just to stir up rebellion among them, not just to endow them with the wealth of the bourgeois and the aristocracy: a new idea of the world must be created, so that revolutionaries would come to see themselves, other men and the entire universe in an entirely new way.

"This operation was called, in Russian, *bogostroitelk´stvo* or "God-building". A perverse but very Russian idea. Modern mankind, the builders of the future, must be endowed with an avant-garde religion. A terrestrial religion, an atheist religion to be brought forth without any reference to God, but by forming a communist society. Do you understand what I'm saying, when I speak of an atheist religion, my good friend?"

"Yes, I understand," I said.

I understood because in Moscow I'd met with Communists like Demyian Bedny, the Enemy of God, head of the League of *Besboiniki*, the Godless Ones, who wrote godless gospels to please Stalin.

"Gorky was the first to develop this theory," Munthe continued, "but there were others with him. The most important of these was Aleksandr Bogdanov."

"Bogdanov was a great mind. Perhaps an evil mind, but a great one," I said.

"Yes, his was a great mind," said Munthe, "the theoretical mind behind the School of Capri. He was, of course, an enemy of religion, because he was at all times a Communist, an atheist, an unbeliever.

But he wanted to introduce God-building, Antireligion. And the time was ripe for that. The Russians were hungry for extraordinary revelations, their regimes had accustomed them to those. In 1914, to announce to the simple people that there was going to be war, the Russian military sent out soldiers dressed as Archangels, with cardboard and feather wings attached to their backs, mounted on white horses, likewise decked out with fake wings. The Russians are like that, a mixture of morbidity, exaltation and political calculation."

Gorky was galvanized by Bogdanov's ideas, said Munthe. He called him to the island to found the School of Capri and launch the new, anti-authoritarian, humanitarian Marxism, nourished by literature, philosophy and science. All these mixed-up ideas were not too far removed from those of the famous Fabian Society in England, which was doing well at the time. Gradually there arrived from Russia dozens of painters, writers, musicians and scientists, but also simple workers. On the island, they were welcomed, found lodgings, fed and looked after. They even had a canteen and an infirmary to themselves.

"They met in Gorky's house, Villa Behring, but also in the open air, on beaches and in grottoes. They were always smiling, relaxed, delighted with the beauties of Italy, the sea and Capri. They looked almost like a group of happy tourists. They'd put on comedies in the grottoes of Capri, they'd sing songs on our beaches, and they'd play at riddles and charades in Russian and Italian, even in English. But in the quiet of their rooms they were preparing the bloodbath of revolution, with its massacres, raids, robberies, mutinies and other atrocities. I know that you, Malaparte, wrote a book about Lenin and the Russian revolution."

"I've written three, and plenty of newspaper reports from Russia. I know Russian quite well too."

"So you'll be perfectly aware that Gorky and Bogdanov were Bolsheviks, members of the party majority, in which the star of Lenin was soon to rise. But between them and Lenin there was deep hatred. And that hatred was caused too by the School of Capri. Lenin was troubled by Bogdanov's project. His political line aimed at something very different from God-building. For him, this was a bourgeois idiocy, a deviation from the revolutionary project."

Munthe broke off, looked up and started whistling in an inimitable style, half way between an ocarina a flute and a cuckoo clock. I was on the point of bursting out laughing when, from the trees came an answering chorus. The birds were responding to Munthe, and not two or three of them, but dozens. He called, they answered. The incredible dialogue went on for a while, then Munthe asked me:

"I adore talking with the birds. D'you ever speak with animals, Malaparte?"

"Yes, sometimes I do. I talk with Febo."

Febo wagged his tail, looking at me with pride in his eyes and showing that he'd understood.

"Ah, very well," said Munthe, a little disappointed not to be the only man on Capri to communicate with animals, and on he went with his account.

Bogdanov was fiery and imaginative, a purifying fire. Lenin, however, was as cold and cutting as the title of his clandestine newspaper, *Iskra*, "The Spark". Lenin despised Bogdanov as a fantasist and heretic. He reminded him of the English Socialists of the Fabian Society, who claimed they wanted to help the poor out of humanitarian concern, but whom Lenin saw as opportunists and spies of the bourgeoisie. For his part, Bogdanov regarded Lenin as cold and without what it takes to stir up the masses and involve them in the struggle, in other words, really to make revolution.

Then there was the problem of money. To finance the revolution, Lenin manipulated gangsters, pimps, arms traffickers and assassins, including Stalin himself, and the money came in fast, so much so that Lenin indulged himself in carriages, luxurious Paris apartments, hotels and vacations. He could afford his mistresses and take a break from his wife who was utterly faithful to the Party, but cold and pedantic.

"But Bogdanov's competing group also raised plenty of money," said Munthe. Here in Capri, Gorky received wealthy sponsors, artists, shipowners. Huge sums of money passed through his hands."

It couldn't go on like that. The split had to be resolved, all had to reach a binding agreement on the future of the revolution, including the fundamental question of money and the common war-chest. Gorky invited Lenin to Capri, where Bogdanov had joined him some time before, setting up house at the Villa Monacone, one of the finest and most panoramic dwellings in the whole island. Lenin hesitated at first, then accepted. Gorky's purpose was to reconcile the Party's two competing Leninist and Bogdanov-inspired souls, in preparation for the revolution. Only, how to go about it? Lenin had no sense of humor, he was rigid, meticulous and mistrustful. Bogdanov was a hot-blooded animal, impulsive and passionate. In open debate there'd be a risk of irreparable damage. Gorky had an idea, then: instead of getting them to talk, let's get them to play.

Lenin loved chess. He regarded himself as an excellent player. He'd learned the game in his family and kept playing it because it relaxed him. In the Bogdanov household at the Villa Monacone, there was a chessboard (what vacation home doesn't have one?). It was a fine wooden chessboard with all the pieces ready to do battle. It was on that chessboard, which belonged to Gorky, that the great challenge took place. Since there's no sport more aggressive than chess, Bogdanov and Lenin could slaughter one another to their heart's content, without declaring themselves enemies and having to go to Gorky for mediation.

The match was held in the presence of a large number of Russian revolutionaries who were students of the School of Capri. For days on end they watched the interminable contest between the two souls of the Party, on the terrace of the villa. Many photos were taken, to celebrate the importance of the event.

"And how did it all end?" I asked.

"Lenin won."

"And Gorky's mediation?"

"No one had explicitly planned that the chess game should decide the political one, but in fact that's how it worked out. Lenin's line prevailed in the Marxist movement, and Gorky fell in line. The School of Capri gradually dwindled. In 1913 Bogdanov returned to Russia, taking advantage of an amnesty offered by the Tsar. In 1917 the revolution broke out and the Tsar was overthrown. But Bogdanov did not join the uprising, because he was against the crimes committed by the Leninists. After the fall of the Tsarist regime, he was sidelined, for while he was even imprisoned. In 1924 Lenin died and power passed into Stalin's hands. Gorky sold himself to theregime, justifying all its crimes. In recompense, Stalin had him killed using a bacteria provided by the secret services. And that brings us up to 1936, just three years ago."

"How can you say that it was Stalin who killed Gorky?"

"Gorky died of a strange pneumonia, and curiously, his son, who was disliked by Stalin, died of pneumonia too. Two weeks earlier, all Gorky's household staff, who were young and strong, went down with pneumonia. Don't you find that a bit strange? I'm a doctor, and I mistrust abnormal situations. Besides, Lenin came to Capri twice, first in 1909, then in 1910. The second time, he came with Stalin, who was incognito, doubtless to make some secret agreement with Gorky at Bogdanov's expense."

"So Stalin has been here too."

"Sure. He knew that to put an end to the School of Capri it would be necessary to go to the place and talk with Gorky."

But, by the time he'd grown old, Gorky was no longer of any use. He'd become a tired and frustrated novelist, celebrated by the regime but unfree and, when all's said and done, not all that happy. He'd ended up approving class hatred, the repression and the massacres.

"He'd been witness to far, far too many inconvenient things. He was more useful as a dead hero than a live witness. So they did away with him," said Munthe.

"I met a whole lot of the big shots in Moscow seven years ago: not just Gorky, men like Lunacharsky and Mayakovsky,. I rubbed shoulders with agitprop men and bureaucrats, I went to the threatre with Karakhan, with Florinsky, with Kalinin... But no one ever breathed a word about all this chess match."

"Obviously! It wasn't fit for too many ears. D'you doubt my word, Malaparte? Just go and ask the Capresi about that chess game and about the School of Capri. You'll see they'll confirm every word I've told you."

"So the inscription *Who is like God?* refers to the discussions that took place here in Capri between Lenin and Bogdanov: Lenin's cold, pitiless revolution against the warm, humanized one of Bogdanov and Lunacharsky's God-building. Is that what you mean, Doctor Munthe?"

"In my view, that's just a comment written by some wastrel. Or maybe even by Gorky himself in a thoughtful moment – who knows? But it was written on the chessboard of the great Lenin-Bogdanov tournament. *Your* chessboard, Malaparte."

"Just one moment. How do you explain that Pam Reynolds' name comes to be on the chessboard?"

"Malaparte, you disappoint me. You know Russian, yet there you go drowning in a glass of water. That word, PAM, only goes to prove my conjecture. Don't forget those revolutionaries were Russians, they spoke, wrote and read Russian, so they were using the Cyrillic alphabet. So PAM doesn't mean Pamela. Because in Cyrillic, a capital r is written P."

I gave a start. I pulled the chessboard out from its packaging.

"Your mystery man, dear Malaparte, wrote not *pam* but *ram*. Of course, that's an English word, meaning the same thing as the Italian *capro*. In the plural: Capri. So all our mysterious scribe did was to write Capri in English, but using Russian characters. That confirms that this was written by a Russian, not an Italian or an Englishman. It was just a joke, a play on words. Didn't I tell you that the School of Capri people liked to amuse themselves with songs and charades in various languages? Theirs was a big motley group with a penchant for merry-making, they'd had no compunction about replacing Capri wine with vodka. Ask whoever you like, there are many who remember them well. Among all those word games between one glass and the next, someone will have dreamed up this silly word-play, *RAM / Capri*, and carved it into the chessboard. That's all there is to it."

Munthe must have read the disappointment on my face, because he hastened to add:

"I'll share a secret from my long experience as a doctor: never think of complicated diagnoses unless it's absolutely necessary."

"Then who put this chessboard in my house?" I said.

"Perhaps one of your workmen, who wasn't expecting you back from Rome, thought you might be interested in buying it as an antique, and left it in your house. Perhaps he'll make you an offer in the next few days. Or perhaps some workman of yours stole the chessboard from the Villa Monacone where Bogdanov lived, and hid it in a very isolated place – meaning Cape Massullo. There could be several explanations, all of them valid. You, Malaparte, are a writer, so you're used to using your imagination. But from what you've told me, you're in serious trouble now. Listen to me and don't waste your time with this chessboard business. And if you still need me, I'll be here at your disposal."

I turned the chessboard over in my hands.

"And then, there's a consolation!" said Munthe, "You're holding a historic object in your hands. Just think of it.   The chessboard of the famous match between Lenin and Bogdanov... If Bogdanov had won, perhaps there'd not have been a Russian revolution, the Tsar would still be there today and the entire history of the world would have run a different course. If it belonged to me, I'd only show that chessboard to my most trusted friends, those able to understand its tremendous historical value. But now you must excuse me, I must go and feed my dogs – they'll be terribly hungry. You will come back and visit me? I'm counting on you."

The Black Wind

Hardly had I and Febo left the gate of the Materita tower behind us than the wind arose, a black wind, black as the black prince who lived in the tower. That black wind drove before it dark, lowering clouds, clouds Turner might have painted over Capri.

It was like the black wind I was to find two years later, in wartime Ukraine in the summer of 1941, in the Cossack lands by the Dnieper, riding on horseback through the woods near an out-of-the way dump called Constantinovka. An episode I'd related so well in *The Skin*. On the trees of that wood, the Germans had crucified Jews, dozens of Ukrainian Jews, with nails and barbed wire. The crucified Jews were still alive, they were dying full of resentment for the world that had condemned them to this death. As I rode among them, they spat at me, they reviled me, they mocked me, an Italian allied to the Germans. I said to them: I'm a Christian, I didn't want you to die like this. I pity you. And they'd reply in Russian: what do you want us to do with your pity? I spit on your pity. *Ya napliwayu! Ya napliwayu* your pity! I spit on your damn pity! While the crucified Jews spoke thus, slowly dying one by one, a black wind howled through the trees, a wind like a black shadow, the black shadow of a night raptor. The same wind blew round Torre Materita after my talk with Munthe, a dense black wind.

As I made my way along the paths of Anacapri I did not know that I'd find that wind again one day at Costantinovka, nor could I imagine the horror that lay in wait for us all. I'd gotten heartburn from the darkness in Torre Materita, from Munthe's antiques, from the sweet, greasy, dusty smell of his junk. All those little tables full of fake worm-holes.

Munthe had carefully avoided asking me who was accusing me of having had something to do with Pamela's death, and why they were doing so. He'd not even asked me how and why I met her. Perhaps because he'd seen me with her on that afternoon four years earlier, when she and I were wandering among the alleyways of Anacapri?

I needed to check on Munthe's account with someone with a comprehensive knowledge of the island, I must go and see Edwin Cerio.

I made a long detour to House like Me, to return the chessboard. Then I made my way to the little town square, where I expected to find Cerio. As the former mayor of the island, he couldn't stop himself from sticking his nose into his fellow-citizens' business. And in the late afternoon all Capri would be in the square.

All places at the café tables had been taken, the piazza was teeming with people and the roads around it were like veins afflicted with thrombosis. The air was thick with stock phrases: "*Eccellenza*, here's a place for you!" – "*Presidente*, this way!" – "Your Highness, permit me to lead the way for you!" Glasses and champagne flutes chinked on the tables or crunched underfoot, in pieces, dropped by fingers full of Tuscan cigars, American cigarettes, long ivory cigarette-holders. The black wind that had arisen when I left Torre Materita was blowing relentlessly. It was making a mess of the women's coiffure, flapping tablecloths, blowing hats far away and staining everything as black as dense octopus ink.

The Marchese del Balzo, standing just near me with a glass of whisky in his hand, was drunk as usual. Luckily for him, Count della Gherardesca was propping him up and listening to his drunken maunderings: "Count, do you remember what Mary Pickford said to me when she came to Capri and I kissed her hand when I was completely boozed up? 'But Marchese,' she said, if you'd kissed me on the mouth I'd have ended up plastered!'" Bottoms up, and a big laugh.

"I told that one to James Roosevelt," said Count della Gherardesca.

"Franklin Delano's son?"

"Franklin Delano's son. But he didn't believe me. He said the Italians eat macaroni but they don't drink. No, Italians don't drink." More laughter.

They were all drinking alcohol but talking about coffee: it was rumored that soon, because of war, there'd be no more coffee and they'd have to drink a revolting substitute made of acorns. No one knew this yet, but it was true, a few years later it really did happen.

Prince Caracciolo passed in front of me, handsome and elegant as ever. "Malaparte, you know the Duce well. Is it true that soon we won't have any more coffee in Italy?"

"That's nonsense. We'll never lack for coffee in Italy. So long, Prince."

"Malaparte *carissimo*!" exclaimed Filippo Tommaso Marinetti, the Futurist poet, coming towards me with open arms. He was followed as usual by his fascinating wife, who was far younger than he.

"Marinetti, what are you doing here?"

"What do you think I'm doing'? I'm enjoying Capri."

"Did you ask Capri if she wanted you to enjoy her?"

Marinetti laughed. "Anyway, it'll soon be all over. War is coming, dear Malaparte, and we'll all be off to fight. You're a literary man like me, so let's not beat about the bush: hitherto, literature has always glorified pensive immobility, ecstasy and sleep. We Fascists want to exalt aggressive movement, febrile insomnia, life at the double, the leap across the abyss, slaps and punches. And war. War is the world's only hygiene," proclaimed Marinetti, trying to make himself heard by as many people as possible, "and we shall win it!"

"The hardest thing isn't knowing how to win a war but how to lose one," I replied.

Marinetti looked at me, amazed and thoughtful.

"D'you think we'll lose?"

"After a war you can be sure of nothing but the dead. And we all know how selfish the dead are."

Marinetti, who was drinking coffee, lost his taste for talk and let his lips dive into the little cup.

Eddie von Bismarck crossed my path swiftly, smiling as ever. His breath smelled of Calvados, a first-class Calvados, knowing Eddie it might have been a Drouin, the ultimate Calvados.

"Pardon my haste, Malaparte. I'm on my way to Phli's place, at Villa Mura."

"Pardon... Who? Ah yes, your friend Philipp von Hessen. Off with you then, don't worry about me."

It was a mystery how Eddie, who detested Nazism, could keep up a friendship with a Hitler devotee. It must have been something to do with nostalgia for money, wealth and power. Eddie von Bismarck came from a great family, but there was not a penny to his name and he'd become court eunuch to Mona Williams. That, I said to myself, must be why he frequented Philipp von Hessen, the son-in-law of the King of Italy. Yes, of course, that must be what lay behind this strange friendship between one of the few German aristocrats not aligned with the Nazis and the mysterious Phli.

Just then, an agitated clamor arose in the middle of the piazza. It was not far off, yet I couldn't see what was causing it. I elbowed my way resolutely forward. In the midst of the crowd, the Sturmbannführer was clearing a path for himself, accompanied by a chorus of protests and dirty looks. He was holding his huge Doberman on a leash and pushing him ahead of himself. Ladies scattered fearfully at the approach of the great beast, which Helmut Aichinger brandished smilingly like a weapon, like the prolongation of his Nazi pride.

A dog is an extension of his master, of his secret nature: the old tale tells that dog and master are always alike, and it's nothing but a reflection of that truth: the dog's a prosthetic extension of his owner, a living one, a projection of his dreams and hidden desires.

The Sturmbannführer and his Doberman crossed the Piazzetta from one side to the other, leaving in their wake ladies' screams and some acid comments in Neapolitan dialect, after which they disappeared into an alleyway. Observing the scene Febo bared his teeth. He despised that Doberman, who was his inferior in all things, but feared his primitive ferocity, the same ferocity with which on the Night of the Long Knives, five years before, the Sturmbannführer's SS had exterminated two hundred SA men, their rivals. (In my *Technique of Revolution*, in 1931 I'd written, three years before it happened: "Hitler will kill all his oldest henchmen".)

"And yet the Doberman's a fine dog," said Marinetti, "it allies strength, speed, power and ferociousness."

"Do you know who developed the Doberman breed?" I asked.

"No, I don't know."

"It was a German called Herr Dobermann. He was a collector of the dog tax, a dogcatcher and gravedigger for dogs."

"One life, one love," joked Marinetti, wiping his coffee-stained moustache with a napkin.

"No. Someone who invents a breed like the Dobermans detests dogs, he hates them with all his soul. In fact Herr Dobermann locked dogs in the kennel, then he buried them, after depriving their owners of their property."

Febo understood what I was saying and began to growl.

"Is it true that we soon won't have any more coffee in Italy?" asked Marinetti's wife, trying to change the subject.

"It's true," I said, without even the shadow of a smile, "and you, Marinetti, have been wise to drink one tonight. Perhaps that was your last cup."

Marinetti raised his eyes to heaven and laughed out loud, as though to exorcise ill fortune. He could not know that he would soon be dead, without seeing the end of the war, and not as a futurist hero, as he had dreamed, but old, poor sick and heartbroken.

I took my leave and made another tour of the piazza. There was no trace of Cerio. Yet there'd be no point in looking for him at home, just when all Capri was making its way towards aperitifs, followed by festivities.

I was waylaid by Commendatore Luigi Freddi and his wife. Freddi was a Fascist cinema bigwig, and was trying to convince Mussolini he should imitate Hollywood in Italy. But the regime mistrusted American cinema and for the time being he wasn't allowed to go beyond kissing Greta Garbo's hand when she visited Italy, or taking Charles Laughton and Ernst Lubitsch to eat spaghetti at some *osteria* on the outskirts of Rome.

"I admire you, Malaparte. One day I'll make a film based on one of your novels. You're a great writer!" said he, squeezing my hand so hard that I came close to letting a groan of pain escape me.

"Then please don't mangle my right hand. It's the one I use for writing."

Commendator Freddi laughed and loosened his grip. He was wearing a fine white suit, which showed up his sun tan and his blue eyes. It was a magnificent suntan, it will surely have gone down well with American actors when they came to see him in Rome.

"Why don't you come with me and my wife?" said Freddi, "We're on our way to Villa Discopoli to visit Baroness von Uexküll. Half of Capri will be there. The baroness will be delighted to have you as a guest."

"No, thanks. I'm looking for Edwin Cerio."

"Our dear ex-mayor? But then you must come with us! Isn't that so, m'dear?"

"Oh yes, Signor Malaparte," replied Signora Freddi in her heavy Russian accent (she was the daughter of the famous Chaliapin, the opera singer). "Edwin too has been invited to Villa Discopoli. Please, please come with us! We'll give him a surprise."

"Then wait a moment, I must talk with Febo."

I bent down and turned to my friend: "Tarapoonchi tarapoonchilah, Febo," and whispered something in his ear. Freddi and his wife watched the scene somewhat taken aback. Off went Febo into the crowd, carrying out my orders.

"I told him he doesn't have to come with us, I've given him his freedom for the rest of the evening," I said to Freddi, "Capri parties bore him."

150

When we arrived, Villa Discopoli was already full of people. The torches on the stone walls of the garden spread brushstrokes of red, yellow and white fire on the faces of the guests. We came to one of the terraces that opened onto the panorama of the sea and the hills of Anacapri. The cicadas were holding their endless meeting, hidden among the maritime pines smelling of resin and damp earth.

Suddenly the black wind grew calm, a light breeze arose from the sea and enveloped us in a perfume of seaweed, salt, freshly fished mussels, that blue and green odor you smell when you take them straight out of the sea and swallow them there and then, sitting on the rocks, with a sprinkle of lemon. Transparent, blending into the breeze, was Pam Reynolds' face, with her sad eyes, her smile, her poems and her chocolate kisses. "It's your fault I died," she said to me, "you killed me. I fell from that cliff because of you. Oh Malaparte, if I'd never met you, if you'd never come with me to Villa Monticello, I'd still be alive."

I tried not to hear that voice, and I said to myself that the dead don't speak, the dead want only to rest in peace and think of their problems and the balance sheet of their lives.

"Ah, at last a few genuine Fascists," said Freddi delightedly pointing out two of his friends. "Malaparte, may I introduce them to you? This is Leonino Da Zara, the eminent journalist. And this is Italo Tavolato, who's a journalist too, and a great inventor of scandals."

A waiter served us cold white wine. I'd not yet eaten, I should have avoided alcohol. The white wine of Capri goes to my head if I drink it on an empty stomach.

"What are you writing? A new novel?" asked Tavolato.

"A writer should never say what he's working on. It brings bad luck," I said, looking all round in search of Edwin Cerio.

"I don't believe in bad luck," replied Tavolato.

"Well then, tell me what you're writing," I said.

"A short, very provocative essay. It will be called *In Praise of Prostitution*."

"But you already wrote that before the Great War... Must have been at least twenty-five years ago!" I exclaimed.

"So what? Can't I rewrite it? A prostitute always does the same thing."

Freddi, Da Zara and Tavolato all had a big laugh. I didn't join in.

"Don't take it badly, Malaparte, we like joking," said Freddi, giving me a disagreeable slap on the shoulder.

At that very moment, greeted by a burst of applause, there entered the garden Mafalda of Savoy and "Phli" von Hessen. They walked arm in arm, followed by an escort of friends and admirers. Eddie von Bismarck followed immediately behind Phli and flashed me a satisfied smile. The daughter of the King of Italy wore a long white dress and, on her forehead, a splendid diadem of emeralds. Phli shook hands to the left and to the right, smiling patiently while his wife made her way through the assembly. The Prince of Hesse, the only man in the world to have access to Hitler at any time, was going prematurely bald, but he had deep, kind blue eyes, revealing a sensitive soul, full of delicacy and discretion, all the qualities to be expected of a king's son-in-law. The Prince of Hesse looked so mild and gentle, it seemed impossible he should have those terrible attacks of rage I'd often heard speak of.

"A lovely couple. A fine marriage," I commented.

"Yes. But every marriage needs balance," observed Tavolato.

"Look, that's Questore Manzi", Freddi broke in, before Tavolato could explain what he meant.

The head of the Naples police, Questore Giovanni Manzi, had entered the garden, using his wife, who came from an ancient and wealthy noble family, to justify his presence.

Baroness von Uexküll extended a joyful welcome to the most powerful cop in that part of the world. "Come, Signor Questore, come with me, I absolutely must introduce you to Curzio Malaparte," said she, leading Manzi towards me.

I put my glass down at the foot of a little palm. As I'd expected, the white wine, only one glass of it, had gone to my head.

"Baroness, Curzio who?" stammered the Questore timidly, but I read the question on his lips.

"The writer, of course," retorted the baroness.

I breathed a sigh of relief. I'd almost feared that Questore Manzi might say "Ah yes, we intend to arrest him for murder" or something of the sort. Instead, as was to be expected from a Questore, a boring cop devoid of any culture, Manzi didn't even know who I was.

Besides, the OVRA, an almost clandestine set-up, was very different from the police, who had arms, uniforms and epaulettes denoting rank.

"Signor Malaparte!" trilled Baroness von Uexküll, "May I introduce you to His Excellency Questore Manzi and his lady, Donna Elvira Borrelli di Sarno Prignano".

Surrounded by Freddi and his friends, Manzi and I shook hands and exchanged a few brief formal courtesies, after which the baroness led the Questore to the retinue of Mafalda of Savoy and Philipp von Hessen, who had just entered the villa garden.

At that very moment I saw Edwin Cerio's little white beard in the midst of a group of young ladies. Perhaps he too had seen me. I dropped Freddi and his friends at once and made my way with some difficulty through the throng of guests, half tipsy as I was, to join Cerio.

When at last I got to the place, before a gigantic vase of oleanders, I found only the young ladies.

"I'm looking for Edwin Cerio," I said.

"But you're Malaparte, the writer!" exclaimed one of the girls.

"It's true what they say, he really is good looking," whispered one of the others, laughing.

"Anyway, do you know where Cerio's gone?" I asked brusquely.

"Malaparte, I've been looking for you all day."

It was the Prince of Sirignano's voice. He took me by an elbow and led me away, trying to avoid the crowd.

"Let's look for a quiet corner. But where the devil have you been today?" said he.

Sirignano never spoke with that tone. Prince Sirignano was a gentleman, and he liked me. If he was speaking like that, he had serious reasons for doing so. We went behind a little wall.

"Malaparte, they say you're in trouble. That you're suspected of having committed a murder."

"That's true. The guys from the OVRA want to frame me. But how do you know?"

"Rumors get around here in Capri. They even say you're about to be arrested."

I looked at the sea, while the sun sank slowly into it, like an outsize round cookie sinking in a silver lake. The sky above the hills of Anacapri filled with cobalt streaks, with violet, brown and red shadows. The gulls dropped from the cliffs with their crazy screams, screams of mad joy, screams of suicidal folly.

"If they arrest me for murder, I'm finished. The news will go all round the world. Do the papers know yet?"

"I don't know. But in the meantime I can help you."

"No, Sirignano, you can't help me. If they arrest me again, not even you can help me. Not even Ciano, nobody can."

I recalled how I'd been imprisoned in Rome, when they were sending me into internal exile. And all the other times the police had come to knock on my door at night, to take me away and interrogate me. I'd had more than enough of being arrested.

"Listen to me, Malaparte. There's a witness. Someone who can say how the girl died."

"And how do you know that?"

"Capri is very small. Our man's someone who chatters too much. He's always boasted that he knows the truth about the death of that English girl, Pamela."

"Where can I find him?"

"He's a waiter at the Quisisana. He's called Carmine."

"Let's go and look for him at once."

"Calm down. He had a day off today and he's gone to Naples to see a sister. He'll be back here tomorrow. But we must get ourselves introduced to him by someone he trusts, someone from the island. For him, you and I are two foreigners."

"What does this Carmine know?"

Prince Sirignano looked at me without managing to conceal a shadow of sadness that crossed his face, almost a grimace of pain, full of friendship and of fear for me.

"I've told you, he's a boaster. He says he knows the truth about Pamela's death. That's all I know, Malaparte."

"Someone left a chessboard in my house with the words: *Who is like God?* and PAM carved on it. Does that say anything to you?"

"No, not a thing."

"Munthe says it's to do with the Russians, the School of Capri, a chess match between Lenin and Bogdanov at Gorky's house…"

I explained to him briefly the theory that Munthe had dished out to me when I visited him at Torre Materita.

"What am I to say to you, Malaparte? Munthe's a bit crazy, like all you great writers. Let's find our witness, then we'll think of all the rest. I'm staying at the Villa Lysis, I've rented it. Come and see me tomorrow morning. But take care. We mustn't give rise to any suspicions." And off he went.

Once again I'd seen on his face an unaccustomed light, a painful patina blending friendship and apprehension.

"Sirignano."

He turned.

"You don't really think I killed her, do you?" I said.

"Malaparte, you're a friend. I want to help you," he replied, and went on his way.

Alone again, I mixed once more with the throng of guests, floating half-stunned in the cloud of chatter, laughter, tinkling glasses, as though I'd been served a mild sedative. The sky was still striped cobalt and violet, the seagulls were still screaming madly. Soon they'd arrest me, I thought, while Pam's hot breath murmured to me: "It's your fault. I'm dead and it's your fault."

Her voice contained a chorus, the hard lugubrious chorus of a Greek tragedy, the chorus of all the women in my life. They were women oppressed, exploited, crushed. "It's your fault," they kept repeating, "Pam is dead, and it's your fault." There was Pam's voice, but there were other voices too, even those of women I'd not yet met. The chorus included Jane, the splendid young American woman who's said to have killed herself for me, throwing herself into the sea dosed up with sleeping pills. Virginia was singing too; she was to die a few years later in a car accident, still hoping to marry me. Flaminia sang, whom I'd disappointed and forced to leave me. Bianca sang, whose youth I'd taken. Rebequita sang, whom I'd brought back from Argentina, from her husband, from her children, all for nothing. Then there was that young English girl whose name I forget, and I'd accompanied her singing all the way to the station, just for the joy of seeing the back of her, while she wept in bewilderment. And Roberta was singing, who ended up as lonely and sad as a corpse, Roberta who, when young, had tried to kill herself over me, because her parents wouldn't let me marry her, Roberta who kept cuttings year in year out for decades of every single word in the papers about me; and wasted thirty years waiting in vain for the day when I'd return to her.

"Malaparte! Have you spoken with Sirignano? He's been looking for you everywhere."

It was Chantecler. He was holding a young blonde by the hand, far taller than him and wearing a pair of bizarre gold and lapis lazuli earrings, surely designed by Chantecler. They looked at me with embarrassment and commiseration, as though I had some nasty illness and little time to live. I passed them with a weak nod.

"Cerio. I have to find Edwin Cerio," I said to myself, "I must think of that and nothing else." I tried not to listen to the chorus, to pretend that my chorus of dead women did not exist.

I shouldn't have drunk that wretched white wine which had gone to my head. A stranger collided with me and I almost fell to the ground, yet I didn't even turn to protest, because my ears were filled with the chorus: "You killed her. It's your fault".

I found myself facing one of the young ladies I'd seen conversing with Cerio. She was wearing a man's blazer with a shirt and tie over a long pleated skirt, and looking at the sea as she nonchalantly smoked a fine Longfellow cigar. She was the perfect prototype of the Capri lesbian, she had the same tender and proud look as Romaine Brooks, Marguerite Yourcenar, Renata Borgatti, and all those unforgettable Amazons who'd chosen Capri to celebrate their strange Sapphic marriages, or to break up the regular relations they already had.

"Excuse me, have you seen Edwin Cerio?" I asked the Amazon dressed in a jacket and tie.

She turned towards me, screwed up her eyes, looked surprised, took the cigar from her lips and put on a soft, welcoming smile. But it was not me she was smiling at, she was looking behind me.

On the back of my neck I felt a warm, honeyed voice, the voice I'd been waiting to hear for many hours, without even realizing it.

"Malaparte, how disappointing to find you here. Still wasting time at parties instead of writing," said Lucia, the little schoolmaam.

Night like Me

It was dark, and we were walking along minor roads in the center, avoiding the crowd, stopping from time to time to peek into some silent villa, with its pergola, its patio framed by white columns, its green, yellow and azure Majolica benches, its garden with those great terracotta jars and little flowerbeds overflowing with succulent plants, haughty cacti, sweet basil and marjoram, turgid pink tomatoes shining like ceramics and cucumbers as big as pumpkins. On Capri the green plants and fruit, and even the flowers, are all outsize, all freaks of nature. Sometimes you seem to be living in a prehistoric dream in which, instead of birds, dragons are flying, the almonds are as big as coconuts and at night you lay down to sleep with a gigantic leaf for a blanket.

Here and there on the walls beside the lane climbed yellow arabesques of broom spreading their drugged perfume, a perfume of oriental spices, of obscure Sufi rites. The aroma of that broom, especially the yellow plant, can be so heady that it leads one astray. The broom on Capri is like a narcotic, everyone knows that.

Walking freed us of the noise of the party, the smell of white wine and cigars and pointless chatter.

"Did you get Baroness Uexküll to show you the little house in the garden where Rilke wrote his poems?"

"I don't care one bit for Rilke," I replied.

"You're envious," said Lucia ironically.

"No. Rilke's fine for you Germans. One day, after the war, you'll pronounce his name and everyone else will think: Rilke who?"

"So you think there will be war."

"Yes."

"Will you too soon be forgotten?"

"I don't know. It doesn't matter."

"You seem out of sorts this evening."

"It's not been a great day. The OVRA want to arrest me. They're accusing me of having killed an English girl, here in Capri, four years ago."

The little schoolmistress gave a start.

"And... you've nothing to do with that poor girl's death?"

"Yes. I mean, no. I knew her but it was not I who killed her. She was very solitary, very sensitive, and very tormented. I think she killed herself. Anyway, I don't have an alibi for the day of her death. But I don't want to talk about that. Come, let's go to the Piazzetta, I have to meet a friend. Then I want to take you to House like Me, the home I'm building for myself."

"Obviously, just for a little chat by moonlight," smiled Lucia.

"Obviously."

In the Piazzetta the crowd saw me reappear without Febo but with a splendid companion. The people sitting at the tables pointed at us and commented. A cheap photographer tried to immortalize us, but I covered my face with my hand.

In front of the post office I found my old friend Tamburi, and beside him, my beloved Febo. My plan had worked.

"Signor Malaparte!" exclaimed Tamburi the moment he saw me appear in the crowd.

"For heaven's sake, Tamburi, talk quietly," I roared, "you're as tall as a lamp-post with two D'Artagnan mustachios and you look like a visionary painter. D'you really want us to attract even more attention to ourselves?"

We'd known each other for years, I'd raised him out of extreme poverty, and yet we still used the formal "lei" when speaking to one another. He was my oldest friend, and yet he came to see me on my deathbed years later, still addressing me as "lei". Perhaps that's because in a real friendship you need to be "familiar but by no means vulgar", as old father Shakespeare puts it.

"But Signor Malaparte, you must understand my agitation! You send me a telegram; you make me rush here, from Rome to Capri, abandoning my work. You make me walk with my suitcase to your new house, where I find Febo who nearly tears me to pieces..."

He pointed at the ripped piece of his trousers where Febo had hung on with his teeth, trying to drag Tamburi away from House like Me. Tamburi had understood, because he knew Febo well, so he'd let my dog lead him to the post office in the Piazzetta. Febo looked at me, almost bursting with pride, as though he expected to be awarded a medal. I lavished caresses on him, whispering words of love.

"Tamburi, you're a great artist, but currently you're employed by the magazine I founded and which I run. I need you here in Capri."

"What for?"

He glanced inquiringly at Lucia. I'd often enlisted Tamburi to help me conquer women, or to get rid of them when I'd had enough.

"I'm in trouble and I need to get out of it. And you, Tamburi, are going to help me. This affects your good name too. If I end up in jail, things will go badly for you as well."

"Does Mussolini mean to arrest you again?"

"No, it's not Mussolini. Someone's accusing me of... Well, these aren't subjects to discuss in public. Find yourself a pensione, obviously an inexpensive one, and tomorrow, come to Prince Sirignano's place at Villa Lysis. All expenses will be covered by the management."

"By the way, Signor Malaparte, those three months' pay you owe me..."

"Come on, Tamburi, are you or are you not going to get moving? We'll deal with your economic gripes at the right time and in the right place."

Tamburi received his orders without any further hesitancy, took his battered suitcase and was off.

"He's a great artist," I explained to Lucia as we left the Piazzetta followed by Febo, "I discovered him purely by chance, in Rome, at a beer cellar party with friends. He'd just arrived from the provinces and painting couldn't keep him from lunch to supper. So I took him on at *Prospettive*. I got him to design the covers, the pagination, the illustrations – why, everything. He owes me a lot. And now I can use his help."

"To get you out of that trouble?" asked Lucia.

"Of course. I need to know who's accusing me. And to find who can get me off the hook. Come on, let's move."

As we walked, we laughed, remembering the Amazon in jacket, tie and skirt, whose cigar had almost fallen from her mouth when she'd seen Lucia. And we laughed at so many other people glimpsed at the party, from hypocritical, puffed-up Fascists, to Nazis ready to burn down the entire world yet incapable of seeing beyond the end of their noses.

"I was looking for Edwin Cerio, at the party, but he just slipped between my hands," I said.

"He went away shortly after the arrival of Mafalda and Philipp von Hessen," said Lucia.

We took the Tragara path, immersed in the freshness of ivy, maidenhair fern and bougainvilleas. We were once again near Villa Discopoli, and we could hear the rhythmic pulse of a little jazz band. A febrile little throng was standing at the gate: starlets fixing their make-up, bejeweled but putrefying old countesses, somnolent husbands reminiscent of tortoises, with their rough necks sticking out from oversized white tuxedos.

Lucia had a silk shawl. A schoolmaam's silk scarf, I thought. We stuck it in front of our faces like oriental dancers and rushed past, so that no one should recognize us, then we kept running and laughing all the way to the viewpoint at Tragara Point.

We came to the great Tragara terrace, suspended above the sea, and our hearts leaped into our throats. In Capri you can take a relaxed walk in the plain with the view obscured by trees and vegetation, and then suddenly find yourself on a clifftop under an immense sky facing a vertiginous abyss.

"It's marvellous," said Lucia.

Before us, under the star-studded sky, lay the silent, mysterious prospect of the sea. If we'd had a magic ship, if we could have launched ourselves into the void, beyond the balustrade of the viewing platform, we'd have crossed the sea all the way to Sicily and, crossing between Scilla and Charybdis, we'd have reached Greece, the Cyclades, the Pelopponese and Euboea, where the first men were to be found who had something in their heads. We were mute, straining our ears to catch the soundless chorus of the stars, absorbed by that black panorama, by that limitless vision full of black light. Febo, too, fell silent, perhaps intimidated by the majesty of the spectacle.

We took the twisting clifftop path from Tragara, excavated from among the rocks and agave roots above the sea, which passes above the Faraglioni and leads to House like Me.

"It really is difficult to get to this new house of yours," said Lucia.

"It has to be. Like everything worthwhile."

Barely a quarter of an hour later, we climbed the steps of House like Me.

In the sky, the white disk of the moon was rolling, its light swallowing up most of the stars. Slowly we advanced onto the roof terrace, towards the sea. To the far right there arose vertically from the sea the vast, gentle silhouettes of the Faraglioni.

I led Lucia indoors. With a little oil lamp, we toured the house, from the living room to the bedroom, and finally, the studio.

"Well, I've been well and truly seduced by this 'country seat' of yours," joked Lucia after I'd shown her round.

Febo understood perfectly that I was busy, and disappeared into some hidden corner. Amidst the boxes containing furniture that had already arrived, I'd found a couple of little divans with a few blankets, and even two cushions. Panting with fatigue, I brought them up onto the terrace.

Lucia was waiting for me, seated on the edge of the terrace and looking at the sea with her legs swinging free below her.

"What are you doing, Malaparte? You don't want to force a lady to camp in the middle of a building site, do you?" she said, her voice suddenly growing serious, when she saw the little divans.

"Really the building site's indoors. Out here, the house is ready," I said with an insolent smile.

"Nothing discourages you."

"No, nothing ever discourages me," I said, avoiding any comment on the triteness of her remark. After all, schoolmistresses repeat the same lines to their pupils year after year. Now Lucia stood up and came towards me, and I went towards her, and our mouths became one, and I knew that I'd found in that predictable little schoolmaam a Woman like Me: a woman from whose black womb the black night is born, a woman more secretive than any nocturnal animal, a woman whose wild hidden nature blends a lizard's agility, a doe's innocence and the dignity of a mare. A woman in whom the human element is light incarnate, whose surging desire has animal strength, the deep, dark power of the newborn.

We needed all night for me to get to know my woman-doe, my woman-horse, to distil our fantasies down to the last drop and discover the mysterious essence of her disorderly abandon.

"Are you calmer, now?" she said to me smiling, as the first light of dawn arose and our bodies at last separated.

"Yes. I am calmer."

Before giving way to sleep, I thought to myself: but where does this woman come from? What merciful deity has sent her to help me? There she was, at Mona's party, talking with someone just a stone's throw away from me, then they had a row, and away she came running and collided with me. Miracles do happen in Capri.

I wonder who that poor bastard can have been who pushed her into my arms, I said to myself. Maybe he too thought she was just a boring little schoolmaam. And then the chorus of dead women raised their hard, sad voices again; and with it, the image of a young girl, weeping, with her eyes closed, barefoot, dressed in white and blue.

I turned on my side and said within myself: "No, Pam, don't speak to me anymore. Please, leave me in peace."

ROME, SUMMER 1957
SANATRIX CLINIC, ROOM 32

The Eyes of Death

"Please, leave me in peace."

I raised my head and saw that the eyes of Death were fixed on me as I dictated that last phrase.

The tall thin Angel of Death who was typing to my dictation pulled at the carriage of the Remington typewriter, sounding the bell that signals every carriage return.

With the suspension of time, the hum of life in the clinic had fallen silent. Not only was Sister Carmelita fast asleep but the unstoppable siege at the door of my room had ceased. The Ministry of the Interior had provided me with a policeman, who stood guard in the corridor outside my room twenty-four hours a day. The paper I wrote for, *Tempo*, had even sent a reporter to record everything I said or did when I died. Maybe they'd fallen asleep too.

The face of Death, still extraordinarily like that of Mona Williams, remained impassive. It seemed as though nothing, not even the gravest setback, could disturb her. I seemed to have been dictating for hours and hours, and yet her pearl-grey tailleur showed not a crease, despite the fact that Death was seated uncomfortably on the edge of my bed.

"Do you like it? Is it coming on all right?"

"It's not supposed to please me, Curzio. Its purpose is not to please. It's to serve your soul, don't you remember?"

"I know. But what matters to me is that it should be well written. I'm a writer, not a typist. I can't write something that has no literary quality. Above all, if it's a complete novel."

"Then I can say I like it. But I still don't see how you are going to undo the knots in your life with this novel of yours. You've spoken of Pam's death. You're tormented by it. Yet it's still not plain where you think all this is getting you."

"Trust me," I said, "I don't want to be like Scheherazade in the Thousand and One Nights, I have no intention to drag things out in order to stay alive a few moments longer."

By now, I had practically the whole novel in my head, except for the ending. A problem that arises for plenty of writers. All in good time, I said to myself, I'll find the way.

My guest picked up her cigarette case, opened it and approached me. I accepted. I found the situation distinctly original: they sometimes say that smoking brings death, not viceversa.

From her bag she drew her gold cigarette lighter and lit it for me. She did it with a gesture at once so elegant and so splendidly icy, that the real Mona Williams would willingly have parted with a couple of million of her dollars to be able to imitate her.

"Cartier?" I asked, pointing at the lighter.

"Dupont. If you don't mind, we'd better be getting on. As you know, our time is limited."

I stood up and served myself a drop of liquor, watered it down, a little and sipped calmly, searching my mind for the words with which to continue. I looked at my legs, once again strong and healthy, and thought of my friend Tamburi, the painter, who'd come to visit me a few days before. "D'you realize we've known each other for twenty years and I've never done your portrait?" he said. He did it on the spot, the last one in my life. In the end I said: "Now lift up the bedcovers, Tamburi, and look at my legs." He saw what was left of them, just skin and bone. When he left, there were tears in his eyes.

The Angel of Death responsible for typing already had his hands on the keyboard, immobile but at the ready. The other Angel, who was likewise tall, diaphanous and thin, had taken advantage of those rare moments when I was standing up to open the window, air the room and redo my bed. I thanked him.

I glanced at Carmelita. The sister who throughout those days of agony had been my guardian angel just kept sleeping soundly on the chair next to my bed, as though nothing in the world could awaken her.

"I'm ready," I said.

"Fine. But remember, don't beat about the bush. This is a novel of expiation. The fate of your soul depends on it," said Death.

I fell silent for an instant, then resumed my dictation.

"In the next chapter," I said, "the protagonist wakes up with just one thought on his mind: he wants to talk to Edwin Cerio as soon as possible."

Death smiled at me. I'd made a good start, I thought.

CAPRI, SUMMER 1939

God Shave the King

"I want to talk to Edwin Cerio. Tell him it's Malaparte. And it's urgent."

The maid at Cerio's house was not used to receiving guests at seven in the morning. I, on the other hand, was very much in the habit of going to bed when the hens go to roost and getting up early. Tormented by my anxiety to find Cerio, I'd forced poor Lucia to get up in the small hours and to leave House like Me the moment it was light. She didn't take it badly: she knew I had a problem to tackle, and a big one at that.

Cerio received me in his studio wrapped in a splendid dressing gown of green damasked satin, his face heavy with sleep, one cheek shaven, the other not. The only thing in order was his magnificent white goatee. I often teased him, calling him the King of Capri. But half-shaven like that, he really didn't strike a regal figure.

"God shave the King," I joked.

"Malaparte, what is it at this ungodly hour?"

"Last night, I was looking for you everywhere at the Villa Discopoli. I even saw you talking to some ladies, but then you vanished into thin air."

"I was rather tired. I went to bed early."

Cerio did not seem so much troubled by my intrusion at that unaccustomed hour, as rather alarmed. I knew perfectly well that I couldn't trouble him, even if I wanted to. Edwin Cerio liked me, he was one of the many people on Capri who liked me. He had me sit down, and tea was served.

"Edwin, I'm in trouble. The OVRA's breathing down my neck over the death of Pam Reynolds."

Cerio hesitated a moment before replying:

"I know. Since yesterday, all Capri's been a-buzz with it. Have you an alibi for the time when she died?"

"No. I don't have one. Edwin, you knew Pam, isn't that so?"

I knew that anyone in Capri who had any connection whatsoever with writing must, sooner or later, come into contact with Cerio, the island's one and only man of letters, the only one to possess an extensive library.

"Yes, I knew Pam. Shortly before she died, she sent me her poems. I had flowers delivered to her, as a sign of appreciation. She was a very precocious talent. No one ever discovered how she came to fall from the clifftop. In any case, her death was something terrible."

"Look here," I said, pulling out the chessboard.

"Who is like God? And then... *PAM,"* Cerio read thoughtfully.

I told him of my meeting with Munthe at Torre Materita, and the chess match between Lenin and Bogdanov at Gorky's house. I told him too of my wartime encounter with the Sturmbannführer, how I'd met Pam, the party at Villa Monticello and, lastly, the duel with sabers, before Pam's death.

"The story of the match between Lenin and Bogdanov is true," Cerio confirmed, "as is Stalin's visit to Capri, and many other details, too. But Munthe took you for a ride," said Cerio in the end.

"Took me for a ride? But why, what for?"

"Have you ever spoken of Pam's death with her father?"

"With Richard Reynolds? No, never. I've not seen him since Pam's death."

"That's a pity. And you won't have a chance to meet him any time soon. Just now he's in England with Mynie, Pam's sister."

"Why do I need to meet him?"

"He might know who's trying to frame you. He has contacts with people who count."

"People who count? Pam told me that her father had been a teacher. These days, a teacher counts for nothing."

Cerio frowned.

"Do you know what the Fabian Society is?"

"Of course. Those English humanitarian socialists. The ones Lenin despised, because he saw them as secret agents of the bourgeoisie."

"Well, Richard Reynolds was one of the secretaries of the Fabian Society. What's more, he'd once been the lover of Edith Nesbitt, the famous children's writer. Edith Nesbitt was one of the founders of the Fabian Society and one of the moving spirits of English socialism. A great writer."

"If he frequents the high and mighty, what's Reynolds doing here in Capri?"

"For many years his secret work involved inspiring and correcting the work of English authors. Norman Douglas, Compton Mackenzie, Francis Brett Young and Algernon Blackwood all made it thanks to his advice. His former students, too, would often send him manuscripts from England. Like a certain Tolkien, Reynolds once mentioned to me, who wanted his help in finding a publisher. At a crucial point in their careers, they'd come to see him and he'd give the key piece of advice they needed to improve their books, or save them from going up a blind alley. When he came to Capri, D.H. Lawrence would meet the Reynolds at the Villa Quattro Venti and spend hours with little Pam and her sisters singing charades and talking literature with their Dad. So you can just imagine where the hand of Richard Reynolds has reached. Even if no one knows that."

"And who told you all this?"

"Come on, Malaparte! My family has always been up to its neck in literature, just like you've been up to your neck in problems. When Joseph Conrad came to Capri he was my father's guest. When he was writing *The Great Gatsby*, Fitzgerald wanted to stay at my house, because that's where Mackenzie wrote *Sinister Street*. Here in Capri so many have passed through: Rilke, Brecht, Gorky, W. Somerset Maugham, George Bernard Shaw, E.F. Benson... If she hadn't died in that absurd way, perhaps poor Pam Reynolds would have seen her name written beside theirs."

Cerio sipped his tea. Edwin Cerio was a gentleman of another era, a gentleman of the old school with a white goatee beard and a steely glance. From time to time he'd look swiftly at me to see what effect his words were having on me.

"So what you mean to suggest," I said, "is that perhaps Pam's death had something to do with the Fabian Society. Perhaps it even has to do with some Marxist movement, with Lenin, with Gorky. Is that what you're getting at?"

"I observe only that Munthe hid the most important thing from you. He wants to sell Villa San Michele".

"To sell it? And who to?"

Cerio scratched his white beard and screwed up his eyes, as though a sudden sunbeam had dazzled him. "Goering," he said, "Munthe wants to sell to Hermann Goering".

"Hitler's Aviation Minister? But Munthe never stopped saying bad things about the Nazis! Every five minutes he'd start crying over Germany's destiny."

Cerio sighed, with a look of long-suffering on his countenance.

"Here in Capri over the past few years we've had one long parade of Nazis. Rudolf Hess, Hitler's deputy, came here. In March, we had the wife of Goebbels, the Propaganda Minister, together with Benno von Arendt, the designer of the Führer's grand rallies. Seldte, the Labor Minister, was here. The place is crawling with Nazis. You know, Malaparte, that I worked in Germany, at the Krupp steelworks, before the Nazis came to power."

"I know."

"That's why, whenever some German bigwig comes here, I'm always pressed into service on the welcoming committee. That means I've had to listen to endless speeches, sometimes pretty curious ones too, about Nazism and Hitler. At times, some of those things are almost unbelievable."

"I'm all ears."

"Very well. I'll tell you it as I heard it. For quite some time, strange ideas have been circulating in Germany. Suddenly, they became obsessed with astrology, with occultism and with secret doctrines. The Nazi leaders are all born peddlers in esoterica, at least they've all got a fine smattering of it. Hess, Hitler's number two, is crazy about the occult. He's quite openly consulting cartomancers and fortune-tellers. He believes in a singular theory, according to which Germany will one day be reunited with Asia, to form an Aryan superstate. Himmler, the head of the SS, takes himself for the reincarnation of the Saxon King Heinrich the Lion. Hitler proclaims himself pagan, he said that quite openly to Mussolini. He spends his days doing nothing and letting problems rot, because he thinks he can resolve them only through sudden flashes of illumination. From time to time he says he despises occultism. In reality he's drugged himself with esoteric rubbish ever since he was a young man in Vienna. Goebbels and his wife devour books about the prophecies of Nostradamus. They're convinced that Germany's destiny is already written in those prophecies, or in the stars. They're all quite mad, the situation's out of control. Five years ago a ban was issued on calculating Hitler's horoscope and that of the other Nazi bosses. Yet, only two years later, there was an astrological congress attended by officials of the Nazi Party and Hitler sent his greetings. The following year, the same congress was banned. There's only one man who plays little part in these speculations, and that's Goering, the Aviation Minister. But he has his own special credo: the Terra Cava theory."

"Terra Cava?"

"The Hollow Earth. It's a doctrine that goes back to the renowned English astronomer, Edmund Halley. Then it was adopted in America by a crazy prophet, Cyrus Romulus Reed Teed, who founded a sect called Koreshanity. Later, it was modified and brought back to Europe by Hörbiger, an Austrian pseudo-scientist, and a certain Neupert, an ace fighter pilot and war hero, for whom Goering has a great admiration. I'll explain it in a few words. Earth, dear Malaparte, is not solid but hollow. The hierarchy of the Nazi Party believes that within the terrestrial globe, there is a sort of subterranean world, a parallel world that's developing under the Earth's crust. In Germany, they organize congresses, they publish articles, they write entire novels based on the idea that under our feet there is another complete world still to be explored, with its inhabitants, its vegetation, its mountains and its rivers. Himmler, the head of the SS, believes almost blindly in Hörbiger's ideas, but in the meanwhile, the man has died. I know, it's crazy. Even Goering, who is not a confirmed occultist, believes in this tall story."

"And what's all that got to do with the Villa San Michele?"

"The Nazis believe that there are hidden entrances to the underground world. In Germany, for instance, there's one on the island of Rügen, in the Baltic. In the Mediterranean there's Capri, and Anacapri which is supposed to be a very special place in terms of terrestrial magnetism. Villa San Michele, in particular, is supposed to be perfectly sited. It's no coincidence that the Nazis involved in these pipe dreams have all visited. Hess came here. Goebbels' wife came. Goering came. Even Hitler has cruised these waters on a warship, in Mussolini's company, while your friend Pippo Anfuso pointed at Capri with his little finger."

"Munthe would have had a big laugh, if he'd known all this nonsense."

"On the contrary. Being Swedish, he knows that the Villa San Michele has a very special value for the Nazis. Besides..." he commented in allusive tones, looking away from my eyes and directing his glance out of the window.

"Being Swedish? What d'you mean?" I retorted.

"In Sweden, too, there are plenty of people imbibing these idiocies. For instance, there's Sven Hedin, an explorer and Nazi fan much admired by Hitler, who discovered in Tibet the source of the Brahmaputra. Hedin has spent a lot of time looking for Shambhala, the mythical lost city, the Asian cradle of humanity in which the Nazis believe. Another famous Swedish professor, Rudolf Kjellén, holds that Germany is the natural and legitimate representative of all Europe and must expand along the Berlin-Baghdad axis, thus forming the Asiatic-Germanic superstate that Hess, the Führer's deputy, never stops talking about."

Cerio really was a man with a brain in his head, I was glad to have him as a friend. For decades he'd been living on a little islet, Capri, and yet he was informed of what was going on in people's heads in Germany, in Sweden, even in America. Only in Capri do you meet such originals, I thought.

"Edwin, you're giving me a headache. What's all this got to do with the death of poor Pamela?"

"I'm getting there. The negotiations to buy the Villa San Michele ended up badly. Munthe cavilled too much, he asked for too much money. Goering got fed up with waiting and did not buy, the Führer launched into one of his furies. So Goering will surely have received the order to do something as a mark of the Führer's displeasure. Only, if they were to harm Munthe, that would have drawn attention to his Villa San Michele, and the Nazis didn't want to give away its importance. It would have to be an underhand blow, in perfect esoteric style, a target that apparently had nothing whatsoever to do with the hollow Earth, with the Villa San Michele and so on."

"I get it. So they picked on poor Pam, because her father is one of those English humanitarian socialists from the Fabian Society, and Hitler detests them almost as much as the Jews. Is it like that?"

Cerio shook his head.

"No. They chose Pamela because the Fabian Society has a connection with the questions of which I've just been speaking. For example, among the members of the Fabian Society was Annie Besant, the famous expert on the esoteric.

"Annie Besant? But wasn't she a student of that other medium of sorts, the notorious Madame Blavatsky? If I'm not mistaken, they both frequented that half-crazy English Satanist Aleister Crowley, the one Mussolini kicked out of Sicily."

"You're not mistaken, Malaparte. As you can see, talk about Richard Reynolds raises names, the names of some pretty weird people. Annie Besant was inducted into the Fabian Society by George Bernard Shaw, with whom she'd had a long relationship. Shaw too had come to Capri. And like the Nazis, Annie Besant believed in Shambhala. Sven Hedin, the Nazi fellow-traveler who was looking for Shambhala, is a friend of Munthe's. So, as you can see, the role of secretary to the Fabian Society, in other words, Richard Reynolds' job, had a special significance in the eyes of Munthe and the Nazis. It was by no means fortuitous that a Nazi from the SS should have been sticking to Pam during her last days. The one who goes around with a huge Doberman."

"The Sturmbannführer?" I broke in. "No, one moment. If it was he who threw Pam off the Òrrico cliff, he'll have done it in a moment of jealous madness. He was in love with Pam, but Pam was drawn to me, and I'd just beaten him in a duel. So there's no need to drag in the hollow Earth, Shambhala or Goering and Hitler's other idiocies."

"Are you so sure the Sturmbannführer had fallen for Pam?" asked Cerio. "And even if he had, how can you exclude that he may have meant to kill her from the outset?"

I fell silent, he'd caught me out. Cerio was studying my face attentively.

"No," I said in the end, "I cannot exclude that. But all this is too complicated for me. I just want to get out of this business. There's a witness who saw Pamela's death. Today, I'll go and find him, but I'm afraid he won't trust me, and he won't want to talk. May I introduce myself as coming from you?"

"Of course you can. I'm respected here in Capri. Even now that I'm no longer mayor."

I noticed that Cerio was still weighing up every single little gesture of mine, every detail, even my breathing.

"And the chessboard? Who d'you think wrote those two inscriptions?" I asked.

"I've no idea. But your problem, your real problem, is that you've no alibi for the time when Pam died," he said, slowly articulating each word of his sentence.

"I need no alibi. There's no motive. I had no reason to kill Pam."

"But of course. You had no motive for killing her," repeated Cerio, with a tone that sounded solemn, yet weakened the sentence, removed all its bite, watered it down.

Before taking the door, I looked him hard in the eyes, his white-bearded satyr's icy eyes, which could sometimes be so cordial, so friendly. I was on the point of asking him, as I'd asked Prince Sirignano, whether he believed in my innocence. But Cerio anticipated me.

"You're my friend, Malaparte," he said, "I want to help you."

By an inexplicable coincidence, he'd used the same words as Sirignano. I understood that Cerio, and Sirignano, and all the others held me in the same secret horror. Not because they took me for a murderer (Mussolini's Italy was full of assassins, crawling with assassins, it was ruled by assassins). But because I was finished as a man, I was a cadaver treading a tightrope above the void, above a prison cell, above a pile of newspapers with my mug shots, above a ruined life – no more parties at Mona Williams, no more Acquasanta Golf Club, no more band playing Cole Porter while the waiters served Chablis. That was what instilled the horror in them.

I took the front door and went on my way, while Cerio stayed on the threshold and watched me go, wrapped in his fine green dressing gown. Suddenly, a question arose in my mind, and I turned.

"But Goering was almost always a long way away, in Germany. How could he manage to haggle a price for the Villa San Michele with Munthe?"

"It wasn't he who did the negotiating. He had an intermediary. The Prince of Hesse."

"Mafalda's husband?"

"The only man who can enter Hitler's apartments at any hour of day or night," said Cerio, impassively.

🪶 🪶 🪶

Du Côté de chez Carmine

Half an hour later I was at the Villa Lysis, where Sirignano awaited me. I was out of breath, because it's quite a climb to get to the Villa Lysis. Seen from above, Capri looks like a fish, but if you look attentively, it's really a woman, with a bosom and hips. There's a fine swelling under the neck, and one at the belly, and all these evoke a special interest in whoever knows how to observe her, above all in males; but these swellings are hard to climb. The protuberance under her head is the great hill facing the coast and looking towards the Sorrento Peninsula. The hips, however, are Mount Solaro and the spreading heights of Anacapri, with their prickly pears, their vineyards, their expanses of olive trees. In the middle, there's the wasp's waist, the narrowest part of the island, where Capri village is situated. Villa Lysis is up on the bosom, just where the breast begins, in one of the most erotic corners. It's no accident that it was built there by Count Fersen, a decadent and perverse French poet, who corrupted his lovers, young, beautiful and penniless Caprese boy prostitutes, who all drugged themselves together, with hookah-pipe and absinthe. Fersen ended up committing suicide out of boredom and excess of licentiousness, leaving posterity the theatre of his vices, his marvelous classical-style villa giving onto the Bay of Naples. Its grand stairway had a handrail in wrought iron with a prodigious, luxuriant flourishing of erect phalluses.

It was precisely on the grand staircase of the Villa Lysis that Sirignano awaited me, wearing an exceedingly elegant linen suit, with a rose in his buttonhole.

"You could have rented another villa. Doesn't it disgust you to live here?" I said, pointing at a photo of Fersen on the wall, with his lascivious moustache and equivocal little eyes. Sirignano leaned calmly on the handrail, with its steamy jungle of turgid penises.

"Quite the contrary. I find it amusing, this is just another side to Capri. Let's go now."

At that moment, Tamburi arrived. He wore the same clothes as the evening before, a tent-like smock and fustian trousers.

"For heaven's sake, Tamburi, we're not in the mountains!" I reproved him.

"Not to worry, the great thing this is you're here," said Sirignano, "even if it usually takes at least eighty people to get Malaparte out of trouble."

Carmine wasn't at the Quisisana, he was back from Naples but he was due to work the afternoon shift. Maybe he'd be at the Torre Saracena bathing establishment, they told Sirignano; he worked there as a waiter in his free time.

We took a taxi to the Torre Saracena, so-called because it was built on the beach in the Middle Ages to watch out for the ships of Saracen pirates. Under the tower, in which Giorgio Cerio, Edwin's brother, lived, there was a fine white, grey and pink-pebble beach enclosed on either side by great black cliffs carved by the wind.

I sent Tamburi on ahead, as I and Sirignano were too well-known to show our faces.

"Tell Carmine I want to see him at once, about a personal matter, and that Edwin Cerio sent me."

Tamburi went down the steep stairs that led from the road to the bathing establishment, a few dozen meters below. He returned moments later, sweating and out of breath.

"Mission accomplished. Carmine said to come down in ten minutes."

"In ten minutes? Why that?"

"I don't know. Maybe he needs to change. He's in his waiter's uniform."

"His mood?"

"Nervous."

"Let's go down at once," said Sirignano.

"Tarapoonchilah," I said to Febo, "wait for us here."

We went down the stairs. On the waves, down below, floated German women, white as mozzarella, freckled redheaded Englishmen and the occasional Italian, as black and as dry as the burnt edge of a pizza. Sirignano and I donned our sunglasses in order not to be recognized by any unwanted persons.

Like almost everything in Capri, the establishment was rustic but very expensive. It consisted of a great wooden terrace standing on concrete piles, a restaurant with a magnificent view over the sea and a series of changing cabins. A little wooden ladder led down to the sea. To the left, on the cliff, the old Torre Saracena stood guard, transformed by the brothers Cerio into a villa out of Paradise. From the restaurant's kitchen issued a great odor of spaghetti in squids' ink, raw mollusks garnished with lemon and orange, and griddled scampi. All the tables were full, the people ate sweating under beach umbrellas while the ice buckets sparkled like fake diamonds. Marchese Verusio and Count Pallavicino sat beside their respective spouses, sipping lazily at a glass of Falanghina, both savoring the décolleté of the American tourist at the next table, while their consorts pretended not to notice.

Tatiana Tolstoy, the writer's daughter, passed us by, chattering away in French with Viscountess Furness. Fortunately, despite the fact that they'd spent a whole night playing baccarat with us only a few months before, neither of the pair recognized us.

We entered the kitchen. "Where's Carmine?" Sirignano asked the chef brusquely. The latter held in his hand an enormous freshly fished octopus, whose tentacles, hanging from his fingers, almost touched the floor.

"Are you asking me? He'd hardly spoken with your friend, that tall guy with a moustache, than he changed and went off without even asking permission!"

Sirignano and I looked at one another.

"Where did he go?"

The cook pointed at the stone steps that led up from the beach to Torre Saracena and beyond.

We rushed down to the beach, then up the stone steps, but a few dozen steps further on we found our way closed off by a little iron gate.

We were trying to climb over it, when from above came an unfriendly voice. It was one of the guardians of Torre Saracena. He told us to clear off or he'd call the police. The people on the beach were curiously observing the scene.

Sirignano tried to get the guardian to recognize him, seeing that he was a close friend of the Cerio brothers, but the man didn't want to know and told us to decamp at once. Carmine had managed to climb over the gate unseen, who knows how often he'd done it.

Rather than pass close to the bathers and risk being recognized, we walked through the rocks and bushes until, weary and swearing, we came to the road.

"But wasn't there any better way up?"

"Don't complain, Tamburi", I yelled, "we're not here on vacation."

There at once was Febo at my feet, wagging his tail and barking, trying to attract my attention. It was just there that the Via Krupp began, the pathway excavated from the cliff face that led from Torre Saracena and, in a series of bold and mortally steep twists and turns climbs over a hundred meters higher to the gardens of Augustus, the park that overlooks Capri village.

"Tarapoonchilah?" I asked, pointing out the Via Krupp to Febo, who barked again, wagging his tail in the affirmative.

"The dog's right," said Sirignano, "that's how Carmine got away. There's a path from Torre Saracena to Via Krupp," said Sirignano.

"Tamburi, follow him."

"But he'll be a long way off by now!"

"Don't argue or I'll sack you. Do what you can, then come and report back to us at Villa Lysis. Come, Prince," I said to Sirignano, inviting him to run towards a taxi parked not far off, while Tamburi, dressed like a scarecrow, ran wearily along the Via Krupp.

A good half an hour later, I was advancing with Sirignano and Febo along a pathway immersed in greenery. We'd stopped by first at the Quisisana where, in exchange for a substantial tip, we had obtained Carmine's private address from a concierge. It was a tumbledown house on the motor road from Capri to Anacapri. Fortunately, the entrance was hidden by a little jungle of hedges and creepers which sheltered it from outsiders' curiosity. We knocked. No one replied from within.

A few good kicks, and the door gave way quickly enough.

The interior was furnished with flea market stuff, apart from a few hand-painted dishes hanging on the wall and a graceful lace tablecloth on the entrance table. We went straight for the bedroom, like thieves. Poor rags of clothing thrown here and there, newspapers already fingered through, old photos.

On a table, a pile of papers. Ferry tickets for Naples, medical prescriptions, a card of condolences to an unknown person, perhaps a relative, never sent. And then, closed in an envelope, a note.

BON BONAD KIND RABAL MERVU

"It looks like a coded message," said Sirignano when I showed it to him.

Febo barked. He was in the kitchen, and he'd found something really curious: a little cage full of lizards. They were all entangled, like a miniature monster with dozens of heads, as many tails and myriad reptilian feet.

"Sirignano, don't you think there's something strange about these lizards?"

"They're blue. But that's normal. In Capri there are blue lizards."

"Are you joking? Round here I've seen lizards, but they were all green."

"You won't find the blue ones in the street, they live only on the Faraglioni. To be quite precise, on the outer Faraglione, the one furthest from the cliff."

"And how did they get here?"

"How do I know? Don't ask me, but in the whole world, that's the only place you'll find them, on that rock."

"And what's Carmine doing with them?" I asked, pointing at the little cage with its tangle of heads, feet and tails.

"The blue lizard is a zoological rarity. You're not allowed to hunt it and many outsiders are prepared to pay handsomely to get one. They'll keep it at home, and when it dies, they'll give it to some museum. There are boys here in Capri who have made a fine business out of selling them. They climb up onto the Faraglione, capture the lizards, then pass them to someone like Carmine who, working in luxury hotels, can speak a little English or French and contact moneyed foreigners."

"The ones who are best at climbing the Faraglioni are very young. Twelve or thirteen. I know one of them."

It took us a good quarter of an hour to get back to the center, and from there Sirignano brought me to an alleyway near Via Sopramonte.

"They're poor people," warned Sirignano, "a widow with three sons. Sometimes she joins the servants at Villa Lysis and does some cleaning for me."

We entered a little slum on the third floor, two dark rooms smelling of food. A woman was ladling out a slop into dishes on the table. I got used to the darkness and saw two children seated before the plates. On the ground, in a corner, was a single broad mattress.

"Ciao Maria. Where's Luigi?"

"Prince!" exclaimed the woman, with her swollen red face typical of poor women who have to struggle to survive. "What are you doing here? *Mamma mia*, to turn up like this without warning, in this poor house…" She made the two children get up from their chairs and offer them to us.

"No, no thanks, we haven't time," said Sirignano. "Just tell us where Luigi is."

"I'll find him for you, Prince", said one of the two kids, and returned a few moments later with his elder brother. He was a boy of twelve or thirteen, as thin as a rake, with the most vivid black eyes, like those of a fawn.

"Listen, Luigi. We're looking for Carmine from the Quisisana. You know, the one who sells blue lizards."

The boy cast a rapid glance in his mother's direction, then again at us.

"Signor Prince, I don't know him.

"Is that true?"

"It's true."

"Come on now, I know perfectly well that you're one of the kids who goes hunting for lizards to sell them. There's no harm in that. But we need to find Carmine, because he's not been sleeping at home in the last few days and we don't know where he's gotten to. D'you want to help us?"

"Tell him!" ordered his mother.

"I don't know, Prince," said the boy, who looked as though his head was trying to shrink into his shoulders.

Sirignano crumpled a large banknote in the palm of his hand.

"Tell him, you fool!" ordered his mother.

"I... I don't know, Prince," said Luigi.

"'O vero?".

"'O vero, principe".

"Just tell us then who the others are who go hunting for lizards with you, and we won't tell anyone your name. Is that all right?"

Luigi hesitated an instant, then broke away and ran. His mother screamed a string of insults after him in pure dialect, of which I understood barely a tenth, and threw a shoe at him, but all in vain. From the surrounding windows, between washing hung out to dry, other swollen ruddy women's faces appeared, likewise entombed in some hovel stinking of food, likewise used to sleeping on a mattress thrown down on the ground and making love with tired husbands in the same big bed as their kids, and, as though in an enormous birdcage, they all began bouncing their – to me, incomprehensible – comments and screams from one window to the next, gesticulating and pointing at Luigi who was disappearing at full speed down the end of the street.

We found Tamburi again at the gate of the Villa Lysis, as tired and sweaty as a packhorse: "Our man has vanished into thin air," he said. He didn't even turn up at the Quisisana for the afternoon shift. His boss was furious."

Sirignano cast a worried look in my direction.

"Luigi will already have warned all his young accomplices," he said, "so it'll already be impossible to find any of that lot. In other circumstances I could have leaned on some friend of mine in the police, or some local Fascist, to convince little Luigi to spill the beans. But now you'll not find anyone to make a move for you, with that charge of murder hanging over your head. Malaparte, why not try a change of air? Go visit your French friends in Paris. Or try England."

"They'd stop me at the frontier, and that would be taken as proof of my guilt. No, I just have to stay here and find some way of proving my innocence. What I don't understand is why Carmine decided to disappear the moment we came looking for him. How did he know what we wanted of him?"

"Maybe he'd already been contacted by the OVRA," said Tamburi, "and they've ordered him to shut up."

"It could have been that," said Sirignano.

"Prince, you'll have to get me a statue of San Gennaro," I said.

"And what d'you want that for? D'you want to pray?"

"No, I've something else in mind. You must find me a statue of San Gennaro, a big, gilded one. And then, a mountaineer. A professional climber."

"Malaparte, you're crazy. Where the hell am I to find an Alpinist in an island in the middle of the sea?"

"Sirignano, you said you wanted to help me. So find me a statue of San Gennaro and a climber."

"I'll do my best."

"Tamburi, just listen to these words: BON BONAD KIND RABAL MERVU. We read them on a slip of paper in Carmine's room. What do they bring to mind for you?"

"They sound like some kind of secret code. KIND means boy in German. But, as for the rest..."

"Right, note it down and rack your brains. Look for a solution, an interpretation."

"This morning, Edda Ciano arrived in Capri, without her husband," said Sirignano, "and this evening there will be a little reception in her villa. Will you be there?"

"Of course, I'll be there. And I'll make sure that everyone sees me. No one must think I'm hiding. Come Tamburi, let's go and take a shower at your pensione. Then I'll pass by House like Me, change my clothes and make my way to Edda's reception. If tomorrow, dear Signora Ciano talks to Papa Mussolini, I'll let him know I'm still alive and kicking."

"D'you really think so?" asked Sirignano.

"Of course. There's nothing Mussolini wouldn't do for his daughter. Edda's the only one who can disturb her father for any reason, even for a trifle."

🌿 🌿 🌿

Roses of Flesh

"Two thousand lire," whispered Edda Ciano.

The Duce's daughter took a quick sip from her glass of whisky and looked around, weighing up the reactions of the other players.

"Too much for me," said the Marchese di Riofreddo, and threw down his cards on the table.

Edda took her cigarette from the ashtray, breathed in hard and puffed out a great cloud of smoke. Under the lamp hanging low over the table, that cloud took on the form of a wave, then a flower, becoming at length an immense Chinese dragon, resplendent with wings and fins, a flying monster hanging over the players' heads. That dragon was the sick womanhood of Mussolini's daughter, her failed woman's soul, but only I could see that, only I knew it existed. The others allowed themselves to be impressed by the number of Edda's lovers, which in reality meant absolutely nothing, because Edda, like her husband, made love out of pure snobbery. That evening at the poker table she wore a low-cut little black dress with two big flesh-colored roses on the bosom, just over the nipples, and they looked like two roses of flesh. They made one want to grab the breasts of the Duce's daughter and squeeze them, as though they were two pieces of dead meat, two butcher's cast-offs.

"Too much for me too," said Filippo Anfuso.

"Ditto," said Marchese Bugnano.

That left Paul Angelescu, the Romanian millionaire.

"I see," said Angelescu.

At the gaming table, Edda Ciano was, as usual, the only woman. She loved being surrounded by men because she herself was a man. Not that she was lesbian or deformed, on the contrary, she was not lacking in charm. But she was a born tomboy and Mussolini had raised her as one, nor had marriage, children and lovers changed her. The grey dragon born from her nostrils continued to fly above the players' heads, threatening them with its tremendous jaws, but they didn't realize it, nor did the people gathered around the table. Only I saw the dragon, for I knew that Edda Ciano was a man, a poor man born with a woman's body.

"Pair of tens," said Edda, showing the cards.

Angelescu laid his cards one by one on the green baize. "Three jacks," he said in a low voice, as though he were apologizing.

Edda laughed. She always did that when a bluff went wrong.

"I'm hot. Will you take me for a walk on the terrace?" she said to Chantecler, who was standing not far from her.

Edda stood up, everyone admired her little black dress with its roses of flesh, those roses of flesh I'd have so liked to squeeze, just to test their consistency – and so what if Edda smacked my face, in fact she'd probably have done nothing. The other players rose too, the game was over, the lady of the house was tired of losing. The flying dragon of grey smoke turned into a mushroom, then a bunch of daisies, after which it dissolved.

The little gathering that had posted itself all round the table dispersed. I knew the routine: after a short walk on the balcony of her villa, Edda would shut herself in her room and call the business manager of the *Popolo d'Italia*, the daily newspaper Mussolini owned, asking him to send her more money urgently for current expenses. Capri's very dear and I need so many things for the children, she'd say (only, that evening she'd lost more than fifteen thousand lire at the gaming table).

For a while I wandered aimlessly round Galeazzo and Edda's enormous villa, just waiting for the party to be over so that I could talk face to face with Fascism's most powerful woman, the only Italian woman appreciated by Hitler, the only one to have made it to the cover of *Time* magazine. In every one of those looking at me, in those who gave me a quick handshake, in whoever spoke to me, I noted the symptoms of my disease, the sickness of someone inches away from the end, and they just couldn't wait to see me in prison, so they could shelve the problem at last.

After 'phoning Rome, Edda returned to the main reception room, followed as ever by dozens of adoring or complaisant eyes. She went onto the terrace and threw herself into Chantecler's arms; and he cuddled her like a little girl. Behind Chantecler stood other handsome young scions of the Neapolitan nobility who'd wait on Edda, refilling her glass or lighting her cigarette, and couldn't keep their eyes off her two wonderful flesh roses.

The guests were beginning to take their leave. I went out onto the terrace. I saw my dear friend Filippo Anfuso, who could not have been closer to Galeazzo Ciano at the Ministry of Foreign Affairs, draw close to Edda and whisper something in her ear with a serious expression, perhaps a request not to overdo her behavior, not to sully her – already shaky – marriage too much.

"We've got to enjoy ourselves while it lasts, Filippo," replied Edda. "It won't last. Soon they'll kill us all."

The guests around her fell silent. "You're upset about losing at poker," said Chantecler, trying to make light of it.

The Duce's daughter took Chantecler by the arm and drew him behind a screen, where the pair stayed kissing, paying no attention to the fact that we were all looking. I felt like crying, I couldn't just stay planted there outside.

I went back in, I passed a group of guests making their way out, I went down the stairs that led to the lower storey of the villa and took the first door I came to. I closed it behind me and found myself in the dark. There was just a weak night light in a corner. In the warm, damp air there rose a slight murmur, a perfumed peace-bringing wave. There lay Edda's three children, sleeping in their little beds. Another door led to the little room where the children's nanny slept. I stood there in silence, like a ghost, hardly breathing, for who knows how long. At length I sat down on a stool and began to stroke the forehead of Marzio, the smallest child, with my fingertips, taking care not to wake him. Outside, I could hear the last laughter, the last clinking of bottles and glasses. I caressed the warm, perfumed foreheads of Raimonda and Fabrizio, the biggest of the three, calling their names in an almost silent murmur, so as not to wake them up. As I caressed them, I thought that Edda was right, the game would soon be over and then war and death would swallow us all up; and it was all her father's fault.

Her father: even during her honeymoon he'd shower her with messages, for he loved her with the visceral attachment of every jealous father. She, Edda, did not yet know that it would be her father who'd have her husband shot, only to end up in his turn massacred, flayed, hanging upside down like a beast with a rope around his neck while the crowd spat and pissed on him; and she herself fled to Switzerland to throw herself on the Americans' mercy, selling off her husband's secret documents to Allen Dulles' secret service for a pittance. Poor Edda did not yet know that, to help Galeazzo, she'd dare blackmail and threaten Hitler himself, becoming the faithful, heroic wife she'd never been. She did not know that her husband, at the moment of his execution, would struggle wildly to turn the chair to which he was tied so he could face the firing squad and take the bullets in the face, not in the back, redeeming in an instant a lifetime of cowardice, betrayals, hypocrisy and lovelessness.

Silently I caressed the warm foreheads of Edda and Galeazzo's children, with tears in my eyes; because I knew Edda was right, the fun would soon be over, soon Mussolini would throw us to the dogs of war, American bombs would rain down and soon we'd all be dead, as we deserved.

From the little room I heard a rustling, a light turned on, the nanny had woken up. I took the door at once and climbed the stairs to the reception room, the magnificent salon famed throughout all Capri because it was said that the blinds over the windows could be lowered at a distance, at the mere touch of a button, something not even the Duce in person had in his house.

The party was over. Edda was alone, sitting expressionless at the card table, still smoking with a glass of whisky in her hand. She must have been thinking of Galeazzo, of his lies, his vanity, his silly dream of replacing Mussolini with the blessing of Roosevelt and Churchill.

She turned suddenly, and gave a start.

"Malaparte, what are you still doing here?"

"I'm waiting to talk to you. I've been waiting the whole evening."

"And why didn't you tell me at once?"

She was pale, her face was tired and her eyes reddened by alcohol and smoke. "Come, let's go outside," she said, "I need air."

She put a white silk stole across her shoulders and led me out onto the terrace. The wind had come up, Edda was trembling a little. We stood there, leaning on the balustrade, one beside the other, gazing towards the distant line of the sea and the stars set in a hard, cold sky. Like me, Edda admired the spectacle, yet she did not care for it. Edda loved only death, I'd always been convinced of that, and at that moment it could not have been clearer.

"I feel sick, I want to go to bed. What do you want, Malaparte?"

"You and Galeazzo are the only friends who could help me. The OVRA has framed me. They're accusing me of having killed an English girl here in Capri, four years ago."

"Did you kill her?"

"D'you take me for a murderer?"

"One can kill without being a murderer. One can have the right to kill."

"Stop joking, Edda. I'm on the point of being arrested. Tell your father or Galeazzo to call off the guys from OVRA."

"Impossible. War's about to break out. My father won't listen to me."

"There's no one your father loves more than you."

"These days I can't even reach him on the 'phone."

"And your husband?"

"Galeazzo can't expose himself over a penal matter. That would be dangerous."

"I get you. You're afraid I might be proved guilty, and Galeazzo would get burned."

"Galeazzo is our Minister of Foreign Affairs, and you know perfectly well how troubled the world is at this time. Who killed the girl?"

"An SS officer. A Sturmbannführer. We first came up against one another at war, at a place called Bligny. Then I met him again here. He was besotted with the girl, but she was drawn to me. We had a duel, and I won."

"So it's all clear," commented Edda. "It was your Sturmbannführer. What are you worrying about? You'll see, the truth will out."

"But Edda..."

"Even the OVRA will understand the situation. You're a writer. A respectable person. You frequent the best society. By the way, they've told me of a theft from the house of Mona Williams. The poor thing's desperate at the loss of her book."

"Edda, I know who stole it. I saw it purely by chance. It was the same Sturmbannführer."

Edda laughed long and loud with her hoarse laugh, then she coughed. Her throat was roughened by too many cigarettes, by vulgar, self-seeking false friendships, by solitude. She took a glass lying on a table and drained every last drop from it.

"And yet I assure you that..."

"The Nazi officer is accusing you, and here you go accusing him of theft! Now, who's going to believe you? – no one!" said she, still laughing.

"I've not understood you properly," I replied, "would you care to repeat what you just said?"

Edda closed her eyes and drew in her breath, perhaps to repress a curse. She put down her glass and began to pace the terrace slowly, with the wind disarranging her hair. She held the stole tightly across her shoulders and bosom, as though to defend herself. I followed her.

"Say something."

Edda avoided my eyes. She let her wind-blown hair hide her face.

"You'll understand, Galeazzo must be informed of certain things. He's the Foreign Minister and the Germans are our allies. But I swear I know nothing else."

She stopped, facing me, and stared me suddenly in the eyes, trying hard to look convincing.

My slap made her head turn sharply.

"Tell me when he knew, and what he said."

She raised her hand to the place where I'd hit her. Her cheeks were flaming and she was speechless with shock, yet she was too proud to show it.

"Papa and Galeazzo tell me nothing."

The second slap made her sway. Not out of pain, but consternation. Not even Galeazzo dared touch her. Not even Mussolini.

I stayed with my hand in mid air, ready for a third smack.

"The Sturmbannführer... The day before you came to Capri. He said you pushed the girl off the cliff."

We both remained silent for a moment. I didn't know what to do with that raised hand and reached with it into my pocket, looking for cigarettes.

"Would you like one?" I asked at length, holding the pack out to her.

"Thanks," she replied, and I lit it for her.

Now the old order, the old harmony, had been restored. She was again herself, the Duce's daughter, with power of life and death over me, and not the other way round. A word to her bodyguards and I'd be arrested at once. But I knew she'd not do that. My slaps were all part of her nights of poker, whisky and Chantecler; senseless, empty nights wasted wondering whether in Rome, at the home of the Princess Colonna, Galeazzo was making it with Buby, or Cicci, or could it be Lilly?

We returned to the balustrade, gazing at the sky and the stars, the marvelous star-studded Capri sky, with its constellations of sand and seashells, salt and wind.

"When war comes, this house will become a bunker," said Edda. "The Americans will land in Italy, and we'll have to turn all our houses into bunkers, so we can die in them."

I felt a stab of pain in my heart at the coldness with which Edda beheld the magnificent spectacle of Capri's night sky while all her thoughts were of death. Edda loved only death, of that I was certain. I wouldn't have been surprised to learn one day that she'd killed someone, or that she had killed herself.

"Who set the OVRA onto you?" she asked, "and why did they kill that girl?"

"I don't know. Edwin Cerio says that Goering ordered the killing, probably with Hitler's consent. He wanted to buy the Villa San Michele, but Axel Munthe dragged things out too long and the deal was never made."

"So what's that got to do with killing the English girl?"

"A symbolic revenge. The Germans wanted the villa for obscure esoteric reasons. They believe the earth is hollow and the Villa San Michele is an ideal point of access to the underworld, or something like that. Cerio says the Nazis are all stuffed to the eyeballs with occultism, astrology and other such crap. The Nazis killed the girl because her father lives at Anacapri, like Munthe; he belongs to the Fabian Society, and they too dabble in the same esoterica as the Nazis."

"I know Goebbels well and he'd not waste a moment of his time on that spiritualist bullshit," said Edda.

"Goebbels is an assassin."

"Goebbels is a great statesman, and he will make Germany great," said Edda. But she was not to blame, she was not to know that less than six years later Goebbels would take poison together with his wife and six children in a Berlin bunker, just before the arrival of the Red Army tanks.

"You, however, *did* get mixed up in an assassination," she added, suddenly turning towards me.

"You know perfectly well that I did what I did to help your father," I said.

Edda did not answer. She ran indoors, crossed the reception room, entered the bathroom and locked herself in. I followed and stood outside the door, waiting for her to finish vomiting.

By pure chance, my attention settled on a marble table, near a light switch. I drew near. There lay a visiting card.

> *Madame Carmen*

I turned it over in my hand. On the back was a symbol I already knew:

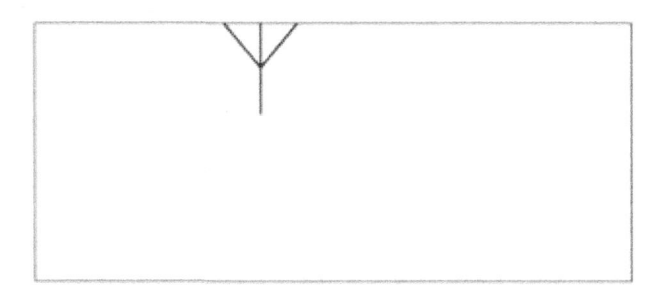

I pocketed the card. Meanwhile Edda was still throwing up in the water closet her whisky, her adulteries, her love-hate for her dictator dad, remorse for her husband, fear for the future and nostalgia for the past. She was vomiting the honeymoon she and Galeazzo had spent in Capri so many years ago, she was vomiting the happy years they'd spent at the Italian Embassy in Shanghai, she was vomiting Galeazzo's first betrayals and the first times she'd drunk herself to a stupor, alone in her room, at the beginning of their unhappiness.

The bathroom door opened. Edda emerged.

"Don't ask me anything, I don't need anything," she said, swaying on her legs.

"Allow me at least to…"

"Shut up."

We went out again onto the terrace.

"It's clear it was your Sturmbannführer," she said. "But I can't help you. This time you're on your own."

"I'll tell you a phrase: bon bonad kind rabal mervu."

"Is that Greek or Chinese?" said Edda laughing and lighting another cigarette.

"It was written on a notepad by the only eyewitness to the girl's death, a guy who has now disappeared. Perhaps it's a coded message. Some military man from the Cipher outfit could give me a hand with it. A word from you would do the trick."

"Times have changed. Things aren't like they used to be, it's not like the time of the Matteotti business. I've told you all I know. Leave me in peace, Malaparte. Go to your American friends. Go to Dumini. Go to Sinclair."

"Dumini was no friend of mine. And he wasn't a real American."

"Go away, Malaparte. Scram!"

Edda always chose her words well, even words that were meant to wound, because she loved death. As I walked away from the villa, I turned back. She was still there, leaning on the terrace balustrade, gazing into the distance. The wind stirred her silk stole and now it was flapping like a banner in the breeze. There she stood with her nose in the air, as though she didn't know I was still down there below her. She knew her words had wounded me; that was the only way in which she could kill just then, and she'd used it, for she loved death.

Edda and Galeazzo's villa was on the top of Castiglione Hill, a quite out-of-the-way place. It was late, but to hell with taxis. I needed to keep walking, I needed to breathe the night air, I needed to get the stink of party smoke out of my nose and the bitter taste of those names – Dumini, Matteotti, Sinclair – out of my mind…

I put those memories in my mouth, and slowly, slowly I crunched on them as I walked.

ROME, JUNE 1924

The Technique of Revolution

It was June 1924, I was a young Fascist, the future was rich in promise, and in Rome it was hot, so very hot.

The front door of the apartment building by the Tiber opened and Socialist Deputy Giacomo Matteotti stepped out into the greasy, dust-filled air of the Roman afternoon. Under his arm, he carried his briefcase, the famous briefcase with its confidential documents, as he set out for his office at the Chamber of Deputies. He was about to put the final touches to his draft, that of the most important speech in his life. He'd been polishing it for weeks, and it was common knowledge that this speech, loaded with tremendous accusations, could bring down Mussolini's government. Already, he'd openly denounced Fascist violence in Parliament: the political assassinations, the intimidations against the opposition, the corruption of the regime, the embezzlement, extortion and electoral fraud. Now he meant to confront Mussolini with a new, even more merciless speech, a lethal indictment: he meant to speak of oil, to expose Sinclair Oil and Mussolini's dirty underhand dealings.

It would bring him scant glory and put him in grave danger, that he knew all too well. He was Mussolini's only serious adversary, not for the votes he won (the Fascists got many more) but because he was such a fine man. There was beauty in his struggle for a lost cause, when even his comrades had abandoned him, he was fine, he was handsome, he had youth on his side, wealth and a good family background (they called him the Socialmilionario), he was fine because he was unbiased and idealistic; fine, because he stood alone. He was elegant, rich, aristocratic and a loner, while Mussolini was clumsy, proletarian and acclaimed by cheering crowds.

The CEKA, Mussolini's squad of secret hit-men, had been lying in wait for hours under Matteotti's house. The government swore that the CEKA did not exist and if it had the same name as the Soviet secret police that was because it was an invention of the Socialist press, conveniently forgetting that Mussolini himself had been a Socialist.

That day Amerigo Dumini was in charge. Dumini, the man they called the Taker of Nine Lives, killer, spy and arms trafficker, my old chum Amerigo Dumini from Saint Louis, Missouri, with his Italian father and English mother. Dumini was my buddy: once I'd even asked him to stand second for me in a duel. I met him in Florence when we were young, at the time of Fascism's bitter and glorious beginnings, when Mussolini was recruiting thugs and hard men. Dumini was one of those likeable bastards, those fine Fascists of the first hours who went trucking around the countryside in gangs of ten or twelve, arriving at dawn at the door of some Socialist trade unionist, breaking it down, tying him to a chair and pouring castor oil down his throat; and if he struggled they'd crack his skull – too bad if he was done for once they'd finished with him. Dumini was one of those bloodthirsty scoundrels that writers like to frequent, for reasons I'd be hard put to explain. If you want to be a writer, you have to make friends with the mob and the mobsters, you've got to become one of them, and get used to the sight of blood.

I know that must sound sick, but that's how it is. Even when I was a boy, from time to time I'd cut my hand with a penknife and just stay there watching the red drops run on my white skin, almost hypnotized. I'd follow them as they formed a narrow rivulet across my wrist, then dripped to the ground, spattering the old bricks in our kitchen smelling of wood and soup, all those droplets as bright red as drops of hot wax from Yuletide candles. It wasn't masochism, it was just a mysterious fascination with blood. Dumini at once repelled and fascinated me, like the sight of my own blood. When he stood before me, I couldn't keep my eyes off his pockmarked face, those cold eyes, one big, one small – those deformed yellowish features. There was something icy about him, a glacial magnetic force field that protected him through thick and thin (during the war in Africa the British had him shot, but he survived with seventeen bullets in his body and escaped to Italy).

Dumini's men had neither nerves of steel nor any sound organization, but Matteotti was alone and they were five strong men – or six – maybe even seven or eight, a crucial detail which, incredibly, was never clarified by any of the innumerable trials that followed Matteotti's death. With political crimes, it's always like that.

It was half past four in the afternoon, a hot, oily afternoon. Hardly had Matteotti left the front door than two thugs from the CEKA jumped on him. He defended himself well, but a third man intervened and knocked him out with a bludgeon to the face, after which they threw him into a car. Once inside Matteotti reacted with his fists, biting, kicking, yelling, even managing to throw his Deputy's card out of the window, to leave a trace. There was no lack of witnesses, but absent-minded cops and strangely prudent judges did the necessary to cover up for the CEKA – with political crimes, it's always like that.

In the car the fight grew so wild that the driver lost control and began to zigzag, while the screams could be heard far down the street. There was really no way of keeping that Socialist quiet. Then out came a knife, they planted it in his chest, and – thank the Lord – he quietened down.

As the blade slipped between his ribs, a cold white light flooded his brain, and death began gently to make its way in, like an old acquaintance. He felt pain at the thought of his wife and children and all the fine things he was leaving unfinished, but he was not surprised. He'd long been prepared for the ambush, the blows, for death itself. He'd warned everyone that his time might very soon be up.

Years before, when he was organizing the Socialist movement and strikes out in the provinces, the Fascists had assaulted him and raped him with a stick, hoping that would break his self-confidence. Far from it. On that hot, dusty afternoon in June 1924, the last afternoon of his life, Giacomo Matteotti was still the same hotheaded Socialist, splendid in his solitude, while around him tightened black pulsating veins of oil and dollars. The dollars were those of Sinclair Oil, in whose hands Mussolini had placed Italy's petroleum resources; money which, as all the headlines were screaming, his brother Arnaldo had received under the counter from Harry Ford Sinclair in exchange for a golden contract: the American corporation was getting ninety-nine years' exclusive oil extraction rights in Italy, tax free.

Matteotti knew. As he lay slowly dying, as he thought of his wife, of his kids, of the battles he was leaving half fought, of his life's innumerable fine unfinished things, his mind turned to his very last trip, to London, where he'd met the leaders of the Labor government and the men from Anglo-Persian Oil.

The Anglo-Persian Oil Company was Britain's biggest operator in the petroleum business. Churchill had financed it secretly as early as 1913, so it was de facto a State undertaking. The British were furious; the Daily Herald accused Sinclair, a bankrupt former pharmacist from Kansas who had mysteriously become a millionaire when he was hardly thirty, of cornering the rich Italian oil market and cutting out Anglo-Persian by means of a shower of cash, some 30 million lire, ending up in the pockets of Mussolini's brother.

In America too the waters became troubled. The Chicago Tribune and other newspapers began to trash the Mussolini-Sinclair compact. The Duce was running scared and bombarding his Ambassador in Washington with telegrams.

Those were the days of hard whisky and easy money, the glory days of the Ohio Gang and the Little Green House nestling in Washington's genteel, tree-lined K Street, where President Harding's men and all Ohio's favorite sons spent the small hours indulging in whisky and women. How do I know all these things? Simple: I had an American friend, a great American friend, a journalist who wore bow ties, and he told it to me in the juiciest detail, all the while conserving that hand-on-heart morality, that cleanness, that clear sense of right and wrong you'll find only in Americans.

Those were, as I was saying, great times, when presidential staff members embroiled in scandals would mysteriously commit suicide, and at the White House the poker games went on till dawn. Meanwhile Americans paid their taxes like good citizens. The Golden Years! But it all came to an end when the Feds blew the stinking top off the Teapot Dome affair. Sinclair had, without any call to tender, obtained in Wyoming, exclusive contractual rights to exploit the rich Teapot Dome oilfield, after injecting rivers of dollars into the coffers of President Harding's Republican Party. What's more, he'd even hired a host of detectives to stick their noses into the private lives of the jurymen who were to judge him. A dirty business that could hardly have ended up worse: The Wall Street Journal threw itself headlong into the investigation, American taxpayers were enraged, really enraged, to learn their taxes had been paying for the poker games of President Harding's cronies; and Sinclair ended up in jail, together – a historical first – with a presidential cabinet member, Senator Albert B. Fall, who'd fattened the cattle on his ranch from the slush funds of the big oilmen.

My buddy Dumini, Amerigo Dumini from Saint Louis, Missouri, knew all about it. He knew there was oil behind it all, he knew that Matteotti must die for oil, he knew that the car they were using to kidnap Matteotti was registered in the name of Filippo Filippelli, lobbyist and financier of Mussolini's brother, whose bank account was flooded with a cloudburst of US dollars only days before the signing of the contract between Sinclair Oil and the Mussolini government. As the car drove on through the stifling clammy heat, leaving Rome, Matteotti's massacred body began oozing not blood but oil. The CEKA hitmen had blood before their eyes but they saw nothing but oil, Matteotti was stuffed with oil, no question about it. The hands of the assassins holding Matteotti down on the back seat were grimy with oil, dripping oil, staining and streaking their white cuffs, their shoes, their fine trousers with turn-ups paid for out of the Ministry of the Interior's special funds. Dumini wiped the sweat from his brow and under his fingertips he found droplets, not of sweat but of crude oil, thick and hot, thick with black stinking lumps, lumps of the hard dry soil of Teapot Dome. And he thought: Matteotti's full of oil. It's for oil that we're killing him, and he's full of oil. And he wanted to throw up, and inwardly he cursed Mussolini, he cursed the Americans, he cursed Matteotti, but he put up with it all, because Mussolini meant to settle the issue of oil once and for all.

While Dumini was ruminating on all this, while his men drove on with their eyes riveted in front of them, hours had passed since the ambush and Matteotti had died.

Who knows what his last thought was before dying? That, I always wished I could have known. I'd have given three fingers from my right hand to know Matteotti's last thoughts, his last words before dying. I'd always been sure it must have been something uplifting, important, moving, like all the things heroes think before dying. If I'd known it, I'd have written it in one of my books, maybe I'd even have made a whole book out of it. Ah, if only I could have found someone who could tell me Matteotti's last thought before dying!

Now Matteotti was as bloated with black crude as an inflatable doll, like some cadavers bursting with worms, with roaches, with cold slimy roaches, and he was dead. But he'd become more dangerous, more violent, more tremendous and aggressive than when he was alive. Matteotti's cadaver was arrogant, intransigent, scornful, and it was terrorizing the thugs from the CEKA. The murdered dead are rabid, obstinate, ferocious. There's nothing more awful than a murdered man staring at you with his unbearable fixed stare, his half-closed dead eyes, his hatred, his terrifying strength. The murdered should be buried blindfold and with handcuffs, in the deepest pits, to keep them from bursting out from the earth and sinking their teeth into those who've just buried them. In the war I saw soldiers open railcars transporting deported Jews, all squashed like sardines and dead from suffocation, but hardly had they opened the doors of the train than those cadavers burst forth and fell onto the soldiers, crushing them, head-butting them, biting them, more furious and violent than the living.

Matteotti's cadaver, lying crushed to the floor at the foot of the back seat, full of oil and as heavy as a cement statue, stared implacably at each and every one of its assassins, calling them by name, whispering with its mute black tongue, while they pretended not to hear. They blocked their ears, they didn't want to hear that dead man's hissed words, that sharp accusing wheeze.

For hours the CEKA assassins wandered across the mosquito-infested countryside, their eyes swollen and twisted, their mouths dry and burning, their hair sticking to their oily foreheads, searching for a place to get rid of Matteotti's body, trying to ignore that oil-bloated carcass which hated them, despised them, scorned them and judged them one by one. In the end they opted for a lonely copse in a place called Quartarella. They'd brought neither shovels nor spades with them, because if the police were to intercept them, Matteotti's killing must not look premeditated. They dug a shallow hole as best as they could and one of them pushed the poor body into it, pressing down first with his hands, then with his feet, stamping it down with hasty rage. But one man wasn't heavy enough, so three of them began to dance on it, then four, then – as though the devil had gotten into them – the whole gang joined in a vile *danse macabre*, and when they heard the poor cadaver's bones crack, they felt a sense of great relief, thinking that there wasn't just that wretched oil in Matteotti, there were bones too; and then they began to laugh, yessir, they began to laugh, and while Matteotti's bones cracked and the oil gushed from his mouth, nose and ears, Dumini and the men from the CEKA felt the soles of their shoes burning, burning, and as they stamped, they laughed and they cried. The tears ran down their faces grimy with dust and greasy sweat, and the CEKA assassins stamped ever harder, faster and faster, laughing and crying for the pain in their feet scalding them in their boiling shoes, and their dance became a witches' dance, a ceremony of murderous shamans, a barefoot dance on the burning coals of the Hell that Dumini and his men had built for themselves when they murdered him for the sake of oil, that curse of humanity.

The body was found weeks later, already eaten by the ants, thanks to a tip-off from a caller who will remain forever unknown, because the Carabiniere who took the message contradicted himself, as he'd doubtless been inspired to do. Obviously, the knife was never found and the autopsy was hard to perform because of the time that had elapsed since death, while the briefcase containing Matteotti's secret documents disappeared, never to be found – with political crimes, it's always like that. The poor widow, ruined by the regime and collapsing under the weight of debts, was first threatened, then silenced with money – with political crimes, it's always like that.

Nevertheless, the Mussolini government tottered for a while, Matteotti's corpse bore its signature. It was inevitable that an honest public prosecutor should arrest the CEKA men, but Dumini blackmailed Mussolini, he had no intention of paying for other people's decisions. Thus it was that an honest judge was transferred to another jurisdiction, then pushed into early retirement, while the mockery of a trial was organized at Chieti, far from Rome and the clamor of the press. What counted was to lighten the burden of the accused, and to arrange a diversion.

That's where I came into the picture.

I knew what the Duce wanted of me. I came to the trial as a voluntary witness and told the judges how Dumini had confided in me on the very evening after the murder. He had not really intended to kill Matteotti, I told them, just to rough up that Socialist subversive a little and teach him a good lesson. Unfortunately, things had gotten out of hand during a struggle in the car, and Matteotti had an attack, he was taken ill, so that the adventure ended badly. Not long before that, an Italian Fascist had been killed in Paris, Dumini wanted to interrogate Matteotti about that murder because he suspected him of being behind the killing. So, Matteotti's death was the result of a political act that had gone wrong, not an assassination.

That was a great help. In the end Dumini and the men from the CEKA got off with a few years in prison for unintentional homicide, some of them were even acquitted, then handsomely paid to keep their mouths shut. Mussolini weathered the crisis: he publicly proclaimed himself to be morally responsible for the crime and the Parliament of the Kingdom of Italy, stuffed with cowards, crooks and swindlers, swallowed the insult. Soon after that, political parties were banned and replaced by the dictatorship which was to drag us into a suicidal war alongside Hitler, who everyone in Italy – starting with Mussolini himself – knew to be a madman.

As for me, with my testimony at the trial, I had blessed Mussolini's coup d'état with the blood of Matteotti. I had mixed it with the black sap of crude oil and with it I had sprinkled the Duce's bald greasy pate, the skulls of the soldiers who were to die in Mussolini's pointless war and the foreheads of innumerable widows, orphans and nameless casualties.

I imagined I'd earned myself a credit that I could always call in. I was badly mistaken. Mussolini's main concern was to get rid of those who knew too much about the circumstances of Matteotti's death. Some ten years later, as soon as he got a chance, he had me sent into internal exile. Dirty work doesn't pay. It brings no profit, nothing but bad luck – with political crimes, it's always like that.

The explosion of the Teapot Dome scandal in America put paid to the Italian government's contract with Sinclair, and the agreement was annulled. But, just to make things easier for the one-time bankrupt pharmacist from Kansas and his cronies, Mussolini had dismantled the entire government department responsible for developing energy resources. All prospecting for oil, together with the exploitation of oilfields both in Italy and abroad, was abandoned. Libya had been our colony for years, yet no one in the Fascist government showed the slightest interest in finding anything of interest under the sands of Benghazi and Tripoli. Only twelve years after the death of Matteotti was the first geological map of the region completed, and then it at once became clear that under the Gulf of Sidra lay enormous oil reserves. But to locate these, seismic reflection devices would be needed, these being the only apparatus capable of analyzing the subsoil. The American firm Western Geophysical had these. At long last the bosses of AGIP, our State oil corporation, made up their minds to order the instruments in America, and they arrived in Italy on June 10th 1940.

That day, which was supposed to mark Italy's accession to oil power status, the dawning of new grandeur and prosperity, turned out instead to be a day of shame and folly.

On that same June 10th 1940, while the Western Geophysics seismic reflection apparatus was being unloaded in Italy, on precisely that day, by an incredible coincidence – or maybe it was no coincidence – Mussolini declared war on France, the country with which Italy had hitherto enjoyed a peaceful arrangement sharing North Africa between them. There soon followed the suicidal declarations of war against Britain, Russia and the United States, none of which Hitler had even requested, and so it was that Italy lost the war, lost face, and lost Libyan oil, and all of us resigned ourselves to dying, as we sipped Mona Williams' Chablis in Capri.

After the war, the British and the French carved up Libya between them. In the end Sinclair spent only a few months in a luxury prison, before returning undisturbed to business as usual. Mussolini had brought off his coup d'état. Matteotti had died for nothing; everyone had blamed his death on the Fascists and on plain political hatred, while the oil factor – which was the key to the whole story – was soon forgotten. With political crimes, it's always like that.

CAPRI, SUMMER 1939

Of their Sweet Deaths

I arrived at the Villa Lysis almost without realizing it, still sunk in a waking dream in which the names and faces of Matteotti, Dumini and Mussolini kept rebounding in my head, like ivory balls bouncing off the sides of a billiard table with no holes.

They'd left the villa's gates open for me. Sirignano was heaven knows where at that hour. Febo, in a state of high anxiety, came to meet me at the speed of light. I crossed the huge garden punctuated by trees, shrubs and hedges and entered the ground floor reception room. Tamburi, still all wrapped up as though we were in Alaska, lay sprawled on a sofa fast asleep.

"Good heavens, Tamburi! I pay you a fortune and all you can do is waste time sleeping!" I said, shaking him.

He came to painfully, his eyes as red as two bloody steaks.

"Have you thought about those mysterious words?" I added. "Bon bonad kind rabal mervu... You've found the answer, haven't you?"

"Honestly, no, I haven't."

"That's bad, real bad! So, what have you been up to while I've been away? Have you no news for me?"

"Prince Sirignano left me a note for you. It was given to him in the town square by that lady," said he, rotating his index fingers next to both ears to mime Lucia's curls. "The lady had heard that you and the prince are friends."

I'll be waiting for you at Villa Ferraro, at all hours.
The party will be long and boring without you.
Your L.

It was a fine handwriting, regular and orderly as only women can make it, but not boring. If I'd ever had a wife, I'd have liked her not to waste time in chatter but just to write me short notes like that, brief and well made, in a noble handwriting. Things like *Dinner's on the table, three days since you vanished but I love you.* Just that.

"Any news of Carmine?" I asked.

"The prince has asked for information everywhere. For the time being he's drawn a complete blank."

"Does anyone know I'm here?"

"Prince Sirignano assures me that he's breathed a word to no one."

"Come on, Tamburi. We're going to a party, at the Villa Ferraro".

"At this hour?"

"At this hour. In Capri it's always late, but never too late. They'll all be there. We need to find a certain Madame Carmen. Febo, will you come with us?"

As soon as we arrived, Tamburi admitted that I'd seen right. It was a complete masked ball, and at past two in the morning no one had the least desire to go home to bed. The garden of Villa Ferraro was teeming with fake cowboys, fake priests, fake Egyptian priestesses, fake pirates, fake musketeers, all strictly dressed in hired costumes. Gentlemen in tux were wandering around, together with ladies in splendid evening dresses with skillfully bared shoulders and youngsters wearing jackets cut with a penknife by the great Caraceni. But a sort of viral infection made them seem fake too, they looked as though their cigars, their hair, their teeth, their faces had all been hired. Chantecler looked more authentic, dressed as a Roman Senator with a laurel crown on his brow, trailing a new woman behind him, small, round and dark, quite the opposite of the one he'd been with the evening before at the Villa Discopoli.

As soon as my presence was noticed, the master of the house, a rich Dutch businessman, came running to greet me with his beautiful wife. On seeing Tamburi and Febo the couple exchanged perplexed glances, but didn't dare ask questions.

When we entered the throng, Count Sanjust di Teulada, the most exquisite gentleman, passed just in front of me without a greeting. Prince Belmonte pretended he'd not seen me. The Duke of Tolve and the Duchess his wife, who were usually so cordial, deigned to give me a constipated little greeting from afar.

"Ah, that's the great thing about Capri, as I always say. So many people who really care for one, and do everything to show it," I muttered. Febo let out a melancholy whimper.

"What do you mean, Signor Malaparte?" said Tamburi.

"Dear Tamburi, by now I stink like a cadaver. They just can't wait to see the vultures come diving down to feed on me."

Most of the guests, curious about my two companions – a dog and a cross between Rasputin and Cyrano de Bergerac – swayed as they stared at me. The orchestra was playing *Lady be good*, the people were dancing without a care for the war about to break out. Febo was disgusted, but he'd come of his own accord so he didn't dare protest.

I grabbed a glass of *spumante* from a passing waiter. I instructed Tamburi to ask around who Madame Carmen was.

"Tarapoonchi poonchilah," I said to Febo, asking him to stay quietly in a corner, and I made for the terrace on the top floor of the villa, surrounded by a crenellated wall, half fake-Moorish, half medieval. On the terrace, someone at last accosted me.

"Hi, Malaparte," said Ivy Earl, a rich American who'd rented an enormous villa in the neighborhood.

"Hi, Ivy."

"Allow me to introduce a friend," he proudly announced, leading me to his friend. "This is Ely Culbertson, the famous bridge champion. A man who makes ten million dollars a year.
He's playing a series of tournaments in Europe."

"Ah, good," said I, disappointing the divine Culbertson with a slack impatient handshake; "Ivy, who the devil is Madame Carmen?"

"D'you mean the one in Bizet's opera?" he asked laughing.

"Oh, to Hell with it," I cut him short and turned on my heels leaving the two poor Americans open mouthed.

Suddenly the whole garden and the villa were plunged in darkness: the usual power cut. Even the little band stopped playing, while the guests vented their frustration with expressions of irritability and more or less loud and clear complaints about the Mussolini regime and its non-services. As usual, it lasted a few minutes, then the light came back on and everything started all over again just like before.

At the far end of the terrace I caught sight of the Duke of Civitella, a great connoisseur of Capri, dressed as a Janissary. If Madame Carmen existed he'd certainly know how to find her. But the moment he caught sight of me, he took two friends by the arm and moved hurriedly down the stairs to the floor below. To Hell with you too, I thought.

But then Commendator Freddi, the confidant of American actors, came to meet me with a broad bronzed smile, once again flanked by his friends Da Zara and Tavolato. They were joined by Assante, the journalist I'd met at Mona Williams' place.

"Malaparte, are you here alone? We can hardly believe you're here without that beautiful lady at your side," said Freddi, bestowing on me his usual handshake that left my arm aching.

"I am in fact looking for a woman. She's called Madame Carmen," I said.

Tavolato and De Zara exchanged an imperceptible wink of complicity.

"Madame Carmen? That sounds like the name of a cabaret artiste. Unfortunately, I can't act as your go-between," guffawed Freddi.

"Then you must excuse me, but I have to find a friend," said I, breaking off.

Hardly had I managed to get away from Freddi and his friends when I heard a woman's voice calling me.

"Monsieur Malaparte!"

I turned and found myself face to face with a sprightly old lady, holding a Venetian-style mask before her eyes. I had no time to waste, so I forced a smile to the importunate old lady and went back down to find Tamburi.

"So?" I asked.

"Nothing. No one knows anything about this Madame Carmen."

"Who did you ask?"

"I don't know. First one guy, then another. They didn't give me their names."

"For heaven's sake Tamburi, you have to get in confidence with people before you go asking them questions!"

"And how am I to do that? No one here lets me near them! The moment I mention your name, they all turn their backs on me."

I held back a curse. Painters make lousy detectives.

"But *I* don't turn my back."

It was Lucia's voice.

"And you, Malaparte, should be ashamed of yourself," she added, "instead of looking for me you've been trying to find out about Madame Carmen. I almost feel like not telling you who she is."

I collected Febo and we left the Villa Ferraro. On the way out, we came upon Sirignano, in the company of a noisy group of young men and girls, all of them rather the worse for drink.

"I came to make sure you'd come," said he in a conniving tone of voice, as he dived down to kiss Lucia's hand.

Then he took me aside and murmured in my ear: "We've still no trace of Carmine. I've unleashed a mass of people throughout the island, including the port. Sooner or later we'll find him. Your San Gennaro statue is arriving from Naples. With the mountaineer, too, we're getting somewhere. I've found a trustworthy person I asked to help you. He'll soon be coming in from Naples too. Meanwhile, take care."

"Prince, listen to me carefully," I said, "There's a saber at the bottom of the cove at the foot of the Migliera, just beneath the viewpoint. We need to fish it out as quickly as possible. The sea's quite deep there. Don't ask me to explain all this, it's a long story."

"First it's a golden statue of San Gennaro and an Alpinist. Now you want a deep-sea diver. It's a lucky man who can understand you, Malaparte. But I'll do it."

With a brief farewell gesture, he turned, moving into the dark.

At last we could get away… But that was not to be.

"Monsieur Malaparte! Je vous en prie…"

It was the old French lady I'd encountered earlier. She was running swiftly towards me with a pen and a book in her hand.

"Another troublemaker," I cursed under my breath, intending to avoid her, but Lucia held me back. Schoolmaams won't tolerate discourtesy.

"Monsieur Malaparte, I'm a faithful reader of yours. Unfortunately relations between our two countries are bad through Mussolini's fault. But, you know, you've many admirers in France. I'm just rereading your *Technique of Revolution*, je l'ai a-do-ré! Look, I've got the book here, an autograph, s'il vous plaît! Up here... please write: A Hermine Dutilleux, con simpatia, Malaparte. There, that's perfect! You know, I've read your *Bonhomme Lenine* too. Ah, mon Dieu, what a masterpiece!"

Lucia was sniggering quietly, I was exhausted.

"Monsieur Malaparte, you know, I've founded a book club in Paris to discuss your books. And do you know, I wanted to come and meet you when they released you from internal exile? I asked the French embassy in Rome for your address, but they didn't even reply – such bad manners! And now I've found you here! C'est merveilleux, n'est-ce pas?"

I knew that my books sold well in France and that I had many enthusiastic readers there, but this was neither the time nor the place. I unwillingly accepted the page on which this lively granny had written her address in Paris, that at Cap d'Antibes, her hotel and room number in Capri, even the details of her sister in Switzerland.

"Monsieur Malaparte, may I put you one last personal question? They tell me that here in Capri you had a row with a major from the SS..."

"That's quite enough, Madame Dutilleux. I'm sorry, but I allow no one to intrude on my private life."

Febo began to growl softly.

"But Monsieur Malaparte, I did not mean to..."

"Don't mention it."

As courteously as possible I dismissed the old French lady, who was visibly disappointed and embarrassed.

Before making our way to House like Me, we accompanied Tamburi to his *pensione*.

"Incredible! You have a conversation with a fellow-guest at a private reception and a few days later all Capri has heard all about it," I commented.

"The trouble is that, when the two party guests in question are a famous writer and a dastardly Nazi," Lucia replied, holding me tightly, "gossip's inevitable."

It was the dead of night, gusts of tepid wind were sweeping the streets of Capri, the air smelled of musk and gentians. Escorted by

Febo, Lucia and I tarried a moment in the alleys at the middle of the village, breathing in those precious perfumes, the silence and the echo of our footfalls on the cobbles. Febo barked. Someone was coming out from a side road.

"Malaparte's dog, behave yourself."

It was Willy Kluck's daft voice.

"Up again in the small hours, Willy?" I asked him.

"You're always up too in the small hours, Malaparte."

"You're right, I'm always up at all hours. But for serious reasons."

"We too have our reasons. There are things in Capri that must be done by night."

Kluck was accompanied by Julius Spiegel and by a third individual, a gangling beanpole halfway between Jesus Christ and a terminal TB patient, a sort of skinny caveman with a long prophet's beard, a white tunic, leather sandals and a threadbare rucksack on his shoulders.

"This is Miradois, the greatest German philosopher in Capri," said Kluck, "just back from Germany."

I didn't want to show it, but I knew perfectly well who that Miradois was. He'd lived for years in a cave on Capri, feeding only on goats' milk and wild plants. Like Kluck, Miradois preached vegetarianism, world peace, the brotherhood of man, respect for Nature, the abolition of frontiers between States, and all the rest. He was the only German to have understood at once that Hitler was a murderous madman, but no one had paid any attention to him. With his ascetic's airs, when he was living in that cave he'd managed to ensnare a young Capri girl who produced a fine daughter for him. When he'd returned to Germany for a while, he'd made out a will leaving his cave and all his worldly goods to the commune of Capri: four stone beds, eight sand and chalk cushions, four walls and the Capri sun. Kluck and Miradois were the quintessence of Capri's mendicant philosophers, all good heart and freedom, people who – inevitably in a country like Germany which wouldn't know what to do with freedom – end up as crazy philosophers, tramps and troglodytes.

"What did you come back to do in Capri, Miradois?" I asked, "soon Italy will go to war. Those will be bad times."

"In Germany the times are already bad," said Miradois sadly, with his heavy Kraut accent.

"Gratìs", said Spiegel chiming in with his friend's sad tones and holding out a hand in supplication. Lucia dropped a coin in his palm.

"Come," said Kluck, "we are going to perform our rite. You're invited."

"A rite? I don't believe in magic, Kluck", I said.

"This is no magic," said Miradois, "it is a philosophical rite, a ceremony auguring peace. Normally only Germans take part. But Italians, too, are admitted."

"My father's German, Lucia's father too. We're all compatriots."

We followed the three philosophers to the Tragara viewing platform and took up position next to the parapet over the sea. There wasn't a soul around.

Miradois opened his rucksack, took out a shoe box and raised the lid. It was full of myriad strips of paper, all covered in minuscule writing. I took some in my hand and made light with a cigarette lighter. It was full of phrases in Latin, German and Italian, written in a calligraphy at once tiny and perfect: *Pax hominibus bonae voluntatis* (Peace on Earth to all men of goodwill), *Friede ist die Stärke der Völker* (Peace is the strength of the peoples), *Nella pace l'uomo trova la vera gioia* (In Peace man finds true joy) and so on. The phrases were so many and so small that the work of writing them must surely have taken days and days.

"You're crazy, Willy Kluck," I said.

"Normally for the launching we use this," replied Kluck imperturbably.

From the rucksack he drew forth a large round metal object. He pulled it at both ends, lengthening it in an instant: it was a telescopic cylinder; it looked like a big spyglass, but without lenses. Miradois put a finger in his mouth then took it out again, holding it straight as though it were an antenna, to check on wind strength and direction.

Kluck extracted from the rucksack a sort of enormous pair of bellows, applied it to the small end of the telescopic cylinder, fed a handful of little paper strips into the big end, crammed them firmly in, then pushed hard on the bellows. The strips were shot down from the parapet and spread all around in the air, but then the wind turned and brought them all back. Some fell at out feet. I remembered how, walking in Capri I'd sometimes found strip like this stuck to the soles of my shoes, without understanding where the devil they'd come from. Now I knew.

"It's not the right evening," commented Miradois scratching his long werewolf's beard, and from the rucksack he drew another large cylindrical object in the form of a projectile. Near the tip of it there was a sort of little box, into which Kluck and Miradois stuffed the paper strips with their message of peace. Then he put the object on the ground, on a sort of perch, in a vertical position slightly inclined towards the sea.

"But it's a rocket!" exclaimed Lucia.

"Who got it for you?" I asked.

"A rather nice gentleman who practices a very delicate profession and insists on discretion," replied Kluck.

"I've got it, it was that nutcase Chantecler," I said, "the only person in Capri who always has a stock of fireworks."

The fuse was lit with a match and the rocket took off with a quiet whoosh, climbed rapidly into the black sky and burst above our heads into a huge blinding flower with fiery red petals. For a few seconds we saw masses of paper strips vibrating in the air, illuminated by the firework, before being lost in the night.

"Why do you do this?" I asked.

"To meditate together on Peace," replied Kluck. "It's important. Don't you agree, Malaparte?"

I did not reply. I was thinking of my meeting with Marinetti in the little piazza, and his public preaching of aggressive movement, febrile insomnia, troops running at the double, the high diver's somersault, blows, fisticuffs and war, the world's only hygiene. I thought of Dumini, of Matteotti's body stuffed with crude oil, of the Sturmbannführer and his Doberman. I thought of Santoni, the lad of the class of '99, screaming as he fired under the rain at Bligny, holding his guts in his hand.

"Stop it. You're all mad," he said.

Silence. In that bizarre little group I was the only one whose name counted for anything. No one dared breathe a word.

"Peace doesn't exist. Peace counts for nothing, you're crazy and that's all there is to it," I said, without even knowing why I said it.

The three Germans let themselves be insulted in silence. Even Lucia couldn't tell me to stop it, the schoolmaam in her would have liked to, but after all she wasn't my wife.

"Who usually takes part in your philosophical rites?" Lucia asked Kluck, trying to calm the waters a little.

"Now that Miradois has returned," said Kluck, "there are many more of us."

Lucia laughed. The night wind deposited a few paper strips on my chest, brought back by some caprice of the breeze. I shook them off.

"Let's go," I said, "let's go to House like Me."

I and Lucia walked on, with Febo at our heels. We left behind us the trio of German philosophers with their eccentricities, while they rather sadly repacked their strange apparatus.

After walking a few paces and breathing in deeply the night air, I understood why that innocent celebration in honor of peace, held by three innocent German tramps, had gotten so much on my nerves. It had been Kluck.

Kluck had been looking at me strangely all the time. His was a look full of fear, a wretched, intimate, cowardly fear. What did Kluck matter to me? I thought. He was a nut, a poor tramp of a philosopher, a burnt out case. And then, he cared for me. They all cared for me, in Capri. What did Kluck matter to me?

In Paris a few years earlier I'd met a Romanian exile who swore at everyone and everything the moment anything went wrong. *La dracu*, he'd say – "to the Devil with it" – and he'd spit on the ground wherever he was, even in the bedroom, even in other people's drawing rooms, on Persian carpets, and even if they took it badly, he didn't care. *La dracu*, he'd say, spitting on the ground.

"*La dracu* Kluck, *la dracu* the whole damn lot," I said, and stepped up the pace towards House like Me, while Lucia held my arm dutifully, and Febo looked at me worried and pityingly.

We arrived at House like Me almost at the double, wide awake. For me, night is divided into two parts: that in which I can't wait to get to sleep and that in which I can't wait to get up and about.

From the boxes of furniture I'd had delivered I pulled out an old gramophone, one of those you have to wind up, in perfect working order. We put it on the terrace and called on Enrico Caruso to give us a free concert consisting of the *Neapolitan Songs* of Master Francesco Paolo Tosti, a genius far superior to Wagner and Debussy even if they didn't give him premières at Carnegie Hall, as he deserved. I rummaged among the boxes I'd had sent in from Rome and at last recovered a case of fine glasses for great vintage red wines, together with a bottle of Brunello Biondi-Santi, one of those Tuscan wines that's redolent of woodland berries, vanilla, cherries and gum arabica, and so deeply, earthily Tuscan that you can sometimes feel on your tongue the sand of the little streets of Montalcino or Greve in Chianti.

After exchanging toasts, clothes got in the way and we lay down entwined on the divans we'd already tried out the night before. The moon wanted to take a look (the Capri moon has always been something of a Peeping Tom) but we frustrated her by hiding under a light woolen blanket. Caruso brought *Luna d'estate* to an end with one of his triumphal high notes, we responded with applause and Febo with a splendid howl in B flat. I slapped another record onto the gramophone without even looking, but we had to replace it quickly because it was Brahms' *Hungarian Dances*, and you can enjoy a Brunello Biondi-Santi with almost any music from Balinese dances to Louis Armstrong, even Stravinsky if you're a bit perverse, but not with Brahms' *Hungarian Dances* because they tickle you under your feet, it's worse than an electric shock. Poor Brahms was torn roughly from the gramophone and rolled to a corner of the terrace, while Febo followed it barking.

"I see you've Glen Gray, Billie Holiday and Guy Lombardo here. What shall we put on?" asked Lucia.

"Ray Noble, *Isle of Capri*."

"How predictable you are."

"I'm keeping fantasy for higher things!"

Later, much later, she asked me how I'd managed to obtain all those American records banned by Fascism. "Does one of your women bring them to you?"

"No, a friend. A very good friend. An American friend. A winner."

"A winner?"

"He's one of those Americans who've already won the war that's about to break out. He's won it in advance. There are many ways of winning a war. The best is to win it in advance."

"Sometimes you really are weird, Malaparte," said Lucia, laughing. "Have you found a way of getting out of that bad trouble you told me of?"

"Unfortunately not. Carmine, the Quisisana waiter who was present when Pam fell from the cliff, is nowhere to be found. He's afraid of being found by me. And now tell me: who is Madame Carmen?"

"Everyone in Capri knows that. She's a clairvoyant. The clairvoyant of Mussolini and his daughter."

"A clairvoyant? That's all I needed. What's Mussolini doing with a clairvoyant? I knew he was madly superstitious but not that he went consulting witches and cartomancers."

"Malaparte, you disappoint me. You frequent the powerful, you travel the world and you still don't know what's going on back home? Everyone in Capri's talking about it. Mussolini's been close to Madame Carmen for quite a while. At the outset, she predicted that a grave incident would endanger his career and his person, but that in the end he'd be saved. A few months later they killed Matteotti, the government was on the point of falling, but by some miracle Mussolini survived. Since then he's hung on Madame Carmen's every word. Sometimes he has her brought to Rome to consult her. If he can't see her in person, he sends Arturo Bocchini, the chief of police. Edda too is a regular client. They say that Madame Carmen predicted Ciano would come to a bad end."

"Good. You'll bring me to her."

"I don't know her, I can't introduce you. But I do know where she lives. The house is called Villa La Madonnina."

"Now, just listen to these words: bon bonad kind rabal mervu. What do they bring to mind for you?"

"Nothing. Perhaps it's because the sun's coming up and I'm very tired."

I stretched out an arm and reached into my trouser pocket for Madame Carmen's visiting card and a little pencil I always keep with me. I scribbled the name of Villa La Madonnina on the card and showed the other side to Lucia.

"Now look at this sign and tell me what it reminds you of."

"Never seen it. What is it, a magic symbol? And where does it come from?" she said with a voice suddenly full of anxiety.

"From the house of Edda Ciano. And I'd already seen it elsewhere on an object which – out of superstition – I don't want to tell you about. It's all a very strange story. I found here, in House like Me, a chessboard left there by goodness knows who, with the inscriptions *"Who is like God?"* and PAM, which is the name of the poor English girl. I thought at the time that someone wanted to suggest a clue about the cause of the girl's death, because *"Who is like God?"* is a biblical expression referring to Saint Michael."

"Saint Michael, San Michele... That's the name of Axel Munthe's villa," said Lucia. "Did you talk to Munthe about it?"

"Sure. According to Munthe that inscription has to do with a group of Russian communists opposed to Lenin's line, who'd worked out theories here in Capri early in the century about some sort of artificial God, a kind of atheistic religion. In other words, nothing to do with Pam's death or the Villa San Michele. But Cerio says that Munthe's laying a false trail with his story of Russian communists, because the thing's really to do with the Nazis. That's because Munthe negotiated with Goering the sale of Villa San Michele, but he doesn't want that to be known because in public he plays the democrat. The Nazis were interested in the Villa San Michele for some esoteric reason. Under the villa, if I've understood correctly, there's said to be an entrance to a sort of underworld, or something of the kind. When the negotiations failed owing to Munthe's exorbitant demands, Goering and his people took revenge by killing poor Pam."

"But why ever should they kill an English girl, for a question that concerns a Swede and the Nazis?"

"According to Cerio Pam's father is well placed in English socialist and literary circles. He's a sort of literary consultant to the Fabian Society, and works secretly on that here in Capri. Some English socialists were always interested in the esoteric. And Munthe's Sweden produced certain occultist theories cultivated by the Nazis. So Pam's murder was aimed at esoteric circles and conveyed an indirect but clear message. I've also spoken of this with Edda Mussolini. However, she's quite sure that the Germans aren't a bunch of crazy occultists as Cerio thinks, that the esoteric trail leads nowhere and that Pam's death is a banal crime of passion. The Sturmbannführer was jealous of me and when they quarreled Pam paid with her life."

Sooner or later, I thought, the subject had to be tackled head on. Lucia might take it badly, but *la dracu* unhappy love stories, and *la dracu* me too.

"So, you and Pam…" said disse Lucia hesitantly.

"No, there was practically nothing between me and Pam," I said brusquely. "But the Sturmbannführer feared me as a rival."

Febo reappeared. Most tactfully, he'd left us alone that evening too. But now the conversation between me and Lucia was troubling him.

"So why can't Edda convince Mussolini to call off the OVRA?" asked Lucia.

"These days her father's not listening to her. Or to Ciano, for that matter. Anyway, someone's accused me of murdering Pam, and I've no idea who it is. And as the key witness who could get me out of trouble doesn't want to be found, I'm left on my own racking my brains with Lenin, Gorky, Goering, Munthe and the Fabian Society. Have you any suggestions?"

"Malaparte, this story's too complicated for me. Only you can help me understand it. If you feel like it, of course," said Lucia.

Lucia's tone was cautious, distant, guarded. *La dracu*, schoolmaams. But then, she didn't know me any better than I knew her.

"I did not kill her," I said, enunciating every single syllable. "Whatever the motive may have been, it was the Sturmbannführer".

Lucia did not reply. *La dracu* the Sturmbannführer, I thought, la dracu Pam's death, *la dracu* the whole damn lot.

She was looking out to sea, towards the Faraglioni, and she was again silent. The first light of dawn, a mere hint of something clearer, caressed her wonderfully well formed shoulders and her splendid black curls. In Capri, the dawn light clothes everything in a purple and light blue mantle. Everything seems to have been painted with that color Homer used to describe the sea, the very color of the Brunello Biondi-Santi we'd just drunk, red with deep bluish reflections. Lucia too had become that color, she looked as though someone had painted her with Brunello and sea water, the water of Homer's sea. I was certain she was aware of my eyes on her shoulders and the nape of her neck, just as I'd felt Munthe's stare on my back. She kept turning her back on me in silence.

"Let's sleep, please," she said at last."

"You're right, let's sleep."She abandoned her head in my arms, without turning towards me. A moment before closing my eyes I noticed that Febo was sleepless. He was sniffing at the air and standing guard.

I felt Lucia's breath grow heavy, then more and more peaceful, until my arm no longer felt her tears.

I closed my eyes, and perhaps I fell asleep. The chorus of dead women did not sing that evening. Even Pam did not speak to me, because she pitied me. She was talking animatedly with Matteotti, she was looking at him scared and trembling, and asking what that black fluid was that ran from his mouth, from his ears, from his nose. Pam was talking with Matteotti, but the pair pretended they didn't know I was there before them. They pretended they couldn't see me because they were dead, but they pitied me.

She asked him: what were the last words you thought before dying? And he replied with a smile: *Of their sweet deaths are sweetest odors made.* Ah, now I knew.

In those last instants before death, rather than weep, Matteotti had understood that he was not alone: he was dying alongside thousands of others, his brothers, all the heroes who have died because of oil, all the cowards who have died because of oil, all the fallen whose names we shall never know, dead because we needed their death, because we needed oil. *Of their sweet deaths are sweetest odors made; And so of you, beauteous and lovely youth...*

These were Shakespeare's verses. I'd so longed to know Matteotti's last thought before dying, and now, thanks to Pam, the poetess, it had been revealed to me. The moment Matteotti had realized that all those who'd fallen because of oil were his brothers, and that they were so many, he'd ceased to suffer. Now he knew that the martyrs like him numbered thousand upon thousand, they were small and light, they were everywhere, they were a perfume lost on the air like Shakespeare's rose petals: *Of their sweet deaths are sweetest odors made; And so of you, beauteous and lovely youth; When that shall vade, my verse distills your truth.*

I too, who had betrayed Matteotti, I who had covered his assassin at the trial, I, the friend of Amerigo Dumini from Saint Louis, Missouri, began to recite those few verses under my breath with Matteotti, and I wept, but mine were not tears of remorse, I wept because no one has ever described the sweetness of death better than Shakespeare. Holding Lucia in my arms as she slept, I wept and recited Shakespeare's sonnet with Matteotti. The black drool on Matteotti's lips formed bubbles, which burst sprinkling stains on Pam's dress. But Pam and Matteotti were pretending nothing, nor were they looking at me, they didn't want to disturb me, because they were dead. I, however, was on the point of being arrested, and they pitied me.

Prison Escapes

"Wake up, Lucia! They're coming to arrest me."

It was Febo who warned me. He was growling and rumbling, gritting his teeth, in a state of extreme tension. He'd awoken me by scratching on my chest with his paws. I looked at him. His muzzle was dry and drawn, hollowed out with fear, he looked as though he'd not eaten for a week. The sun had hardly come up, and someone was about to arrive at House like Me. Febo knew it, his instinct was infallible.

"To arrest you?" Lucia exclaimed with a start. "But I can't see anyone," she added, staring with sleepy eyes at the road leading from the center of the island to the rock on which House like Me stands.

"Febo's never wrong. They'll be here in a few minutes."

I threw her shoes to her unceremoniously, put on mine and began to make my way down the steps to the little cove under the house.

"Where are you going? We can't swim away from here," said Lucia fixing her clothes in a wild rush. I'm afraid schoolmistresses just don't have what it takes when it comes to life on the run.

"Shut up and run for it."

Moments later, I'd pulled out the little boat I kept for emergencies from its hiding place of seaweed, leaves and pebbles and launched it. All three of us got into the tiny craft, I took out the oars and began rowing hard.

We were just in time to turn the cape, when two figures appeared in the distance, on the roof of House like Me.

"Febo was right," said Lucia, "at this hour in the morning it can only be the OVRA."

"And we've fooled them," I said, while Febo flattened himself against the bottom of the boat, as though he wanted to make himself invisible. A moment's hesitation, and the men from OVRA would have seen us getting the boat out under House like Me. Of course, the little divans and the gramophone on the roof made it clear that someone had spent the night there. But my pursuers had no idea where to begin looking for me.

"What now?" said Lucia, all pale and confused.

"Don't worry. I'll not make you a fugitive's accomplice," I said.

I set her down in a cove where a not too steep path led back towards the center of Capri. I put out to sea with Febo, while Lucia waved to me with her eyes full of tears, unsure whether she'd ever see me again. I hate tearful farewells: mine was a joyful and chivalrous greeting. Febo would have liked to salute her with a fine loud bark, but sensibly abstained from doing so. If our pursuers had good ears, they might have heard. A few more oar-strokes and Lucia had disappeared.

At the first possible opportunity we abandoned the boat on a pebble beach, not far from the Via Matermania, which links the eastern part of the island with the center. Jumping from rock to rock we managed to find a mule track that led to safety. By now I was feeling safe, when I heard a voice coming from down below:

"Curzio Malaparte, stop! You're under arrest!"

It was the Harbormaster's motor launch. On board were two or three men – no more than that. My response was to climb faster.

"Tarapoonchi poonchilah," I said to Febo, who was scared stiff, to give him courage.

"Stop or we'll shoot!" said the voice with the megaphone.

Moments later, the first shot came from the launch. The pistol had a silencer, it must have been one of those caliber 9 Berettas with which the police and Carabinieri had been equipped for the last four or five years. I heard the bullet whistle above my head and hit the rocks a little higher up. They wanted to scare me, but without making too much noise. It's not nice to shoot at a famous writer who's escaping unarmed with his dog; and even at dawn, someone might have heard shots. I continued my desperate climb and a few instants later I heard another two dull detonations. The first shot hit a huge rock a few paces from me, the other kicked up the dust a little further forward. The marksman was adjusting his aim.

I was breathless, my hands and arms were grazed and bleeding.

"Malaparte, stop!"

The fourth shot rang out, the last one.

ROME, SUMMER 1957
SANATRIX CLINIC, ROOM 32

Once More, a Splendid Woman

It was hot in Room 32. I got up, went to the window and opened the top button of my pajama jacket. Nothing had changed during the second round of my dictation: dear Sister Carmencita hibernating by my bedside, the fastidious youngster in a grey suit tapping away implacably at his typewriter, while his companion looked after small chores (opening the window whenever necessary, refilling my glass of water, bringing reams of paper to his typist colleague) and the splendid lady with the aquamarine eyes, sitting on the edge of the bed and listening absorbedly to my narration.

"What do you think of it?"

Death's eyes were closed. She remained silent.

If only the parrots and bloodsuckers had been able to get their claws on this posthumous masterpiece of mine! All those opportunists glued to the legs of my sickbed, gnawing and nibbling at it in the hope of tearing off some shard of notoriety. A rival of mine, the well-known journalist Indro Montanelli, had publicly offered to donate his blood to me, perfectly aware that I'd refuse it. The very idea of filling my veins with another's blood, above all Montanelli's, filled me with horror; our soul is in our blood.

The head physician, Professor Pozzi, kept looking at me with a strange appetite in his eyes. He had published a book entitled *Thus have I seen Them*, in which he described the death of famous personages who'd passed through his hands. I had read it and learned that all his patients had died at three in the morning. Once Pozzi had shown up in my room at some unearthly hour. I said to him: "Listen Pozzi, d'you want to know something? When you come into my room late at night I don't feel at ease. You can at least make an effort not to come at three." He went away, blushing, and left me in peace.

"What do you think of it?" I repeated to Death, thinking she'd not heard me.

Her eyelids opened and she looked at me with a pensive stare.

"You tell me. Judge for yourself," she replied.

"The tale seems to work. For a balanced judgment, you'd obviously need to get to the end. But I think there's everything we need for it to be a success."

"But I don't think you're on the right track."

"Why ever not? If you'll excuse my brazenness, the main character's an interesting guy. The characters are well drawn, and so are the settings. So what's missing?"

"You tell me."

"Oh, come on, haven't we had enough riddles? Have you a cigarette?"

"Sure," said Death, handing me first the cigarette, then the flame of her Dupont.

"Is the plot perhaps too complicated?"

Death did not reply. She just went on smoking in silence, blowing an enormous, utterly delicate pearl-colored cloud upwards, full of infinite doodles and arabesques. It seemed to be a representation of her thoughts, Death's obscure thoughts about my novel.

"Maybe I've got it. You don't like the fact that I'm the narrator. I should have written in the third person. That would have been more modest, more prudent."

Death gently shook her head.

"Then it must be the love scenes," I said. "Too cold. Or maybe too artificial, I don't know."

The Queen of this world looked at me compassionately, with a sad, tender smile.

"Malaparte, you're the lord and master of your book. I neither want nor can tell you what to do. You'll be judged on the basis of your goodwill, and that alone. You're a great writer, aren't you? Use your art."

Saying which, Death stared fixedly out of the window. She had nothing more to add.

"OK then, OK," I said, trying to save face. After all, she was right. Death is a woman, and when it comes to words, women are always right. I've never managed to understand how they do it, but that's how it is. I was the author and I could perfectly well manage on my own. I was pleased with how the book was coming on, wasn't I? After all, I had every reason to be pleased, it was flowing more naturally than many other of my novels, which I'd sweated blood to complete. Besides, I said to myself, I'd better just keep going without any fuss. Writing is also a problem of self-confidence, everyone knows that: you need stamina, you need persistence, you need balls.

I nodded to the Angels of Death, and at once the Remington started rattling away again, like a machine gun.

CAPRI, SUMMER 1939

Blood like Me

The shot whistled past to my left and slammed into a rock. I felt a burning whiplash on one cheek, touched it and saw that I was losing blood. A little splinter had shattered from the rock and hit me in the face. At that very same moment, I'd reached my goal, high up, in the green undergrowth where the trees would hide me. I had an advantage: the launch could not effect a swift landing. The bottom was shallow and rocky, to land there, the crew would have to use the life-raft. That would take a few precious minutes and meanwhile I could make my getaway. Febo stayed by my side, more worried for me than scared. At last he was getting a bit of movement, I thought, after all those boring parties, all that silly chatter, all those pretentious people he so despised.

"Tarapoonchi poonchi poonchilah," I said to him, "we mustn't be seen."

It was a tremendous advantage to have Febo with me: a dog's sense of smell (and Febo's was superb) would warn us at once if there were human beings in the vicinity.

Obviously, I already had a plan in mind. For days, I'd been obsessed by images of my imminent arrest. With the eyes of the imagination I'd viewed the scene over and over again and every conceivable variation on it: an arrest while eating at a restaurant, while swimming in the sea, while shaving in the morning. I had to get away from that part of the island, I had to go to Anacapri. Only up there, far from the tourist circuits and the metalled roads, would I have any chance of avoiding arrest. At least until Sirignano found Carmine.

We'd reached the Via di Matermania, the long track that leads to the center of Capri. I left it at once and we hid behind a big bush. Febo looked at me with pity, but also with some irritation.

"Well yes, we're in trouble again," I whispered to him. "But it's not my fault. It's Mussolini's doing. He's set the OVRA onto me."

Meanwhile, I used a few leaves and a bit of saliva to wipe the blood running down my face as well as I could, and to clean it from my hands and arms, all scratched and grazed during the mad rush of the scramble over the rocks of the cliff. Febo just kept looking at me, with that patient look of which only he was capable, full of pity, understanding and even a touch of canine humor, that special sense of humor, at once so innocent and so subtle, with which dogs look on us men, wearing ourselves out with a thousand worries, and just wonder why we can never find the time to stretch out in the open with them on a sunny afternoon, to follow a couple of cats, to rub our backs against the roots of a tree and just to take an easy nap by their side.

"You're quite right, I'm an idiot," I said, "but now we've got to save our skins. We'll have to hide in Anacapri. Then I'll give you a very important mission."

Febo growled with satisfaction. He hated to run away, he'd always rather take the initiative. The police and the OVRA would be lying in wait for me in the center and along the main roads. It wouldn't have entered their heads that I and Febo would head at once for the opposite end of the island; but we'd better get a move on.

We began our forced march, keeping well away from public roads, and making our way swiftly across orchards and gardens. Thank heavens the island was still sleeping, the people were recovering from the excesses of the night before and there wasn't a living soul in sight. Suddenly Febo stopped and flattened himself against the ground. I lay down by his side. We heard steps running down a nearby lane, and excited voices. It must have been the men from the OVRA and the Police searching the area. We remained hidden for a few minutes, holding our breath. Febo was aware of the danger, but galvanized by the adventure: at last his rather luckless master could show himself to be a hero.

When everything seemed to have calmed down again, we resumed our march. Strangely, there was no sound of megaphones or of police vehicles. It was clear that the authorities didn't want to disturb island life with a manhunt.

To catch me quickly, they'd have had to comb through all Capri, with surprise raids on every villa and private house, including those of V.I.P.s. And not just with a couple of discreet OVRA spies, but swarms of gendarmes who'd have been wide-eyed on discovering the true face of Capri the sewer, shit under a mink coat. Masses of ordinary cops and Carabinieri would have been eye-witnesses to the fact that this or that party boss was sharing his bed with a fifteen-year old boy or had in his house pictures taken from a museum, or that half of his villa had been added to illegally or that his chests of drawers contained banned imports of English books or American gramophone records. If you want to get at something in a pile of shit, you must probe gently, with tweezers; otherwise you'll achieve nothing but to shift the shit and, as we all know, it stinks. They wanted to let the news out only when there was a *fait accompli* and they had me in handcuffs.

That was plainly the reason why they'd used a silencer when shooting at me from the launch. They'd not start their trumpeting until they'd caught their criminal, and then they'd crucify him in all the papers.

It was going to be a hot day, a very hot day. Moving at breakneck speed, in not even half an hour we came to Due Golfi, the place under the great jutting crown of rocks that divides Capri from the heights of Anacapri. It takes its name – meaning "Two Bays" – from the fact that there you have a view over both the bay of Marina Grande, facing Naples and the coast, and that of Marina Piccola, on the opposite side of the island. Before us rose the rocky heights of Anacapri and Mount Solaro, and we had to decide how to get there.

There was certainly no question of taking the high road along the coast where we'd surely be seen by some passing car. Likewise, I ruled out the Phoenician Steps, the old stairway with its eight hundred steps carved out of the rock-face, which leads to Anacapri just under Axel Munthe's Villa San Michele: a tourist trail, which would have been too exposed. There remained only the Passetiello, the ancient path across the fields that the young men of Capri take at night to go courting their Anacapri belles. The island was slowly awakening, the sun was beginning to beat down.

"Get ready for a hard climb," I told Febo, and we began the long upward slog.

Moving away from Due Golfi we passed alongside Villa Quattro Venti, the big oriental-style house build by that paunchy old Elihu Vedder, the American painter who'd frescoed the Library of Congress and who, with his swollen pot belly and his Roman-style togas, looked like a caricature of Nero. We were walking very fast; I saw with disappointment that the tree cover was growing thinner; at any moment they might catch sight of us, even from far off. I was sweaty and covered with dirt from head to foot; I'd have given my right leg for a glass of water and a crust of bread, a little shade or somewhere to sit down. I owned the finest house in Capri, and just look at what I'd come down to.

I turned to look at the tower of the Villa Quattro Venti with its oriental-style windows, its red-tiled pagoda roof and cursed at the heat and the flies that were swarming in on me. Suddenly, Febo stopped, petrified. Someone was passing, not far off. I dived to the ground, flattening myself in the dust under a sort of hedgerow. It was two peasants, and they were talking in dialect. They talked about money, about a bad harvest, about the depredations of the Fascists, and Mussolini who protected them. They passed a few meters away from me and it was frankly a miracle that they didn't notice my legs sticking out from under the hedge.

I stood up. "You're beginning to pay for my death." I closed my eyes and thought: what do you want of me now, Pam? Leave me in peace, can't you see I'm on the run? Please...

Then I remembered: Cerio had said that D.H. Lawrence, sad, noble D.H. Lawrence, would meet with the Reynolds family at the Villa Quattro Venti when he came to Capri and they'd all play charades together. They played charades, said Cerio, and Pam was there too.

We kept climbing. How lucky I was to be wearing those strange new shoes with rubber soles! As we scrambled among the rocks, hidden by the shade of the agaves, holm oaks and bushes, I turned to get an idea of how far we'd come. By now we were high up, perhaps some four hundred meters. The lower part of the island lay stretched out at our feet like a great dead fish floating in the sea, with its scales glinting in the sun and its tail open and motionless. Its great soft green body was pocked with the sparkling white of the villas and luxury hotels. Only House like Me lay hidden behind its distant rocks, proud in its solitude.

After another half-hour of forced marches, we reached our destination. We were on the great rocky outcrop that marks the border between Capri and Anacapri. From here, one could scan at a glance the far side of the island, all the way to the Roman ruins of Damecuta, and the Punta del Faro – Lighthouse Point – Capri's signaling tower, looking across stretches of olive trees, vineyards, fruit trees, bare rocky spaces that suddenly turned into cliffs and fell vertically to the sea. Febo sat down to admire the vertiginous view, exhausted but happy. I touched my face: I was still bleeding. My hands and arms too were still bleeding but there was no time to do anything about that.

We were on a little shelf hanging between heaven and earth, dotted with maritime pines, oaks and beeches. Here too, nature had exaggerated; narcissi, broom, lithodoras and the rarest wild orchids sprang up everywhere as in a little earthly paradise. Only the flies, swarming in their hundreds to quench their thirst on my face and arms, spoiled the pleasure of the moment.

Febo went scouting ahead, in search of any possible dangers. We took a path that led to the top of Mount Solaro. The area was not completely uninhabited; we needed to be on guard.

We wandered on the slopes of Mount Solaro, looking for a cave, a hut, a ditch in which to shelter from the sun, but found nothing. The flies followed us like vultures, feeding on my sweat and my blood. At long last, we caught sight of a sort of hovel, a long-abandoned tool shed cobbled together from sheet metal, old planks and sheets of plywood. I just prayed that no one would catch sight of us from far off and rushed to the refuge. There was no lock on the door, I went in and let myself collapse on the ground. I touched my forehead and felt it was burning; I'd hardly slept that night, I must have a fever. In the little shed there were sticks, pickaxes, a billhook, dusty old wooden boxes and masses of rags. I prepared myself a place to lie down. But first I rummaged in my pockets. I fished out a pencil and a leaf from one of the notebooks that I used to carry around with me, and wrote on the back:

Unexpected guests came this morning.
Urgent to find Mr. Q.
Send reply through our gourmet friend.

If the note were intercepted by strangers, they'd need time and luck to decipher it. Sirignano's, however, was a fine intelligence. He'd understand at once who the unexpected guests were, And Mr. Q(uisisana) could only be Carmine. Our "gourmet friend", poor Febo, deserved to be fed and watered accordingly. Last but not least, Sirignano was to entrust Febo with his reply. I added no clues as to my hiding place, so as to avoid any betrayal or leakage of information. I slipped the message into my faithful friend's collar. I stroked him and whispered in his ear:

"Go to Sirignano, at the Villa Lysis. Tarapoonchi poonchi poonchilah, Febo. Then come back here with his reply. Understood?"

Febo wagged his tail and smiled his special canine smile, a lovely smile, full of innocence, all teeth and tongue. I pushed him gently out of the hovel and watched him through the half-closed door. He moved off a few paces, then turned, to make sure I was safe and sound. Then he trotted off at a fair pace, moving in the right direction. Descending from Mount Solaro he'd cross the Migliera path which, moving to the right, would take him to the center of Anacapri village. From there, he'd take the Phoenician Steps or the motor road. Febo knew well how to behave with passing cars, it would be difficult for him to be knocked down. How he'd move on from there, only God and his mysterious canine intellect knew.

I felt a pain in my right arm. Something had pricked me – no, bitten me. It was not a fly. It was a big ant, a red ant. It had found one of the wounds on my arm, it had smelled my blood. Nearby, there were others, many others, attracted by fresh meat. I tried to blow them away, but they stayed at their post. They were like the ants at Sala Dingai, the enormous red ants at Sala Dingai, the desert plain in the Horn of Africa where that mysterious Carolingian castle stands which, in the last ten centuries no white man but me has seen. I'd been there a few months before, when I was a war correspondent in Ethiopia. When a man was wounded, an ant would come, but without attacking him. It would smell the air, the odor of blood, and if it felt that the man would live a while longer, it would go away. It went to call its companions. They'd all wait patiently somewhere underground for death to do its work. Only when the soldier had died did they come in their masses, covering his corpse in a heaving red blanket.

The fever was making itself felt, my forehead was a hot coal. I was intolerably thirsty, I was exhausted and in my heart I felt I no longer had a drop of blood. I thought of my friend Piero Gobetti, Piero Gobetti the Communist, who died in Paris of a heart attack after being assaulted by Mussolini's thugs. He too lay under two meters of earth, like Pam, like Matteotti, like Santoni, eaten by red ants. So let the red ants come and eat me – *la dracu* – to hell with the red ants, after all I could do nothing but wait. My life depended on Febo and his mission, it all hung on an Etna Cirneco. If someone noticed that strange solitary dog, instead of Febo I could expect an OVRA commando.

I stretched out on my filthy bed of rags and boxes, said a prayer for my dog and fell asleep.

I dreamed of dogs, just dogs, so many dogs, packs of dogs all just like Febo, dogs walking under the Capri sun and suffering from heat, thirst and flies, but all smiling at me, smiling and advancing. I was in a yellow, grey and brown world: the grey of mud, the brown of rusty barbed wire and the yellow of gas and explosives. I saw other packs of dogs coming, the dogs of war from all the world's armies, Dalmatians, Pomeranian sheepdogs, Border Collies, bomb-dogs loaded with explosives and trained to kill themselves exploding underneath tanks, telegraphist dogs carrying on their backs spools of telephone wire which they unrolled surreptitiously in the midst of the enemy lines, dogs pulling machine guns that weighed five times more than themselves, dogs bearing an order to move an army of three hundred thousand men, dogs out looking for the wounded and the dying in the midst of dead bodies on the battlefield. We'd send them on a distant errand with some message, meanwhile we'd move on kilometers further, yet they'd always return to us, they never failed. When it snowed, we put sardine oil on the soles of our boots so that they wouldn't lose track of us, but it was not necessary. A war dog always finds the soldier who's his master, even when he's dead –

above all when he's dead, because he wants to stay there and die with him. I saw the war that was still to come. I saw the German soldiers of General von Schobert enter villages to the southeast of Kiev and at once exterminate all the dogs with machine guns and grenades, even before killing the Jews, lest they be enrolled by the Russians. I saw Rin Tin Tin, the German shepherd which an American corporal found in the French Ardennes and which went on to become a Hollywood star, dying in the divine arms of Jean Harlow, but I know that even when he lay dying in Jean Harlow's arms the heart that was beating within was that of a humble war dog, and he was thinking of his first master, a nameless German soldier who died in the Ardennes.

And then I dreamed of carrier pigeons, immense flocks of white and grey doves, identical to those which the banker Nathan Rothschild sent from Paris to London with the latest news, in order to speculate in the Stock Exchange on Napoleon's victories and defeats. I saw acrobatic doves, freed in mid-flight at crazy speeds from military biplanes following from on high the troops on land, following ships, even submarines, doves flying heroically above the enemy lines, while shots from below exterminated them; yet on they went, onward, ever onward. I dreamed of the German dove I'd shot at in France and which fell at my feet with a message still tied to its legs: *Before Vauquois. We are only 28 men now. The Americans are attacking us in a thick fog of gas. We shall resist to the last cartridge. Pray for our souls.*

Then came the horses, colossal multitudes of military horses at the gallop, horses white, black and piebald, French horses, English horses, Italian horses, Russian and Finnish horses with long blonde manes, Moroccan and Berber horses, the Indian horses of Maharaja Sir Pertab Singh, horses dragging carts, machine guns, stretchers, horses wearing gas masks, sick and underfed horses, dead horses that did not know they were dead and kept running. I saw the stallions of the Algerian Goumiers, which their riders used in gun battles as flesh shields, stuffed with bullets. Before me passed hundreds of headless horses, and I still did not know where they were coming from, because I was to see them with my own eyes only two years later, during the war, in 1941: they were Russian horses used against the Finnish infantry, dead horses caught in the ice of Lake Ladoga, which the squads of Finnish *sissit* had to decapitate and saw to pieces to be able to bury them. Then I felt the earth tremble and saw half a million Cossack horses charging across the snowy steppes of the Bucovina amidst a chorus of wild neighing, and behind them, galloping along the banks of the Dnieper, the Tartar cavalry of Marshal Budyonny in a suicidal charge against the armor of the German *Panzerpferde*, and the smoking carcasses of the Hungarian and Galician horses that died in the Carpathians, among the marshes of Jaroslawice, where Russian cavalrymen and Austrian dragoons massacred one another with sabers in August 1914 in the last great equestrian battle of all time. I saw the thousands of white chargers that lived free on the immense grasslands of the Gojjam, in Ethiopia, and the warhorse which my friend Teklit Unturà, the Ethiopian soldier Teklit Unturà, stabbed to death with a knife. I saw Bulgarian mules, harnessed together two at a time, transporting medicines and the wounded on litters, like walking hospitals, and putting up with the enormous weight without a complaint, because animals at war are far more generous and noble than us soldiers, they strive, suffer and die with never a lament, never asking for anything in exchange. I saw the Italian mules, the humble Italian mules, the glorious Italian mules, which in the eleven battles fought alongside the River Isonzo during the Great War had daily transported cannon into the mountains on their backs, right up to the glaciers, only to die smashed and forgotten at the bottom of some ravine.

As in every military parade the minor regiments came last, and I saw squadrons of camels, Turkish and Kurdish camels, German camels, Kirghiz camels charging across the vast plains of Petropavlovsk. Behind them, the Croatian pigs killed with hatchet blows and roasted in the trenches, Czechoslovak bears forced to play for the troops, African and Austrian roe deer, Montenegrin sheep, Polish cows from Lida, Russian geese, Istrian hens, Serbian bees confiscated from civilians and kept in old wooden hives by the Austro-Hungarian troops so that they could have fresh honey every day. In my dream I stuck a hand into the hives, took it out and licked it, tasting on my tongue the sweetest honey of the Ottynia bees, the Carpathian bees, there's no honey better than that from the Carpathians. There was a wonderful cold snap at Ottynia, it was 20 degrees below zero and all the Austrian soldiers froze to death. I licked my hand again, it was yellow, sweet and yellow as asphyxiating gases. As I looked at my yellow hand I realized that another tongue was licking my hand, no longer my own. I awoke, still looking at my hand. A dog's tongue was licking it. Febo was back.

He'd made it. Neither the OVRA nor the police had intercepted him. He was even filthier than before, his legs were still trembling with fatigue and emotion, but his muzzle was dirty with bread and milk: Sirignano had fed and watered him.

The first thing I did was to celebrate his return with endless embraces and kisses, while he tried to keep up virile restraint but in the end tears welled up in his eyes. Then I looked in his collar and found a piece of paper. Sirignano had replied as I'd hoped he would. I pulled out the paper and unfolded it:

> *Guests on vacation everywhere, but discreetly.*
> *Friends and girlfriends asking for news of you.*
> *Mister Q. still AWOL, but now I know why.*
> *A great friend is now at your disposal.*
> *We'll be delighted to welcome you on your first visit.*

As I'd imagined, the OVRA were searching for me but meant to go about it discreetly. Tamburi and Lucia ("friends and girlfriends") anxiously awaited my news. Carmine ("Mr. Q.", Q for Quisisana) was still nowhere to be found, and now Sirignano had found out why. I must know that as soon as possible, I said to myself. Perhaps Sirignano's mysterious helper ("a great friend") could also help me, besides offering me a hiding place.

I'd best not leave my den, I thought; Sirignano knew what to do, but Tamburi was unreliable and Lucia might easily make a false move.

My fever still raged, I was still intensely hungry and thirsty, dreaming of some cultivated field where I could sink my teeth into a nice juicy red and green tomato, but daylight exposed me to too many risks, I must wait. I lay down again on my foul couch and napped a little longer. Why should Carmine want to keep away from me? I couldn't think of any reason but Sirignano had managed to find out. *La dracu* Sirignano, *la dracu* Cerio, in that island they all had better brains than me. A red ant was tasting the flesh on my wrist. I was too tired, I let it be.

A voice awoke me when sundown came at last. "You're paying for my blameless death."

It was Pam's voice, but this time I shut her up. You're dead, Pam, you can't speak any more. You're dead like Matteotti, like Santoni, the lad of the class of '99. You're all a meter under the ground, eaten by red ants, and you can't speak any more, you no longer count for anything, nobody's thinking of you, of your poems, of your mouths full of crude oil, your guts spilling out on the ground.

The time had come, enough of foolish thoughts. I got up and went out from the hovel, spat on the ground and began walking, followed by Febo. *La dracu* Pam, *la dracu* Matteotti, *la dracu* Santoni and the lads of the class of '99.

The wind bore an odor of sulfur from the island of Ischia, whose distant silhouette lay in the midst of the twilit sea like a great sleeping turtle. The sky was rent by invisible lightning, sudden gusts of air bearing whirlwinds of sand and salt and depositing them on one's skin, in one's hair, up one's nose. It's going to rain soon, I said to myself. The air was as dense and heavy as a woolen blanket and it smelled of woman, it smelled like a hot woman with a deep voice. God, how I longed to see Lucia. We'd been apart for less than twenty-four hours yet it seemed an eternity. Who knows what she'll be doing, who knows if she really wants to see me or is it that she's just afraid. Will the OVRA have come to interrogate her too? Soon it'll rain, God, bring Lucia back to me.

We passed close to the old house of Norman Douglas, the great writer Norman Douglas, the house where that old swine Norman Douglas received his well-paid young Capri lovers. The boys sold their bodies with their families' consent, that way they'd earn a bit of money, nothing wrong with that, is there? He was a great artist, Norman Douglas, he was a benefactor of Capri. If he'd not been a great artist he'd not have been able to write *South Wind*. Norman Douglas was a great artist, and Capri was a marvelous place, there was nothing like it in the whole wide world, no one would ever get me to change my mind about that.

We took the Migliera trail. We were a stones-throw from Axel Munthe's property, the Villa San Michele, where Goering thought there was an entrance to the Underworld. What crap! It was a senseless delirium, a joke in bad taste, yet the Nazis believed in it. How was that possible? I turned towards the seafurther, just a few hundred meters further, the Migliera came to an end with the abyss into which the Sturmbannführer had almost skidded. The Migliera abyss, the Òrrico abyss where Pam had died, the abysses of Count Fersen and Norman Douglas, with their little boys – in Capri it's all one abyss. I mustn't think of that, I said to myself, or else Pam would start talking to me again, and that I did not want.

A sudden shock. The two guys from the OVRA, Bianchi and Marelli, those who'd interrogated me at House like Me. They were walking along the Migliera in the direction of the center. I ducked among some bushes, but there was no need. They were walking at a deliberate pace, without looking around them, they weren't searching for anything. They'd gone up there without having the least inkling that I was hiding in the vicinity, that was perfectly obvious. We followed them from afar, among alleyways and little stairways, until we saw them get into a car and drive off at full speed, heading for Capri. I'd come close to being found by chance. Febo gave a deep sigh of relief.

Once we got to the center of Anacapri we took care to use only rarely frequented alleys. I met the occasional old woman, a few groups of children and a trio of peasants, no one paid the least attention to me or Febo. I saw the evening papers on sale in the news stalls and the headlines. Not a word about me.

We ran into a boy with a battered straw hat. He'll have been eleven or twelve. I asked him if he'd give it to me and he said yes at once. He was barefoot, a poor child, but for him giving a present was no problem, only the rich are incapable of making gifts. I told him I'd pay for it, I'd have the money on the next day, but he didn't understand, he said I could keep it and that's all there was to it.

With the hat, I could hide my face a bit, and I prayed that the poor light would do the rest for me. We went down the Phoenician Steps. In the dark that posed no problem. Once we were back down from Anacapri the greater part of our troubles were over: our goal was a stone's throw away, facing onto the loveliest bay in Italy. It was a risky move, but it was well worth attempting.

✒ ✒ ✒

Naked Men

"Whom am I to announce to the Signora?"

"Tell her I'm a friend. A friend who prefers to come when her husband's far away, in America."

The maid left me outside the gate and hurried back to the house. No one could be permitted such insolence with Mona Williams. The lady of the house would have me thrown out, for sure.

Instead, five minutes later it was the Kentucky filly in person who came to welcome me. I saw her approaching down A the driveway at a slow, gentle pace; only she walked that supple walk, she must have learned it from the fillies in her father's riding stables. She was pleased I'd come but took good care not to show it. As I'd hoped, she still knew nothing about the arrest hanging over my head.

"I'd understood it was you, Malaparte."

"You're a very smart woman. A smart filly from Kentucky."

She smiled, but did not reply. She went to such immense pains to force that lah-di-dah British accent to please her husband. She said London but her thoughts were of Owensboro, she said Devonshire but her mind moved to the Appalachians, she said cricket but she meant baseball, she said pudding but thought Kentucky fried chicken. Nowadays, horses and fillies turned her stomach. She opened the gate and looked at Febo with some perplexity. Mona liked miniature poodles, an Etna Cirneco had too proud a personality for her taste.

"Eddie detests the smell of dogs," she said, using the pretext of her supposed lover. "Now he's in Naples, but he'll be back here tomorrow."

"Don't worry," I said, "Febo's not coming. He's got better things to be doing. Tarapoonchilah, Febo."

My beloved Cirneco made off after casting me an understanding glance. He had a new mission to accomplish.

"No alcohol, just water. Plenty of water, please," I said, collapsing onto one of the Fortino's oversized sofas.

Mona served me in person, and had herself brought an orange blossom. She was splendidly slim, and dazzlingly lovely, as ever. Only her hands were not as slim as all the rest, they gave away her family's old trade, they were tough hands used to holding reins and shifting bales of hay in the stables (and that's perfectly visible if you look at her old photos, even those by Cecil Beaton). She wore a fine blouse, black silk pants, black moccasins and around her neck a double necklace of enormous natural pearls, bought in ports on the China Sea during her honeymoon cruise on Harrison's yacht. Hers was a superb suppleness, she didn't even seem to be made of flesh. I've got to keep a cool head, I said to myself, I'm here to save my skin and I can't allow myself any distractions. Under Mona's skin, I thought, there's no flesh, just masses of money, Harrison Williams' dollars. Mona's liver was made of banknotes, I repeated to myself, her stomach was made of banknotes, her pancreas and her spleen were banknotes, her intestine a long tube of rolled-up banknotes. When she blew her nose, bits of banknotes issued from her nose together with the snot. She was a Fifth Avenue shopwindow manikin stuffed with banknotes. If a surgeon were to open her up with a scalpel, instead of a heart he'd find a pocketbook with a press stud that went tick when you opened and closed it. Mona studied me closely from head to foot.

"Good heavens, Malaparte, what ever has happened to you? You look as though you've been robbed and beaten up."

"I've been out for a walk in the country with Febo. You know how it is, you get dirty out there among the brambles, and you ruin your clothes."

"I can get you some clean clothes. Harrison's size is close to yours."

"I'll accept that willingly. But first, I need a shower."

Mona rang a little silver bell and a couple of maids arrived like lightning. The lady of the house gave her orders rapidly and one of the maids asked me to follow her. The guest house of the Fortino was a separate building and one had to cross the garden.

"Are you leaving me alone?" I said to Mona.

"Oh all right, I'll come with you. You're insolent and egotistical, Malaparte. Just like they say," she replied with a smile. She sent the maids away, took her orange blossom and led me across the garden. As I followed her, I thought that everything in the Fortino, in the air, even in Mona's voice, betrayed the absence of a man. Harrison was always in America, Eddie von Bismarck lived in the Fortino but he was not a man, he was something less and something more.

Through the park of the Fortino wafted perfumes of gentians, bougainvilleas, orchids and bushes bearing the rarest of roses – Perle d'or, Fellemberg, Mermaid, Blush Noisette, and Princesse de Nassau – roses worthy of Mona and Harrison Williams. The palm trees swayed lazily in the wind, like lascivious ladies massaged by a slave. The sky was streaked with pink, it was all cobalt blue but crossed by long rosy streaks, streaks of pink raspberries, rosé champagne and pink bananas, those little pink bananas you find in Peru.

We came to the guest house. It was a large apartment at garden level. We entered a suite with a bathroom.

"Take care not to scratch that. It's made of Cinnabar lacquer," said Mona anxiously, pointing to a red Chinese table, all decorated in intaglio with Buddhist lotus flowers, Buddhist lions, Buddhist foliage. I sat down on an 18th century Italian chair and took a look around me at the English carpets, the Staffordshire chandeliers, the George III mirrors and the late 19th century French table clock. The maids came in and placed two wicker baskets on the bed on which were piled up a bathrobe, towels and a change of clothing, all splendidly ironed and perfumed with lavender. Mona was on the point of making her way out with the maids. I stopped her.

"I detest having to take a shower all alone. Stay here, outside the bathroom, so we can keep chatting." I took off my shirt and threw it on the ground, remaining bare-chested.

Mona grew pale. All alone with a half-naked Italian Aborigine. If the people at *Vogue* were to learn of this, it would be all over for her. But now there was no escape, Harrison's money couldn't defend her from me. Great ladies are to be treated like flower-girls, and flower-girls like great ladies. I forget who said that, but it's gospel truth.

I unbuttoned my pants, without dropping them. Mona stared at me through half-closed eyes, trying hard to hide her surprise.

"Don't worry, you're not embarrassing me one bit," I said to her, "I don't have complexes."

Hers was the same confused, defenseless stare as my own, a few years later, when in a sauna in Finland I ran into Heinrich Himmler, the head of the SS, naked and sweating, all pink and flaccid, wearing only a little towel to cover his private parts, while his men beat him on the back with birch twigs. Naked men have that effect, even on men themselves; they always make one feel uncomfortable. Naked men are unnatural.

I went into the bathroom and turned the shower faucet. I took off my pants and threw them out of the bathroom door, at Mona's feet.

"On the contrary," I continued while turning the faucet to get the right jet, "we Europeans need to learn from you Americans how to live without complexes. America's the future, while Europe's rotten. She's our mother, but a rotten mother. She's rotten inside. That's why we have Hitler and Mussolini. Hitler and Mussolini are weeds growing out of the same shit. But America will teach the world democracy and culture. I'm reminded of Emily Dickinson: *Water is taught by thirst; Land, by the oceans passed; Transport, by throe; Peace, by its battles told; Love, by memorial mould; Birds, by the snow.* And to this I'd add: *Culture, is taught by America*". D'you know Emily Dickinson?

"No, I don't know Emily Dickinson".

"A pity. She was a great poet. She lived in Massachusetts. Massachusetts isn't *that* far from Kentucky, is it?"

Through the crack between the door and the wall, I could just see Mona in the little sitting room, inwardly cursing Kentucky. Why wasn't that wretched Kentucky swallowed up by the earth, together with all its horses? That evening Mona was aching to make love, I could read that in her face as she slowly sipped her orange blossom. I simply love orange blossom, I thought, it's a damn delicious cocktail. In summer one should drink nothing but orange blossom, all other drinks should be banned. Free of my filthy clothes, I was beginning to feel better, almost good humored. It was a wonderful evening, the sky was all streaked with pink bananas. What a pity I was there to talk of disagreeable things: I had to speak to Mona of the stolen book and the Sturmbannführer. I entered the shower cabin, under the tepid cascade, and let the jet massage my back.

"Why do you say that America will win the war?" asked Mona.

"Because there's no choice. America must stop Hitler. You'll have to enter the war and fight here in Europe. You've already done just that, twenty years ago: you waited until the European states were massacring one another, then you landed in Europe and won. America is the future of the world. America and the world are one item, and that item is America."

Mona laughed out loud. "You're crazy, Malaparte."

"Why should we Americans stop Hitler? To do the Germans a favor, maybe?"

"Hitler's not German, he's Austrian. By the way, have you ever noticed the shape of Austria? It's just like that of Kentucky. Wide on the right, narrow on the left."

"You're crazy, Malaparte. You're a crazy Eyetie. And you Tuscans from Florence are even crazier."

"I'm from Prato, not Florence."

"So what? In America no one's heard of Prato, but they all know about Florence."

"Prato's magical. If you go to Prato and you feel hungry, you can eat the earth."

"The earth?"

"I'm quite serious. I grew up as a kid eating earth in the country round Prato. One day I'll tell you about that."

"You're mad, Malaparte."

The water was pouring down and working wonders for me. I'd regained my strength. The fever had gone, too.

"I'm not mad. I just have the guts to say what others don't want to hear. America should invade the world. In any case, it's already doing just that. D'you know what Mussolini once said to me? He said that Hitler hates Berlin. He hates Berlin because he says it's too Americanized. Berlin's a city without German culture, says Hitler, it's in the hands of American culture. D'you get it? The capital of Nazi Germany is too Americanized. That just goes to show I'm right."

"You're mad, Malaparte. You're raving mad. You want to build yourself a villa on Cape Massullo and change the place's name to Cape Malaparte."

I'd scrubbed enough, I turned off the shower. I tied a towel round my waist, like a skirt, and came out of the bathroom still dripping.

Mona avoided looking at me. These millionaires are all kids, I thought. I sat down on the chair opposite hers, the 18th century Italian chair. I was soaking wet and I wet the precious satin cushion on the 18th century Italian chair. Despite being morbidly jealous about her furniture, Mona pretended she'd not noticed. I could have just picked her up, dumped her on the nearby bed and started undressing her, and she'd not have offered the least resistance. That's just what she herself was hoping for, she'd have liked to beg for it, but she was too wealthy to lower herself to that. She'd buried her face in her orange blossom, like an ostrich. I stood up, snatched the glass from her hand and poured it away.

"I detest orange blossom. It tastes of nothing," I said, returning her the empty glass. Mona's mouth stayed hanging open.

"You're crazy, Malaparte. Presumptuous and crazy. Everyone says so, and it's true."

From the pile of clean clothes, I grabbed one of her husband's shirts and put it on. It was of the finest cotton batiste and it smelled of lavender, it had mother-of-pearl buttons and two ivory cufflinks, it really was very well made. Maybe Harrison Williams had worn it, I thought, when he was kissing Coco Chanel or his other mistresses at Oak Point, at Palm Beach, in New York, in those long months when Mona in Capri thought of nothing but getting herself photographed by Cecil Beaton, watering her roses and, to ward off boredom, going to bed with some plebeian waiter. Mona had a son by a previous marriage, but she never spoke of him, it was as though he didn't exist. Sometimes she and Harrison did not see or speak to one another for months, though each regarded the other as the best possible accessory for his or her life. Harrison had allowed Mona an official lover, Eddie von Bismarck, because he was homosexual. The shirt really was beautifully made, I thought, Mona and Harrison dressed with taste. They had a wonderful life.

"No, I'm not crazy," I said, "I just say what everyone thinks but they haven't the courage to say. American culture must be spread worldwide. Only that way will the world be safe. Talking of culture, did you find the book that was stolen?"

"Not yet."

"Did you call the police?"

"I don't want to involve the police in this. That would be useless."

"You're quite right, that would be useless. In Italy the law is like a harlot's honor, it's always useless to call the police. Not just useless, but dangerous. If the police come into your house, they'll find other books."

"In Italy it's also dangerous to let someone like you into the house," said Mona laughing.

"Who do you think stole the book?"

"That is none of your business, Malaparte." She'd spoken with her insufferable fake British accent.

Very well, I thought, now's the moment. I stood up, I took the empty glass from her hand and framed that little face with its huge aquamarine eyes with my fingers. She accepted my kiss passively, without giving much. She took my hands from her temples, they were ruining her perm. Plainly, a stronger approach was called for. I lifted her up bodily and slung her across one shoulder.

"What are you *doing*? Then you really are nuts!" she screamed in her real accent, her healthy, sincere, honest Kentucky accent.

I entered the bathroom, turned the shower faucet and brought her into it. Mona was squawking and flapping like an enormous bird, like a bald eagle from Kentucky. As we struggled locked to one another, the water soaked us from head to foot, flooding Mona's shoes, and causing her make-up to run down her cheeks and neck. As she wouldn't stop squawking and wouldn't make up her mind to undress, I tore off her blouse and all the rest of her clothes, and in the end she burst out laughing and tore off my shirt in her turn. The fine mother-of-pearl buttons and the ivory cufflinks went flying and slid one by one down the plughole. Mona didn't move. I was bewitched by her look when she let them go down the drain; it was a cold look, a look with a fake British accent. The water was overflowing from the shower, it was flooding the floor.

I closed the faucet, we left the bathroom laughing and swaying from side to side. We dried ourselves by rolling on a king-size bed big enough to take an entire family. Even Mona's lovemaking had a fake British accent, it was a poor imitation of British lovemaking. It had nothing to do with how English women make love. I've made several long stays in England, I know what I'm talking about. Mona was playing a role like an amateur actress hamming it up, she was hurrying along, it was like a forced march, like someone who wants to play Shakespeare but has never seen Laurence Olivier on stage and has never heard of Edwin Booth. With her fake-British lovemaking, Mona was throwing to the wind her hot, explosive American woman's lovemaking, which I'd have far preferred. Mona said "I'd like" but meant "I want". She said "Take your time" but meant "It's time". She said "We could" but meant "I can". She said "I feel" but meant "I want to feel".

It wasn't her fault if everything she did was fake. When I squeezed her, I felt the banknotes crumpling under the skin of her belly, under that soft skin I felt her liver, her spleen, her guts, all made of banknotes, of watermarked paper, her guts of a woman stuffed with dollars, a stuffed dummy. Afterwards, she let her head fall on my chest and slept.

When she woke up, she had us brought dinner. We ate like two lions, laughing and stealing eggs and fish from each other's plates, competing to see who could drink more glasses of Veuve Clicquot. Perhaps that was the only moment when she really broke free of her assumed self, of that British Mona, and returned to her childhood, before her father divorced and ruined her family and her life, perhaps for an instant she became again young Mona Strader, proud daughter of a Kentucky groom, a lovely girl with rather large hands. I even teased her for her fake British accent.

"Mona, you Americans will never understand a thing about Europe. If you want to cut a fine figure, these days you should have a cockney accent. The children of the old European aristocracy all have governesses who speak with a cockney accent, and they grow up speaking cockney, thinking cockney, even governing cockney. You really must learn cockney, or you'll not be worth a thing."

"You're nuts, Malaparte," said Mona laughing, and at last laughing a bit even at herself. The terrain was well prepared.

"I know who stole your book," I said suddenly.

"Then, out with his name."

"It was the Sturmbannführer. During the party."

"Give me proof of that."

"I saw it with my own eyes."

"That's not good enough."

"I could make a witness statement. Even to the police. Why is that book so important to you?"

"The book is not important. But inside it there's a memento. A memento of a dear friend. Someone very special. I got all the servants to search for it, but then I became resigned. The book's been stolen, that's for sure. In any case, I've promised a fat reward to the maid who finds it. I'll leave no stone unturned. But now, won't you tell me about the Sturmbannführer and the theft? Did anyone else see him besides you?"

"No one else, I think. Who else would be interested in that memento?"

"Someone who holds a very important position in a foreign state. More than that, I can't tell you."

"You're not generous. I've revealed to you that the thief was the Sturmbannführer," I said smiling. "Now you can report him."

"No, it was *not* the Sturmbannführer. He came to take his leave at the end of the party. He could perfectly well have left before the end, without coming to say goodbye, like so many others, with the book hidden in his jacket. Instead he came to me. His conscience was clear. That was obvious."

"I assure you that I saw him take it with my own eyes."

"You must have been mistaken. I know these are hard times for you."

"What do you mean?"

"Come on, come on. The OVRA means to arrest you. They've been searching for you high and low, all day. But don't worry, I'll tell no one you're here. And here tonight no one will come looking for you. I'm an American citizen. They must respect me."

I was thunderstruck. I'd thought I had her in the palm of my hand, I'd thought I could squeeze out of her whatever I needed, instead of which my life was in her hands.

"I... Thank you, Mona".

"What for? You're insolent and presumptuous, but I like you. One day I'll read one of your books. Why did you kill that girl?"

"I didn't kill her, for heaven's sake. It was the Sturmbannführer."

"Why does the OVRA suspect you of the girl's death?"

"Because someone's trying to frame me. Unfortunately, I don't know who. What's more, the Sturmbannführer has given evidence against me. False evidence."

"Poor Sturmbannführer. You really do want to get him into trouble, don't you?"

I cursed. I was almost on the point of getting dressed and leaving, slamming the door behind me. Then I calmed down and explained it all to her: the chessboard inscribed with the words "who is like God" and PAM, Munthe and Cerio's versions, Goering and Lenin, Reynolds and the Fabian Society. She listened to me slowly sipping the last flute of champagne.

"As you'll have understood," I concluded, "they've told me nothing but nonsense. Poor Pam's death has nothing to do with Russians or with Nazis."

"Poor Malaparte," said Mona, standing up and looking at the sea from one of the great windows. "You've not understood a thing."

"What do you mean?"

"You see everything divided, separate. I have a very different view. You speak of the Russians and Germans, you speak of the revolutions as though they were distinct from one another. But they aren't."

"And what d'you know of that?"

"My husband Harrison works with money. He's a financier. He knows many things. He explained to me that the Russian revolution was financed by the Germans and Americans. He knows what he's talking about. He knows all the big bankers. Come, I want to show you something."

We went out and crossed the garden, wrapped in two white bathrobes. The pink banana sky had gone, the cobalt had veered to dark grey with a few warm purple streaks. The rocks on Mount Solaro were still highlit by a few weak glimmers of sunshine which transformed them into mysterious yellow and reddish patches of light, reminiscent of details you'll find in the work of artists of the Hudson River School, or how Thomas Moran painted Grand Canyon and Yellowstone landscapes, that stubborn, meticulous way of handling yellows, reds and ochres.

Returning to Mona's apartment, we entered her bedroom, walking barefoot on an immense English Saint Cyr carpet. Mona approached an 18 century trumeau where, in the midst of Meissen porcelains, Worcester bowls and green lacquer Chinese boxes stood a photo of Mussolini. She opened a drawer, rummaged among some papers and pulled out a large envelope. She extracted a newspaper cutting and showed it to me.

It was a cartoon from the St. Louis Post-Dispatch dated 1911:

"Don't you see? The richest and most powerful men in America. George Perkins, J.P. Morgan, John Ryan of the National Bank, John D. Rockefeller, Andrew Carnegie and Teddy Roosevelt. All friends of Marx, all friends of the Marxist cause in Europe and in Russia. Harrison kept this cartoon. He finds Marx's expression so amusing, He shows it to all his friends. Harrison told me that when William

Boyce Thompson ran the Federal Reserve, he arranged for the loan of a million dollars to the Russian revolutionary government. It was our very own President Wilson who enabled that Communist subversive Trotsky to return to Russia and join the revolt against the Tsar, by giving him an American passport."

"Come on, Mona. Are you trying to use a twenty-eight year old newspaper cutting to convince me that the world is the opposite of all that we see and that Marxists and capitalists are really going arm in arm?"

Mona continued her spiel as though I'd said nothing.

"You know that Gorky founded his revolutionary school here in Capri. But when that same Gorky was seeking public subscriptions for the revolution, where d'you think he went? To us, in America. The money Lenin used to finance the Russian revolution came from the Germans via Finnish and Swiss banks. At the same time our banks were financing the Japanese who were fighting Russia in the Far East. Bankers are like that: if it suits them to lend money to someone, they just go ahead and do it. If they want to create a new market, no matter where, they just bring in the money. It's quite natural, just a matter of weighing up the pros and the cons, and it's their job. Bankers aren't people who know how to make political distinctions. They do business. I know these things, Harrison and his friends often talk about them."

While Mona was warming to her subject, wrapped in her fine cotton bathrobe with appliqué lace trimmings, I seemed to be seeing her elsewhere, dining in her house on Fifth Avenue, sheathed in a *grande soirée* gown by Robert Piguet, in the company of her husband and a select group of the Upper Ten Thousand and listening to phrases that even she couldn't understand, yet soaking them all up and preparing herself mentally to repeat them one day in fashionable salons. She must have felt herself to be the depository of Wall Street's most complicated and exciting secrets, and while she gave discreet nods to the waiters, she'll have been praying that no one would talk of Kentucky or horses.

"What you're saying doesn't make sense, Mona. The Germans who financed Lenin weren't bankers," I said, "It was the German government, it was Kaiser Wilhelm, those men were politicians."

"Of course. Governments engage in politics and they use money for their purposes. In the Great War the Germans were fighting on two main fronts, against the Russians in the East and the other allies in the West; so they wanted to promote revolution in Russia in order to force that country's withdrawal from the war and concentrate all their forces on the western front. And by financing Lenin's revolution, they succeeded, that's all there is to it. It's their job. It's all a great game, that's what Harrison keeps telling me. The major bankers are friends of the Socialists too, even of your friend Richard Reynolds' Fabian Society, and they rain money on all of them. Why are you surprised? There are things you can't understand, Malaparte. This is *big* business, and I mean big – it's not for common people."

Mona is a great lady, I thought. She really doesn't know what she's talking about but she keeps on talking, she won't be ignored, she won't retreat. I found her like a child who's barely been weaned and wants to eat her soup all alone and unaided for the first time; and, as no one has given her a spoon, she uses what she finds to hand, a piece of wood, a pen, a little brush.

"Why have you a photo of Mussolini here?" I asked her, pointing to the portrait of the Duce.

"He's a good man. He knows how things work. He used to be a Socialist, now he's the Fascist leader. He's been financed by the French and the English, he's taken money from everyone and now he's become the Duce. Frankly, my dear, I don't give a damn. I don't mind the Fascists. In England, too, there are Fascists. There's even a Fascist Party, the party of Sir Oswald Mosley. Mosley used to belong to the Fabian Society, he was a Socialist like Mussolini. Sir Oswald and his wife Diana are good friends of mine, I know what I'm talking about. There are plenty of people in England who look on Hitler with sympathy and don't want war with Germany. There's Lloyd George, who calls Hitler *the George Washington of Germany*. Then you have Lord Halifax, Lord Londonderry, Lord Lothian and Lord Beaverbrook. And there's Lord Rothermere with his *Daily Mail*, and the Duke and Duchess of Windsor, who are dear friends of mine and who came here to Capri last year, you saw them too when they gave the Roman salute in public, like a pair of good Fascists. D'you remember? We all went together to see *A Yank at Oxford*, at the Capri

Film Festival, the people were acclaiming them, and there were the Windsors, returning straight-arm salutes. Only that swine Churchill wants war with the Germans at all costs. Good heavens! Where did I leave my pearl necklace? It must have come off in the shower."

She rang her little bell and within fifteen seconds a maid arrived, Mona gave her instructions, the maid disappeared, and we were alone again.

"You're getting muddled, Mona," I said. "I too know Sir Oswald, the head of the English Fascists. We lunched at Larue's in Paris, together with Harold Nicolson, and it was a really delightful luncheon, Mosley has a marvellous sense of humor. But the English aren't like him. The English are a noble people, they're no Fascists. The English will never be Fascists. They don't have the heart for that kind of thing, they don't have the stomach for it. And the Americans aren't Communists. They're good people, they're human. Americans are pure-hearted. Communism's a monstrosity. I've been in Russia, I know what Communism is."

Mona did not reply. From a silver box, she took a cigarette and a lighter and took a few puffs, slowly, calmly, decisively, all the while looking at me with great green-blue eyes. She drew near and caressed my face and my neck, slowly. She liked having me there before her, she liked having me available. She couldn't imagine that in a few months war would break out and she'd have to flee Capri; nor could she imagine that in New York the authorities would withdraw her passport, treating her as a Nazi, while her husband's best friends would denounce her to President Roosevelt.

"So," I continued, "in your view what Munthe and Cerio said could be true after all. You think there's a connection between the death of Pam Reynolds and quarrels between Nazi occultists and Munthe – and perhaps even with Russian Communists, Lenin, even the Fabian Society."

"Exactly. But you should be aware that Edwin Cerio's word is worth nothing."

"Why is that? After all, it was he who said the Fabian Society had something to do with this affair."

"Poor Malaparte," said Mona with a smile. "Come, let's go back out."

There was quite a wind, the great heat was over. We stretched out on two chaises longues in the middle of the lawn. The sea was black and troubled, it was rough, it couldn't get to sleep. On the wind was a smell of seaweed, of fishing nets, of waterlogged wood, of dead mollusks and crabs. A smell of fishermen, a smell of those boats which put out at nightfall to catch lobsters with a lamp. I'd gotten to know that smell on Lipari, when I was in internal exile, and I'd never forgotten it.

It was almost chilly, and Mona took out two light blankets from a white-painted wooden box and covered us with them.

"Malaparte, don't ask me how I know this. Cerio has already been interrogated by the OVRA. That was before you arrived in Capri. They asked him if you were the murderer of that English girl."

I said nothing, holding my breath.

"Cerio replied," Mona went on, "that writers are a strange bunch, people with unpredictable reactions, so you might perhaps have been prompted by passion."

I remained silent. Memories of my conversation with Cerio at his house were beating in my temples, memories of his fine green dressing gown, of his way of looking at me and studying my every reaction. Edwin Cerio was a true gentleman, he had a lovely white goatee which he always kept perfectly trimmed, and it became him so well. Now I understood why he'd sloped off like that, when I was looking for him at the party at the Villa Discopoli. By going to his house on the next day, I'd forced him to hide that stab in the back from me.

"Munthe too was interrogated before I went to visit him at Torre Materita, is that not so?" I asked.

Mona sighed. "Yes. He said he'd seen you with the English girl at Anacapri, hand in hand, a few days before the murder."

"Did he say he thought I could be the murderer?"

"I don't know. I swear I don't."

A few seconds passed in silence.

"It's nice of you to tell me all this," I then said, looking far across the cold black sea.

"Don't mention it. Capri's small, rumors travel fast. People meet often, at receptions or by the seaside. You think you're entrusting a secret to someone you can rely on, and by the next party everyone knows it."

I'd had enough talk, I'd said and heard too much. Mona too was gazing at the cold black sea, she too felt she'd spoken enough.

I heard Febo barking, outside the Fortino. I stood up, it was time I was on my way. Mona had me accompanied into the house so that I could choose more clothes.

I looked at the young maid who was escorting me and I thought: Mona will have made her, too, take part in the search for the book. So she too will have been promised a fine reward if she finds the book. But just suppose now that the precious 'memento' kept in that book, that concerns a person 'who holds a very important position in a foreign State'... just suppose it should have slipped out of the book. That was by no means impossible. If that were the case, the 'memento' could still be in the Fortino. So, at the start of the search, Mona must have described it to the servants. The maid was very young and very pretty, jet black eyes, a lovely little snub nose and long curly hair. Once inside the villa, I decided to take my chances.

"Are you free or d'you have a fiancé?" I asked her point blank, as she led me along the corridor.

"I'm engaged," she said, turning and blushing slightly.

"Is it serious? How many days has it lasted?"

"Days? Nearly two years!" she replied with a malicious glance.

"Two years, what a good girl! And what's your young man's name?"

"Rocco, he's called Rocco."

"And I imagine you'd like to get married soon, you and your Rocco," I continued in conspiratorial tones.

"Of course, we'd like to!" nodded the little maid, opening a wardrobe full of men's shirts.

"Well then," I added, "you should try to find that wretched book your mistress lost, or at least that thing inside it, what was it?"

"You mean the postcard with a crucifix but no cross...? Ah, if only I could! Then we'd be able to settle down properly, me and my Rocco, with the prize the Signora has promised. But it was inside the book, and that's surely been stolen."

A postcard. That's what was so precious inside the book. A postcard with a picture of a crucifix, but without any cross.

That was all I needed. It would make no sense to anyone else, but not to me who'd fought in the Great War.

I asked no more questions and began delving into Harrison Williams' rich wardrobe in search of something suitable to wear.

"I'll have your dirty clothes washed," Mona said, once I'd returned to the garden. "When all of this is over and you're sleeping in your own home, I'll get Eddie to bring them over to you. Eddie Bismarck really is a dear, don't you think so too?"

"Yes, it's true. Eddie Bismarck really is a dear fellow."

In Mona's language, that meant this was the only evening *en tête à tête* she was granting me.

I thought again of Cerio, and then of Axel Munthe, buried in the gloom of Torre Materita, of his greasy smell of old powder and fake antique furniture. I thought of the lies with which Cerio and Munthe had been having me on. I'd imagined I could play the Mona card, but I was the one who'd been played, and for quite a while.

"Thanks," I murmured to Mona as I kissed her for the last time, taking the driveway that led to the gates of the Fortino. Mona Williams liked me, she really liked me. She'd done me a great favor. Capri is a marvelous island, full of people who cared for me, who'd really put themselves out for me, that was for sure.

"And now what will you do?" she asked when we came to the gate of the Fortino.

"There's someone who can get me out of this. I must find him at all costs."

"And if you don't find him?"

"I'll try to arrange matters in such a way that the Sturmbannführer is interrogated. If I know him, his nerves aren't that steady. He might break down and confess."

Mona opened the gate.

"Where will you sleep tonight? You've wounds on your arms and on your cheek," she asked at the very last moment, betraying a slight anxiety, which was most unusual for her.

I smiled at her and went out through the gate without replying.

"Good luck, Malaparte."

The gate closed, Mona walked straight along the driveway and disappeared into the park.

As I watched her disappear among the trees of the Fortino, my thoughts turned to what I'd just discovered in Mona's house, something that seemed to be mysteriously connected with my destiny.

The Saarburg crucifix. The crucifix without a cross could only be the Saarburg crucifix. Mona probably didn't even know what it really was or what it meant for someone who had fought in the Great War and had known gas and the trenches. The Saarburg crucifix!

For twenty-one years I'd been wearing civilian clothes and still I felt it fixed and weighty in my head, like a lead dart. When you're at war, you think that one day it'll come to an end, they'll tell you that an armistice has been signed and it will be all over. Nothing of the sort: it is precisely at that very moment, with the armistice, that the war enters you and becomes a part of you, your secret eternity. The war begins when you hang up your rifle on a nail.

I heard a sound of panting, and found Febo between my legs, happy yet somehow bothered. He nuzzled the clothes I was wearing suspiciously, clothes that smelled of Harrison Williams and perhaps even of Coco Chanel. This time too, he'd done his work well, in wartime he'd have made a first-class messenger dog. As I expected, two silhouettes emerged from the gloom.

Sirignano and Tamburi had come running the moment they received the latest note I'd sent through Febo. I'd given them an appointment at once at the gate of Mona's property, recommending that they not let themselves be seen.

"Don't tell me that you took refuge with Mona to avoid getting arrested," said the prince.

"I'm not that dumb. I found a lonely rather out-of-the-way place for myself."

"Signor Malaparte, we've been waiting out here for nearly half an hour. You had us worried!" murmured Tamburi.

"Come, come, what an idea!" said Prince Sirignano gaily, "Malaparte was having fun with Mona Williams."

"Are you quite sure you weren't followed?"

"Relax, Malaparte," said Sirignano. "We've taken all the necessary precautions."

"I really hope so. They came close to catching me today. I nearly bumped into those two guys from the OVRA, the ones who interrogated me, when we were on our way back from the Migliera viewpoint."

"What were they doing there?" asked Sirignano.

"That, I'd really like to know. Maybe they were looking for me around there. They can't conduct a broad manhunt, they have to fish for me discreetly, taking careful aim. Here in Capri there are too many bigwigs. They can't scour the whole place and go searching Ciano's villa or that of the Queen of Sweden or the Prince of Hesse. They'll smear me in grand style in the papers, but only once they've caught me. My only hope is to keep constantly on the move, sleeping somewhere different every night, in places no one knows of."

A third silhouette appeared. A short, stocky, badly dressed individual, with a square jaw, a squashed nose, two burning eyes, massive shoulders and coal-black curly hair.

"This is Ciro," said Sirignano, "the friend I told you about. He's *'nu bravo guaglione*, a great guy. A guy who knows how to live." The vaguest of phrases, yet enough to tell those in the know that Ciro was a gangster, a member of the Camorra.

"If you're a friend of Prince Sirignano," said Ciro, "Prince Sirignano's friends are my friends."

What an introduction! Prince Sirignano, who had the guts to collect songs and verses against Fascism just for the hell of it, simply couldn't fail to pick the right man for the risky undertakings I had in mind.

Adolf Kaputt

There was plenty of news for me after my first day as a fugitive. In the first place, the golden statue of San Gennaro had been raised to the top of the outer pinnacle of the Faraglioni.

"I went to see Ciro, and he was just great," said Sirignano. "The climber he found me habitually uses the Faraglioni as a training ground and he knows them like the back of his hand. I insisted on absolute discretion about his mission and he placed the statue early this morning. Of course, that cost me a bomb, but I don't want a penny from you. It's for a great writer, and many other things. Even if I really can't see what the hell's the point of sticking a golden statue of San Gennaro on the Faraglioni," said Sirignano".

"Thanks, Ciro," I said.

"Prince Sirignano's friends are my friends," the Camorrista repeated with a certain haughtiness.

"And thank you too, Prince. One day I'll find a way of paying off my debt."

"Forget that now and think of the present. Things are not going well. Unfortunately your builder has been visited by the OVRA."

"Amitrano? But why?"

"I asked him to get information about where Carmine could be hiding. And he did that. But everyone knows he's your builder. Some snooper must have followed him; there are plenty of those here in Capri. Well, the snooper must have thought poor Amitrano was going around answering questions on your direct instructions. So they arrested him and turned the screws on him. After that, he ran away from his home, fearing that the OVRA guys might come back for him. Tonight he's sleeping at some friends' place, in Via Marucella. It's not far from here."

"Let's go," I said.

"Tell me something about yourself, Ciro," I said while we walked in the moonlight. I needed to know whether the newcomer suited my needs.

Sirignano answered for him:

"Ciro knows how to keep his mouth shut and he gets on with everyone. The only ones he doesn't like are Mussolini and journalists."

"That's fine," I said, "just the same people I have to be on the lookout for. But why exactly Mussolini and journalists?"

"Since the Duce's been around we haven't made a penny here in the South, Signor Malaparte," said Ciro. "First Mussolini had many of us teach them Socialists an' trade unionists a good lesson. We didn't mind doin' that, I'd no objections 'cos that lot was trash. But then, when he comes to power, the Duce forgets about us and gets it into his head he's goin' to restore law'n'order in Naples and Caserta *his way*, so he does a lot of lousy things. He has masses of good men arrested, he gets a heap of lies published about the folks of Naples and Caserta, and he makes thousands of innocent families starve. If you read the Fascist papers, you get the idea that Naples and Caserta are under the heel of shady customers. Whatever goes wrong, they blame it on the Mafia and the Camorra, jus' think of that! Those are exaggerations, Signor Malaparte, slander, all made up by newsmen who got nothin' else to write about. You got no idea how many people I know who had to emigrate and now they're all working in America, in Chicago and in New York City, in Broccolino."

"Brooklyn," Sirignano corrected him, "We Italians say Broccolino, but in English it's pronounced Brooklyn."

"Yeah, that's it, they had to go all the way to Brooklyn to find a bit of work. I got a cousin in New York who buys and sells booze, another cousin in Boston who runs a gambling racket, another who gets protection for the unions, and another who's in the arms business, they're all good guys, good family men, they make good money and there's no Mister Mussolini around to pester them, and yes, they keep on writing that America's a great country. I always say: when a man dies, he hopes to go to Heaven, but when I die, I want to go to America. D'ya get me, Signor Malaparte? Nine years ago, in my town, Caserta, they arrested four thousand people in one night. Four thousand! Now, can ya imagine that, Signor Malaparte? The same year, that English minister came, what's his name…?"

"Churchill," said Sirignano.

"Churchill, yes, that's it, Churchill came to Italy an' complimented Mussolini on how good he was changin' the country. But d'ya really believe that in a city like Caserta, where they're gennelmen, there could be four thousand people to put in handcuffs?"

"In Caserta they're all gentlemen," said Sirignano.

"I know, that's known all the world over," I added.

"Mussolini even went an' did away with the province of Caserta," Ciro went on. "I just can't tell ya, Signor Malaparte, how many good folks from my parts have been reduced to misery. Just think of it, once they even arrested *me*, on some old charge of armed robbery, all a misunderstanding, of course."

"Of course," I said.

"Of course," said Sirignano.

Ciro was barking angrily, he was gesticulating and waving his arms frenetically as only we Italians know how to, but his expression remained cold and clear. A good Camorrista, used to risking his freedom and his skin, stays cool even when he's angry, above all when he's angry.

"It was jus' dawn, and when the police dragged me outta the house in handcuffs, guess who was in the street outside waitin'? Newsmen! They even took my photo, the filthy rats. And who d'ya think told them to be there?"

"Mussolini," I said.

"Of course, Mussolini or his men! Before him, things like that never happened, we was free to work and live in peace. But now you got newsmen here, newsmen there, and during the trials my face got plastered all over the world, along with the faces of lotsa my friends, and I, a gennelman, end up with a reputation like shit. One night where nobody was around I jus' happen to meet one of them newsmen, an' I explain my point of view to him, I explain it rather warmly, d'ya see, Signor Malaparte? An' what does that guy go an' do? As soon as he gets out of hospital, he squeals on me, he gets his news buddies to write articles about me, an' again the police come to my house, again the newsmen under my windows, again a trial... An' you just can't imagine what they put me through when the newsman in question is found in a ravine with his brains spillin' out! They wanted to accuse *me*, me, a gennelman, and the day of the murder – which I think must have been an accident – I was miles away, miles away from there. Signor Malaparte, life without Mussolini and without newsmen wasn't paradise, but at least I could feed my family."

"Ciro's very much a family man," explained Sirignano, "especially since his sixth son was born."

I made up my mind I liked Ciro, I really liked him. He talked like every true Camorrista, and to get out of the fix I was in I needed someone just like him, neither more nor less.

A few minutes had gone by, and we were already there. The place was a little house with a garden. Sirignano knocked hard at the door. A little while later, a woman's voice replied cautiously from behind it.

"We're friends. We want to visit Adolfo," said Sirignano.

They made us wait a little longer, then at length the door opened. A young woman peered cautiously at us, then gave a start when we emerged from the dark and she saw who'd been knocking.

"Prince Sirignano! Come in, please come in! These are friends of yours, of course?"

"Silence, and no names," I said.

All four of us entered. The entrance and the kitchen were all one. The rest of the family was sitting by the hearth, the father and four children. They were still eating, the father told them to get up and greet us, but Sirignano stopped him with an imperious gesture.

"Let us see Adolfo," he ordered.

Suddenly the place was plunged in darkness.

"The usual power cut," said Sirignano, "damn those tourists and that mean bastard Mussolini who can't do a thing to improve our energy supplies."

The blackout lasted only a few minutes.

We then crossed the little house, the house of poor people, too small for six. We went out behind, into the garden. There was no rest room in the house, just a little shed outside, under a tree, with a black well for bodily waste. The young woman opened the door and we were immediately overwhelmed by a stifling stench, a hot, damp, repulsive blast of air. But it did not come from the black well. It was not the usual odor of a latrine. It stank of vomit, of blood, of rotting fecal matter.

"Adolfo!" I said.

He was slumped on the ground. I wanted to approach him but I had to stop my nose and mouth with one hand. Sirignano, Tamburi and Ciro couldn't stand it and drew back.

"Signor Malaparte, is it you?"

"Yes, Adolfo, it's me," I said, kneeling at the entrance to the shed.

"Don't come any nearer, Signor Malaparte," he said, "I don't want you to see me like this."

My eyes had grown accustomed to the dark, I could see Adolfo's outline better. He was immersed in a morass of feces and vomit. I asked the others for a lighter, and Ciro passed me one.

"They used castor oil, didn't they?"

"Yes, Signor Malaparte," said Adolfo.

He tried to get to his feet but could not. He slipped, lay down again on the ground and crawled to the middle of the shed, where the chamber pot was. The white porcelain pot was covered with squirts of liquid and blood. Adolfo leaned over the pot and vomited.

I looked at him carefully. There was not a single place on his body that was dry. He had become a disgusting reptile, a green and grey crocodile with its own bodily fluids for a skin, he was sheathed in those fluids, and the more he tried to draw himself up from the nauseating puddle in which he was drowning, the more he sank into it. He was a green and brown crocodile of a man, all clothed in vomit and shit.

"Why doesn't he stand up?" asked Tamburi.

"Because he can't," I said, "he's too weak. With that loss of fluids, his legs won't support him."

"There's blood in his vomit," said the young woman. "And in the diarrhea. We were going to call the doctor, but Adolfo didn't want to. What do you think we should do?"

I knew Adolfo Amitrano well, he never spoke lightly. If he said something, that's how it was. Now he was sitting on the ground with his shoulders up against the bowl. I held the lighter flame close to his face.

"Let me take a look at your face," I said to him.

"Yes, Signor Malaparte."

He turned. His face was covered with brown splashes, it was all bruised and as swollen as a rubber ball, from the sides of his mouth two streaks of blood ran, he had lost a front tooth and another one was broken. Castor oil always worked like that, I'd seen it with my own eyes in Tuscany, in Emilia, in Rome. I knew the whole scenario by heart, I knew exactly what had happened to Amitrano. Once they'd immobilized him, the *squadristi* had begun to work him over with their fists, with sticks, with pistol butts. To complete the treatment, they'd kicked him in the stomach, in the kidneys and in the ribs. Once they'd broken Adolfo's teeth, once his eyes were so swollen he couldn't keep them open, once his cheeks were blue and green, the Fascists had tied him to a chair, tightening his pants with a cord, and with a funnel, they'd poured the oil down his throat.

Castor oil is not a food oil; it's a first class lubricant, a useful cosmetic, a pain killer, it's even used to induce birth, but it is about as edible as petroleum or bleach. Ricin plants are poisonous: if you eat three or four seeds, you'll die in atrocious convulsions. In Eritrea I'd seen some enormous bushes, as big as a large house. It's not by chance that the good Lord put ricin in Africa, where people have a robust constitution, as they have to face up to lions and elephants. One glass of castor oil will produce strong diarrhea, you'll be sick all night and well again the next day; obviously, the problem is how to go back home on foot with your pants full of excrement, while the Fascists follow you, laughing and belaboring your back with sticks. With a dose of five glasses, you'll be sick for three days, the first one, vomiting, the next two with dysentery, when you won't spend one single moment away from the rest room. With a liter, the process lasts weeks: diarrhea and dehydration are catastrophic, with intolerable cardiac arrhythmia, vertigo and headaches, sleep is out of the question and the whole body is shaken by convulsions, while your face becomes as yellow as a lemon. More than a liter, and there will be hemorrhagic gastroenteritis and crises of tetany, you'll go into a coma and end up in a hospital's emergency department, where you can only pray the Lord to send an embolism to put an end to you without too much suffering.

"How much oil did they give him?" I asked the woman.

"They stuffed him with it," she replied. "But what scares me most is the blood coming out from his mouth. They gave him too many kicks in the stomach."

"D'you want us to call a doctor, Adolfo?" I asked.

"No, Signor Malaparte. It's all right like this. I'll make it," answered the crocodile man.

"Still, let's call one, for heaven's sake," said Tamburi. "Let's not take unnecessary risks."

"A doctor would be no use," I replied. "Adolfo has made his mind up, and we'll respect his decision."

"But there's an internal hemorrhage!"

"Shut up, Tamburi. Let's leave that to Adolfo. If he says he doesn't want a doctor, we must respect his decision. Besides, it's a slight wound."

That was obviously untrue. The internal lesion was no light matter, he was bleeding copiously, anyone else would be ready for the morgue. But Adolfo would make it, I could see it in his eyes, and that made all the difference. In wartime, some died of septicemia after a ridiculous little wound. Others lost legs, arms, eyes, got themselves roasted by a flame thrower, stuck with bayonets, torn apart by barbed wire, and survived it all. After the war they married and had eight children. The only difference between one lot and the others, between those who died of a silly infection and those who survived infernal ordeals, lay in their eyes. Those who were destined to die were already dead the moment they'd been wounded, they were dead in the eyes, they had dead man's eyes, eyes that turn upwards to heaven, calling for mercy. Sometimes they were already dead the day before dying. Above all, when they were very young, like the lads of the class of '99. I'd see their sad faces, in the trenches, playing cards before an attack, or before the enemy began an artillery barrage. Perhaps they were even smiling, those boys, but the light in their eyes was a dead light, I could have gouged out those eyes with my fingers and they'd not have reacted. Their body was alive, they ate, drank, talked, pissed, but their eyes... no, their eyes were already dead. I'd look at one of those and I'd think to myself: tomorrow we'll be digging your grave. I couldn't tell anyone they were already dead, they'd have thought I was casting the evil eye, so I kept it all to myself. Next day, a grenade, a rifle shot, and that very evening I'd have to write the letter, *that* letter, to the soldier's mother, to his wife, to his brothers... you must know, Signora, what a fine soldier your son was, how he died a hero... you must know what dead eyes he had the day before he died.

The others, however, those destined to live, always had that strange, crazy light in the middle of their foreheads, just above the nose, at the point where they say there's a third eye, that half animal, half human flash that Nature gives us when it means to continue pulsating in our arms in our legs, in the spongy flesh of our lungs, in the black flesh of our liver, in the green flesh of our bile, in the white of our bones and cartilage.

"Signor Malaparte".

"Tell me, Adolfo."

"I found out something that could be useful to you."

"Is it about Carmine?"

"Yes, Signor Malaparte, it concerns him. I found out something that can help you. But no one knows that, I'm the only one who knows. I've told no one. The guys who gave me the oil wanted to know, but I didn't tell them."

"Bravo, Adolfo. What did you find out?"

"You must go to Spadaro. He can help you. He knows why Carmine doesn't want to be found by you. Go to Spadaro, Signor Malaparte, he'll tell you."

"Good, good, so I'll go and see Spadaro. Are you quite sure we shouldn't get you a doctor?"

"Yes Signor Malaparte, I'm quite sure. And pardon me, I didn't want you to see me in this state. When I'm better, we'll finish building the house."

"Yes Adolfo, when you're better we'll finish building it. But first you must rest. Do you promise me you'll rest?"

"Yes, Signor Malaparte, I promise. Now go to Spadaro, Signor Malaparte, talk with Spadaro. He can help you."

He was shaken by a great tremor and bent sideways. From his pants issued a sort of gurgling. I stood up and left the shed.

"As soon as possible, strip him, let him drink and wash him, I said to the woman of the house. "Then give him fresh clothes."

"We've already done that. But half an hour later everything's filthy again."

"No matter. Just keep going like that and it will pass in the end. He's not going to die, believe me."

Walking to Spadaro's house, I put Tamburi through a third-degree treatment.

"Well then? Did you find out anything about that mysterious phrase?"

"I have some clues, Signor Malaparte. After lengthy research I was able to establish this: *kind* means 'child', in German. *Bonad* can mean 'money' in English slang. *Rabal* is a place in Portugal. *Bon* can mean 'good', or 'a coupon' in various languages. So, *bon bonad kind rabal mervu* potrebbe could mean something like 'A cash credit for a child in Rabal'."

"But the meaning of *mervu* is missing," I pointed out. "Without *mervu* the sentence is incomplete."

"Oh, I hadn't given any thought to the word *mervu*. It's the only word that means absolutely nothing. I 'phoned our office in Rome. I asked them to go to the library and look up all possible words in all possible vocabularies and all languages, even in the strangest ones like Urdu, Gaelic, Sanskrit, Arabic and the languages of the American Indians. Nothing doing, I could find *mervu* nowhere. There are similar words, of course, but *mervu* doesn't exist. It's an invention."

"Tamburi, if I weren't in this mess I'd already have given you the sack!" I blurted out. "If you don't understand every single word, the sentence can make no sense, even a kid can see that. And you have the nerve to come to me with this half-baked crap you call a translation! Do I have to withhold more of your pay?"

Febo did not bark as he usually did when I raised my voice, because he knew Tamburi well, and he was sorry for him; besides, he liked his painter's moustache.

"I'm sorry, Signor Malaparte, I'll try to adjust my aim," said Tamburi.

Sirignano was stifling his laughter, Ciro stood by with a look of mute superiority, typical of plebeians when they have dealings with bourgeois in trouble. Tamburi shut himself up in a contrite silence. He was a great artist but you couldn't ask him for anything outside his art, *la dracu* – to hell with painters!

"Give me news of Lucia," I said.

"Lucia's fine, she wasn't arrested or interrogated," said Sirignano. "After you'd put her down on that little beach, she managed to get back to her *pensione*, where she stayed barricaded in her room all day. She came out only when she was sufficiently sure that none of the OVRA men who'd come to arrest you had seen or recognized her. This evening towards seven I met her in the town square. She told me what had happened at House like Me, and then she asked if I had news of you. She was very worried. Obviously, I told her I knew nothing."

"You did well, Prince. Lucia mustn't get mixed up with this, the game's too dangerous for her, and we can trust no one. I've just learned that Munthe and Cerio led me up the garden path. They'd already spoken with the OVRA before they met me, and they didn't breathe a word about that to me. Mona told me. Despite that, she thinks Cerio's idea is valid. Pam's death could have to do with some kind of backhanded revenge against Munthe on the part of the Germans."

"Not so," said Sirignano.

"Why not?"

"I understood that today, while we were waiting for Febo at the Villa Lysis. It was just a matter of a few simple calculations. Munthe began negotiating the sale of the Villa San Michele with Goering about two years ago. But Pam died four years ago. So Pam's death has nothing to do with any revenge for failed negotiations. Mona's good at her sums too, she should have thought of that."

"Hell, that's true," I cursed.

"Did Mona by any chance try to feed you her theory that American capitalists are behind Communism and that Mussolini was financed by the English and French?"

"Why, yes, she did say something like that. In some detail, too."

"It's one of her warhorses. I've already heard her come out with that kind of spiel several times. She'll have tried to make something of a smokescreen, concealing the fact that Pam could not have died because of the negotiations between Munthe and Goering over the Villa San Michele. Mona just loves bundling everything together so as to confuse people. Never trust a woman who's too rich, Malaparte."

He stopped, and looked me severely in the eyes.

I told Sirignano too of the last revelation I'd winkled out of Mona's chambermaid: in the book they'd stolen from her there was a postcard of the Saarburg crucifix. That was why she cared so much about the book.

"What is the Saarburg crucifix?"

"It's a great mystery," I said. "A mystery that concerns the death of twenty thousand men, killed twenty-five years ago."

BLIGNY, JULY 1918
SAARBURG, AUGUST 1914

The Blind Sun

How hot it was that night at Bligny in July 1918, a warm damp night, a lovely summer's night, one of those hot French nights smelling of summer and death.

I was a young officer who believed in the war, at least I still did then, and I'd returned to the front only lately. For three days we'd somehow withstood the German attacks, by now we were without water, without food, without medicine. I'd been knocked out by mustard gas, spending a long time in hospital. To get rid of the burns and blisters caused by the gas, they'd had to wash me with bleach for days and days, but I'd survived. (I didn't yet know that the mustard gas had already done for me and that I'd die of it many years later, mustard gas and war will always get the better of you in the end.)

At first I'd cursed fate, but then I'd calmed down. I'd understood that all this was part of my destiny as an Italian soldier: the French, the British and the Americans all had new, efficient gas masks, the Italian ones were old and they leaked. The British, the French and the Americans had anti-tank guns, we Italians had none. The British, the Americans and the French were peoples full of pride and dignity, while we Italians were nothing but a mass of sweaty bodies thrust forward towards death. We had no right to a glorious death, because we were not a people, just a herd of tramps, a bunch of poor fatheads like Santoni, my lad of the class of '99.

At Bligny we were having a lovely night of death, the battle raged along the river Ardre, the Italians and French were not allowed to retreat, the order was: "Die at your posts". The British too and the Americans were to die at their posts, and whoever disobeyed was shot. The only way not to be shot was to fight to the death, only death could save us.

General Ludendorff's Germans had tanks, against which we'd never fought, so that we didn't know how to defend ourselves. Then we had an idea, an idea for ragged, desperate Italians: to burn the whole wood. That created an enormous barrier of fire, the German tank commanders were scared their fuel would explode and they had to withdraw amidst our howls of joy. I was howling too, I was shooting and howling for joy at miraculously staying alive. When the mustard gas had made me lose my senses, an officer had taken me for dead, and I'd come within a hairsbreadth of being buried alive.

(All my life I've been tormented by the thougt that I might have made a mistake when I said, "Yes, he's dead, take him away". When they clean up the cemeteries, opening soldiers' caskets, from time to time they find one who's all contorted in a grimace of pain, with his bayonet stuck into his belly: when someone who's been buried in error wakes up in the casket, rather than die of asphyxia, he kills himself with the bayonet buried by his side).

During the nth German attack, one of my superiors panicked and was on the point of turning back towards our lines, taking all his men with him, and opening up a dreadful gap in our front. I aimed at him and fired. My shot only grazed his neck and he fell to the ground. His men stopped, regained control of their nerves and started firing again at the Germans. The entire unit had seen this but no one had the nerve to reproach me because I'd behaved well, I'd done what was expected of a good officer.

Suddenly we found ourselves surrounded by the Germans. We were under the command of the only senior officer left alive, Lieutenant Colonel Chiodelli. The rumor spread that he wanted to order us to retreat. All the surviving officers, about a dozen of us, went together to his tent to try to get him to change his mind.

"Colonel," I asked him, "is it true that you want to order a retreat?"

His face was as white as that of a cadaver. He'd come to the front only three days before, after months in a rearguard posting in Libya. He had no experience of war and he'd lost his head.

"Yes, it's true."

"But that's madness!" I cried, "next to us there's Colonel Morand's 408th French regiment, and they're resisting for all they're worth.

Besides, the Germans have surrounded us, so to retreat wouldn't only be cowardly, it would be suicidal."

"Captain, obey orders!" bawled Chiodelli.

"We received our orders before you came here, Sir: to die at our posts."

Chiodelli was becoming paler and paler. He was as pale as a corpse, as pale as his own corpse if he'd died that day.

"Captain, for the last time: obey."

"No."

The other officers hadn't the nerve to open their mouths. Chiodelli drew his pistol from its holster and pointed it at me.

"Obey or I fire."

He was as pale as a corpse, as pale as his own corpse, and his hands were trembling.

From under my jacket, I pulled out a hand grenade, ready for use.

Chiodelli saw it and smiled: "You'll come to a bad end."

"I know. But you too will come to a nasty end, Colonel."

Absolute silence in the tent. Outside we could hear bursts of machine gun fire, rifle shots, the crump of shells exploding. Ten, fifteen, twenty seconds passed. Chiodelli lowered his pistol.

"We're retreating," he said, turning to the other officers.

"Yessir!" they all chorused, rushing out from the tent to pass on the order.

"I and my men will not come," I said.

"Do as you please," said Chiodelli.

The retreat began. As I'd expected, on that night the fine flower of our units met their deaths, wiped out in the dark as they withdrew without being able to defend themselves. My section, the 94th Flame Throwers, stayed on to defend our lines. All night long I stayed up listening to the screams of our men, massacred by the Germans. Our wounded lay on the ground in agony, calling to one another for help, while the Germans advanced and finished them off one by one. I too was dying with them, I knew them all by name and I was dying with them, with every burst of fire I was dying with them, without being able to do a thing to help. I heard the officers' screams of rage when they no longer knew what orders to give, and then the death song of the German machine guns, always the same, always that unbroken ra-ta-ta-ta-tat...

Dawn came, with its cold light. It was a blind, lifeless sun, a cold, dead sun. When death passes over the battlefield and takes many soldiers, the sun is always a blind sun. I don't know why, but it's always like that, I've seen it time and again with my own eyes.

I couldn't stand the sight of that blind sun; I went into our foxhole and squatted down, trying to stifle my sobs. My body was empty, eaten up from within, as though they'd torn out all my innards and replaced them with something else. I felt like a stuffed animal that looks alive from outside (still the same eyes, the same fur, the same limbs) but it's a poor dummy within, a poor straw-stuffed dummy.

When I raised my head, my eyes still red and swollen, I noticed a postcard on the little table by my side. I picked it up. It was a half-naked Jesus, his arms raised and his head bent to one side, as though sadly crying victory, and he was balancing on tiptoe. An impossible equilibrium: he looked as though he was about to fall at any moment. One of my men was there with me. I asked him what that strange image meant. "Captain, d'you really not know it? It's the Saarburg crucifix."

"But it's not a crucifix. There's no cross."

"It's a miracle, Captain. No one knows how it happened. I read about it in a newspaper sent to me from home by post. My mother knows German, together with the article she sent me the translation. The postcards are German, but they printed so many of them that some have even reached us."

It happened at the beginning of the Great War, in the battle of Lorraine, the first great clash between French and German troops. In mid-August 1914 the 1st French Army marched on Saarburg, in Lorraine, one of the regions Germans and French had fought over for centuries. The German 6th and 7th armies were deployed there, under the command of Prince Rupprecht. The French continued their advance for about twenty kilometers; at that point, the German counter-offensive began.

Near Saarburg, beside a tree-lined road called Bühlerstrasse, there is a great crucifix, mounted on a pyramid of rocks in the midst of the Lorraine countryside. This is no invention: if you take the Bühlerstrasse you'll still find it there today; perhaps they'll have built some houses around it, but the crucifix is still there, just as it appeared in contemporary postcards. It stands out so much, in that gentle and rather bare landscape, that you can see it even at a great distance. By a caprice of destiny, the clash between the French and Germans took place in that very plain, around that crucifix. The holy image did not occupy any strategic position, it had no special symbolic value, it wasn't even very old (it had been erected in 1875, some forty years before). It was just there, in the middle of the battlefield, and that's all there is to it.

For three days Frenchmen and Germans engaged in desperate battle. August 19th began with violent artillery barrages. The infantry took refuge in the craters left by enemy shellfire. Whenever they tried digging to build a real refuge, the shovel would at once unearth the bodies of comrades, buried under landslides. Every single shell would raise enormous fountains of earth, burying and crushing dozens of men, after which a second explosion would exhume them, blasting into the air corpses torn to shreds, and all around would fall a rain of heads, arms, chests and feet. The stink of death was everywhere, above ground, underground, in every lump of soil. When someone was buried by a shell blast, they'd dig for him for a quarter of an hour, sometimes even half an hour, trying to save him. Soldiers were dragged out in a state of total asphyxia, grey in the face; they'd be trembling from head to foot, as though they were freezing, like broken automata. Then another shell would fall and again bury everyone, even the rescuers, it had all proved pointless. They couldn't defend themselves, they could only wait to die, night and day, closing their eyes and tightening their fists with every new cannonade and thinking now I'll die, now I'll die, now...

The constant thunder of the big guns, the German Krupp and the French Schneider heavy guns, monsters weighing tons that no soldier in human history could ever have conceived of, shook the earth, shook men's innards and wrenched their backs, setting off searing headaches, with every single blast it seemed one's head was split in two, expelling something black and unspeakable amidst demoniac birth pains. Hundreds of recruits, boys of twenty, could not stand it and went mad, their pants swollen with feces and piss, no longer obeying orders, they wandered slowly here and there outside the trenches, pale as ghosts, caring about nothing. Their commanders called them back, screaming, weeping, threatening, but they no longer responded, they just kept wandering around like dead men, with empty upturned eyes until some projectile struck them down and they collapsed into the mud in a last fit of disjointed tremors. Those who came out of it alive became *Kriegszitterer*, puppets shaken by perpetual trembling, night and day, they couldn't stand on their feet, they could not eat, they could not speak, and one had only to show them a pair of shoes or a hat for them to burst into tears for no apparent reason.

Every now and then, some reconnaissance plane would pass, but the pilot (who'd tell this in the following days) could understand nothing from the map, the roads had disappeared, the villages had disappeared, bombs and shellfire had cancelled out everything, civilization and nature, they'd transformed the entire landscape into a foul grayish slime that stank of cadavers. It began to rain, foxholes became mud-filled tubs, everything turned into an enormous bog; water got into boots, mud swallowed them and sucked them off the men's feet. In those holes, full of torn bodies, the survivors dragged themselves along, barefoot and as haggard as ghosts. High-ranking officers arriving from the rearguard and knowing nothing of all this insulted them for not wearing their uniform boots, but the soldiers had lost their voice from the influenza which was decimating the front lines, and remained silent when the officers whipped them across the face with their riding crops.

The hot greasy smell of cadavers got into clothing, into your skin, under the fingernails, making you feel rotten although you were still living, and already you knew that you would never forget that stink, by now it was part of you, the most important part of your future as a man, and the most important part of your future as an animal, a man downgraded to the rank of a beast.

The day after the earth had ceased to be shaken by artillery barrages, what remained of the infantry was sent out from the trenches. Forward, boys! And the infantry advanced. Slowly, inexorably, impelled by no will, yet not like a flock of sheep. A flock moves forward without understanding: the infantry, however, understands, but doesn't want to know. What does it matter to know why you're dying? You must die.

The terrain offered little cover, fighting was at close range and every single house, every chapel, every little wall was fought over. When bullets ran out, men would switch to hand-to-hand fighting with bayonets. They'd advance like ferocious beasts, driving the enemy out from behind each rock, each tree, maybe the same young German or French boy who, one day before the war, when you were vacationing in his city, in Nancy, Metz or Baden-Baden, had given up his place at a café table to you and your wife, recommending you a good restaurant and making efforts to speak your language out of courtesy, and now you have to creep up on him behind that tree and plant your bayonet in his belly, so that his mother or his wife will receive a military postcard a few weeks later and fall weeping to her knees.

By the third day of the massacre it became clear that the Germans had won; the French withdrew to the Marne, blowing up the bridges once they'd crossed them. No one knows how many had died, perhaps ten thousand on either side. Thousands of civilians were massacred by the artillery, flames engulfed houses, churches and schools.

The crucifix on Bühlerstrasse was in the midst of that inferno for three days, struck by who knows how many bullets and shrapnel splinters. It should have burned or been blown apart, it should at least have been smashed. Yet, after the massacre, the German soldiers found themselves faced with a mystery: the cross had been destroyed, while the statue of the Redeemer remained in place, intact, standing straight and quite unsupported. He stood, thanks to some invisible magnetic force, on the one nail transfixing his feet.

The falling away of the cross had not caused the statue to bend at all. The nails that had fixed Jesus to the cross were still visible: those in the hands were driven through his palms, and their sharp tips pierced the sky where before they had sunk into the wood of the cross.

It looks as though he is speaking to the German infantrymen: I have won through, yes, I have overcome, and he is saying it sadly, but he's saying it, what's more, he's shouting it. The soldiers kneel by the dozen before that miracle: that statue is the image of the fallen, another of the thousand upon thousand fallen at Saarburg, pulled out from the mud half naked, without boots and by now as rigid as wooden statues.

Christ wanted to transform himself into one of us, think the soldiers, he wanted to stay by our side like any ordinary soldier, he too is maddened with fear, he too has been buried under an avalanche of mud, he too has been horsewhipped for losing his boots, and he has chosen to cry out alongside us to the end, to die under Satan's body blows, to perish with us, and at last he will open again eyes that closed on Horror, to a vision of Love.

Saarburg's Christ without a cross was portrayed on innumerable postcards and circulated throughout Germany. Those who held the card in their hands came to hope that the world would not end in a cloud of fire and blood, and that human beings would not all be turned into straw-stuffed dummies.

"Many bigwigs in the German army wanted to see this marvel with their own eyes," said my soldier, concluding his account.

It was said that at the very moment when a shell smashed the cross to pieces, leaving the Christ almost suspended in mid-air, a second miracle took place at the foot of the statue. A French soldier, who was wandering about lost, found himself facing an Austrian recruit, a youngster from Upper Austria, between Linz and Salzburg. The young man was a *Meldegänger*, a messenger. He was armed with a pistol and kept it aimed at the French soldier, but fear made his hand tremble so much that he wasted the three remaining bullets in his magazine, missing every time. The French soldier, who had somehow ended up miles from his lines, had lost his helmet and seemed to be in a state of shock. However, he held a Lebel rifle in his hand and, after miraculously escaping the three shots aimed at him by his adversary, he calmly pointed his weapon at him. The distance between the two was minimal, the young Austrian was almost paralyzed with terror, sure that he was about to die full of lead. The French soldier aimed, had his finger on the trigger and was just about to fire when a loud report rang out and his head split in two amidst a shower of blood.

At the same instant as the shot which struck down the French soldier, the shell which destroyed the cross on the statue of Jesus struck its target. In other words, two miracles had taken place at the same instant; for days and days the troops in the area talked of nothing else.

As soon as he realized he was alive, the Austrian soldier turned to the man who'd saved him, a very young recruit who had aimed at the head of his assailant from a distance of only some twenty paces. The two comrades approached one another and embraced. Later, it became known that this recruit, apparently a very ordinary boy, was in reality a member of an ancient and high-ranking noble family.

My soldier concluded: "A few days after the battle, when an automobile of the regimental commander came to drive him away, word spread that the recruit was the young Prince Philipp von Hessen".

CAPRI, SUMMER 1939

Warm Beds

"That's why Mona cares so much about her book," Sirignano remarked, "or rather, about that postcard: it has to do with Philipp von Hessen, who happens to be in Capri just now."

"Yes, it obviously has something to do with the Prince," said Tamburi, "but how?"

"You'd have to ask Mona," I said, "but she's shut up like a clam. I've already tried by all lawful means to get that out of her."

Sirignano gave me a conspiratorial wink: he'd surely not failed to notice the clean, well-ironed clothes I wore after my visit to the Fortino, but he asked no questions. Sirignano was a true gentleman, he really liked me, as did so many people in Capri, and he changed the subject:

"Malaparte, I did what you asked me to and sent a team of boys to find the sword in the cove under the Migliera viewpoint. All expert divers. But there's no sword down there. They looked everywhere. Are you quite sure it fell there?"

"Absolutely sure. Couldn't they make another search?"

"They could. But I don't think there's any point in it. And now we've arrived," announced Sirignano, knocking at our man's door.

Spadaro's home was a hovel, a decrepit little house, a sort of ruin between two other old houses whose paint had likewise all peeled off. But it was more than good enough for young Spadaro, it was already a great deal for someone like him to have a roof over his head.

"Good heavens, did Adolfo really have to send us to this tramp Spadaro?" I couldn't help muttering while we waited at the door.

"Capri's like a family. You don't choose your parents, Heaven does that for you," said Sirignano, knocking a second time.

Our man was not in fact the real Spadaro but an impostor who'd taken his place: his son. The real Spadaro had originally been called

Francesco Spadari; he had a long thick beard and wore a fisherman's striped vest, threadbare trousers, a strip of cloth round his waist and a shapeless old woolen beret on his head. He went barefoot, with a pipe in his hand or solidly lodged between his yellow teeth.

Dressed like this, he seemed just to have disembarked from a fishing boat, he was the living image of your old Capri fisherman, the true unmistakable symbol of the island. In reality Spadaro was no fisherman at all, he'd never held a fishing rod or a line or a net in his life and he didn't even know how to swim. What's more, he hated the water and he'd never even dipped a toe in the sea of Capri. There was, however, one thing he'd understood perfectly well: what counts in life is not who we are but who we appear to be. And, day in, day out, come rain come shine, Spadaro would take up position at the entrance of the little town square, all done up with his beard, pipe and beret, and the smile of an old sea dog, in the strategic place where anxious tourists first set foot in the pulsating heart of Capri, the Piazzetta. There, they'd bump into Spadaro, the prototype of the Capri fisherman, and they'd be overcome by the vertigo of the picturesque. Berlin beauticians, Parisian nurses and Liverpool typists would offer huge tips to have their photo taken with him, and with those tips Spadaro lived more than comfortably; no one wanted to return from a trip to Capri without a photo of him. Now there was a veritable flood of postcards, calendars, newspaper articles, even oil paintings; old Spadaro's face had ringed the world. He'd become the Eiffel Tower, the Statue of Liberty, the Big Ben of Capri. Even the great philosopher Walter Benjamin had written about Spadaro, his symbolic value and his significance as a mass phenomenon. At the age of 81 Spadaro had caught pneumonia and been taken back by the Creator. Next came the struggle for the succession. One of Spadaro's brothers grew a beard and got hold of the dead man's clothes. But Spadaro's son beat him to it. True, he was a bit tubbier than his dad, and he didn't have that marvelous white beard worthy of an old sage. But the general resemblance was there, and the boy got there before his uncle. It was he who, not long after his father's funeral, was first to dress up as a fisherman and take up his customary place at the entrance of the Piazzetta. No Berlin beautician, no Parisian nurse, no Liverpool typist realized there'd been a changing of the guard.

At long last, the door opened a crack and through that we saw a face with greasy pallid skin, a long unkempt beard and a bald shining head.

"Who are you? What do you want at this hour?"

"Spadaro, let us in. We've been sent by Adolfo Amitrano," I said.

"Amitrano? Ah, I get it. You're here for Carmine. Is the prince there too?"

"Here I am," said Sirignano stepping forward. "Let us in – and... no names."

"*Va bene, va bene,* come in."

We came into the dreary bare room. To one side were Spadaro's unmade bed, a table with a few dusty papers, a sideboard, a washbasin, a crucifix on the wall, a little statue of the Madonna with a little candle before it, and a few chairs. Without his stage costume, with that shining bald pate, that scraggy beard and pale starveling's face, Spadaro Junior looked like a vision from beyond the tomb. He stared suspiciously at Febo: he'd not expected to have to play host to a dog as well. Febo paid the fake fisherman back with his own coin, looking at him with just as much mistrust and coming close to me.

"Please take a seat," said Spadaro pointing to his rickety old chairs. "But please make it quick. I was already in bed." He was looking at his feet, like so many poor, insecure people in Italy.

"We'll not keep you," I said. "What have you got to tell us?"

"Me? Nothing, to tell the truth. But Adolfo Amitrano told me you needed something."

"I get it," said Sirignano with a resigned, patient expression. He stood up, approached the man and held out a bank note.

"That really wasn't necessary, you shouldn't have bothered," said Spadaro pocketing the money at lightning speed.

"Spadá, stop being a hypocrite. And now tell us about Carmine, 'cos we're in a hurry," said Sirignano.

Spadaro looked around himself calmly for the first time. He made a rapid scan of every one of our faces: first, Prince Sirignano, then Ciro, then me and lastly Tamburi. This diagnostic art was necessary to place the tip as high as possibile: a swift look, and he knew all he needed to know about rich and poor, people pleasant and unpleasant, ingenuous and crafty, sincere and hypocritical, and that evening he seemed to have intuited what mattered in every one of us. Perhaps only Tamburi, an odd fellow with his head in the clouds, will have seemed a bit obscure to him. Spadaro turned to me and said:

"You're the man who's been hunting for Carmine all this time, aren't you?"

"Correct. Where is Carmine?"

"I don't know. If I knew I'd tell you, because I've the greatest respect for the Prince Sirignano. Now listen: Carmine is scared."

"But why? What harm could I do him?"

"You, nothing. But two days ago, just before he disappeared, he comes to me and asks if he can sleep at my house. I ask him why, and he says that someone's looking for him, an outsider who's building a villa at Cape Massullo. He explains that he doesn't want to be found, because the affair is dangerous. It's about the death of that English girl at Anacapri, a few years ago. Carmine's always said he knew how that girl really died."

"We know that," said Sirignano.

"Fine. Very well, then, Carmine explains to me that the outsider with a villa at Cape Massullo is suspected of having killed the girl, and he knows it wasn't like that, it wasn't that man who'd pushed her from the Òrrico cliff. But if he'd spoken out, he'd have gotten himself in bad trouble, because the Germans were involved."

Sirignano, Tamburi and I exchanged knowing glances.

"It was quite obvious, Signor Prince," Spadaro continued, "that I couldn't put him up, 'cos I'm already leading a life *'nu sfaccimme* as they say in Naples, I'm already up to my nose in the shit and I don't need any other trouble. When I tell him that, Carmine takes it rather badly; then he says he'll find another solution, but he doesn't say what. I ask him: why don't you go to your sister in Naples? But he says they'll be quite sure of nabbing me there, maybe they'll even catch me when I go to take the ferry in Capri. Before leaving he repeats that he has a solution in mind, but it's a bit risky and he doesn't know if it will work. But I say to him, Carmine, you can't just keep on running away like that, it's got out that you know how the girl died. Sooner or later, someone's sure to come and ask you for explanations, aren't they? And he: I don't want to know, 'cos it would get me into no end of trouble, cops, trials, lawyers, newsmen – you name it. But if the truth comes out on its own, no one will come for me, 'cos that way no one will end up in jail. Then off he goes."

"What d'you think he meant by 'that way no one will end up in jail'?" asked Sirignano.

"What do I know of that, Signor Prince? Carmine didn't want to talk clearly, an' I don't have no glass ball like the magicians and fortune tellers. Maybe he meant to say that the girl's death was to do with someone who'll never end up in jail 'cos he's looked after by some saint in Paradise. Didn't you think of that one too, Prince?"

We heard voices from the road, then a car passing, footsteps coming and going in a hurry, then – fortunately – all became quiet again. Time to move on, any moment might bring some unwelcome visit. Spadaro wasn't to breathe a word of our visit to a soul, or he'd be in really bad trouble, the kind you never get over; Sirignano and Ciro reminded him with two or three syllables and just a couple of glances, as they do in Naples when they're talking serious business; and Ciro had "Camorra" printed on his forehead.

The fake fisherman promised obsequiously and unendingly that he'd keep his mouth shut and bid us farewell with exaggerated bowing and scraping, even kissing Tamburi's hand. Febo followed us out of that wretched hovel all proud and happy that Spadaro had in the end treated me and my friends properly. Febo hates it when someone's lacking in respect for me, he feels he's been insulted too.

Outside it was pitch dark by now. An army of cicadas in tuxedos were singing *Ain't Mishbehavin'* at the top of their voices, fireflies in high heels were brazenly cruising in the dark, some philosophical toad was burping his damp green thoughts. From the gorges of Anacapri wafted the musk-laden odor of pines, holm oaks and sky-blue lithodoras, while the stars and the moon, those great snoopers, spied on us but pretended they too weren't misbehavin'. In that marvellous night time I felt out of place; to me the singing of the cicadas seemed like the clicking of the handcuffs that were waiting for me, the fireflies made me think of the flashguns of the photographers at the moment of my arrest, and the gurgling of the toads of the jailer's voice that would soon be addressing me when I arrived in a Naples prison. How lovely it would be, I thought, if there in the grass at our feet we were to find three or four warm beds to sleep in, a bed for each one of us, and then wake up when the nightmare was over, when no one any longer accused me of Pam's murder. It was irresistible, that longing for warm beds, I wanted a whole row of warm beds all for myself, Tamburi and the others. I'm becoming melancholy, I thought, maybe it was time for us to go our separate ways.

"Now I absolutely must get myself seen out and about in Capri, Malaparte," said Sirignano. "At some party, in the street, in the Piazzetta: the one thing that counts is that there should be plenty of people. If anyone were to notice my absence from my usual haunts this evening, our dear spies would understand that I'm with you. We must take care: Villa Lysis has a side entrance, so I can always go into and out of the house without being noticed. But if your enemies start following me all day long, sooner or later they'll get back to you too. The same goes for Tamburi. We mustn't forget that Questore Manzi is in Capri. Did you see him the other day at the Villa Discopoli."

"Manzi? He doesn't even know who I am. When they introduced me to him, they had to repeat my name."

"Are you sure? I know Manzi. He reads plenty, he's a bookworm. Strange that he'd not heard of you. In any case, his men will do all in their power to lay hands on you. It would be humiliating for a big noise like him to be on vacation here in Capri with an important fugitive like you getting away right under his nose."

Sirignano left me some money, cigarettes and matches. Tamburi passed me a little picnic basket of his in which he'd packed water, bread, hard-boiled eggs and ham. For a while at least I'd not die of hunger.

"I promise I'll decipher that sentence, Signor Malaparte," said Tamburi.

"Sure, sure," I said. "The main thing for now is to keep me informed of the effect the golden statue of San Gennaro has on the people. And let me know if they find the sword that ended up in the sea. We'll keep in touch through Febo, who's been great so far. If I say the magic word, Febo never gets it wrong. Isn't that true, old thing?"

My beloved Etna Cirneco wagged his tail happily, standing up and placing his forepaws on my thigh, seeking a reward for all his exploits.

"Tarapoonchila poonchi poonchila," I murmured in his ear, pushing a fine hunk of bread between his teeth. Then I drew Madame Carmen's visiting card from my pocket and showed it.

"That Y-like symbol means nothing to me. But everyone here in Capri knows Madame Carmen," said Sirignano.

"Do you think that Madame Carmen knows my face," I asked.

"I don't think so. She doesn't read the papers and I myself haven't seen any picture of you recently in the Naples press. And she certainly won't have read your books."

"Sooner or later I'll have to pay her a visit. What do you say, d'you think it'll be fun?"

"I don't understand what you've got in mind, and I'm not going to ask you, but if I can I'll help you. And remember: if you get a chance, try to sleep."

"Tonight I'll be thinking of Saarburg. Every now and then I dream of what happened in Saarburg. D'you understand me?"

"No, Malaparte, I don't understand you. You'll explain it all tomorrow."

I smiled to him. Of course he couldn't understand. He was younger than me, he'd not seen war, he'd been neither to Bligny nor to Saarburg. He couldn't understand war, perhaps he couldn't even understand my yearning for warm beds on the grass.

I set my employee one last task: "Tamburi, you must absolutely find out for me what that strange symbol means. If you like, 'phone the office of *Prospettive* in Rome. But whatever you do, don't mention my name! The police will certainly be listening in on public 'phone booths in Capri."

Sirignano, Tamburi and I parted as brothers. Ciro meanwhile stayed with me. "Now you and I will go and have a chat with someone," I said to him.

Almost a Crime

As I expected, the lights were on in the Villa San Michele. By day, Dr. Munthe received visitors in the austere ambience of the Torre Materita, but in the evening he returned to sleep comfortably at the Villa San Michele, his kingdom, with its garden, pergola and panoramic view over the Bay of Naples.

"Is this it, Signor Malaparte?" asked Ciro.

"This is it."

Villa San Michele, Munthe's villa, was one of the biggest estates in Capri. It comprised a vineyard, fruit trees, an ancient chapel dedicated to Saint Michael which Munthe had converted a panoramic living room overlooking the sea, a park, and then the main building, built on several levels. Starting from there, a colossal pergola with a view over the sea, describing a curve that seemed to prolong into infinity. Along the pergola, supported by thirty-seven white columns bearing an enormous verdant vault on their capitals, there stood at intervals antique stone and bronze statues, amphoras, fragments of mosaic, marble busts and columns, in other words all the junk dear to Munthe, half of it authentic, half not, so that the fakes could never be distinguished from the genuine article, but dazzled the spectator as though they were the real thing, indeed even more so.

Joined to the one-time chapel of Saint Michael, which had been transformed into a sort of enormous panoramic living room giving onto the sea, was a little loggia out in the open, crowned by a cupola and supported by little columns, which offered an idyllic view over Capri, the port of Marina Grande, the Bay of Naples, the sky and the sea. When you came to this place after crossing the chapel, you seemed to hear the trumpets of Paradise. Within this little loggia stood Munthe's umpteenth, his supreme find: a red granite Egyptian sphinx, crouching at the corner of the parapet. The sphinx turned her back on the visitor, fixing her gaze on the horizon and enigmatically hiding her face. To see her face to face, one would have had to climb the parapet of the loggia, risking a fatal fall to the Phoenician Steps which lay below. A clever, romantic and deliciously kitsch idea, like everything that came from Axel Munthe's head.

The garden and pergola of the Villa San Michele were, thanks to their owner's loving care, something of a miracle. I've never been able to understand how the devil he managed it, but Munthe had succeeded in getting even Scandinavian birch trees to grow there, trees that needed three times as much water as was available in Capri. Munthe spoke with his beloved birds like Saint Francis, but I suspected that he was also capable of giving orders to plants. He loved plants, he loved them passionately, far more than he loved men, I'd say he loved them more than he loved his sovereign, Victoria of Sweden, who was also his mistress. Northern men, starting with the Germans, are far closer to the vegetable kingdom than we Mediterranean people. For an Italian, a flowerbed is a stolen space that should have been given over to houses. For a Swede, or at least for Munthe, a human being took up space that should have been given over to plants. He said: "Live!" and the freshly planted birch, delighted that someone was talking to it in Swedish, its native language, simply obeyed.

We entered the garden furtively, climbing a wall. I told Febo to wait outside, I didn't want to involve him in the unpleasant business that lay ahead of us.

The perfume of Munthe's garden was irresistible. It was a mingling of camelias, cinerarias, azaleas, wisterias, hortensias, roses, agapanthus, jasmine, Japanese pittosporum and hundreds of other plants from the Mediterranean basin and other parts of the world, lovingly cared for by the master of the house. Everywhere, ivy served as both carpeting and wallpaper. And then came the spontaneous species like acanthus, myrtle, broom, rock roses and many more. Among the trees, pines, palms and cypresses, the mysterious Swedish birches stood out. In the pergola, honeysuckle and morning glory climbed over the long line of white columns. In a hidden corner of the park, near the chapel, a statue of a dancing Faun skipped on a little column of cipolin marble in the midst of a clump of Tuscan cypresses. Munthe loved birds, but how he loved his plants! He could never have lived without them. He really was a fine Swedish gentleman, I thought, a dear old Swedish doctor, mild-mannered and true to his patients. How I longed to have a little chat with old Munthe, ah yes, it would be quite a chat.

From the park, we moved to the garden, and from the garden to the pergola. From the outside, the Villa San Michele looked like the realm of some oriental satrap, with its terraces all decorated with pseudo-Moorish castellation. I was glad to be entering that unbelievably eccentric dwelling like a thief, the place was so perfectly suited to springing surprises. Ah, what a surprise I meant to give old Munthe!

Once inside, we made our way downstairs in the dark and came to the kitchen. And there he was, the old lover of birds and plants. I caught sight of him through the walnut doorway and saw that he was sitting at table all alone, eating. When I'd visited him at Torre Materita he'd mentioned that his servants didn't sleep at the Villa San Michele, but in the tower. So there was no one else in the house.

From the oven came the smell of roast meat. Pork? Veal? No, something else. Before him, on a little wooden table Munthe had a glass of *grand rouge*, a swelling *ballon* for vintage reds, and he was just pouring from the bottle. Then he took the *ballon,* shook the wine about with a firm hand, slowly breathed in the bouquet, sighed and put it down on the table, to air it well before tasting, as one does with well-structured reds with personality. You old swine, I thought, you do like coddling yourself. The blind man's spectacles lay on the table, near the glass. I screwed up my eyes, trying to see what he had on his plate: game, perhaps. I recognised the label on the bottle: it was a Château Clos Labarde Ducasse. Now, I like Château Clos Labarde Ducasse very much, it's a high-class Bordeaux, a connoisseur's wine. One drinks Château Clos Labarde Ducasse only on solemn occasions, to celebrate some historic news, an anniversary, to meditate on the death of a great enemy or a great friend. Ah, you old swine, dear Dr. Munthe, you adorable liar. I stepped forward.

"Good evening," I said, flinging the door open.

Munthe screamed with terror. The *ballon* fell to the ground and shattered into a thousand pieces.

"Nothing to be afraid of, Doctor Munthe. This is only a ghost, and ghosts never harmed anyone."

"Malaparte! You... you... you frightened me to death."

His hands were trembling, his face was as white as one of the marble statues in his garden, he looked as though he needed a doctor. He stood up, feverishly looking for something on the table.

"Water, where's the water? I need to drink."

"A little water for Dr. Munthe," I said to Ciro. My companion found a jug full of water near the stove and handed it to Munthe, who poured himself a glass, and then another one. While Munthe was drinking, I looked at the remains of his meal. It was as I suspected: Munthe, the bird lover, the worshipper of our feathered friends, was eating pan-fried quails.

"How did you get here? Where did you get in?" he asked in dismay.

"From the garden, climbing the wall. How did you manage to recognise me, Doctor Munthe? Was it perhaps my voice?"

"I... I... don't know. Where are my glasses?"

"Please," I said to Ciro, "be so kind as to look for Dr. Munthe's glasses. He's blind, you know."

Ciro picked them up from the floor: they'd fallen with the *ballon*, but they were still intact. Ciro drew near with them, but Munthe pretended he'd not seen. Panic was written all over his face: he knew perfectly well that, without his dark glasses, he couldn't hide his ever-shifting, watchful and evasive blue eyes, eyes that could see perfectly. He kept fumbling here and there on the table, like a real blind man groping for his stick. To complete the comedy, he came too close and trod on my foot.

"Oh, excuse me, but you know...my eyes..."

That was one too many. "Come here, Ciro. Let's begin that chat with Dr Munthe I just mentioned to you," I said.

"Who is this gentleman?" asked Munthe.

"A friend. *'Nu bravo guaglione*, a good lad, don't you worry about him."

Ciro grabbed Munthe by his shirt collar, pushed him towards the chair and sat him down by force. Munthe was too taken aback to protest, he just whimpered with terror. That's the positive side of the Camorristi: when you need them to do you a favor, they do it quickly, without hesitating, and they do it so well. Ah, if only Tamburi had been in the Camorra!

"But what are you doing? Take your hands off me!"

"Doctor Munthe, I mean only to settle one or two small scores with you. What did you tell the OVRA about me?"

Munthe gulped for air: "The OVRA? But I've never met anyone from the OVRA."

"Ah no? So what were two guys from the OVRA doing today snooping just around here?"

"How should I know? They certainly didn't come to see me!" gasped Munthe.

There was still a pan on the stove. I went to take a look at it.

"Besides, I'm in my own home here! Get out at once," squawked the old doctor, but Ciro kept him firmly in his seat.

I took the top off the pan and was overcome by a whiff of perfume. Quails cooked in wine with a sausage stuffing, flavored with sage, rosemary, garlic, herbs and fennel seeds, accompanied by peas. De luxe quails, still piping hot.

Munthe again tried to get up, but Ciro sat him back down again with a big slap on the shoulder.

"Malaparte, my friend, you're getting yourself in deep trouble. I shall submit a protest to the Duce through the Swedish Embassy! They'll be hearing from me in Rome, ah yes, they'll be hearing from me!"

"Ready?" I asked Ciro.

"I'm ready," he said, and he took up position behind the chair on which Munthe was sitting. With one hand he encircled his neck and with the other he blocked his arms behind his back.

With a napkin I took one of the roast quails from the pan and approached Munthe:

"So, what did you tell the OVRA about me and Pam?"

"I don't know what you're talking about."

I forced Munthe's jaws open and pushed the quail in with my middle finger. It had already been deboned, and it looked quite delicious; the skin was perfectly crisp. Munthe screamed, the hot meat was burning his palate and his tongue. I closed his jaws and kept them shut. His face became as red as the mouth of a blast furnace. I took the bottle of Château Clos Labarde Ducasse and sipped a little from the bottle, seeing that the *ballon* was in pieces at our feet. As Bordeaux wines go, it was a little too young, but excellent.

Munthe was chewing desperately, he'd understood that another mouthful would soon be on its way.

"A drop of wine, Doctor?" I asked.

Munthe couldn't reply, he was still struggling with the burns to his palate and the quail wouldn't go down. He was horrified to see me drink his nectar after the manner of the tramps. I grasped the bottle firmly and shoved it between his teeth, pouring wine into the nice Swedish doctor's mouth. He drank a little and coughed up a little, belching and gasping. Only by a miracle had he managed to swallow the first quail.

After removing the bottle from his mouth, I poured half the contents down his shirt collar. Munthe's face became purple; he was probably thinking of the jingling of all those Swedish Crowns that were vanishing with every drop of that precious Château Clos Labarde Ducasse. Then I took another scalding hot quail, again opened the jaws of the master of the house and stuffed it well down his throat. Munthe made as to vomit, but managed not to. Another shower of wine down his collar and his shirt-front refreshed him a little. Château Clos Labarde Ducasse is a fine Bordeaux, its bouquet is graced with those notes of fresh fruit, cinnamon, almonds and prunes that make it a rich, complex wine, one that defies description. Come to think of it, it was wasted on quails: it should accompany a *cordon bleu* or an *entrecôte à la bordelaise*, in other words, something stronger. Munthe was chewing almost as fast as an aeroplane propellor, and he was on the point of suffocating.

"An' what about the peas?" Ciro asked me.

"Ah yes, the peas."

I took a portion from the pan, but they were scalding. I got rid of them slapping down the whole generous handful in Munthe's face and spreading it over his nose, cheeks and forehead. Now Munthe no longer had that ugly red complexion, caused by the burns to his palate. He'd become as green as the flowerbeds in his splendid park, a fine military green that suited him down to the ground.

"Courage, Doctor Munthe, now we're going to take a walk." And I shoved another hot quail down his throat, together with all its exquisite stuffing of *fines herbes*, fennel and garlic. Munthe was close to collapsing. When I was pushing down the quail he tried to bite me, but Ciro gave him a slap that shook even the table, and the old man calmed down. I motioned Ciro to take our victim outside. Even if he'd wanted to scream, his throat stuffed with birds would have stopped him from doing so. Knowing that if he spat them onto the ground I'd cram them all back into his mouth, he kept frenetically chewing the quails, desperately trying to free himself of the gag. I poured the rest of the Château Clos Labarde Ducasse, first down his throat then over his head, which I then gave a quick rub with both hands. Now Munthe's head, his hair and the nape of his neck had that subtle note of prunes, almonds and cinnamon of Château Clos Labarde Ducasse. It was a matchless bouquet, one to be found only in certain great Bordeaux; an expert will recognize it at once.

Kicking and pushing from behind, we drove Doctor Munthe into the park, amidst the southern pines, the cedars, Aleppo pines, the precious tea trees and oaks. While Ciro kept him still, I inserted the last quail, which Ciro had brought with us wrapped in a napkin, rather energetically in his gullet. This time Munthe hadn't managed to chew quickly enough; he crouched down and threw up part of what he had on his stomach. Doctor Munthe was in good health and had a robust constitution.

"Well then, tell me something about your dealings with Goering? You never even mentioned those in our little chats!"

"Malaparte... I... you... cannot treat me with this violence."

"C'mon, c'mon!" said Ciro moving towards the chapel at the far end of the park, and kicking Munthe forward like a rag doll. By now the quails were finished but in a nearby flowerbed was a rose, a magnificent velvety red Conrad Ferdinand Meyer rose. Taking good care not to prick myself (the Conrad Ferdinand Meyer is well known for its thorns) I picked it and handed it to Ciro.

"Come on, offer a rose to the Doctor."

Ciro didn't have to be asked twice. He opened Munthe's jaws and stuffed into his mouth the rose, its leaves and the tender stem with its sharp little thorns. Munthe moaned with pain, had a spasm and twisted as though a harpoon had been planted in his esophagus.

"C'mon now!" said Ciro encouraging him with a couple of clouts. Munthe tried to eat it, but the thing got stuck in his gullet. Then we took a watering can and pushed Munthe to the ground face upwards and, holding his mouth open, we poured a good bucketful onto his face, between his lips and down his nose. He sat up, dripping; even his hair had lost that fine aroma of Château Clos Labarde Ducasse. From the nearest flowerbed I picked a bunch of clover. It was tender and sweet-smelling. I put it on my fingertips, grasped Munthe's face and forced the grass and clover up his nose. He tried to break free but Ciro held him in a vice-like grip, he could do nothing. Then I plucked another tuft of grass and pushed it into his ears, first the right one then the left. Munthe was moaning, he was weeping, but he wasn't speaking. Ciro took some little yellow flowers from near the wall and shoved them down his throat.

"Answer, Doctor Munthe!"

The Swedish doctor shook his head and Ciro gave him a great backhander.

I must say I wasn't expecting such obstinacy from our good old Axel. But I couldn't very well take my leave as matters stood, saying "Eminent Dottore, seeing as we've not managed to get a word out of you, we must be on our way, and please remember us to your bloody little birds." What kind of an idiot would that have left me looking like?

"Let's see, then," I said, switching sharply to gentler tones, "Shall we take one step at a time? What were these flowers? You are an excellent botanist and you can see perfectly well. Tell me their Latin name. I've always wanted to know it."

"*Mahonia aquifolium*", mumbled Munthe after a few moments in which he'll have tried to understand if I was crazy. It was hard for him to speak with his mouth all stuffed with leaves and stalks.

"Ah I see. And how about these?" I said, pushing another bunch down his gullet, while gesturing to Ciro to hit him again.

Another refusal, another smack.

"*Nephrolepis exaltata*," he murmured. He'd decided to humor us, but he still wasn't spilling the beans.

We kept feeding him, and he sampled *Lantana montevidensis*, *Rhododendron simsii*, *Iochroma cyaneum* (if I remember rightly) and so on. Doctor Munthe really was a great botanist, and I really did admire him. I've always had the greatest respect for those who learn all those names of plants in Latin, I think it's a really cute occupation.

"Come on now," I said, "What a perfect evening: first we dealt with birds, then with plants. Two of your favorite hobbies. Now we come to the last and most important item: recitation."

Ciro had kept Munthe's spectacles, his fake blind man's glasses. He carried out to the letter what I'd asked him to at the beginning of our expedition: he took one of the lenses out from the frame and inserted it like a monocle in Munthe's right eye socket, then slammed it in hard. Munthe screamed with pain.

"Is that OK?" Ciro asked, showing me the result.

"Perfect."

A fine blue circle was left in the eye socket, it looked almost as though a lens had been fitted under the skin. Ciro repeated the operation with the left eye: lens placed in the eye socket, a punch, Munthe's scream. Now the Swedish doctor had two splendid blue circles around both eyes. Ciro let one of the lenses fall to the ground. The glass broke. To complete the good work, Ciro picked up one of the fragments and, while I held Munthe down, with the sharp shard he traced a sign on Munthe's nose, between the eyes, then two lines from the outer edge of each blue circle to the ears. While the glass splinter ploughed through his face, the Swedish doctor screamed, but with Scandinavian dignity. On the features of Doctor Axel Munthe, physician and famous writer, a magnificent pair of glasses was now drawn, glasses made of bruises and blood. They'd take some two to three weeks to disappear.

"So now, Doctor Munthe, you'll be the first blind man to wear incorporated specs. As genuine as your blindness," I commented.

Munthe did not answer: he was panting and massaging his eyes, bruised and swollen by Ciro's fists. He was spitting out a bizarre mixture of saliva, blood and leaves.

"You see, Doctor? What with living in Italy, even your spit has become white, red and green like our flag. You're a true Italian, my compliments."

We dragged him to the chapel. There we were almost overcome by the perfume of the azaleas and the wisteria. How clean that perfume is, I thought, there's such innocence in its primitive essence, it makes you want to enter again into union with Nature, to regain your original purity, to return forever to the Truth. Ah, now, if Munthe were only to return to the Truth, or at least to the truth about the OVRA!

We entered the little chapel. "Why are you bringing me here?" whimpered the Swedish doctor. "Malaparte, I don't want to die!"

He was expecting me to reply "Well then, speak, once and for all!"

But I said nothing.

In that great space with its columns and volutes, antique furniture, a number of pictures, imposing antique iron candle-holders, spiraling columns supporting masonry arches, old services of dishes hanging on the wall, an old wooden statue of Saint Michael and other church furnishings, stood the grand piano which Munthe was wont to pound away at on the long winter evenings, when no one came to see him and he was left alone with his dogs, his birds, his Château Clos Labarde Ducasse and his pan-fried quails. The windows were of magnificent Gothic tracery with wreathed mullions, it felt as though one were back in the Middle Ages, when Capri was full of monks and hermits. We came to the far end of the chapel and emerged into the open, that little panoramic loggia giving onto the sea, where the red granite sphinx scanned the horizon.

"What do you want to do with me? No, please no, I beg of you!" gurgled Munthe.

We hoisted the old man over the parapet, next to the sphinx. Beyond that little wall, many meters below, the stone of the Phoenician Steps awaited him. By day, the view from that position was simply breathtaking. If the sun hand been up, we could have seen the Fortino, I thought, and with a telescope, one could have admired Mona Williams watering her roses. Dear old Mona, dear old friend.

"No! Don't kill me!"

"Dear old Axel," I thought without opening my mouth, "why don't you sing once and for all?" This wasn't just stubbornness with a vengeance, it couldn't just be fear of the OVRA, no, there was something else behind Munthe's bloody-minded refusal to sing – unlike his wretched birds – but what could that be?

We pushed Munthe over the edge, holding onto his legs. The rest of his body, head and chest, hung from the parapet. He was struggling, trying to cling to the wall like a lizard, as though he had suckers under his fingertips. He was pitiful; faced with death, even Swedes lose a little of their sangfroid. Munthe had every reason to be scared; I was rather attracted to the idea of giving him a nice flight. No one except for Febo knew that I and Ciro were at the Villa San Michele that night. We could get clean away.

"OVRA," I said, just to remind him of the business in hand.

"Pity!" was the only reply I could get from that pig-headed Swede.

Very soon he'd be falling. We jerked on Munthe's legs, just to let him know that we were on the point of dropping him. Our guest would have fallen through the black night onto the black Phoenician Steps, he'd have broken his head and out would have flowed the old Swede's dense black blood. It would have formed a black circle around his broken head, a big black circle. A second tug, Munthe trembled, but still said nothing.

"Well then, shall we drop him?" Ciro asked impatiently. He too wanted to see that black circle. Suddenly, I've no idea why, an image returned to me from the nothingness of the remote past.

Third and last tug...

Damp Fire

After pestering my eyelids for quite a while, the sunray managed at last to awake me. It was late, almost two in the afternoon. It was hot and my back was soaked with sweat, boiling sweat, like damp fire. The flies were regaling themselves with my forehead, my neck and my eyes.

I couldn't stand having that damp fire on me, I sat up on the sofa and slowly opened my eyes. I was famished; I grabbed the little knapsack with food and water that Tamburi had given me, and served myself.

Febo whimpered.

"You're quite right, you did plenty of walking too last night," I said, holding out a piece of bread to him.

Then I stretched out again and closed my eyes.

Febo too began dozing. He was happy with how we were fixed up: he too had the feeling that no one would be coming to look for us. How lucky we were to be able to hide in the house of my friend Guglielmo Rulli! After seeing Bianchi and Marelli at Anacapri, on the Migliera path, I absolutely needed to find myself a new refuge.

After we'd completed our little job at the Villa San Michele, Ciro and I each went our way. The Camorrista went off quietly to spend the night at the house of an acquaintance, recommended by some Naples mafia boss. I for my part had to take on a tremendous nocturnal uphill scramble with Febo, crossing thickets and orchards until I at last made it to Rulli's house. No one would every have suspected me of hiding there, a stone's throw from House like Me: it was the last thing any rational fugitive would do.

Rulli was a diplomat friend of mine and we'd bought land and built our houses on Capri at the same time. His charming little villa was high up, set down on the rocky heights behind Cape Massullo; from up there one could see House like Me, resting on its great clifftop. Rulli's fine villa was almost completed, and I knew which stone in the garden to raise in order to find the key to the front door. Rulli was in Rome, and perhaps he'd paid someone to look after the house, but in Capri such people make a check once a month.

I thought with a smile of Axel Munthe. At that moment, I'd have been willing to bet, he'd be in one of the many bathrooms of the Villa San Michele, dabbing the new spectacles that I and Ciro had drawn on his face with ice and disinfectant. He'd stay buried in the Villa San Michele until the bruises and wounds had healed, and after that he'd never speak of these things with anyone. It didn't suit him to report me and Ciro: he'd have had to accept a medical examination, they'd discover that he had the eyesight of a falcon, and so farewell to his fame as a blind old novelist. What's more, before leaving the villa, Ciro had advised him to keep his mouth well shut, otherwise someone would come back to visit him, and this time it would end up badly. The lazy old so and so had made us work like slaves! And all that to unbutton next to nothing: when all was said and done, Munthe hadn't revealed much to the OVRA. He'd seen Pam hand in hand with me at Anacapri two days before her death. That much he'd said. He'd confessed to me that the OVRA knew he was not really blind and claimed that was why he'd had to talk. Obviously, that made no sense. He could perfectly well have said he'd not met us. No, old Axel had betrayed me for some other reason. Just then, however, I preferred not to think about that. I was too relieved to know that what he'd told the OVRA was not in contradiction with what I'd stated during the interrogation by Bianchi and Marelli (if that's what they were really called) at House like Me.

Far more to the point, however, was what the OVRA had told Munthe: there was a *written* summons against me, or at least someone had signed a document heavily compromising me. So that was what lay behind the trouble I was in: a scrap of paper about which, for the time being, I knew absolutely nothing. The mysterious document must be locked away in some safe at the main OVRA office in Naples, which handled the entire region.

Lastly, something had emerged which had nothing to do with the OVRA: for the sale of the Villa San Michele, Munthe had never dealt directly with Goering. The go-between had been Philipp von Hessen. "The only man," Munthe had said, "who can get to…"

"…the Führer at any time," I interrupted him, "I know that one by heart."

The name of the Prince of Hesse kept coming up under too many circumstances: Mona's party, the Saarburg crucifix, the theft of the book, the sale of the Villa San Michele… What got on my nerves was the fact that there didn't seem to be any logical connection between all these strange manifestations, each one so far from the others.

For two nights I'd had no decent sleep, and the snooze on the sofa after a pretty full day hadn't helped. And then there all those damned thoughts that just wouldn't stop coming. There was a charge against me, so Munthe had said. Who had an interest in reporting me? In Capri I'd had no enemies until then, apart from the Sturmbannführer; and, however dangerous he might be, he was cited only as a witness in the nebulous investigation against me. I couldn't think of other enemies. Minister Balbo had had me sent to Lipari a few years earlier, but he'd been in Libya for quite some time now. Giovanni Agnelli, boss of half Italy, detested me but no longer had any cause for concern: Virginia, his son's widow, had given up the idea of marrying me. So, what then? I felt that something must be escaping me, something horribly banal.

God, how I wanted to see Lucia. I must get to her. I'd send her Tamburi at nightfall. I'd not tell her anything about Mona: when all's said and done, that had been a work meeting, to save my skin. Lucia, where are you? And what about Carmine, that wretched Carmine, where the hell's he gotten to? I couldn't do a thing until it was dark. All I wanted was to fling the doors and windows wide open and enjoy the vast panorama. Rulli's place was several dozen meters higher up than mine; I had a house for seagulls, Rulli's was a house for falcons.

Once again sleep weighed on my eyelids. Through the cracks in doors and windows wafted a perfume of pines, cypress resin and sun-dried earth. It was the smell I'd known in my childhood, the smell of those long summer afternoons in the country near Prato, with my band of footloose brats. Why in the country? Ah yes, that was it. My mother hadn't wanted to breast-feed me. With those words, my memories kept on coming, but now they came in my sleep: I was dozing and remembering. And I said to myself: why all these memories? A voice replied – I don't know whether it was my own or someone else's…

"Because the truth is staring you in the face, and you can't see it."

PRATO, 1912

Earth like Me

On the night I was born I had two mothers. The first one, as soon as she'd given birth to me, had me wrapped up at once in a blanket and sent to the other one. The second Mama was called Eugenia; she'd just lost her newborn son and she'd been chosen to be my wet-nurse. All that was quite normal: it was seen as vulgar to suckle one's own children – that was good for the lower classes. So it was Eugenia who gave me her milk, even if she'd have preferred to give it to her dead son. I'd grown sucking the milk of a dead child, the milk meant for a dead child.

Perhaps it was then that a strange and powerful sense of death entered my mind, the sense that death is part of us, that death is making its way within us, even while we're living, even when we think we're alive.

Eugenia and her husband Milziade were simple country folk, and they had other natural children. But the moment Milziade saw me all red and trembling in that blanket, he grew attached to me, and with time I became his favorite son, even more beloved than his own. I used to joke that Milziade was my wet-nurse.

My real father was German, and he was hard and unhappy like so many of his compatriots. With age, he lost his mind, and he'd call me names like varmint and whoremonger. When the ambulance was carting him off to die in hospital, he called for a beer, but the nurses didn't want to give him one. He kept on threatening and insulting them until they gave in. At the bar, he offered a round to everyone then returned to his ambulance and kicked the bucket a couple of hours later, swearing like a trooper. That's how he was.

From time to time Mama, my real Mama, the one who hadn't given me milk, would come and collect me from Eugenia and Milziade's. She'd arrive in a carriage, with a white dress and a parasol. Those were still the days of top hats, frock-coats and velocipedes. She was beautiful, that Mama of mine, all rosy and wreathed in smiles. The summer air was dense and compact, it smelled of ripe corn, thyme and cypresses. The carriage would stop in Eugenia and Milziade's yard and they'd all start yelling: Curtino, come out! Curtino, your Mama's here! No one ever knew where I was, maybe throwing stones at the pigs, catching frogs out in the fields, swimming in the stream or crouching under a bush eating chestnut polenta. Once they'd found me, I'd run to the carriage to kiss Mama and drown in the folds of her white dress. She'd tick me off at once: "Hey, careful! You're getting me all muddy." I'd smile to her, but then a moment later I'd break away and run, cursing myself for muddying her white dress, for being a boy who dirties his mother. And then I'd hide where they couldn't find me; I was happier there, with my nurse-dad, the frogs, the cicadas and the pigs. At last I'd see my mother's carriage go on its way, raising a great cloud of dust on the avenue, while I stayed hidden in a field of Indian corn, feeling my tears fall on my dirt-caked little feet. In the evening Milziade would close his blacksmith's workshop and come out looking for me. When he found me sitting under a tree, all sad and thoughtful, he'd say: "Curtino, sooner or later, you'll have to go home. Your parents are waiting for you". And I'd say to him: "Nobody loves me, you're all I have in the world, I don't want to go home." But then a tree-frog would jump near my feet, in the midst of the corn-cobs, and I'd follow it without another thought.

For years I thought I didn't love my mother, but I was wrong. I couldn't know that one day I'd be with her dying, staying till her last agony, with a son's gentle, loving patience. I couldn't know that I'd open my heart to her, the last time I saw her, just before she died, although I'd never really opened up to a woman, a friend, or anyone at all.

When Mama came for me at Milziade's, we kids were always barefoot and dirty with earth, we were part of the earth we lived in, we were made of earth like Adam. It was just so normal to be made of earth, to live with earth and in earth, that sometimes we'd eat it. From America to Japan, everyone knows Florence. As for Prato, no one knows it, we had no Lorenzo the Magnificent and no Botticelli. Yet

Prato's superior, because it's magical. We'd learnt that around Prato every lump of earth had not only its own strange, special name, but its own taste: the earth of Le Sacca tasted of juniper berries, that of Mount Spazzavento crackled between your jaws like breadcrumbs, the earth of Poggio al Fossino tasted of oranges and made you shiver, that of Il Soccorso, down in the plain, you could spread on bread because it was greasy and strong and black like olive pâté. I wasn't afraid of dying, because if I died I'd get myself buried in the orchard next to our house and I'd have so much good earth to eat, and with it I could nibble carrots and onions, tomato roots and salad from our garden.

Every now and then I'd run a long way away, into the woods, with a box of matches stolen from the kitchen, trying in vain to start a fire. Sometimes I'd disappear for two or three days, then I'd come home covered in scratches and soaked with rain, quite unable to explain what the devil I'd been up to. Sometimes I'd pretend that they'd stolen a toy of mine and, crying like crazy I'd make everyone search for it, wreaking chaos for the family, though I was the first to believe my tale and search for the thing desperately with all the others. I'd even invented a god, the great Auramada, cruel and all-powerful, and I'd built him a totem in the woods (the name I'd gotten by mangling that of a famous Iranian deity). I'd explained to the other kids that I alone could placate him, so long as they buried all their coins before him. After that the coins would disappear from the hole (I'd steal them by night) and everyone was convinced that Auramada had taken them. At night I'd write dozens of novels and poems, and the first one (which I burned in the fireplace) was called *The Stink of Women*.

On some full-moon nights I'd go out from the house and wander round with the ghosts of dead kids, the dead kids of the neighborhood and the ghosts of their dead dogs. I was the only living kid who dared go round at night with the ghosts of dead children. From them I learned so many things about life and death which I've put in my books, wonderful and terrible things, but in those days I could tell them to no one, they'd not have believed me. One night a hunter saw us, he got scared and fired; it was a miracle I wasn't killed. They found me bleeding and unconscious; I was between life and death for days and days.

Setting out in the morning, I'd go out courting the country girls, all of them bigger than me; I'd meet them in the middle of the fields, in groups of three or four, half naked because of the great heat, and they'd scream, pretending they were scared, but every one of them hoped I'd like her.

I was a star pupil at the middle school, no one was better than me at Greek or Latin: but I was absent-minded, closed and taciturn, and in the end the teachers and my fellow pupils left me to my devices.

Then I grew up, I became a youngster, and a few hairs sprouted under my chin. I ran away from home in 1914, at the age of sixteen, to volunteer for the Great War against the Germans. I spent my teenage years in the mountains of France, in the Argonne, amidst handgrenades, trenches and baggage trains. I fought the Austrians in the Alps, then again in France, I fought the Germans. When peace came, I was twenty, with my lungs wrecked by mustard gas and disgusted by all I'd seen, suffered and understood of war. I was taken into the diplomatic service and went to Paris, on to Warsaw, and then back to Rome, all the while trying to make myself a name. But when I could, I'd return to Tuscany, to my beloved Prato, and I'd go to the country fairs and dance in the village squares until I got backache. I'd spend hours playing cards, chess and bowls with the old men, and I loved cheating. I'd go to the feast of San Michele a Carmignano, where there was a chess competition and there I'd find three half-crazy noncoms, Alcide, Paolo and Moreno, who'd spout about God and the saints with the parish priest after downing two or three bottles of Chianti, and if I was on form I'd let them drag me around through the fields singing at the top of our voices while we stole fruit from the trees and even carved our names into the bark, and every single time some mean bastard of a peasant would shoot at us and we only just got away with our lives.

I couldn't do without returning to those places where as a kid I'd eaten earth, adored the powerful Auramada and followed tree-frogs through the corn. I went back to spying on those peasant wenches half-naked out there in the fields, I got drunk with my friends composing verses in octaves, as the old Tuscan peasants have been doing for centuries, marvelous exhilarating verses that died with the next day's hangover. I came back to kiss my old nurse Milziade, and sitting on the farmyard steps he'd ask me why I'd gotten it into my head that I wanted to be a writer instead of finding myself an honest job, and why the hell I had to keep travelling to Paris, London and Moscow, and whether it was true that Mussolini was *un gran bischero* – a great big dope, and I said to him: yes, Mussolini's a *bischero* – only, Milziade, don't you go saying those things to anyone, ordinary people can't say things like that, only we writers can. And Milziade would ask: are you really sure, Curtino? Don't you think you'll end up in trouble? And I: I'm a writer, Milziade, I know what I'm doing. Those in power are scared of us writers, we stand above and beyond power.

He'd nod in agreement, looking at me with concern, his eyes veiled with tears, but I could see that he didn't really believe me. Oh! How sweet old man Milziade was, as sweet as a calm summer's night on the summit of Spazzavento, where my grave would lie one day, the grave of my strange, wild childhood, the grave of *a young Apollo magnificently unprepared for the long littleness of life.*

CAPRI, SUMMER 1939

Awakening

I woke up. My back felt broken. I twisted and turned on Rulli's sofa, trying to find a more comfortable position, still groggy: it was dark. I flicked my lighter on and read the time from an old clock: midnight! I'd collapsed again and slept like a log, it was about time for me to go out and join the rest of the group.

I felt a pain in my stomach. *La dracu* Prato and Tuscany, *la dracu* my childhood. I had an arrest warrant hanging over my head like a huge boulder, I couldn't waste time dreaming of a past that would never return, I had no right to do that. *Ya napliwayu* childhood, I spit on my childhood. Febo gave a vague start, gave his back a good shake and licked his paws thoroughly. He too had slept heavily, he too was ready to go out. We had a perfect understanding with Tamburi and Sirignano. If there'd been no hitches, they'd have prepared everything that day.

I went out and returned the key to its place, under the stone in the garden. It was dark enough, I just had to keep away from trodden paths and to hide in the vegetation.

As usual, I sent Febo scouting ahead. It wasn't very far from Rulli's house to the Villa Lysis. I slipped a card with the place of our appointment under Febo's collar, murmured the usual magic word and watched him set off swiftly towards his destination.

Before setting out in my turn, I wanted to take a glance, just one, at House like Me. Obviously, I couldn't go and visit it: the path was too open, the risk of being seen was far too high.

I looked, and for a moment my heart sank, but then I said to myself: no, there was no light in there, I must have been mistaken. There's no one in House like Me.

Quisisana Chaos

It had all worked out perfectly. We'd met at the agreed time and place: the Natural Arch, the extraordinary rock arch at the eastern tip of the island, surrounded by prickly pears and agaves against the background of a wild, enchanting bay. It is one of the most magical and bizarre of Capri's attractions, and they call it the Natural Arch, but I have never believed that: it is far too big, too fine and slender to be a work of Nature, some good-for-nothing must have built it by night. Just go and take a look at the Natural Arch for yourself one day, and then come and tell me if I'm not telling it like it is. I kissed and hugged Febo for having accomplished his mission so well. Once again I'd succeeded in giving no advance notice of a meeting with yours truly. I trusted Sirignano and company almost blindly, especially in dealing with the gentlemen from OVRA and the police, but an involuntary leakage of information was always possible. When I arrived, I saw that I'd done well to stick to my cautious approach: at the Natural Arch, Sirignano, Tamburi and Ciro were accompanied by Chantecler, who had no lack of idiocies to his name.

Once together, Sirignano as usual wasted no time in chit-chat, and reported succinctly on the main events of the previous day.

A little less than three hours earlier, at 10 in the evening, parties in the private villas were in full swing, while all was quiet at the Quisisana. Those who wanted to stay up into the small hours were at the hotel's bar, in the gardens or on one of the terraces. Only two members of staff were left at the reception desk and the long corridors were empty, apart from the occasional guest returning to his room to sleep. When Prince Francesco Caravita di Sirignano turned up in the lobby, he at once captured the entire attention of the two concierges. He asked whether his friend John Rockefeller was in his room, thus setting off total panic: no one in the hotel knew a thing! Immediately the two concierges began to enquire whether a Rockefeller was in fact on the guest list, perhaps under a pseudonym for reasons of privacy. Sirignano, who really did know John Rockefeller, had also been waving a visiting card of his on which the 'phone number of the

Quisisana had been written (but by Sirignano). Frantic telephone calls to the other departments of the hotel, checking the guest list, vain attempts to get through to the hotel manager (who was obviously elsewhere at that hour, at some party).

At the same time Chantecler arrived in the hall, announcing that he'd lost an earring of inestimable value that afternoon in the hotel lobby; obviously, a dirty trick prearranged with Sirignano. So, laborious searching for the earring underneath sofas, carpets and chairs in the lobby and all adjoining spaces, and growing nervousness among the hotel staff, while Chantecler threatened to call the police and get them to close the hall of the hotel until the jewel was found.

That afternoon Tamburi had obtained the number of the Sturmbannführer's room, telephoning reception on behalf of a dealer in exotic animals and telling them he had to deliver a cage containing an African parrot of a particularly talkative variety to a German gentleman with a name like Helmut Aichinger. The receptionist at the Quisisana quite willingly authorized Tamburi to deliver the talking parrot directly to the consignee's room, instead of to reception. As soon as he'd obtained the room number, Tamburi repeated the name more accurately, and found there had been a misunderstanding: the person to whom the parrot was to be delivered was called Altinger not Aichinger, and the hotel in question was another one situated in the center, while there was another client of the dealer in animals at the Quisisana, which explained the mix-up.

While the two receptionists tried to cope simultaneously with the Rockefeller enigma and Chantecler's protests, Tamburi slipped into the hotel, accompanied by Ciro. The two made their way rapidly to the Sturmbannführer's room, where Tamburi acted as lookout while the Camorra man forced the lock with little difficulty.

There was no risk of the Sturmbannführer being present in the room: he'd been kept under observation all afternoon.

A romantic young couple consisting of two elegant young Neapolitans had taken up position in the hall of the Quisisana that morning, as soon as they'd received instructions from Tamburi. The young lovers were in reality two youngsters recruited by Ciro and Sirignano. They lounged around in the hall of the Quisisana browsing through newspapers and magazines or sipping coffee at the tables of the hotel bar, just in front of the entrance, while they were in fact waiting for our man to pass. When the time came, the two observers had no difficulty in recognising the Sturmbannführer, thanks to his SS uniform and the enormous Doberman. Protected by their innocuous appearance, the fake fiancés tailed Aichinger as closely as two lice. The SS officer left the hotel towards lunchtime, took a long walk, ate in a modest tourist restaurant and returned towards 4 p.m. The young lovers were beginning to wonder whether the SS major was ever going to come out from his room, when at last, on the stroke of 8, Helmut Aichinger crossed the hall of the Quisisana followed, as ever, by his huge beast. The pair again tailed him, this time from a distance, fearing he might notice them. The Sturmbannführer met with a group of German tourists in the town square and they all sat down at a café and ordered a few hectoliters of beer. One of the two fiancés, specifically the young gentleman, stayed in the vicinity so as not to lose sight of the target. Meanwhile, the girl went to warn Sirignano, Chantecler, Tamburi and Ciro, who were awaiting their cue for action in a nearby alleyway.

As soon as they'd gotten the door open, Tamburi and Ciro turned the whole room upside down, but still found no trace of the book stolen from Mona. They did find a number of books (tourist guides, a novel in German, an SS photograph album) but not *Bestie delinquenti*, the tome that mattered.

Just before getting out, however, rummaging through the Sturmbannführer's personal effects, Tamburi noticed an interesting detail. It was a scrap of paper with just one solitary sign on it, and Tamburi reproduced it for me at once:

EDDA

"Good lord, that's a clear sign that the Sturmbannführer and Edda Mussolini have something in common!" I exclaimed.

"What do you mean," asked Sirignano.

"First of all, tell me, is there any news about the sword I asked you to fish up?"

"Yes, that old French lady, Madame Dutilleux, came and gave me excellent news for you: it has been found."

"The saber? And it was the old French lady? But how the hell did she manage that?"

"You must thank Heaven that you've admirers like her. Four years ago, shortly after your duel with the Sturmbannführer, your second, who was probably one of the many penniless Capresi, spread the juicy news that a beautiful brand-new saber had fallen into the sea from the Migliera viewpoint. So one of the many equally penniless village kids ran to look for it. But then he found he couldn't sell it, because it was a military sword, and what's more, it belonged to an SS officer. The local fences will surely not have been willing to touch it. So the sword stayed in the home of a Capri family, naturally, well hidden in a cupboard. Now last year, an English friend of Madame Dutilleux rented a room from this family. Like many women of advanced years, this lady was a dreadful busybody, and she found the sword in the cupboard. Astounded, and also somewhat suspicious, she got the Capri family to tell her where it came from. The answer could hardly have been more fascinating: a duel between an SS officer and a good-looking young Italian, rivals in love for a young English poetess. The Italian won and the saber went flying down into the sea. As though that were not enough, the young poetess had a mortal fall from a cliff, immediately after the duel. The English lady told the tale to half Capri, and it came to the attention of Madame Dutilleux. As our old lady is anything but stupid, she put two and two together and suspected that you were involved in the duel, and at the masked ball at Villa Ferraro, she wanted to ask whether you were by any chance the handsome young Italian who won that duel, as everyone knows of your swordsmanship, your reputation as a womanizer, your dislike of Nazis, and last but not least, that you've a house here in Capri."

"In other words, Madame Dutilleux wanted to ask whether you were interested in getting that sword back when she buttonholed you at the Villa Ferraro. But you didn't want to listen to her..." added Chantecler sarcastically.

I bit my lip in shame: so, when the old French lady came to talk to me at the party and asked about my clash with the Sturmbannführer, she'd not been talking about the row at Mona Williams' house, as I'd thought, but about the duel four years earlier, and the saber that had fallen into the sea

"Shut up, Chantecler, we're talking serious business," Sirignano continued. "Well, today poor old Madame Dutilleux saw me in the town square and asked if it was true that you and I are friends. Obviously, I said yes, and she told me the whole story of the saber fished out from the sea just as I've told it to you. Obviously, recovering the saber cost me some money, but that's on me."

"Prince, may Heaven reward you for this one too. So where's the saber?"

"I've hidden it in a bush, just in case anyone caught us waiting for you here."

"Like some news-hound," broke in Ciro, "those bastards are a menace."

"Let me finish, Ciro. As I was saying, it is after all the sword of an SS officer on vacation here in Capri, and it could get one into trouble. The family that sold it to me had heard that the Sturmbannführer too tried to recuperate it from under the cliff, but he got there too late. Come, Malaparte"

We came to a big thick laurel bush and Sirignano drew the long blade out of the earth and handed it to me. It was still the shining saber I'd seen on the day of the duel, four years before. So the thing that interested me was still perfectly visible.

"Look," I said, showing Sirignano, Chantecler, Tamburi and Ciro the little symbol enclosed in an oval, where the hilt joined the blade:

Then I drew Madame Carmen's visiting card, which I'd filched from Edda's house, from my pocket.

"It's the same sign as the one on the sword. Where did you get that visiting card of Madame Carmen's?" asked Chantecler.

"At Edda's place, the other evening, not long after you'd been necking with her on the terrace. The card was on a marble side-table, next to the switch that controls the automatic shutters."

"Ah yes, Edda and Galeazzo Ciano's sublime automatic shutters!" sighed Chantecler ironically.

"Has the statue of San Gennaro had any effect?" I asked.

"Not yet," replied Sirignano, "the climber placed it right on the tip of the central Faraglione, and until someone goes up there, it won't be easily seen."

"Tamburi, where are we with *mervu*?"

"Still nowhere, Signor Malaparte. I've got all the staff of *Prospettive* working on it. They're asking linguists, crossword experts, decoders and even poets but no one has a clue what that wretched word could mean ."

"*A cash credit for a child in Rabal*", I repeated to myself, remembering the partial interpretation we'd arrived at. "And then there's... *mervu*. It feels almost like a joke. And the mysterious symbol? Do we have any results?"

"Here, yes we do. They told me from Rome that it could be a rune."

"A what?" said Ciro.

"A rune. A letter from an ancient north European alphabet. We'd need to talk to an archeologist, someone who deals with antiquities."

"Sirignano, d'you know any expert antiquarian in these parts?" I asked.

"I don't," said Sirignano, "How about you, Chantecler?"

"Antiquities are your business, I only frequent young women."

"Wise guy. Ciro?"

"Prince, I think I got an idea to give a hand to Signor Malaparte. I'd have to go to Naples early tomorrow and get help from a couple of guys. If you'll let me, that is."

"Sure I'll let you," said Sirignano.

"Then, if you don't need me, I'll be off," said Ciro, and saluting us with all due deference, he withdrew. Chantecler left us too, not without first giving me a brotherly embrace.

"We're doing all we can for you. But take care, and always stay on the lookout for idiots."

"So what are you doing here?" sniggered Sirignano.

"Go to Hell, Prince. See you, Malaparte," said Chantecler, moving off into the dark. So now we were three, with Febo making up a foursome.

"Follow Ciro's example, dear Tamburi," I said, "he never whines, never complains, he's always ready for action."

"I'd be like him, Signor Malaparte, if I got paid regularly."

"If I paid you on time, you'd be away from the office every other day."

"But that's what the contract says."

"Exactly. It's a lousy contract. Now let's go.

Sirignano gave me the razor and shaving soap I'd asked him for the day before.

"Thanks, Prince, but I've changed my mind. Tonight I'm sleeping at your place, at the Villa Lysis. Is all quiet?"

"I think the timing's safe. This afternoon, I invited a group of people from Rome and Naples for drinks at my place, including some friends who've excellent connections with the police and Interior Ministry. I let them wander all around the villa, just to show that I've no secrets. By the way, they'd all heard of your failed arrest. We joked about that quite a bit. I'd say that, if they catch you, there'll be quite a big noise in the papers. For the time being, there's no news out. They'll all be waiting for the big bang. They must have had orders from Rome."

"That's what I was afraid of. All they want is to report I've confessed to the crime, regardless of whether that's true or not. That way all my friends will drop me, even outside Italy. Let's get a move on, tonight I want to sleep instead of schlepping around. Tomorrow we'll be up at dawn, even before the sun comes up. And let's hope the cops sleep heavily."

Febo's head jerked from the one to the other of us, trying desperately to follow our conversation. He had the same ingenuous optimism as I did when, on sleepless nights I'd sit up on the terrace of House like Me patiently following for hours and hours his dialogue with distant dogs, and in the end I was convinced I could understand the messages he'd sent with his never-changing barking.

When we got close to Villa Lysis, Febò growled quietly. Sirignano stopped sharply: someone was waiting for us in front of the gate.

"Wait for me here," he said, gesturing that we should stay hidden.

He returned a few minutes later, both reassured and excited.

"We'd forgotten the boy."

"What boy?"

"The one we sent to check on the Sturmbannführer's movements. We all kept our rendezvous, but the boy kept tailing his man."

And here's what had happened: while Ciro and Tamburi were getting into the Sturmbannführer's room at the Quisisana, the SS major was drinking beer with a group of Germans on the town square. But the fun didn't last long: Eddie von Bismarck came to his table.

"Mona Williams' homosexual official lover," I explained to Tamburi, who didn't know who this was. "He's the grandson of the famous Chancellor Bismarck, the Iron Chancellor, who ruled Germany for so many years. He doesn't like Nazism, and he doesn't hide it, despite the fact that his brother works for the German diplomatic service in Italy."

Eddie was on his way to look for the Sturmbannführer at the Quisisana, and we were very lucky that he'd found him in the square. Otherwise he'd have met Chantecler or Sirignano when he got to the Quisisana, just when they were playing charades with the concierge, and that would have gotten them into difficulties.

Eddie von Bismarck had invited the SS officer to follow him: once they'd bid farewell to the group of Germans at the café, the two had moved off rapidly on foot.

"Where did they go?"

"To the Villa Mura, the villa of Philipp von Hessen and Mafalda of Savoy. And there must have been a row there, because the windows were open and at one point, shouting could be heard from the road. Of course our lad couldn't understand a thing, because the argument was in German. He waited quite a while, maybe half an hour, until the Sturmbannführer came back out. But this time he didn't go straight back to the Quisisana. He wandered around for a while, looking rather lost, as though he'd had one drink too many. As soon as he got back to the hotel, our informer came here to report to me at Villa Lysis. I paid him well, he'd done a good job."

"At the Quisisana the Sturmbannführer won't have been exactly happy," Tamburi remarked. "Ciro stole the little money he had left in the safe, to camouflage our break-in as an ordinary burglary."

My eyelids were weighing down on me like two millstones. I chose one of the servants' rooms to sleep in, far from the front door. If some unwelcome visitor came to the villa during the night, I'd maybe have time to make a break for it through one of the windows.

Fortunately, nothing happened. I soon fell asleep, happy to have a real bed under my back. After struggling, as ever, with the thousand fears of every fugitive, my last thoughts before sleeping were of Carmine, to Hell with him, and then of Lucia, and I had peace at last. But not for long.

"Malaparte, wake up."

"How long have I slept?"

"An hour, you've only slept for an hour. The boy who tailed the Sturmbannführer has come back."

"So, what did he want?"

"The Sturmbannführer was found dead at the Quisisana not long ago. Hanged."

"Oh for Heaven's sake," I said, slowly raising myself and sitting on the edge of the bed.

"The hotel manager's doing a cover-up," said Sirignano, "by arrangement with the police. They're telling people it was a heart attack. News mustn't get around that you can commit suicide in the best and biggest luxury hotel in Fascist Capri. Least of all when the suicide is an officer from an allied country who's a witness in a case being brought against one of our writers. What splendid publicity!"

It was an absolute disaster. I'd ardently hoped I could so manage things that the Sturmbannführer would end up in the dock. Anyone who heard how Pam died could only conclude that the murderer must have been him. What use was his dead body? None at all, it was absolutely useless. What's more, with one more dead body, my case would become even more juicy for public opinion: "EX-LOVE RIVAL OF MURDER SUSPECT FOUND DEAD". *La dracu* that coward Helmut Aichinger, I thought, *la dracu* him and his fears. I should have known it would end up like this when I saw him shoot poor Santoni at Bligny, firing at that poor cadaver with his guts spilling out on the ground. A guy who shoots corpses can only end up committing suicide, I thought.

"I'm beginning to understand something," I said to Sirignano.

"To understand what, Malaparte? It all seems very obscure to me."

I lay down again, with a very perplexed Sirignano looking on, and fell asleep at once.

Sleep didn't last long, maybe a couple of hours. I'd been wrong to confess to Sirignano, and to myself, that I was beginning to understand something. In my half-sleep the sentence kept repeating like a hiccup, and I just couldn't stop it. God, how I wanted to see Lucia. I needed someone to caress my head, to hold that sore head gently in her arms. I felt I was on the point of developing a dreadful headache, like those that split soldiers' heads at Saarburg. I felt myself suffocating; I just couldn't face a headache, I must come up for air.

I dressed in total darkness and wandered like a sleepwalker through the rooms of Villa Lysis, with its enormous neoclassical reception rooms full of Corinthian stucco and Greco-Roman motifs – all crap for the tourists.

I wrote a note for Tamburi, with a series of tasks for the next day. I left it next to his bed, then entered the round room where Count Fersen entertained his young male prostitutes and his favorite, the wonderfully handsome Nino Cesarini, inhaling opium from the narghile and sprinkling cocaine in champagne glasses. In that very room with its Arab motifs, so they said, Fersen had committed suicide by dropping five grams of coca in his glass, a dose to kill an elephant. Capri's a wonderful island, I thought.

I needed air. I went down the great stairway with its wrought iron balustrade replete with erect penises and, I don't even know how, I found myself at once in the garden.

The park of Villa Lysis, crowns Capri's most spectacular and dizzy heights and dominates the entire island, Mount Solaro and the Bay of

Naples. In all that immense landscape the only things visible were points of light from the few houses where someone was still awake.

I was on my feet, I wasn't asleep but I was not awake either. Villa Lysis is Greek, it is an excessive, vulgar, ingenuous and perhaps successful allusion to Greek architecture, or to the architecture which the symbolist poets and secondhand decadents like Fersen, with their black masses, their metaphysical witches' brews and their mercenary perversions, thought of as Greek. But there really *was* something Greek in the air, something that tasted of Euripides, and the language of Homer and Pindar, and that was what wouldn't let me sleep. I tried to think of Lucia and the way she stroked my hair, but I couldn't; the mute cold choir of my women had returned, that icy chorus from Greek tragedy in which Pam's voice stood out from all the others and said: now you're beginning to understand something of what's happening to you, so come to me, come to the Truth, console me and come and die with me, I beg of you, Malaparte.

Human Meat

I left the Villa Lysis well before sunrise, when no one, not even the cops, would be around setting traps for me. I had an appointment I must keep on time. This meant a long walk; the Faro was at the tip of the most remote tongue of land in Capri, at the opposite end from the Villa Lysis: a wild and solitary rocky cape on which stood the island's only lighthouse.

The road from Anacapri to the lighthouse winds lazily in a series of soft descending curves amidst rows of trees and a rustic landscape of cultivated fields, until it comes gently to an end among the rocks at the Faro. As I walked in the early dawn, I was enveloped in the blue diamond of the Capri sky. The road to the Faro ran downhill, the cobalt plane of the sea drew ever nearer and seemed to hold out a promise that I'd end up walking miraculously on the waters.

Just as I'd hoped, on the road I met no one; but sooner or later they'd get me, I thought, so *la dracu* caution, *la dracu* thinking all the time of all possible contingencies, the Sturmbannführer was dead and

amazon.com

SGk90DsZFT

Your order of August 15, 2023 (Order ID 111-8786808-7021018)

Qty.	Item	Item Price	Total
1	**Death like Me (MALAPARTE)** SORTI, MONALDI --- Paperback **1790261775** 1790261775 9781790261772	$17.99	$17.99
This shipment completes your order.	Subtotal Shipping & Handling Tax Collected Order Total Paid via credit/debit		$17.99 $11.17 $1.17 $30.33 $30.33

Return or replace your item
Visit Amazon.com/returns

0/Gk90DsZFT/ 1 of 1 //LGB5-DAY/std-intl-us-eur/0/0817-02:30/0815-22:23   SmartPac

I was the one who'd end up on trial for Pam's death, not him. Unless I could find Carmine, they'd stick me in a cell and throw the key into the deep blue sea, that was for sure. I needed help, so in the end I'd turned to someone who could give it.

Already two days before I'd gotten Tamburi to contact an old friend of mine in Rome, the only one I was quite sure would not disappoint me. He'd decided to come to Capri to meet me, despite the intricate and dangerous circumstances. He'd arranged everything by 'phone with Tamburi, and in order to meet me far from indiscreet eyes he had – typically – found an intelligent and original solution. It was from details like this that one could recognize the man; he was a champion, a man destined to make the best of all that fate brought him, and it was no accident that he bore the prophetic name Percy Winner.

Winner had worked for Associated Press, for the *New York Evening Post* and for the International News Service of the Hearst group, but war was drawing near and he was turning into something else, something he could not say.

He was the only American male in this story, but he'd prove decisive, driven by that can-do spirit every American male shows once he's made up his mind to do something, damn it! I love the Americans. I love the Americans because, every single thing they do, whether it's bad or good, they do seriously, they put their heart and soul into it, with all the honesty and goodwill of which they're capable. I love the Americans because they sincerely see themselves as gentlemen. I love the Americans because they regard all other peoples – some more, some less – as perverted or crooked, yet they feel it's their duty to re-educate them, even if that sometimes means strong-arming them. I love the Americans because they despise cowards, dime-store intellectuals, guys full of complexes and those who are ashamed of pissing in company. And they aren't like this because it suits them (on the contrary, it brings them heavy labor and no end of trouble), but because they really believe in what they're doing with all their heart, with that incredible purity of heart only Americans have.

I could already imagine how Winner would greet me: "Remember our walks in Rome, Malaparte?" And I'd answer: "Sure, I remember, Winner, and how…"

For years we'd met once a week in Rome at the Caffè Aragno. We'd sit in the open and drink an *Americano* — Cinzano with seltzer, bitters and lemon peel — and then we'd make our way to the Spanish Steps, and from there we'd take long walks, talking of Fascism, of Italy, of so many things. He adored gossip about Mussolini, his phobias and his ridiculous fears. It was I who revealed to him that the Duce suffered from stomach trouble and that for a year he'd eaten nothing but milk and crispbread, and how he couldn't keep still in a chair for two minutes and was as superstitious as a gypsy woman, but also, his relations with the Fascist hierarchs, with the King, with the other European leaders, all of which things Winner had often written, arousing the Duce's wrath.

Winner always wanted first-hand information, but did not always publish it. There were so many things he kept for himself, or for other persons whose names he never mentioned – also because I never asked him. It was a game in which each of us gave and received without asking questions, knowing instinctively what would please the other. I loved it when Winner talked to me about America, about how they live, love and die in America, and then he'd tell me many old tales from the glorious days of President Harding, about American oil, about Sinclair Oil, about the oil with which Matteotti's body was stuffed.

It was almost nine and the sun was beginning to beat down hard on the rocks of the Faro. As ever, Winner was absolutely punctual. Ah, if only all men were like Ciro, Sirignano and Winner! The world would run like clockwork, even boredom and sadness would sail gaily like yachts, or at least like the little fishing smack that was now approaching the Faro point. Winner had opted for the most discreet way of coming to see me in Capri, by not setting foot in port. He'd hired a fishing boat and come to take me on board at the Faro. With one hand I waved to the crew while the little boat approached the rocks, and they waved back. On board I could pick out Winner's mustachioed features in the distance, his bald head, his white shirt, his philosophical pipe. Dear Winner, I'd known him for fourteen years, but he'd returned to Rome only recently; for almost nine years the regime had barred him from Italy because of some articles he'd published in America that were anything but soft on Fascism.

A quarter of an hour later a small boat had taken me aboard the fishing vessel, which was drawing away from Faro point and taking us out to sea, towards freedom. From the fishing boat, Capri looked now like a great whale floating on its belly and slothfully showing its fat, flaccid flesh. The moment I boarded, Winner and I embraced like brothers.

"Well then, Malaparte, what can I do for you?"

"Plenty of things, dear Winner, plenty."

"You may be a great writer, but you're always getting into the shit."

"We writers are made for getting into the shit."

"It's dangerous to be a writer in Europe. It's not like it is for us in America. In your country the authorities crush you."

"No, it's not like that," I said. "Someone's gotten me into trouble, that's for sure. But Mussolini's been in power for over fifteen years and I'm still here. Those in power are scared of us writers. We're outsiders, we stand above and beyond power."

Winner needed less than three minutes to size up the gravity of my situation. He listened gravely and courteously to what had happened to Pam, the Sturmbannführer's suicide, my trials as a fugitive writer and our adventures with Tamburi, Sirignano and Ciro. He laughed heartily at the confused mystery of Gorky's revolutionary school of Capri, the Fabian Society, the Nazi occultists, Munthe and Goering.

"Why don't you make a break for it abroad? You've friends in France, in England and so many places."

"No, Winner. The OVRA would catch me. Besides, I couldn't stand life as a fugitive. Injustice gets me in a rage. I'd end up sick if I had to live on the run."

"I can understand your rage," said Winner, "for example Munthe made a fool of you. But you were wrong to humiliate him in his own home. That was not the action of a gentleman."

We sat barefoot on the deck of the fishing boat, with our shirts unbuttoned and our pants rolled up on our shins, like vacationers. The day was fine, the group of fishermen worked silently alongside us, checking on the nets, going below then re-emerging, and piling up wooden cases. They asked no questions, their eyes didn't even touch on us. For mysterious reasons, Winner seemed to have a long-standing familiarity with those fishermen, they knew how to behave. Had he perhaps used them on other occasions? I didn't ask him, that would have broken the rules of the game. They served us two dishes of squills and a fine *fritto misto* of calamari and prawns, freshly cooked in the fishing boat's tiny galley. They also produced a bottle of white Amalfi wine, two glasses and even a pair of napkins. For ages I'd not felt so coddled, safe and free from worry. I felt the muscles of my neck relax and become as soft as dough.

"It's in your honor, Malaparte," said Winner smiling and handing me the bottle of white wine together with a corkscrew, "and enjoy it – you need to relax!"

I trusted Winner. Sometimes I'd passed him the proofs of my novels, to get his opinion. While I was opening the bottle, he smoothed his moustache, with a discreet but unmistakeable gesture. That delightful moustache was Winner's very soul, that of an amiable upper class New York gentleman of the class of 1899 who'd studied at Columbia University and the Sorbonne, a masterly journalist, expelled from Italy for nine years for having published a not-too-amenable portrait of Mussolini, the juicier details of which had in fact been dictated by me. Winner was the best American patriot that America, the splendid, brave America of those days, could ever have bestowed on Europe. From Savile Row he'd order only genuine Scholte coats, cut from the softest wools, while concealing his baldness with splendid grey Homburg hats no less distinguished than those worn by Edward VII. At table, he'd not drink the best Champagne if the year was not the right one, and in conversation, to put the person with whom he was talking at ease, he'd even descend to quoting *The Citadel* or *The Grapes of Wrath*; but with me he'd spend hours discussing discutere Mallarmé, Joyce, Max Jacob or Apollinaire, while giving me precious advice for the translation of the passages from *Finnegan's Wake* which I was editing for *Prospettive* during quiet periods, between one arrest and the next. Way back at Columbia University, Winner was buddies with refined spirits like Kenneth Burke and Matthew Josephson, big names at the time, though one day they'll mean nothing to anyone: the sort of Americans who are happy to be exiled to Europe and who'll die of boredom if you don't quote Nietzsche, Thomas Mann, Rimbaud or Marx every five minutes.

I trusted Winner. Before bringing the wine to his lips, he tipped his glass towards me in a benevolent gesture. I was a fugitive, a suspected murderer teetering on the edge of ruin, but Winner made me feel like an Indian Maharajah. That was his secret art, his enigmatic *savoir vivre*. His smile was open, frank and disarming. His lips overflowed with things wise, sincere and loyal, and when they smiled it seemed the sun was rising. When we'd stroll together through Rome, along the alleyways off Via del Corso, women's heads would turn more for him than for me, above all when he smiled. Winner's smile was extraordinary; it was contagious, luminous, and so generous.

I still could not have imagined that my dear, generous Winner was soon to become a big noise in the Psychological Warfare Section of the Allied armies in North Africa and later, head of the Office of War Information for Europe: duties, co-ordinating military espionage throughout the continent, that could only be placed in the hands of someone like Winner, so open, so loyal and so generous.

There was just one thing Percy Winner denied the world: his eyes. He always kept them hidden behind sunglasses. Those dark glasses were his only defense, the only barrier between Winner and the world. He wore them even in the evening and on rainy days. Sometimes it was hard to remember whether I'd ever seen his eyes or whether I knew their shape, color or expression; I was tempted to ask him why he didn't take them off, but then, no, I didn't dare. He was never separated from his sunglasses, dear Winner. But I trusted him.

While the fishing smack forged steadily ahead, we drank toast after toast, nibbling away at squills and eating that pan-fried seafood, as fragrant as the roses in Mona Williams' garden, with our hands. The wind was laughing and ruffling our hair, sticking its fingers down our shirts and getting between our toes. I'd almost forgotten what I was there for. Meanwhile, we rounded the Faraglioni and passed in front of Cape Massullo. I pointed out House like Me to Winner.

"That's your house?"

"Yes, that's it."

"It's beautiful, I like it. One day I'll come and visit you there, when you've finished it. After the war."

"D'you promise me?"

"I promise."

We were a long way from House like Me, yet I seemed to glimpse a movement behind my study window, perhaps a shadow. But no, I guess I was mistaken.

"Why did you say I wasn't a gentleman with Munthe?" I asked. "After all, I had to teach him a lesson. I had to make sure people treat me with respect."

"Oh, of course. It's just that sometimes I'm thinking in different terms from yours. That's not your fault," said Winner.

I understood that he meant to tell me something. He left off speaking Italian, his delicious Italian full of bright Yankee stripes, and continued in English so as to be sure that none of the fishermen on board would understand more than they ought to.

"Munthe's a real bon viveur. A gentleman. The British think the world of him."

I really liked Winner's way of expressing some things. He'd found such an elegant, discreet way of getting it across to me that Axel Munthe was an British spy working for MI6, something of which neither Goering nor Philipp von Hessen, with whom Munthe had conducted lengthy negotiations about the Villa San Michele, could have had the least idea. Only Winner, among all my acquaintances, was capable of using such an elegant, discreet and appropriate forms of words.

I trusted Winner. I couldn't imagine that after the war he'd betray me and that he'd never come to see me at House like Me, nor that he'd return to America where he'd publish a novel that revealed everything about us and our secret relationship, because by then I no long served any useful purpose. Those were the hard rules of war. Once a network of confidants is no longer of any use, you blow it.

"The problem's always the same," he said, "you need to understand who you're dealing with. You ran into this with Munthe. That's why you had so much trouble getting old Axel to sing. He'd been trained by our friends in MI6 to resist far worse. It will have suited him fine, I thought, to pretend he was loyal to the OVRA, telling them without too many scruples that he'd surprised me in Anacapri with Pam.

"Dear Malaparte, Munthe conducted the negotiations with Goering and quite deliberately let them drag out. It was an interesting situation, and it provided him with plenty of useful information. But he didn't want to talk of that with you because he feared you might take some unfortunate initiative. For example, that you might write about it in a newspaper. Or in one of your books. You must understand him."

"So what was I to do? I don't understand what you're getting at."

"I'm just trying to help you. I repeat, you must always know who you're dealing with. Commendatore Freddi, the American actors' friend and his journalist buddies Tavolato and Da Zara, all work for Manzi, the Naples police chief."

Winner did not spell this out, but since these persons were all civilians, apart from Questore Manzi, it was clear that they worked for the OVRA. That's why I had seen them all together, first at the Villa Discopoli, then at Villa Ferraro. That's who was keeping an eye on me in Capri.

"But there are others like them in the area," he added. "We know there are two of them. And I'd like to know who they are. All this information will be useful to us when we land in Europe."

"If I can, I'll give you a hand," I said.

"We know we can count on you," he said.

It was always like that, when each of our confidential meetings was coming to a close, Winner would pass from "I" to "we".

Winner would say "we" and I didn't ask "we, who?" because I knew he meant "we in America" or "we, the US embassy in Italy", "we the world's liberators", "we who'll save your rotten Europe from itself".

"So you Americans will land in Europe. You're speaking of the war?"

"Yes, the war. The war that's on the point of breaking out in Europe. We've spoken of that so many times, haven't we? Sooner or later, we Americans will have to join in. We'll have to fight against you. And we'll have to win. For your own good. To free you from your leaders, from Mussolini and Hitler."

"You're right, Winner. You'll have to free us from ourselves. D'you know who'll win the war?"

"The stronger side will win."

"No, victory won't go to the strongest. The winners will be the dead and the whores."

"Then your dead too will win."

"No. Our dead will be like the dead in the Great War, in 1918. Our dead will be ragged, dirty and miserable. Your dead, the dead you'll bring back to America with your ships and aircraft, will be rich, happy, free dead. And that's the difference between Italy and America, between our rotten Europe and America, between our enslaved Europe and free and happy America."

"Sorry, Malaparte. Someone has to win this war."

"True. Someone has to win the war, when all's said and done. But you won't win it. The dead and the whores will win."

"So what is it you're trying to get at?" said Winner, frowning a little.

In a flash of inexplicable precognition I saw a series of hutments in the middle of a high fence, and piles of naked shrivelled corpses, SS soldiers barking orders [in German], and long columns of emaciated human beings marked with a yellow star, files of human fantoms, men who were no longer men, entering cells where in deference to the aberrations of a racial pseudo-religion, Satanic experimenters would massacre their flesh, their eyes, their hearts, even the grey tortuous mass of their brains. That is what I meant, I thought, it was all a matter of meat, a matter of human meat.

"Malaparte, what do you mean?"

Winner's fishing smack sailed on its placid way, a seagull screamed a strident greeting, but I remained in a state of absorption, in which I was borne to the coast right opposite Capri: to Naples, the future postwar Naples, Naples at last liberated by the Americans, pocked with bomb craters, plundered, burnt, raped, that Naples with its revolting stench of death in which a filthy, mass of famished women and boys would be free at last to prostitute themselves for a crust of bread, where in improvised lupanars among the ruins and cadavers, in schools, offices and latrines, raven-haired Neapolitan girls, their hair too dark, their skin too dark, waited holding in one hand tiny blonde wigs with an elastic and a hole in the middle: these had been made to please their new masters. The wigs with a hole had been invented for the benefit of fair, pink-skinned Australian, Canadian, English, Scottish and New Zealand soldiers; they were for their pleasure as victors, to rid them of the inconvenience of skin that was too dark, hair that was too dark, and they wore those fine wigs between their legs. This too was all about the same thing, human meat.

I shook my head, I couldn't understand those all-too-premature visions, those images of death and aberration. While they were disappearing, a familiar voice sneaked in: come and die with me, Malaparte, now you've seen where I and the Sturmbannführer are, and remember that I died for you; it's your fault I died.

"C'm on, Malaparte, what do you mean?" Winner repeated, growing impatient.

"It's all about human meat."

"What?"

"Oh, sorry," I said, "forget what I was just saying. I was thinking of how to solve my problem."

"OK. Then let's forget the war. Let's deal with Eddie von Bismarck and his friend Phli," said Winner. "Because that's where the problem lies. And here too, as with Munthe, you need to understand who you're dealing with."

And he explained to me how to go about it.

The Traveling Companion

The day on board Winner's fishing boat had renewed my spirits. I was bronzed, rested, even optimistic. I'd had my fill of brilliant conversation, as ever with Winner, and in the end I no longer felt myself hunted. When a coastguard launch drew up alongside the fishing smack, I'd had to hide in a galley closet, but the officials didn't even ask to come aboard; they just stayed near the boat and kept it under observation, then went their way.

I showed the crew where I wanted to land. Winner and I embraced in farewell.

"So, d'you promise that one day you'll come and see me at House like Me?"

"Sure, I promise."

"'Bye, Winner".

"Goodbye, Malaparte. You'll see, it will all work out."

By now it was evening. We were at Cala del Rio, a little cove on the Anacapri coast, enclosed between high rocky walls, so much so that it was almost impossible to see into it. As planned, a shadow was waiting for me among the rocks: Ciro had carried out the orders I'd passed on through Sirignano.

As soon as the fishing boat had gone, Ciro tugged at my shirt. There was a little fishing boat at the end of the Cala del Rio.

"Signor Malaparte, we gotta get a move on," said Ciro. "I want you to meet the traveling companion I brought you from Naples. We need to do our talking fast, I gotta take him back as soon as possible."

"OK, let's go and see this traveling companion of yours."

We boarded the boat. We were met by two youngsters, smart young Camorra recruits, who hardly deigned to glance at me, while I did likewise (sometimes it's better to pretend you've neither seen nor met people). Followed by Ciro, I descended the steps and lowered myself into the half-covered cockpit. The traveling companion was trussed up, blindfolded, gagged and lying on the ground. He'll have been well over fifty, and in that state I felt really sorry for him.

"You jus' can't imagine how much trouble it was calming him down, Signore," said Ciro. "I wanted to treat him like a gennelman, but then he starts talking of goin' to the cops, an' it gets worse – articles in the papers – so I just had to fix him up. You know me, Signore: newsmen give me a fit, if I could I'd drown 'em all in sulfuric acid. Now he's fine, except at the start of the trip he wet himself a bit."

The hostage's pants did indeed smell rather of urine.

"Good Lord, Ciro, did you really have to bring him all the way here?" I whispered in the Camorrista's ear. "And are you quite sure he doesn't know where you've brought him?"

"Couldn't be more sure, Signore. He thinks we've brought him to Posillipo, and we're still on the coast. If we're quick, in three or four hours he'll be back in his bed and he'll think he just had a bad dream, that I guarantee ya."

Ciro did nothing by half measures. We'd asked him to find someone who knew Oriental languages and he'd not only picked the right person, but he'd even kidnapped him and brought him fast by sea to Capri. The nice Camorra guy had the same wild enthusiasm as some dogs that risk smashing themselves to bits in a ravine to fetch the stick thrown by their master. But he did know just where to find information: thanks to the Camorra's tomtom he'd selected no less than Amedeo Maiuri, Professor Emeritus of Greek and Roman antiquities at the University of Naples, raised to that prestigious chair solely on the basis of his remarkable reputation. He'd been the hero of innumerable digs and explorations at Rhodes, Crete, in the Dodecanese, but also Pompeii, Herculaneum and Capri. That was the disadvantage of his choice: Maiuri was famous in the area, he even had a house in Capri, so the abduction had better not last too long or it would set off serious enquiries and be far too risky for us. The abduction had to look like an attempted robbery; fortunately, just when Ciro and some of his acolytes bound and gagged the archeologist, he had with him a considerable sum of money, enough to justify the criminal undertaking at least in part, while it was really all about something quite different.

"We asked you to find a specialist in ancient languages, not to kidnap him," I said to him.

"Sorry Signore, but if I'd asked him to come here to Capri, d'ya really think he'd have come?"

"Maybe yes, maybe no. That was the trouble with this job."

"Right. But in any case he wouldn't have come at once. Instead, with a little friendly persuasion, so to speak, we got results pronto. S'cuse me, Signore, I like things quick an' done right."

For all his brutality, Ciro was right. We removed Maiuri's blindfold and the professor gave a start.

"C'mon, Prof," said Ciro, "take a good look here."

Providing a little light with a flashlight, Ciro shoved a piece of paper with the strange symbol on Madame Carmen's visiting card and on the Sturmbannführer's saber under the poor man's eyes.

Poor Maiuri was both stunned and terrorized. The piece of paper was pushed under his nose. He tried to look upwards towards us but the flashlight blinded him and a hard smack made him bend downwards.

"Eh no! Jus' ya look at the drawing, Prof," warned Ciro, "an' s'plain to us what it means."

"But what do you want of me?" whined the learned archeologist Maiuri, incredulous at being consulted about a scribble.

"C'mon, c'mon, what is it? A magic symbol?"

"Please, don't hurt me again."

He was trussed up like a salami and he couldn't move. His arms and his shoulders must have been hurting a lot, judging by how his hands were tied tightly behind his back. Maiuri was still scared that the question about the mysterious drawing might just be the pretext for some torture. Only after hesitating for a long time did he decide to answer.

"It's a rune. A character, or rather a symbol of the ancient Nordic peoples."

"And what does it mean?" asked Ciro.

"It's a symbol of death. They put it on tombs. Have you never seen it?"

"Prof, you're the expert here. Where would we have seen it?"

At that moment the archeologist became convinced that the symbol they were showing him, the rune, really was of interest to his abductors. He seemed relieved.

"For instance, the SS put it on their uniforms. And on their arms."

"On their swords, too?"

"I think so, on their swords, too."

"And where do these runes come from?"

"I don't want to say something silly. I'm not a specialist in Nordic languages, My field is Greco-Latin culture."

"Keep talkin' anyway, keep talkin', Prof. Don't worry about that."

"God how it hurts, can't you sit me a little straighter?"

Ciro did so. He turned the poor professor's chest a little, which had been resting all on one shoulder.

"As far as I know," he continued, "the runes were codified in an ancient poem, no, a collection of poems, written down for the first time towards the middle of the thirteenth century, I think around 1240 or so, but their origin must surely be far older. It's a series of rhymed sagas on the Vikings, composed in ancient Icelandic. I repeat, that isn't my field, and what I'm telling you is in very summary and perhaps imprecise form."

"Keep talkin', Prof, don't ya worry about that," Ciro repeated.

It was just as well that the lamp was pointed in the middle of Maiuri's face, and he was screwing his eyes up with discomfort. As a precaution, I kept my face well covered behind a shirt, which had been given to me by one or Ciro's two assistants.

"Well, among other things these poems sing of the mysterious origins of the runes, their quality, their meaning, and so on. In Germany, there's a whole series of studies on these runes, in some circles they believe them to have almost magical powers, what nonsense. Of course, I don't mean to speak ill of anyone! But the SS symbol present on their uniforms is also one of these runes, as is their double S that's all spiky, like a Z, which is the symbol of victory, or something of the sort. In Germany they've even built a typewriter with a special key to type the double S using the runic symbol of the SS. If you like, I can draw it for you."

"No, Prof, I can't untie you. But we believe you, we believe you." I had a question but I didn't want Maiuri to hear my voice, in case he might recognize it some day, so I whispered in Ciro's ear, and he repeated:

"What's the name of the ancient poetic cycle written in runes?"

"The title means something like "great grandmother" or "great-great grandmother, and it's easy to remember: *Edda*."

Tomorrow's History

Damn all those occultists, I said to myself half an hour later, as I walked the dark lanes of Anacapri. I'd always despised all things esoteric from the bottom of my heart, and that had been a mistake. If I'd chewed on a little Nazi occultism, I'd have known what runes were, the name Edda would have meant something different to me and I'd have been able to extricate myself rather better from the entanglement I'd gotten myself into. It was logical enough that the rune of Death should be among the Sturmbannführer's papers, together with the name Edda – which therefore had nothing to do with Mussolini's daughter. Yet it was a fact that in Edda's house there was Madame Carmen's visiting card with the rune of Death on it. Edda Ciano did not frequent SS officers or Nazi-style esoteric circles, but she was, like her father, a client of Madame Carmen. Perhaps I should clarify matters with Madame Carmen? Let's hope she's a surly ignorant old witch, I thought, who knows nothing about novels or writers and has never seen a photo of Curzio Malaparte.

By the middle of the night I was at the center of Capri, quite exhausted, in front of Lucia's pensione. Her window was on the ground floor giving onto a little courtyard; I knocked a few times on the window until I heard light footsteps and at last the click of the lock.

Lucia smiled. She was half asleep and had trouble keeping her eyes open.

"Come, Malaparte, if you only knew how I've been waiting for you," she said in a voice heavy with anxiety.

We remained a few minutes entwined on the bed, without doing or saying a thing. How full of warmth and perfume it was, that modest room in an even more modest pensione. I felt safe from everything, even from the Greek chorus of my dead women, their litanies of death and their icy, pungent reproaches.

"Lucia, you and I are half German. But you're more German than I am, I can feel it. And I'm sure you speak good German too, am I right?"

"*Jawohl, mio tesoro*," she nodded, caressing my head.

"But my father didn't teach me a word of it. Lucia, please, speak to me about Hitler."

"And so you came here at the dead of night, embracing me tenderly, just to talk about Hitler?"

We both laughed until we cried, stifling our laughter in the pillows so as not to make a noise. Once we'd gotten over our fit of hilarity, I said to her, wiping my eyes:

"Lucia, this is perfectly serious. What kind of soldier was Hitler?"

"Malaparte, I'm a woman, I don't make war."

"I'm not talking of how Hitler really was. I want to know what he *thought* he was."

"I was only a little girl but... yes, I remember my father talking about him with friends. I think that, for a while, it was in the press too. In the schools there were books praising the Führer's courage in the Great War, the dangers he'd run, his valor. It was all part of the propaganda. But some newspapers wrote that Hitler had always stayed far from the front and he wasn't the hero he wanted people to believe he was, but actually a coward."

"But wasn't Hitler decorated during the war? He got the Iron Cross, second class," I said.

"You're right, that's true. Yet I remember that someone used this word when speaking of him: *Etappensau*. That means "rearguard sow", in other words a soldier who doesn't risk his life on the front but keeps well behind the lines, in safety, while others risk their lives for him. If I remember rightly, my father spoke of a trial, perhaps Hitler sued someone for libel. I remember the name of a paper, *Echo der Woche*. I don't remember quite how the story ended or whether anyone was condemned or not, but surely Hitler came out on top. Why does that interest you?"

"The Sturmbannführer hanged himself."

"Hanged?" said Lucia with a start; "I heard of a German officer who'd died of a heart attack in his room at the Quisisana."

"That's the official version of the hotel and the police. The Sturmbannführer killed himself after a row with the Prince of Hesse and Eddie von Bismarck, over a postcard stolen from Mona Williams' house on the evening when you and I met. A postcard that seems to have had something to do with Hitler. Eddie von Bismarck says it affects the security of the Reich."

Lucia worked free of my embrace and fell silent, with her eyes lost in the void. Perhaps she was wondering how the hell she, with her regular schoolmaam's life, could have ended up in such a mess.

"Malaparte, you're not a man one can marry. They're searching for you by day, you knock smiling at my window so that I expect some good news, but instead everything just gets more and more complicated and absurd. What has Hitler to do with the death of that English girl or with the charges against you?"

"In theory, nothing whatever. But in fact, everything's strangely linked together."

I explained her the riddle of the rune on Madame Carmen's visiting card, identical to that on the Sturmbannführer's saber, and all the connected details, including the name shared by the Duce's daughter and the ancient Icelandic poems that bore the first runes. Obviously, I said nothing about Ciro's break-in to the Sturmbannführer's room or the abduction of Maiuri, the archeologist, because I didn't want to implicate Lucia: it was I who'd inspired Ciro to commit a number of serious crimes.

"The worst news of all," I concluded, "is that Carmine still hasn't emerged from his hiding place."

"I imagine you've some idea of how to get yourself out of this mess," said Lucia.

"I've an idea, but I daren't say it out aloud. I've got to find my way out of this wretched intrigue without having understood what it was all about," I said, rising from the bed.

"Don't go away, stay here with me," said Lucia as I made my way to the window. She took my hand and squeezed it hard.

"How can you ask me that? In the morning I'd end up straight in a cage."

"Then go to Sirignano at the Villa Lysis. You'll be safe there. I imagine you'll already have slept there, am I right?"

"Yes. But it's better to change places every night. That's a ploy that always works."

A sad silence fell between us. If things went wrong, we'd never see each other again.

"Leave me something of yours," I said.

"I'll bet you never ask that of the others," said Lucia, forcing a smile.

"There's always a first time."

She rose and turned on the light. She opened a drawer and took out a silk handkerchief, a lipstick and a little silver box. She colored her lips than pressed them hard onto the handkerchief. The imprint was clear and distinct, a fiery red. She folded the handkerchief, put it in the little box, placed it in the palm of my hand then closed it with a squeeze of her fist.

"Will it stay eternally red?" I joked.

"Till we're through with one another. Once it's faded you'll know it's all over."

Thunder made the window frame rattle. It was a summer storm. The first heavy drop fell at once.

"Lucia, I must go. I can't run the risk of them catching me here. I'll find shelter somewhere."

"Don't be silly, Malaparte. Try to sleep somewhere dry. You can't spend hours and hours under the rain. Go to Villa Lysis."

"I don't know where I'll go, I still have to make my mind up."

I couldn't tell Lucia where I was hiding. She'd not have been able to stand up to a hard interrogation.

I detest farewells. Without wasting time on further chitchat, I opened the window and swung myself up on the sill. Before I dropped to the other side, I waved gaily, pretending I couldn't see her face bathed in tears, pretending I'd not seen that light from Lucia's Italian side, that gentle fantasy Italian women have written on their faces, like a loving look forgotten between half-closed eyelashes.

The downpour had chased everyone back into their houses and the streets had that unmistakable smell of hot wet asphalt, a smell you associate with country outings and running like hell under the lightning. It was raining cats and dogs, I'd need to hurry if I didn't want to get to my destination completely drenched. But I never got as far as the Villa Lysis.

Pulsing stronger and stronger as I drew nearer, I sensed an alarm in the air and there could be no mistake about it. It was a sort of siren that spoke as clearly as a war bulletin. I felt it drawing ever nearer, ever clearer, it was beating rhythmically in my temples. It was Febo.

He was howling with a special tone he rarely used, perhaps because he knew perfectly well it gave me gooseflesh. It was a howl of rage, of anguish, of affliction, a howl that expressed pain in the face of betrayal. I stopped, about-turned and started to run.

What had happened at the Villa Lysis? Perhaps Sirignano and Tamburi had been arrested? The raindrops were falling as heavy as oranges; in Capri it rains little, but when a summer storm breaks out, it's painful. Where was I to go? I'd already been at the Fortino, I could expect an ambush there too, as at the Villa Lysis. The same went for Rulli's house, I didn't feel like tempting fate twice. My salvation had until then been to sleep every night somewhere different, in a place no one knew about. No one would help me; the family that was putting up poor Adolfo Amitrano was mistrustful; without a guarantee from Prince Sirignano they wouldn't let me stay at their place. They'd seen what had happened to Amitrano, they were scared. Even Spadaro wouldn't be particularly keen to put me up without Sirignano's backing. For the time being, I had no other options.

For a moment I sheltered under a little tree, just not to get soaked to the skin. A massive thunderclap made me jump. I was worried for Febo, just as I knew he was for me, but his howl was loud and clear, perhaps he was in the garden, so that he could get away at any time, while Sirignano and Tamburi would surely find it far harder to escape. The rain did not let up; a cave! I thought, that's where I must take shelter. Capri was full of caves; I'd be able to shelter all night, perhaps even to dry my clothes. I knew the grotto under Castiglione hill, the height on which Edda Ciano's villa stood. It would be enough to get to the little green oasis of the gardens of Augustus, then to go down a few turns in the Via Krupp and climb the slope to the right that led through rocks and rare bushes to the mouth of the Castiglione grotto. Yes, the Castiglione would do fine, at its mouth the hollow was very high and would let in the wind and the rain, but it narrowed, once inside. The Cerio family, which also owned the area around it, had built a hut there where I could rest. Yes, that was it, I'd go to the Castiglione grotto.

On the road, I crossed quite a few people, all running towards some hotel, or cramming into the entrances of restaurants or night clubs, watching the black sky vomit all that water, all soaked and almost amused by the novelty of it, so that no one paid any attention to me walking fast in the midst of the deluge. I was like an enormous wet matchstick, the rain had drenched me through and through. Now the storm had calmed down a little, it had become a thick warm drizzle, almost a light shower. The torches at the entrance of the gardens and the big hotels had all been dowsed by the storm and from them spread a smell of burning, their drops of red wax mixed with the silvery drops of the cloudburst: I was reminded of the rain at Bligny and the stink of bodies burnt by flame throwers, the white and red drops that fell to the ground from Santoni's guts and mixed with the rain, that rain which was not only French but Italian, German, American, English – the rain of all the Bligny dead. One fine day I'll free myself of Bligny, I thought, please give me another war fast, I must get away from those memories of Bligny.

To get to the gardens of Augustus, the fine park through which you get to the Via Krupp, I had to pass behind the Quisisana, near the Carthusian Monastery of San Giacomo. Here the wilderness was absolute, there wasn't a soul around, not even tourists who'd lost their way.

I'd always loved the old Charterhouse. A place like that, older than any other building in Capri, brings a dissonant touch of spirituality and medieval mysticism to the island, one that it hardly deserves, worldly and ambitious as it is.

All around, besides a tower and the church, stood buildings with cupola roofs, almost level with the road I was walking along, behind the Quisisana. The fine but dense raindrops made it feel as though I were looking through a glass pane streaked with rain, as in one of those cruel portraits Francis Bacon painted after Velázquez, slashed with vertical lines like the trickling of water and blood.

Suddenly above the cupolas of the Charterhouse, I saw an enormous cat jump, a sort of big feline on two paws, a wild black lynx utterly indifferent to the rain, to the night, to the lightning. I could not believe my eyes. I drew nearer.

Yes, it was an enormous black cat, a human cat that loved death and playing in the dark, leaping on tiptoe from one cupola to the next with superhuman strength, never setting a foot wrong and defying death as only cats can.

"Edda!" I called out.

She turned. From her eyes black streaks of make-up ran down her cheeks. Her evening dress, dripping with rain, was glued to her so that it looked like an old sack. Her shoes were as full of water as two sunken boats. Her hair was plastered against her forehead like a battle headdress, giving her a proud, wild look, the tragic caricature of a war goddess.

"Edda!" I called again.

She seemed to be smiling, but it was an empty, pallid, put-on smile. Her eyes were directed at me but went beyond me, they went straight through me, they did not perceive me.

So it was true what they said in Rome, I thought. It was true that Edda, Countess Ciano, had been seen at night in Capri all alone, leaping without a care on the brink of some ravine, or dangling her legs over the edge of the high cliff at Ventroso Point, in evening dress and perfectly made up, humming popular songs while the wind whipped against her, and she'd return home at dawn, whistling to herself as though nothing had happened, when her three children's nurses, by now desperate, were calling Mussolini in Rome, begging for someone to come and search for the countess, for someone to talk to her and get her to change her lifestyle.

At that very moment Edda started jumping again from one cupola to the next, as though she wanted to offer me a show. She loved making her longest leaps just where the roof came to an end and certain death began. The rain began pelting down again, but it was as though Edda, Countess Ciano, Italy's most lauded wife, did not feel the heavy splash of the raindrops on her shoulders, her neck and her face.

"Edda, it's me!" I called out even louder, but to no effect. Where was her husband, I thought, where was Count Galeazzo Ciano, Foreign Minister of Fascist Italy? Where was her father, Benito Mussolini? Where were her merry partners at poker, where was the Italy that had applauded her marriage and her honeymoon on Capri?

There was no one under the cupolas of the San Giacomo Charterhouse, no one under the rain. They'd all abandoned Edda to her love of death, her secret folly, her tomboy fantasies. They'd let her bite into the fatal apple, and she'd turned into an unhinged whisky- and- poker sozzled Cassandra, foreseeing tomorrow's history, that obscene comedy she called "They'll kill us all", hearing years in advance the overhead rumble of American B-17 engines and the whistle of their magic eggs raining down to flatten our cities, seeing Fascists magicked overnight into antifascists, seeing the lovely Naples brunettes selling their bodies to the victors, with a blonde wig between their legs, and offering our new masters an abasement they themselves hadn't asked for and maybe didn't even want, just like Mussolini (ah, Mussolini!) who'd one day declare war on Russia and America without Hitler's even having asked him to, and maybe without him having even wanted it. They'd all left Edda alone with her visions of her father, the father she feared, loved and hated, the vision of her father having her husband shot, the vision of herself at the end of the war, left without a cent to her name, without so much as a hair left on a head that had known too much pain, in Capri begging Chantecler for one last sad night of love. It wasn't right, I thought, that she should have been allowed to know all this, and to live through it all before it even happened.

"Edda!"

She had stopped. She held an arm out in front of her and stared at the raindrops striking the palm of her hand and splattering into a thousand droplets. Perhaps she'd stop playing cat-on-the-roof, I said to myself, but at that very moment she gave a start and disappeared from view.

I started running, turned back then turned around, entered a few alleys and found myself at length at the entrance of the Charterhouse. A small monastic community lived there, Canons Regular of the Lateran, but the Charterhouse was far too big for them and, despite restoration work, it just kept on falling to pieces. The entrance was a great wooden door in a very bad state of repair; I pushed vigorously and went in, crossed one or perhaps two spaces – I don't recall properly – and found myself at length in the middle of the great cloister of the Charterhouse. It was a vast quadrangle, delimited by a colonnade supporting the portico. It was still raining. The darkness was dense and heavy. I felt that Edda was near, she was not calling me but she wanted my help.

The cloister was all muddy. The soil with which neglect had covered the paving had turned now into a layer of dark slime in which every footstep left a sharp imprint like a bad memory.

"Edda!" I called again, once, twice, three times, but this time under my breath. What would the Canons Regular of the Lateran think, I wondered with a shadow of amusement, if they found the Duce's daughter wandering within their walls like a madwoman?

"Edda, where are you?" I cried out.

Suddenly from behind a hand touched my shoulder.

"Edda, you're trying to scare me to death!" I said, with my heart beating like a drum. I turned.

"Good evening. I am Madame Carmen, a friend of Countess Ciano. To whom have I the honor?"

The Amazons

Madame Carmen was wrapped in a black cloak that covered even her head.

"Kurt Suckert, I too am a friend of the Countess. How do you do?"

"A friend of the Countess? That's curious, Edda never mentioned you to me."

"Edda hasn't mentioned you to me either."

"On what occasions do you frequent her?"

"When she's not dancing on the rooftops."

I looked more closely at the lady. You couldn't tell her age, perhaps around forty-five, with a high pale forehead and permed hair pulled back and kept in order with a curling iron. Her eyes were grey and glassy, wide open but distant, possessed, a true priestess. Her cheeks were white and covered with a thick coating of powder, her neck, long and rigid. The overall effect was at once majestic and disturbing, the very portrait of a cartomancer who knows how to play her role.

"Ah, if only you knew how I'd looked for you," I said.

"Really? And how come?"

"I've heard so much about you. Oh yes, so much. And it's really a surprise to find you here now," I said, continuing to look all around me for Edda.

"I and Edda came here after spending the evening at my house," said Madame Carmen. "The Countess wanted to take a little walk," she added, as though I might believe her.

"Where's she gotten to?" I said. "If she falls down from up there, it's goodbye to our Contessa".

"Don't let that worry you, Edda's sometimes like that. She's an inconstant character. I'm here to protect her."

I turned my back on Madame Carmen and walked towards the portico, still calling Edda. Meanwhile, Madame Carmen remained in her place like a statue in the middle of the cloister. There she stood, draped in her black cloak, as upright and immobile as a pole. I understood that the gossip about Edda and Carmen was true, and all that I'd suspected was true, as well as all that Winner had confided to me while we tucked joyfully into the *fritto misto* washed down with Amalfi wine. Thank you, Winner, it's good to have a friend one can trust.

"Edda, where are you?"

"Don't scare her, Suckert. You mustn't disturb her, she's a big-hearted woman and very sensitive," said Madame Carmen. She'd spoken in a low voice, but in the desert of the great cloister, despite the persistent rain, every sound could be heard distinctly, as within a glass bell jar. By now I could imagine the speeches with which that witch kept her client under control: you have a heart of gold and everyone takes advantage of you, but you'll see, I shall defend you.

I kept running around the cloisters calling Edda in vain. A door opened a crack. A faint light shone from within. I approached. Behind the narrow opening stood an aged friar with a long beard wearing a white cassock.

"Father, it's an emergency, call someone. The Countess Ciano is here in the cloister."

"It's no emergency. She often comes here to do her crazy thing, and if we say anything she threatens to have us arrested," the friar answered before slamming the door in my face.

At that moment I at last heard her voice:

"I told you to go away, to go to your American friends."

She was a few paces from me and she was smiling at me. Her face was devastated by make-up; long black streaks of rain and mascara ran down her cheeks to under her chin. She too looked like an Amazon, a warrior from the forests of the Amazon, her face striped as in the strange disguises worn by some head hunters, those indigo and red marks they make on their cheeks to terrify the enemy, or wild beasts. Water ran in rivulets from the hem of her dress to the ancient flagstones of the Charterhouse.

That water, I see it now, was extraordinarily like the sweat I was to see three years later dripping from Himmler's pink, flaccid chest, neck and limbs in a Finnish sauna, while his SS beat his back and shoulders with birch sprigs, just an instant before the SS Reichsführer opened a little wooden door and rushed out into the snow to hurl himself into an icy stream. Only then, in that sauna on the outskirts of Rovaniemi, did I realize that there was something monstrously in common between those bodies, the pink, naked, vaguely feminine body of Heinrich Himmler and Edda Ciano's angular body, wrapped in a soaking, vaguely masculine suit. The luminous madness of the SS Reichsführer, the luminous madness of Nazism, was the same monstrosity as the dark madness of Countess Ciano and her father.

"For heaven's sake, Edda, just look at the state you're in," I said to her, trying to caress her face, but she drew sharply away from my hand.

Madame Carmen still did not approach. She had remained immobile in the middle of the cloister, waiting.

"Edda, the Sturmbannführer has hanged himself."

"So what?" she replied.

"It matters to me. Capri is small, they'll soon find me and put me on trial. You knew the Sturmbannführer, didn't you?"

She took out a cigarette and put it in her mouth. It was completely soaked, the paper was on the point of tearing. She drew a sailor's lighter from a pocket, brought the flame close to the cigarette, returned the lighter to her pocket and began to drag hard on the cigarette and to turn it in her hand, as though it were lit.

"The Sturmbannführer? Never seen him in all my life," she replied.

"Liar."

She smiled, looking me fixedly in the eyes, then opened the silver box with her drenched cigarettes and offered one to me. The cigarette was still between her lips and she even screwed up her eyes as though the smoke might get in them. I declined, pushing the box roughly away, and two or three cigarettes fell to the ground but Edda retained her composure.

"So why was this on the Sturmbannführer's ceremonial saber?" I asked.

I took out Madame Carmen's visiting card and showed her the other side of it, the one with the rune drawn on it.

"It comes from your house. It was on a marble side table, next to the switch controlling the shutters," I added.

Edda took the card delicately in her hand, turned it over and returned it to me. Then she started laughing, quietly at first, then louder and louder.

"The OVRA boss for this zone is Questore Manzi," I said. "His assistants are Freddi, Tavolato and De Zara. You knew that, didn't you?"

Edda kept on laughing, she was looking at me with a shade of compassion in her eyes, and laughing.

"You could have spoken directly with them," I went on, "without having to go to your father or your husband. You could have stopped them. You could have saved me when the investigations were just beginning. Now it's too late, there's already an arrest warrant out for me. Why didn't you help me, Edda?".

But Edda did not answer, she just kept laughing and laughing, with her damp cigarette in her mouth, she was shaken by tremors of hilarity and she just couldn't stop.

I grabbed a forearm and squeezed it. "Who are the other two OVRA agents that have been keeping an eye on me in the last few days?" I said, shaking her hard, but Edda kept on laughing.

Finally, she said: "You shouldn't treat me like this. I like you. All my family likes you, my husband got the Ministry to buy forty thousand copies of your magazine, *Prospettive*, even if we Italians only went to Spain to massacre innocents. You shouldn't treat me like this, it's not fair."

She freed herself from my grip and went out into the open, outside the portico, returning under the pelting rain. Walking slowly and stumbling every now and then in a puddle, she moved towards Madame Carmen. The clairvoyant took her under her cloak as though under the wing of an enormous bat, covering her neck and her shoulders.

Slowly, unwillingly, I followed and joined the two women. Madame Carmen was covering Edda as though to protect her from me.

"Edda, is this person perhaps annoying you?" she asked, looking at me with a theatrical air of mistrust.

"No, he's a friend."

"A friend of the Countess," I added, "and of her father. A friend who's done the Countess's father many favors."

"What do you mean to say, Signor Suckert?" said Madame Carmen.

At that moment, Edda could have said: he's not called Suckert, he's called Malaparte.

But at that very moment I heard a noise, and I seemed to see on the road overlooked by the Charterhouse, the road I'd been on when I first caught sight of Edda, a number of figures, maybe in uniform, advancing under the rain.

"I... I'd like very much to come and see you," I said, turning to Madame Carmen. "I'll come and visit soon, very soon indeed. But now you must excuse me, I must be on my way."

I couldn't take any risks; I quit Edda and her clairvoyant abruptly and rushed at full speed for the exit from the cloister.

As I fled, I could hear in the distance the confused sound of voices, people calling to one another to coordinate a team. Perhaps, after waiting in vain for me elsewhere, they had set out to search for me. I was really lucky this time and I managed to get quickly onto the Via Krupp without being intercepted. In a few minutes I was scrambling uphill towards the Castiglione grotto, and in a quarter of an hour I was inside it. In that pitch darkness, the climb to the grotto was, to say the least, hair-raising, and as usual I grazed my legs and arms badly. The rain was abating, it was getting hot again and I took off my wet clothes. It was too dark to make my way to the hut inside the cave, I'd risk falling and hurting myself badly; better to run no risks and curl up among the rocks. I gathered a few leaves and twigs at the entrance of the grotto and made myself a sort of couch on which I collapsed. Now I'll sleep, I said to myself, I'm freezing, I'm hurting all over, above all I'm exhausted, now I'll sleep for sure. Maybe they'll think of coming to look for me here but *la dracu* the OVRA and the cops, they're all morons, they'll not find me, no, they'll not find me. And now to sleep, I'm not a kid any more, I'm too tired to think, I'm too tired even to breathe, now I swear I'm going to sleep.

But I didn't sleep; jingling non-stop in my ears came the words of Edda, Countess Ciano, the lover of death who knew how to use words to hurt so smoothly, so delicately, so compassionately.

Edda had drawn from her Pandora's box full of mischief the issue of *Prospettive* on the Spanish civil war published three years earlier. In Spain, when that war broke out, we Italian Fascists had helped General Franco to exterminate the Communist and Republican opposition. Dear Edda knew perfectly well which words to utter, even when she was a prey to the fits of madness that set her dancing on the rooftops under the rain. She'd gone and fished up that gigantic bloc of forty thousand copies, a complete printing run of *Prospettive*, bought up by the Minister of Foreign Affairs, His Excellency Count Galeazzo Ciano. In that number *Prospettive* had glorified the Italian massacres in Spain, in the Balearic Islands. Legitimate, patriotic massacres, war's like that. So you might think. But I knew what had really taken place. In Spain, as with the Matteotti trial, I had a friend from the canaille, another character like Amerigo Dumini from Saint Louis, Missouri. His name was Arconovaldo Bonacorsi, but everyone knew him as Count Rossi, the *nom de guerre* he'd chosen for his mission of death. In the Balearic Islands there was no front in the war between Franco's Nationalists and the Republicans, there was fighting here and there but military actions were pure guerilla warfare. Anyone could die from one moment to the next, no one could sleep quietly in his bed. It was my friend Count Rossi who organized "preventive executions", the house-by-house murder of trade unionists, schoolteachers, members of religious communities, Communists or just ordinary citizens suspected of Republican sympathies. Count Rossi and his Italian Fascists were called "the early morning ones" because they came at dawn, dragged men and women from their beds and shot them without a trial, without explanations, without any real motive. Their squads, *Los Dragones de la Muerte*, Death's Dragoons, entered hospitals to shoot the sick in their beds, to rape the nurses, to wreck the clinics and operating theaters. *Los Dragones de la Muerte* entered the prisons and exterminated the prisoners one by one, in the courtyards, in the cells, behind bars. These were the assassinations that *Prospettive* had glorified, under my signature, in that famous issue three years previously, with its colossal print run. Oh, Edda, why did you remind me of that? Ciano wanted that, and I did it to please him. I hoped I could get clean away with lying to myself, I hoped I could lie to the refined and courageous Malaparte who'd built House like Me, written *The Technique of Revolution*, mocked Hitler and jeered at Mussolini. Instead, three years later the memory and the shame of that article were imprinted in my memory and my consciousness like the fresh slime of the Capri Charterhouse. Mine, the suffering of those murdered, mine the black fluid that flowed from their noses and their ears as they rotted in the sun of Palma de Mallorca. Mine, that tremendous scream *¡Viva la Muerte!* which I'd used in *Prospettive* as the title of my article. Mine, that *Long live Death!* which the Spanish Falangists chanted in the lecture halls of the University of Salamanca, mine, the cry *Down with Intelligence and long live Death* which General Millán-Astray, cursing the entire human race, screamed in the face of the great philosopher Miguel de Unamuno, mine that cry *¡Viva la Muerte!* with which Millán-Astray led the squadrons of the Foreign Legion into villages, to rape, massacre and burn, after which in the evening he'd pray that every human being should end up like him, without an arm and without an eye. Mine that cry – I had glorified it in my articles, and no one could ever again free me of what I had done. But mine, too, the suffering of the victors, mine, those seventy days in which Colonel Moscardó in the Alcázar of Toledo resisted the siege of the Communist soldiers, mine, the telephone call in which his seventeen year old son Luís announced "Papa, the Reds have taken me hostage and if the Alcázar surrenders they'll spare me," mine the broken voice of Moscardó, replying "Son, commend your soul to the Lord, cry ¡*Viva el Cristo Re!* cry ¡*Arriba España!* And die like a hero". Mine, the bullet with which the Communists shot Luís Moscardó in the right temple, blowing half his head off. Mine the tears of General Varela when he succeeded in relieving the Alcázar, and Colonel Moscardó, who had just received his son's last telephone call, the last call before a bullet entered his son's head, met him, standing at attention, dirty and half-starved, in the midst of the ruins: "Here at the Alcázar, nothing to report Señor General." Ah, Edda! Why did you have to remind me that all those things were my doing, when I pretended not to know it?

Lying there in the Castiglione grotto, I ought to have concerned myself with my own circumstances, the arrest that was drawing ever closer and with it the prospect of rotting in prison with a murderer's reputation; instead of which I was thinking of Count Rossi, the nurses gang-raped by his *Dragones de la Muerte* and all those young Spanish women who in the evening made love with their husbands and in the morning saw them die shot by Count Rossi's men in the courtyard of their own house; thinking of the Spanish children touching with their incredulous little fingers those holes in the courtyard wall left by the bullets that had just killed their fathers. I was tired, chilled to the bone, famished, thirsty, and I was thinking of the trembling little fingers of the Spanish children in the Balearic Islands. *La dracu* Edda, *la dracu Prospettive, la dracu* Count Rossi, I babbled in near delirium.

La dracu you too, Pam, now don't you too come hounding me with your dead girl's voice and your chorus of women chanting ¡*Viva la Muerte!* I owe you nothing, now you're all dead, you and the nurses raped at Palma de Mallorca, you and Santoni, you and Matteotti, you and the Sturmbannführer. Please now just let me collapse onto this bed of leaves, I need to be in good shape tomorrow, I want to be in good shape when they come to arrest me, don't make me think of the trembling, incredulous little fingers touching the bullet holes in the walls of their houses in Palma de Mallorca. And don't talk to me of pity, I know how selfish you dead are, you think of nothing but yourselves and settling scores with your past, and you want our pity.

But *ya napliwayu* your pity, as the crucified Jews said in Ukraine, *ya napliwayu*, I spit on it, I spit on pity.

I thought this delirium had lasted only a few minutes, but it had lasted all night. When first light came, I was still there murmuring *ya napliwayu*, grinding my teeth and arguing with the dead, coming to blows with them, detesting them. I've never hated the dead as I did that night, I'd have liked to see them die all over again, but this time for good, swallowed up by the dark once and for all; but I knew that was not possible, because the dead die only to obsess us, to torture us with their absence, to spit us in the face with their cold, useless absence.

As sunlight reached into the Castiglione grotto, there I lay on the rocks, with my back utterly wrecked. I felt my eyes swollen, my legs shattered, I hadn't the strength to make a run for it, perhaps I should give myself up. Then I heard distant shouts, a clamor of boys' voices, excited voices calling everyone to come out and announcing something strange and exceptional. That's wonderful, I thought, rising to my feet, at last some good news, that was just what I needed. I got dressed and began to make my way back down to the road, stumbling among the rocks in the grotto.

The sunlight made me feel reborn, its warmth went right into my bones. It felt as though I were emerging from the gates of Hell: I needed love, laughter, warm voices that smell of honey and pineapples. Oh God, how I longed to see Lucia. When I came to the Via Krupp I found a group of old people discussing animatedly. I looked like a cave man and I was coming straight down from the Castiglione grotto, yet they didn't so much as spare a glance at me. I went on towards the center. You could feel a sort of electric charge in the air, an over-excitement so dense that you could almost touch it. From the middle of the village came the sound of music, at first distant, then more and more distinct. It was a brass band, the village band, yes, it was Capri's famous Putipù brass band, led by Mastro Scialapopolo, specializing in tarantellas and fairground cacophony.

As I drew near to it the crowd grew thicker and the hubbub, noisier. Swarms of barefoot brats were converging on the piazza, fat peasant women, whole families, all the real people of Capri and Anacapri.

"What's happened?" I asked a little boy.

"Come on, don't you know? A miracle, a miracle!" he said, then rushed away, following a little friend.

A miracle! The chaos was indescribable. Outsiders don't realize that the people of Naples, and those of Capri too, indeed all southern Italy, simply lives for miracles. They still have a capacity for marveling at mysteries, they can believe in the age-old blood of San Gennaro which turns liquid in the phial held in the bishop's hand in the presence of thousands of the faithful, they eat and drink miracles daily, their very life is a miracle, and it's a miracle too if you can understand what they mean when you ask them to explain you a miracle. That's because the Italians down south, above all in Capri and Naples, live on familiar terms with God, they know Him well, they invite Him home to drink coffee in the living room with the grandchildren playing all round Him and patting Him hard on the shoulder. For them, God's still a friend, even when they betray Him, spitting in His face, stabbing Him in the back, kicking Him into a ditch and throwing a lighted cigarette in after Him.

By now I was quite near the Piazzetta and the crush was such that you couldn't move a step further. The place on which all those people were converging was surely the church of Santo Stefano on the town square. I decided to let myself be carried forward by the throng and let myself be pushed forward without attempting any resistance. In the crowd I couldn't see any face I knew, it was only the humble part of the island, the poor, the servants, the waiters, the peasants, those you'd never see at the Fortino, at the Villa Discopoli or the night clubs. The only face I recognized for a fleeting moment was that of Spadaro, the pseudo-fisherman, his hawk's eye searching for some rich foreigner to take his photo. But the rich weren't there, the rich still lay sleeping in their villas, and the very thought of waking up and taking part in a religious ceremony, what's more, in the company of the common herd, would have been enough to make them feel ill. Still borne onward by the multitude, I entered the Piazzetta at last: the band was going full blast, a Mass had just finished and other people were swarming out from the church of Santo Stefano, adding chaos to chaos. I felt quite safe in that morass: an early morning religious ceremony attended by hundreds of people is, I thought, no place to look for a fugitive. The main door and sacristy of the church had been decorated with red curtains, meaning that a solemn ceremony was taking place. After a thunderous burst of applause, a trio of priests emerged from the darkness inside the church bearing a great painted wooden crucifix. Behind them a procession was forming.

"But what has happened?" I asked a bearded youngster standing next to me.

"How's it possible you don't know? A miracle, a miracle!" he said, and disappeared into the throng. I repeated the question to a couple of young girls, but the two were already staring at the great processional crucifix, rosary in hand, reciting an unending ejaculatory prayer.

La dracu the miracle, I thought, I can't get anyone to talk here. But at that very moment the crowd exploded into resounding, emotional applause. Emerging from the church, on a platform borne on the shoulders of four young priests, was a gilded statue of San Gennaro.

"Did they find it at the Faraglioni?" I asked the crowd around me.

"At the Faraglioni, at the Faraglioni! A miracle, a miracle!" came the enthusiastic reply.

My stage management had worked. It was so difficult to get a statue that size to the top of the Faraglioni that everyone had regarded it as a miracle. Near me the throng was praying, they were falling to their knees, reciting the rosary and slowly joining the procession. I felt guilty for having duped the people's faith, but then, didn't I have the right to save my skin?

At that moment a hand touched my shoulder and a voice whispered in my ear:

"Signor Malaparte, what ever are you doing here? There are cops everywhere!"

Knowing my habitual prudence, poor Tamburi was utterly appalled.

"Don't worry your head about that, Tamburi. Who found the statue of San Gennaro?"

"That's what I'm trying to find out, but I'm afraid it won't be easy. Prince Sirignano sent me out to make enquiries, and I was wondering what criterion to opt for…"

I didn't even let him finish what he was saying. I saw a small kid next to us and asked him in dialect: "Tell me, *guaglio'*, who found the statue of San Gennaro?"

"It was Giuseppe Gargiulo, the baker's son," said the adorable little urchin.

"Did you see, Tamburi? The criterion to adopt was: *ask*. And now we're off to Villa Lysis."

"But yesterday evening there were masses of cops all round the villa."

"I know, I heard Febo howling. But with all this chaos there's a good chance no one will notice me, so long as we walk separately."

When I arrived at the Villa Lysis it was hard to tell which was greater: Sirignano's astonishment or Febo's joy.

"Malaparte, you're crazy," said the prince as I let myself collapse onto a sofa and Febo washed my face with his tongue. "What's come over you that you go walking around in broad daylight? Yesterday evening the whole area round here was crawling with cops."

"Prince, rejoice! There's absolute chaos outside. The golden statue of San Gennaro is driving them all wild. We have to trace a certain Giuseppe Gargiulo, the kid who found it. If he climbed up to where the statue is he'll certainly be a hunter of blue lizards, so he'll bring us to Carmine".

"Wow, I'll get down to that at once! But now you tell me what you've been up to during all this time you've been out of contact! We've all been getting as jittery as a bunch of old ladies round here."

I told in few words of my meeting with Winner, Ciro's lightning abduction of Professor Maiuri and the spooky nocturnal encounter with Edda Ciano and Madame Carmen.

"About Madame Carmen," said Sirignano, "we've checked out everything you asked us to. Tamburi, you tell us all about it as it was you who handled the business."

"Well, it was like this… Greasing the palm of one of the Communal registry clerks with some cash generously provided by the Prince, I received the following information: First, Madame Carmen's real name is Carmela Capasso, married name Buronzo. Secondly: the husband's name is Vincenzo Buronzo".

"Buronzo, Buronzo... the name says something to me," I said. "Ah yes, now I remember! He's a Deputy."

"Exactly, Signor Malaparte. Vincenzo Buronzo, poetaster and man of letters, a Fascist bureaucrat from Asti, previously married and widowed, entered into a second marriage with Madame Carmen. The marriage was difficult to arrange: Madame Carmen had been abandoned by her first husband, who'd fled to France and disappeared without trace. The woman asked Mussolini for help and he got the first marriage annulled so that she could marry Buronzo. The Deputy's an old man, but he still has plenty of influential supporters and he's very well off indeed. Without him, Madame Carmen would have had it. When she was abandoned by her husband, she had three children on her hands and, for a long time she looked desperately for a social position and financial support. At this moment, however, the couple is again in trouble. Buronzo has just undergone a major operation, he's still convalescing in Rome and psychologically he's not quite all there. Before he fell ill, he was planning to get the Duce to appoint him Senator of the Kingdom, so as to round off his political career with a rich stipend. But now, after the operation, there could be difficulties. Madame Carmen and Buronzo are not the perfect match: the Signora tells her women friends that he's a querulous old grump. Fortunately, he spends plenty of time at Asti and in Rome, so she's delighted to be left alone and in peace here in Capri. To sum up, I'd say that the two pillars of Madame Carmen's life are Mussolini and hubby Buronzo's money. Oh, I was forgetting: Buronzo is an amateur poet. He writes eulogies and then pesters the Duce to read and comment on them, to authorize their publication or have them broadcast by radio, and to return them to him with his autograph. It seems his house is chock full of autographed photos of the Duce."

"Good, good, the picture's clear enough. Well then, Tamburi, run at once to the public telephone office."

"Back to the Piazzetta all over again?"

"Don't argue or I'll leave you without pay for the next six months. Prince Sirignano's 'phone will certainly be tapped. Call my secretary in Rome, tell her to run to the Foreign Press Club where all the foreign correspondents in Italy have their offices. They have an archive of German newspapers there and she must get them to give her all the back numbers of the *Echo der Woche*. I want to check on all the articles that deal with Hitler's role in the Great War. It'll be a long boring job and she'd do well to get herself helped by someone. At the club, she could talk to Cecil Sprigge, the correspondent of the *Manchester Guardian*: he's a friend of mine, he'll willingly provide her with a desk and perhaps even with an assistant. Have you understood my instructions clearly, Tamburi?"

"I've understood, I've understood. But I've run up some expenses recently, and I wanted to ask if..."

"Did you make any progress with that riddle? I'm referring to *bon bonad kind rabal mervu...*"

"Really, there's been nothing new..."

"And you want me to cough up more cash now? Off with you now... At the double!"

"I'll go and look for this Giuseppe Gargiulo," said Sirignano, while Tamburi took the door, not in the best of moods. "Let's hope the kid can at last lead us to where Carmine's hiding. See you later!"

"Wait, Prince. I've another favor to ask of you. You must tell Chantecler to organize a big masked party this evening, here at Villa Lysis. It should be the pagan sequel to the religious festivities for today's miracle, the finding of the statue of San Gennaro on the Faraglioni. In other words, we want hubbub and havoc."

"A masked ball, here this evening?" smiled Sirignano, as ever delighted by my eccentric ideas.

"A mask is the only way I'll ever get out of here," I explained.

"Malaparte, you're lucky to have met someone as nuts as yourself, namely yours truly. And you're lucky to have a certain Chantecler in these parts, whose sole interest in life is organizing parties. We'll have to get a few friends to come, of course. What do you have in mind to do while I'm out?"

"To eat and have a wash. Then sleep a few hours. Prince, d'you still have that collection of antifascist verses and doggerel somewhere around?"

"In the safe in my room. But what do you want that for?"

"I want to change the authorship of a poem."

"It's a great man who can understand you, Malaparte. I really hope they don't arrest you, otherwise I'll never know what all your crazy ideas of the last few days were meant to achieve."

He left me the key. Once I was alone, I spent a few minutes playing and exchanging endearments with Febo. Then I ate, had a good bath and made my way to Sirignano's room. At my side, Febo was trembling and yelping with contentment, but also with fear. From the tone of my voice he'd understood that in a few hours I'd be risking my all in a desperate gamble.

ROME, SUMMER 1957
SANATRIX CLINIC, ROOM 32

¡Viva la Muerte!

"Let's stop here," said Death, "there's something that just doesn't square."

The typist angel stopped. The queen who reigns over the things of this Earth wore on her features an expression of suspicion and vague hostility. It was the first time she'd interrupted my dictation.

I rose from the bed, went to the washbasin, opened the faucet and gave my face a quick wash. I didn't like the way things were going. It's no fun to see Death looking askance at you, it's unpleasant and hardly sets you at ease.

The Angel of Death at the Remington folded his arms placidly. The other angel, the one who looked after small tasks, came to the washbasin and handed me a clean face towel. I thanked him; he responded with an elegant little bow.

"Well then, what is it?" I said. "We're just coming to the finale, I suppose everyone here's happy."

"You're cheating, Malaparte," said Death icily.

She rose from the edge of my bed with a sensual and extraordinarily elegant movement, just like those of the real Mona Williams, yet at the same time imbued with terrible solemnity. It's no fun to have dealings with Death when she's in a bad mood, above all when it's you who are the cause of that mood.

"I'm cheating? What do you mean?"

"Do you think I was not at Saarburg too?" said Death. "In those days, I harvested thousands and thousands of young lives! I crossed that countryside from end to end, gathering cadavers among the trenches, the guns and horses' carcasses. That's why I can tell you for certain that the Prince of Hesse was not there. And nor was a certain Austrian soldier from near Linz, as you've written. What you've written is a straightforward falsification. The young soldier of whom you speak was Hitler – that much I've understood! But Hitler hadn't yet joined up in August 1914, when the battle of Saarburg took place. It was only in the Fall that he arrived at the front."

I'm willing to put up with all sorts of things, but not to be called a counterfeiter. Writing is a creative act and there's nothing doing, I just get very awkward when people confuse creation with falsification. Besides, I was beginning to understand what sort of woman Death was. The kind of woman who merits respect, but whom you must absolutely not allow to browbeat you. She had to be treated just as I'd done with Mona Williams, no more, no less.

"I don't like the way things are turning!" I replied, "This is my novel, if I'm not mistaken. Anyway, it's you who made that clear at the outset! So please leave me free to write what I think. I'm not in the habit of taking dictation."

Caught off balance, the lady with the wonderful aquamarine eyes fell briefly silent. Her frown was at once proud and tender. Ah, how adorable Death could be! There were millions of living girls who hadn't a fraction of Death's sweetness: to be really alive, maybe they needed first to be dead.

She looked at me pensively. She had again sat herself in that same elegant but uncomfortable position on the edge of my bed.

Unaware of all this, Sister Carmelita slept away placidly, uncomfortably seated on my bedside chair. It was good to have that dear sister's silent, peaceful presence there beside me, the only living link with my past life.

"In other words, you're really not pleased with all the work I've done up until now?" I asked in a rather more conciliatory tone.

Death rose and went over to the window, which one of her acolytes had opened, and there she stood, with her back to the windowsill. It was as though the room was too small for her, she seemed to find it oppressive. She closed her eyes and gently breathed in the air coming from outside, perhaps to taste the smell of the maritime pines in the garden below, or to ready herself for what she had to tell me. In that exquisite pensive pose, she was more beautiful and desirable than ever. At that moment, I'd have liked to be a great poet. Verse was never my strong point, apart from a few comic items I managed to bring off well, and very few more serious ones; but out of pride, I'd never admitted that to anyone. As I was saying, I'd have liked to be a great poet, to be able to write a poem on the beauty of Death, the beauty of the Death with aquamarine eyes who stood before me, and if she'd not been Death, I'd have asked her out for a romantic dinner date, closing with a chaste kiss on her doorstep.

"Ah, Curzio Malaparte," said Death, "how you disappoint me."

"I disappoint you? Just because I invented a historical detail from the battle of Saarburg? Because I used my freedom as an author?"

"No, that's not where the problem lies. I offered you an opportunity for expiation through the art of which you're a past-master, the art of writing."

"I don't get you. Isn't that just what I'm doing? You've heard my tale. I've written of my sufferings, my weaknesses, my remorse, even my stupidity. I've humbled myself, showing my silly, presumptuous side. Isn't that expiation?"

"No. It's not good enough."

"And what else am I supposed to do?"

"It's certainly not for me to tell you that. This is your book, I told you that before you started. No one else can tell you what you have to write."

"That seems to me a rather silly rule, if you'll allow me to say so".

"It's no rule. It just can't be otherwise. The good and evil you've done or not done in your lifetime are your business. No one can tell you if or how you're to expiate them. That has to come from within."

"But you can at the very least tell me what I'm *not* to do if I'm to bring this off."

"There, I can help you. Don't bother about style. Don't get bogged down in gossip or name-dropping. Don't lose sight of the goal, go straight for it. It's your soul that's in the balance. And you don't have much time."

"Eh, one moment. Is it a book you want me to dictate to your friend or a shopping list? If I'm to write a novel, and you know perfectly well that's my line in trade, I must be able to do it properly. This kind of sweeping criticism is beginning to get on my nerves."

Now even Death was beginning to treat me as an exhibitionist. Despite the fact that it was the newspapers and radio that had turned my death into a social event, the fault was mine. "The usual show-off", "He's titillating the public's morbid curiosity", "He has turned dying into a show" screamed the headlines. All lies. Do you really think that someone who feels the icy cold slowly eating his legs, someone the veins of whose hands are bloated with black, coagulated blood, has time to think of advertizing for himself?

I was, on the contrary, trying to be as little of a nuisance as possible. I didn't even want to weigh on the clinic's expense sheet. I always sent back the clear vegetable soup that Sister Carmelita brought me. I asked a friend to go to some Roman trattoria where they knew me well and order something fit to feed a man: say, a chicken *alla diavola*, a steak *alla fiorentina* or a dish of tortellini. I recommended him to tell the cook that the dish was for Malaparte, so that he'd make the necessary effort. I was never short of fine liquor, even if it was watered down. It made me feel better.

On one of the last days, when I'd almost stopped eating, I got a hankering after milk. The oxygen cylinder had left me with burnt lips and nostrils; phlebitis had swollen my legs; the metastases were so many that almost nothing in my old carcass was working properly. I thought a bit of milk was the one thing that might help. So I asked them to go and get a good glass of milk from the farm at Torre in Pietra, in the Roman Campagna, near the sea, towards the Fregene pinewoods. Torre in Pietra milk is delicious, once you've drunk it you'll not want to drink any other. It's a return trip of almost a hundred kilometers, but of course I paid for the trouble and they brought me the milk. Was that exhibitionism?

If I'd been an exhibitionist, I'd have gotten myself a tomb in fashionable Capri, a place I love anyway. Instead I decided to have this old carcase of mine buried in my Tuscany, on the mountains of the Val di Bisenzio, up on the summit of the Spazzavento, in the hope that nothing would stop me from raising my head from time to time and spitting into the cold draft of the north wind.

Death did not reply. If there's something I can't stand, it's when I'm talking to someone and I don't get a decent answer. I hate that, it has always made me mad. What's more, writing had made me feel good, full of energy, and even if I was dealing with Death I had no intention of letting myself be messed around.

"I repeat: these criticisms of yours are beginning to get on my nerves, d'you understand? I didn't ask to die! I'm writing this novel because I ran into mustard gas when I was a young man at Bligny. One fine day, they diagnosed a rather nasty illness and in a few months, there I was under an oxygen tent. Then here you come and tell me that to save my soul I must write a novel. Fine! I'm doing my best. I'm putting all I've got into it, I'm showing up Curzio Malaparte in the worst possible light, and here you come telling me my best isn't good enough, without explaining why or how. I'm very sorry, but I can't work on those terms."

The sweet woman looked at me again, and in her eyes I glimpsed a bottomless abyss of compassion. Yet her eyes also expressed a secret, ardent will not to deviate by one iota from the path she'd set me. She did not even need to speak. In the blue-green eyes of that adorable Mona in a Chanel tailleur, eyes lovely but adamant, eyes overflowing with regal dignity, I clearly read that she would not give an inch.

"I've understood, there's no point in arguing," I said. "I'm someone who takes things to the bitter end."

"I know, Curzio," said Death, "It's a lifetime I've been observing you."

Another thing I can't abide is when someone, Death or no Death, tries to patronize me. I'd far rather be taken for an idiot, so long as I'm accorded the honors of war.

"Ah, so it's a lifetime you've been watching over me?" I replied. "Well, you're going to have to wait a moment longer. Now I'm going to complete this novel and I'll do it *my way*. You know your job, I'm not contesting that, but I'm a writer and, for goodness sake, I do know what I'm doing. You say there's something missing? Well, the story isn't over, and I'm sure that in the end you'll change your mind."

I felt like that old man I saw in Florence in 1944 in the middle of the road, when the British tanks were entering the city to free it from the Nazis. The old man was pushing a shaky old hand-cart down the street, loaded with wine flasks, and he wouldn't get out of the way. Behind him, the tanks were thundering menacingly, the soldiers were cursing, they were spitting and throwing stones at him, but he just went on, tranquil and stubborn, neither turning nor moving to one side. Only when he'd got to where he wanted to go did he take a side street, at last allowing the interminable, deafening column of British tanks to go on their way. That's how I was now: Death was breathing down my neck, but I wouldn't give way. I wanted to decide the if, the when and the how.

"So you really think I'm going to change my mind, Curzio?"

"Yes, I think so. *Prego, Maestro*", I said turning to the Remington-wielding Angel of Death, "please start the last movement of the symphony."

Thin – so thin – pale, febrile, the lanky youngster reminded one of Dinu Lipatti, the greatest pianist of all time, at his last concert in Besançon, shortly before he abandoned the podium, consumed by leukemia.

With his fantastically light touch, the angel in a pin-striped suit began striking the keys the moment I pronounced the first syllables.

CAPRI, SUMMER 1939

Cricket in Capri

Chantecler had performed miracles – mere routine for him, when there was fun to be had. Besides, it was high summer and the cocktail and reception industry was in full swing. The costumes for the masked ball were ready by eight o' clock, together with refreshments, a little jazz band, and above all a fantastic quantity of gorgeous young girls (English, American, French, Swedish…) whom Chantecler and his friends had picked up in the course of a brilliant recruitment drive in the bars of luxury hotels, always finding the trick to part them from aged parents, jealous fiancés and fat, spotty girlfriends.

He'd even managed to take on a few extra staff, whom Sirignano didn't normally employ at the Villa Lysis, so that the drinks and canapés would be properly served. The bill would be astronomical, but Sirignano had confessed to me that he'd just sold a little farm, so liquid cash and refreshments posed no problem and, as ever, his money flowed fast and freely into other people's pockets. My princely friend stubbornly pursued his genial pauper's destiny, the destiny he shared with the true, great, generous aristocracy of the Kingdom of Italy, engaged in its final pirouettes on the stage of history before the war reset its wealth to zero.

The servants had carried out the instructions of the master of the house to the letter: no mask, no entry. Those who'd not come in fancy dress had at least to accept a fine black velvet mask on their noses, enough to make them practically unrecognisable. Villa Lysis had been taken by storm. It had been off limits for many years, and now all the island's well-born males were excited at the idea of getting into one of Capri's most famous residences and seeing at last for themselves the place where Count Fersen, prince of perverts, had lived among his mercenary young lovers, his hookahs and the wrought iron stairway with its erect phalluses.

While the band played *Happy Days are Here Again* (I had that disc too, I've always loved Ben Selvin), I stayed closed in a room on the first floor, surreptitiously spying from the window on the guests whom I myself had brought there by the dozen, like some bargain-basement Great Gatsby.

"Well then, what now, Signor Malaparte?" said Ciro.

"I'm ready, soon we'll be on our way. Are you quite sure there's enough confusion on all sides?"

"Ah, no question about that," Ciro continued, "there's one hell of a ruckus. And they're still carrying that statue round the whole island. Did you hear the fireworks? I've never seen such a mess in the street. People put tables outside the front door, eat in the middle of the traffic, hand out bread, wine and tomatoes to whoever comes by. Just as well they've not yet heard about this on the mainland an' there's no news-hounds around. I can't stand it when there's snoopin' newsmen."

Febo was lying at my feet, with a forced, unnatural smile. He'd been watching me on the point of leaving for more than half an hour, and he'd understood perfectly well that the coming hours would be decisive. His nerves were on edge, even if he wasn't showing a thing.

"This confusion is just what I need to pass unrecognized. Even if the real purpose of the statue was quite different. But it's all gone wrong, and no one could foresee that."

The discovery of the San Gennaro statue had been a disappointment. My plan had apparently succeeded: the statue had been discovered by one of the kids paid by Carmine to climb up the Faraglioni in search of blue lizards. Without the extraordinary bait of the golden statue of San Gennaro we'd never have been able to track them down. Little Giuseppe Gargiulo had found the statue; yet, despite Sirignano's offer of money, first to the parents, then to his other little friends, he'd not been able to help us. Neither he nor any of his friends had the least idea where the waiter from the Quisisana was to be found. That had been a nasty surprise; we even began to wonder whether Carmine wasn't dead or hadn't perhaps escaped from Capri by night on some fishing boat; maybe he'd even left the country.

To get out from the Villa Lysis I'd donned a splendid cowboy outfit. I looked at myself in a mirror: with the ten-gallon hat, leather waistcoat, spurs and a Venetian mask that covered almost all my face, I was just another of the swarm of spongers currently infesting the Villa Lysis. Ciro was even worse: he was dressed as an oriental satrap, complete with turban, scimitar and pointed slippers, and looked like a cartoon version of one of the Three Magi. On my advice, Tamburi was disguised as a musketeer: the seventeenth century costume with sword and pistol suited him down to the ground and justified the mustachios sprouting from under his black velvet mask.

"Signor Malaparte?" said Tamburi, "I just don't understand what you want to do with the information I've gathered for you."

"It's better that way, Tamburi. Otherwise you'd be so scared you'd start trembling like a leaf, and I'd no longer be able to enjoy your dubious services. So, please just go on not understanding."

"And what about the Prince? Didn't he understand anything either?"

"On the contrary. My friend Sirignano has a subtle mind and he'll probably have guessed at what I'm trying to do. Most people haven't a tenth of his sense of humor, his intelligence or his cash. But he gets a kick out of helping me, and he just can't resist an unusual, risky challenge."

"Jus' excuse me one moment, Signor Malaparte", Ciro broke in, "but you been to school and you prob'ly even know English, so why don't you go to America and open a nice casino? If I were in your place, I'd be off like a shot."

"A casino, what an idea..." sniggered Tamburi.

"C'm on. My relatives in Broccolino made a sack o' dough off the gambling racket!"

"No Ciro," I said, "America's not for me. America's the future. I'm a poor guy from the past, I was born in old Europe, in our rotten old mama Europe. Just wait and see, after the war, we'll all become old and rotten like Europe."

Sirignano joined us at last. He was impeccably done up as a Caribbean pirate, complete with sword and black hat.

"Come on Malaparte, let's get out now," he said, "the car's waiting for us in the center, just outside the town square. You two, meanwhile," he said turning to Tamburi and Ciro, "stay here and stand guard."

Febo whined, but he didn't ask to come with me, he'd understood the situation. I adore dogs with self-control, and Febo was one of those.

Sirignano and I went downstairs to the ground floor when the music and the hubbub from the guests were at their loudest. Black Velvet was flowing, dozens of sweaty, masked figures were gaily thrashing about on the dance floor, a Turkish odalisque tripping over the halbard of a lansquenet, a Roman senator throwing his laurel crown to a mustachioed youngster dressed up as a valkyrie, and no one paid the blindest attention to us as we crossed the villa's reception rooms. To exit the garden gate we had to force our way through a throng of youths kept out by the servants because they had no mask, all begging to be let in.

Out in the street, amidst the euphoria caused by the miracle of the San Gennaro statue, our costumes drew us greetings and gaiety. They were well made disguises and in the dark they made us practically unrecognizable. I shivered briefly only when we crossed the path of Italo Tavolato, one of the journalists sold to the OVRA; fortunately he spared us no more than a distracted glance.

Eddie von Bismarck had returned from a trip to Naples the evening before. Sirignano had gone to fetch him at the Fortino, without warning, so that he'd not have time to prepare any snare. While he was ringing the bell of the Fortino, Sirignano got me to wait some way off, so I'd be safe from any unpleasant surprises. Eddie's profile was hardly that of a traitor, but there are times when you can't be too careful.

Eddie came out from the Fortino and climbed into the car. The moment he saw me get in behind him, he turned to shake my hand, smiling.

"Ciao Malaparte, good to see you."

"Ciao Eddie, I'm glad to see you too."

"So it's true: you're still free, they've not arrested you."

"No, Eddie, they've not yet arrested me."

"You've done a good job. You've managed to dodge them."

"Every night I sleep somewhere else. And they're not making house-to-house searches. In Capri there are too many villas where the police prefer not to go nosing around. They're keeping the news of my flight almost secret. Only until they've caught me, of course. When that day comes, the news will spread as far as Patagonia."

"I'm quite sure it wasn't you who killed that girl."

"Thanks Eddie, it's good to hear that."

Sirignano started the engine, and the car started climbing the road to Anacapri.

"I'm in a car with you," he said with a nervous smile, "with a fugitive. I'm running a risk."

"Thanks Eddie, it's good to hear you say that too. But you shouldn't worry. No one will get you into trouble. You know I play fair. I always play cricket by the rules."

"Me too, I always play a fair game of cricket."

"Bravo, Eddie. The great thing is always to play a good game of cricket, and to keep up the cricketing spirit – that's even more important."

The place that had been chosen for our little talk was a little shed in a vineyard alongside the road to the Blue Grotto. In the shack there was nothing but a table, a few chairs and an oil lamp. Sirignano knew the owner of that field well, he'd even lent him money, we could spend a while there without anyone disturbing us.

Outside the corrugated iron walls of our refuge, the countryside was teeming with secret life. Fretful mosquitos buzzed here and there, melancholy grass snakes dreamed of having arms and legs, romantic little lady frogs waited in the shade for some gallant bullfrog to make an appearance with top hat and stick. All the animal world was throbbing with warmth and life; only inside our tinplate shack was the air cold and stagnant, smelling of human infamy.

"We've not much time," I said as soon as we were seated.

Eddie shifted on his chair, vaguely anxious.

"I want you explain to me," I said, "what took place at the Villa Mura yesterday evening between you, Philipp von Hessen and the Sturmbannführer."

"What do you want to know?" asked Eddie von Bismarck, looking thoroughly alarmed. "And how do you know that the Sturmbannführer was with me and Phli at the Villa Mura?"

"I know, and that's good enough for you. There was a row between you."

"Did you set spies on us?"

"People heard you. Your friend Phli was yelling, and you'd left all the windows open," I said.

"It's true," he said thoughtfully, "We'd left the windows open."

"Speak up, Eddie. I've told you, I don't have time to waste. And I need your help."

He looked all around, embarrassed because I was asking him for help. I was a famous writer, someone above and outside the world of power, and I was asking him for help.

"I don't like what's happening in Germany," he began, "you know that perfectly well. But this is a delicate matter. It affects the interests of the German Reich."

Eddie said "German Reich" but in his voice I heard "Phli", he said "a delicate matter" and I heard "the Prince of Hesse".

"The interests of the German Reich? All that for a postcard of the Saarburg crucifix?" I said.

Eddie's jaws tightened. He wasn't expecting me to be privy to that detail. He was in two minds; he'd have loved to pass on some juicy revelation, some detail of the crass cruelty of the Nazi regime, but he was held back by fidelity to his dear Phli.

"Well, that's how it is," said Eddie von Bismarck, "it's a matter of State security. That explains why I can't tell you what's in that postcard. But anyway, what does it all matter now? The card's been lost. Sturmbannführer Helmut Aichinger is dead, officially of a heart attack. He insisted that he knew nothing about the card, he repeated that to the bitter end. Expletives were flying in all directions. Phli became furious and threatened to bring in Himmler, even Hitler. He even spoke of the strange death of that English girl the Sturmbannführer was involved with. The poor Sturmbannführer had been drinking before I brought him to Phli's place. Once he got back to the hotel, he found that his room had been ransacked by thieves. He'll surely have thought this was the work of someone sent by Phli, that it was a warning... He'll have felt he was done for. He was rather highly strung, I think he was suffering from depression. He left a short note addressed to no one in particular, in which he swore that he hadn't stolen the card and he hadn't killed the English girl. The note was impounded by the police, who'll have arranged for it to get lost. The dead man was a bachelor; his parents will be notified by his superiors in Germany. There will be no autopsy. End of story."

"And what about Phli?" asked Sirignano.

"He's very sad. He never thought it would come to this."

"That postcard has something to do with Hitler, isn't that so?" I said.

"It's you who say so," replied Eddie, growing more and more ill at ease.

"Yes, I'm saying so. You'd have to be an idiot not to think of that one. Your Phli has unlimited access to the Führer."

Eddie von Bismarck did not reply.

"Eddie, my life's at stake," I said. "Sooner or later they'll catch me, and I need to know what's behind this story. What's hidden in that bloody card? Murder? Coups d'Etat? Wars? All those things are Hitler's specialities."

"You've forgotten his mania for persecuting Jews," said Sirignano.

Eddie's expression set into a bitter smile.

"The matter's rather more subtle than that," he said. "I'm sorry, I've already said too much."

"You promised to play a fair game of cricket."

"That's just what I'm doing."

"Then if you won't talk, I'll do the talking. During the war, Hitler was a *Meldegänger*, a messenger, isn't that so? His job kept him moving all the time. One fine day, at Saarburg he found himself facing a stray Frenchman who was on the point of killing him. But he was saved by Phli, who shot the French soldier dead. That's how the Führer and the Prince of Hesse came to know one another," I said.

Eddie stiffened, it was as though someone had stuck a pin in his behind – Sirignano too caught onto this. Eddie had a kind heart, he didn't know how to keep secrets, kind-hearted people are like that.

"How do you know?" he asked.

"I've only just understood it this very moment, thinking back to what one of my men told me at Bligny, when I was at the front. He knew that the Prince of Hesse had saved the life of an Austrian soldier at Saarburg. When he told me that story, I couldn't know this, because Hitler was still a nonentity. But now it's all quite clear to me. That's not the end of Phli and Hitler's tale, is it now, Eddie?"

Eddie would have liked to vanish like a wind-borne cloud. He kept looking all around, exasperated and impatient.

"Talk, Eddie!" I yelled. "I've jeered publicly at Mussolini and Hitler. Can't you even give a little discreet help to an innocent man?"

He stood up, showing he meant to leave: "I'm sorry, Malaparte. I hope you understand."

I watched him make his way to the door of the shack.

A moment later I'd jumped on him. I threw him to the ground and dragged him back in.

"You bastard, you coward!" I panted, landing a few desultory and rather innocuous blows on his face. I was too tired, too desperate to hit anyone. Above all, I'd no desire to hit Eddie, that was something I'd never have wanted to do, because he was a gentleman, a grandson of the great Chancellor Bismarck, and I liked him. Dear Eddie may have been an asshole, but I liked him, and maybe he liked me too, like so many people in Capri.

Sirignano parted us with some difficulty, panting and swearing. While Eddie wiped a rivulet of blood from the corner of his mouth, I shook the dust from Mona Williams' husband's shirt. It was a lovely shirt of the finest cotton, it must have spent plenty of time in the drawers of the Fortino; maybe Eddie von Bismarck would have recognized it.

Suddenly I felt very weak and very much alone, but I still wanted to keep playing scrupulously by the rules and respecting the man facing me. That's how they've always played cricket in old England. Because rules count in cricket, but the spirit of the game counts for even more.

"Eddie, if you don't want to talk, I'll do the talking. Let's speak of a cinema in Rome. Let's speak of the Cola di Rienzo cinema."

Eddie von Bismarck stared at me through narrowed eyes.

"What are you referring to?"

"I'm referring to how, four years ago, during a film at the Cola di Rienzo cinema, your friend Phli took advantage of the darkness to place his hand between the legs of the spectator sitting next to him, not realizing that he was an off-duty police officer. I'm referring to the occasion when Phli was arrested for this, taken to the police station and interrogated. I'm referring to when he got away with it by presenting the police his visiting card bearing the inscription *His Royal Highness the Prince of Hesse,* and the chief of police ordered his immediate release on grounds of political expediency. There, that's what I'm referring to."

I'd spoken clearly, like a proper cricket umpire, one of those noble spirits properly indoctrinated at the Marylebone Cricket Club. Eddie smiled sarcastically.

"You're not playing by the rules, Malaparte. You're inventing everything, the Prince has nothing to do with all this," he said.

His mouth was dry. He sat down.

"All right," I said, "then tell me about the Prince of Hesse's relationship with that English poet, Siegfried Sassoon."

"I repeat, I don't know what you're referring to." Eddie's mouth was very dry and he was pale, as pale as a dead moon.

"Really? I was hoping that you'd talk to me about the love letters which your Phli and that well-known English poet Siegfried Sassoon exchanged when they were young, and which told of the nights they'd spent together travelling around Italy and sharing the same hotel room in Rome, at Castel Gandolfo and on the Lake of Como. I was hoping you'd talk to me about the fact that Sassoon was half Jewish. A detail which the Führer might perhaps not appreciate, don't you think? I was hoping that you'd talk to me of how Sassoon kept Phli when he was indulging a pastime as interior decorator to the Roman nobility. I could spice this up with some rather dirty details, but that wouldn't be cricket. Would you like me to go on?"

"That won't be necessary. These are all lies, you can spare yourself repeating them. It's quite true that Siegfried Sassoon was a friend of Phli's, but that doesn't mean…"

"Eddie, Phli's wife, Princess Mafalda, the daughter of the King of Italy, knows none of these things. The Italians don't know of them, perhaps even Phli's father-in-law doesn't, and nor do the Germans. It really wouldn't be nice if some journalist were to spread the news everywhere, now would it?"

"Phli is a decent person and an exemplary husband."

"Very well, Eddie, as you wish. So then let's talk of the Prince of Hesse's friendship with Ludwig Curtius, the director of the German Archeological Institute in Rome, a well known pederast who advises him when he has to make important purchases of works of art for Hitler. Would you perhaps prefer to talk about that?"

"That's quite enough, Malaparte, otherwise I'll really be on my way. I won't put up with your provocations one moment longer."

Eddie was again on his feet, trying hard to give the impression that he'd soon be leaving, but he just wasn't up to it. He wanted to see what else I knew, he wanted to know how much of a danger I might be to him and Phli, his dear Phli.

"So shall we go on to your own sexual preferences?" I said. "Perhaps Princess Mafalda will have wondered how come you and the prince her husband are so inseparable. I could always arrange for her to receive some information. But that wouldn't be cricket, now, would it?"

"You're quite right, it wouldn't be cricket," said Eddie von Bismarck, wiping away the sweat between his mouth and his nose.

"An article in some French, or British, or American paper might perhaps speculate on the Prince of Hesse's nocturnal visits to the Führer's room. Is it or is it not true that some fifteen years ago the Bavarian police kept documentation locked up in a safe on Hitler's encounters with some young aides? That too might be of interest to journalists."

"Enough!"

Eddie von Bismarck, my dear friend Eddie, was burned out. He'd yelled, he didn't want me to go on, and he was quite right.

Mentally, I gave silent thanks to Percy Winner, my dear friend Winner, one of the few friends I trusted. It was he who'd told me, in his delicious Yankee accent, the details of the Prince of Hesse's private life: his preference for occasional encounters at the cinema, his tender friendship with the English poet, the Jew Siegfried Sassoon and his relations with other German homosexuals in Rome. Thus I at last understood what that journalist, Italo Tavolato, was alluding to when Phli and his wife arrived at Baroness Uexküll's party. "A lovely couple, a fine marriage," I'd said. "But every marriage needs balance," Tavolato had replied.

Without Winner, without his perfect acquaintance with the American Secret Service's reports on Philipp von Hessen, which he'd told me as we crunched seafood on the fishing boat, while the wind blew through our unbuttoned shirts, I'd never have been able to make Eddie von Bismarck tremble and cause his mouth to dry up, I'd never have been able to make him as pale as a dead moon, or to make him howl with that depth of utter desperation.

"Now it's your turn to talk, Eddie", I said.

My voice was worn down to a raw gurgle. I was tired, so tired, yet I'd spoken urbanely, respecting my adversary. It was all in the cricketing spirit.

Actually, I'd reconstructed the first part of the story on my own, on the basis of a few articles which my secretary in Rome had traced in the Foreign Press Club, and then summarized to Tamburi over the 'phone.

According to the official version told by German propaganda, Hitler had enrolled in 1914 as a volunteer in the army of Bavaria, the so-called RIR 16, the 16th Bavarian Reserve, in the List Regiment, and he'd served as a *Meldegänger*, or staff messenger, on the French front, which meant being continuously exposed to enemy fire. According to the official version of the Nazi regime, it was at war that Hitler had come to know the Jews and their vile cowardice. In 1918, a few months before the end of the war, he had been decorated with the Iron Cross, 2nd Class. It was life at the front that had forged the Führer, making into him the man of destiny who would take in hand the future of Germany and rid the land of Jews. According to the propaganda, there was one in his own regiment, Gutmann by name. He and Hitler could not stand one another. When they met, they avoided all verbal exchanges. Hitler was disgusted by people like that. Already before receiving the Iron Cross he had performed heroic actions. Once, throwing himself into a ditch between the enemy lines to shelter from the bullets and shells whistling on every side, he had found himself in the midst of a group of English soldiers. He had drawn his pistol and arrested them, after which he'd led them back to the German lines as prisoners. In France, during the Picardy campaign, in clashes along the River Aisne, he had captured twelve French soldiers during a patrol, thus enabling his regiment to advance and inflict grave losses on the enemy. That was the official version, repeated *ad nauseam* by newspapers and school books in Germany.

Eddie hesitated a moment, before starting. Then he said:

"The truth is that Hitler ought never to have received the Iron Cross. Not one of the deeds attributed to him during the war is true. The tale of the Englishmen the Führer took prisoner single-handed, armed with only a pistol, is a propaganda invention. The other story, that of the twelve Frenchmen taken prisoner, is quite true. But it wasn't Hitler who captured them: it was Gutmann the Jew."

It was precisely thanks to Gutmann, explained Eddie, that Hitler had been awarded the Iron Cross, it was Gutmann who'd proposed that the honor should go to the young Austrian corporal. For his part, Gutmann was one of the bravest men in the RIR 16. He had received the Iron Cross a long time before Hitler, and he was rated by his superiors as one of the most generous, fearless and capable soldiers in the entire List Regiment.

"Is it true," I asked, "that, despite being a *Meldegänger*, Hitler always stayed in the rearguard, as some newspapers have written?"

"He was responsible for communications with regimental HQ, not with the front line. So he could stay kilometers from the line of fire. He was regarded as an *Etappensau*, a "rearguard sow", one of those soldiers who kept well away from the deadly fire of our front lines."

Of course, continued Eddie, things could go wrong for him too, and once he was in fact wounded in the thigh by a piece of shrapnel. But Hitler's risk of getting killed was infinitely lower than those run by front-line soldiers and *Meldegänger*.

Sometimes he visited positions closer to the line of fire, and everyone there could see quite how terrified he was. At mess he'd unbutton his NCO's epaulettes, as some do in order not to be identified in forward positions, within range of enemy binoculars, while all the other soldiers calmly went on wearing theirs, because they knew that the real front line was quite another story.

One of the worst weeks of the war was in August 1918, but this time too Hitler didn't get a taste of it: on August 21st, the first day of a terrible English offensive, he'd left the front to attend a signalers' training course in Nuremberg, hundreds of kilometers away. A few months after attending the course, in the fall of the same year, Hitler again left the battlefield, after getting himself granted a furlough, and, straight after his return, he was off again, this time to a military hospital, a *Kriegslazarett*, the Pasewalk Clinic, about a hundred kilometers north-east of Berlin. Hitler had become blind.

He told the doctors that he had been hit in the eyes during a gas attack. A small taste, in other words, of what his comrades-in-arms had suffered: the British used mustard gas, the same gas that had put me out of action and wrecked my lungs. This gas corrodes the mucous membranes and can cause blindness. Later on, Hitler is said to have liked putting it about that the injury had been extremely severe, and that for some time the gas had left him blind.

"What no one knows or is supposed to know," said Eddie, "is that at Pasewalk they discovered that Hitler's blindness was not due to gas, but to a hysterical reaction, as often happened during the Great War with soldiers lacking in courage."

The section of the Pasewalk *Kriegslazarett* handling this kind of condition was known as the section of the *Kriegszitterer*, those whom war had reduced to trembling, and was led by an energetic and rather unusual man: Doctor Edmund Forster.

Forster had discovered and concentrated his study on the fact that many soldiers' illnesses at war were simply hysterical phenomena, in other words, manifestations of cowardice on the part of psychopathic personalities. In 1917, he had published a number of papers setting forth his theory. The entire consciousness of hysterics is in itself, said Forster, utterly different from that of normal persons, and the origin of this is to be found in a profoundly infantile character, at once fearful and megalomaniac. According to Doctor Forster, every man tends towards hysteria to a greater or lesser degree, but it attains pathological levels only in minds afflicted by excessive self-esteem. This is in fact quite normal in children, but when they become adults, they acquire a better perception of their worth and duly adapt to reality. Hysterics, however, remain children, they regard themselves as the center of the universe and always attribute their failures to external factors. Lulling themselves into a state of excessive self-esteem, they take refuge in the analysis and study of their own emotional reactions, and this in turn leads to a gradual detachment from objectivity, in which they accord paroxysmal attention to their own emotional sphere, in a vicious circle that leads them to further inflate their own importance. Hysterics thus develop a special fantasy and an exceptional capacity for make-believe, which Forster calls autosuggestion. Their self-awareness is very different from that of normal people.

Forster studied and described cases of soldiers who were fearful but wanting to be praised, who had a congenital tendency to react hysterically in the face of danger, to save themselves without revealing their own cowardice. The hysterical reaction consisted of the apparent manifestation of serious illness, such as paralysis, blindness, epilepsy and tremors. Not only were these persons incapable of repressing these symptoms but, on the contrary, they turned them to their own advantage: this was the only way to stay far from the front without losing face. It was no accident that many of the patients at Pasewalk declared themselves impatient to get back to the front. This was, in Doctor Forster's view, nothing but a piece of semi-conscious play-acting, a risk-free ploy for making a good impression.

Forster had designed a highly successful cure, one that worked for almost all his patients.

He had his own rough and ready method: he treated the soldiers suffering from it as frauds, targeting their self-respect. During treatment sessions, Forster would insult his patients, accusing them of simulation, upbraiding them for having abandoned their comrades at the front and being a bunch of little women. Sometimes he employed electric shock treatment, but above all he shook hysterical soldiers by handling them roughly, insulting them and screaming at them. Thanks to this somewhat homely technique he had cured hundreds of them. Thus the Pasewalk doctor had become famous after the war. The fact of being among Doctor Forster's patients meant only one thing: that one was a coward so sick with terror at the mere idea of having to go and fight that he tried to hide this by faking illness. An unbearable dishonor for an ex-combatant in the Great War!

"The section of the Pasewalk clinic that treated mustard gas cases," Eddie explained, "had examined Corporal Hitler and diagnosed that his eyes were fine. So they'd sent him to Forster. Nor was their diagnosis mistaken: Forster did indeed cure him, but by then the war was over."

Subsequent Nazi propaganda had succeeded in turning the truth inside out. They'd managed to hide the hysterical origin of Hitler's blindness and the fact that Hitler had been cured by Forster, so that Pasewalk had become a sort of shrine. An entire mythology had been built up around Hitler's military service, thanks to the complicity of former RIR 16 comrades, who publicized a whole series of the Führer's heroic deeds, every one of them invented. Some were generously rewarded with party and government positions.

Other soldiers, however, had been bold enough to bear witness to the truth of the matter, and articles had appeared in some newspapers which had gravely embarrassed Hitler and the NSDAP. But once Hitler had become Chancellor and controlled propaganda, the fable of the war hero had gained the upper hand.

"The very next year, they even organized pilgrimages to Pasewalk," said Eddie, "publicizing the clinic as the place where Hitler, after recovering his sight, had taken the decision to enter politics and save Germany from ruin and the Jews."

"But in actual fact Hitler was treated by Forster as a poor madman, a liar and a simulator. Isn't that so?"

"For sure. Only, there was no clinical report to show that."

"But Dr. Forster will surely have had one!" I said.

Eddie guffawed again:

"The moment Hitler became Chancellor, Forster was denounced for sentiments hostile to the government and suspected pro-Jewish sympathies. At first he fled to France, but then he realized he couldn't stay a step ahead of the Gestapo, so he went back home and shot himself. It was certainly a strange suicide: no one, not even his wife, had ever imagined that Forster owned a pistol, but that's how it happened. And Forster himself had recently confided to a journalist: "If I should die, it will not be suicide". Just to make it clearer, the only other two men who'd managed to find Hitler's health records, a general and an officer in the secret service, were both killed.

Malaparte, you're a writer, don't you find that tale quite extraordinary?" said Eddie.

He had spoken with an empty smile, a smile that expressed empty joy, a purely abstract, cold, solitary joy, the kind of joy a cricketer experiences when he's bowled out an ace batsman with a brilliant googly. In that smile was all his paltry pleasure at being a Bismarck, the scion of a glorious German family, his pleasure at having kept well away from the Nazis while being the heart companion, perhaps even something more, of the man who enjoyed access day and night to the Führer's room. What an immeasurable demonstration of power! Eddie was admitted to the magic circle of Nazism, yet he spat on it. *I spit on Hitler, I spit on Phli.*

"All right, it's quite clear to me," I said. "Hitler's a cowardly hysteric who's conquered Germany by getting them all to take him for a hero. If someone had managed to publish at the right time the fact that Hitler had been cured by Forster, maybe he'd never have made it to Chancellor. He certainly wouldn't have been able to present himself as a war hero capable of saving Germany. But you, Eddie, have gone on for a long time, yet you still haven't answered my question: what has all this to do with the postcard stolen by the Sturmbannführer?"

Once again Eddie stiffened. He looked to his right and then to his left, as though he was trying to find a way out, while he was really seeking one within himself. He was making his mind up whether he really liked spilling the beans, or whether he was going against the grain.

At length he said in a very small voice:

"The card once belonged to the Führer. Forster gave it to him with a written dedication on the day when he was released from Pasewalk."

Doctor Forster had a rather surly character, explained Eddie, but he allowed himself to be moved by his *Kriegszitterer*, the lads returning shell-shocked from the war, and sometimes he made them little presents. In this case it was Hitler who'd asked him for one: Forster's autograph behind a postcard, the card of the Saarburg crucifix. For Hitler it was a fine souvenir, the souvenir of when Philipp von Hessen had saved his life. He could certainly not have imagined at the time that Doctor Forster was to become famous for having cured so many hysterical soldiers.

Years later, When Hitler had become the new star of politics, half of Germany hastened to clamber onto the victor's chariot. Philipp von Hessen went several times to see the Führer and pick up the threads of their old friendship that had begun at Saarburg, the friendship that had sprung from a double miracle, as my soldier had told me during the war: Philipp had killed the French soldier at the very moment when German and French crossfire had destroyed the cross, leaving the crucified Christ inexplicably standing unsupported.

Today, only today do I know the real meaning of that miracle: that naked Christ marked the Fall of Man, and God falling with us; it announced every one of the Jews who was to fall, naked and tortured like that Christ, with arms raised to Heaven like that Christ, in the extermination camps where Hitler had brought them. At his feet, when Hitler was miraculously saved from death, began the road that led to the abyss of Auschwitz, Treblinka and Bergen-Belsen, to the slaughter of millions of soldiers and civilians. The Saarburg crucifix was a warning, an early warning of the Abomination of Desolation.

Eddie continued his account.

"In Capri, we often have electricity blackouts. But years ago, during the long drawn-out economic crisis that followed the Great War, they often had them in Germany too. One day, Hitler had been called away unexpectedly to attend a meeting and just at that moment there was a blackout. A damned nuisance. Phli then offered Hitler his personal manservant to pack the luggage he'd be taking with him on the trip. As he and his manservant were rummaging by candlelight in his friend's room, Phli chanced upon a series of postcards that had been well hidden. They all depicted the Saarburg crucifix, from different angles. Phli picked them up and noticed that one of them dated 'Pasewalk 1918' was signed by Forster on the back."

Phli's first thought had been to ask Hitler if he could take one of these as a present, a memento of their first, memorable encounter. But when he found the postcard bearing Forster's signature, he slipped it into his pocket without saying a thing.

He then deliberately caused an "accident", dropping his candle among Hitler's postcards and feeding some old papers into the flames, so that the loss of the card could be put down to the blaze. His manservant was completely taken in, anxiously putting out the fire with a jug of water, after which he told Hitler of the accident, as Phli had intended.

"Phli doesn't know whether Hitler ever realized that the card had disappeared, but even if he had done so, the Führer would have put it down to that accident," Eddie concluded.

"What ever can have been written on the card?" asked Sirignano.

"Nothing much. A well-wishing phrase addressed to the soldier Adolf Hitler and signed Professor Edmund Forster – Kriegslazarett Pasewalk, November 1918."

The problem was not the content of the postcard, but the signature and the date. With time, Forster had become well known. His work on the curing of trauma-induced mental illnesses had circulated among all the specialists. His signature on the postcard to Hitler was evidence that Hitler had been in his care, and the date corresponded with the period when Forster was working at Pasewalk. In the 15 years between the end of the war and the time when Hitler became Chancellor (1918-1933), the importance of those few lines had grown out of all proportion. In 1918, those clichéd words meant only that an obscure soldier called Adolf Hitler had been hospitalized at Pasewalk. In 1933, however, they revealed that the hero of the German people, Chancellor Adolf Hitler, was no war hero but a pusillanimous hysteric and an impostor.

Meanwhile a number of newspapers had entered the fray, including *Echo der Woche*, publishing statements by Hitler's comrades-in-arms: the Nazi boss had not been an exceptionally brave soldier, but if anything the opposite. There was a risk the public might learn the truth: Hitler had not been a war hero, but a mediocre phony of a soldier. Yet no one could make the decisive link, connecting his name with that of Forster, the specialist in cases of war neurosis. Only the postcard and the clinical records made that possible. That was why Forster had been eliminated; and that, too, explained the killing of the general and the secret service man who had consulted the Pasewalk clinical records. Rebellious newspapers like the *Echo der Woche* were silenced by a series of trials and the regime's powerful propaganda machine. Thus, the only threat from Hitler's past was the postcard from Saarburg.

Getting rid of the postcard put Phli in a fix, given its importance. One day it might prove useful: Germany was like a ship in the tempest, and even if the Princes of Hesse and the Nazi leadership got on fine, one never knew what the future held. It might always be useful to have the means to blackmail Hitler or launch a hostile campaign to turn public opinion against him. So Phli decided to entrust the card to Eddie, who'd put it in a safe place in Capri, well away from Germany. Eddie and Mona had decided to hide it at the Fortino, but not in some safe or strongbox, which might always be forced by thieves.

"If there's one thing that doesn't interest burglars," said Eddie, "it's books: they're hard to resell and their cash value is low. So let's put the card inside a book, hidden in a cover flap. For years, nothing happened. Then the Sturmbannführer had the crazy idea of taking the book, and you know all the rest."

"One moment," I said, "I saw the Sturmbannführer making off with the book. But he didn't look at what was inside it, between the pages."

I saw Eddie grow thoughtful. Then he said:

"Yes, it's true, when Phli was screaming at him and threatening him with the most dreadful punishments, the Sturmbannführer kept saying that he'd never stolen a postcard. He didn't even seem to understand what we were talking about, and he kept denying it all categorically. That was what made Phli lose his temper: he can't stand someone denying evidence. Phli easily loses patience. When he began screaming and yelling, the discussion went to pieces."

"I think the Sturmbannführer hadn't the least idea there was anything else in the book," I replied. "He had some other motive for stealing it."

"What was the book?" asked Sirignano.

"The only thing I know is that the title was BESTIE DELINQUENTI," I replied.

"Curious. Eddie, why did you and Mona put the card inside that particular book?" Sirignano asked.

"So as not to lose sight of the hiding place, even years later. The title served as a memo: Hitler's a beast and a delinquent. We'd never be able to forget where we'd put his postcard."

"I wonder why the Sturmbannführer stole that very book, if he didn't know the postcard was inside it," said Sirignano.

"I'd like to remind you that Mona still doesn't believe the Sturmbannführer was the thief," said Eddie, "and Mona has an excellent intuition."

"I know," I replied, "but I saw our man taking the book with my own eyes."

It was time we were on our way. Eddie seemed relieved to have gotten these things off his chest. He'd spilled the beans, and he was happy to have done so under threat, without having to feel guilty for his actions. He'd enjoyed learning all the foul gossip that was circulating, about Phli, about him and even about the Führer. He knew what threats might hang over him, even in the near future. And now we were friends again, as though nothing had ever come between us, the old harmony had been restored. Everything was fine, and we were good old friends once more, all's well that ends well.

"I know I can trust Sirignano," said Eddie, "he's a gentleman. But you too, Malaparte, must promise me that this business will never come to other ears. Neither the postcard nor Phli's occasional peccadilloes. That wouldn't be cricket."

"You're quite right, Eddie, that wouldn't be cricket. So, you've nothing to worry about."

"What d'you mean to do now?"

"I must think things over. I've got to work out my next moves."

"I hope I've been of use to you," said Eddie, who'd started out not wanting to help me.

Eddie was like that: he was a generous soul, but to be really generous he needed some threat. I'd threatened him to get him to speak, and that suited him down to the ground. Like all Germans, he had no use for freedom. He preferred to obey. Eddie's game of cricket was one in which you did what the captain told you to.

In the war that was about to begin, those were the rules the Germans would play by. They'd stand by them faithfully, even in the camps, the gas chambers, the cremation ovens of Auschwitz: they'd carry out orders, oh yes, they'd carry out their Great Captain's orders, just as the members of the Marylebone Cricket Club obeyed Lord Harris on the pitch at Lords.

That was cricket for you.

The Guardian of Disorder

After the nth night spent out in the open, in a copse on the outskirts of Anacapri, I came early in the morning to the Villa La Madonnina, the residence of Carmela Capasso in Buronzo, alias Madame Carmen. I got there strolling like any ordinary tourist, expecting at every step to be recognised and arrested. But nothing happened. I didn't know how to interpret this nth miracle; it will all work out fine, I said to myself; either that, or it will all go as badly as possible.

Madame Carmen: she was my wild card. It was she herself who'd opened my eyes, in the Charterhouse cloister, when she took Edda under her cloak like an Amazon protecting her daughter. It was there, on the spur of the moment, that the idea came to me. Madame Carmen held the reins of Mussolini's superstition. She was the key to stopping the OVRA and the police. And just as Mussolini's weak spot was Madame Carmen, Madame Carmen's weak spot was her husband.

The garden of the villa gave access to a big living room full of old sofas in dark walnut, old mustard-colored armchairs, dusty lampshades with switches covered with a plume, glass gewgaws, china dogs and cats and a broken down piano that looked like a coffin. It was a classic old-fashioned sitting room, and anyone who used to visit some old auntie with his parents will know what I'm talking about, because that's the kind of sitting room in which a child can't move without breaking something, so that the afternoon invariably comes to a close with the kid getting a good hiding and cursing the old auntie and her wretched sitting room through his tears.

I kissed the cartomancer's hand and announced in imperative tones: "I need a consultation, and I need it now. I'll brook no refusal."

I was ill-shaven and my clothes were crumpled, but I was decisive and wide awake. Taken by surprise, Madame Carmen didn't know what to answer. As I'd imagined, she was used to receiving only adoring devotees. She had no defenses against brusque, unceremonious manners.

We sat at a card table with four chairs around it. A young maid served us an espresso coffee as black as pitch.

"Oh, I'm so tired today," said Madame Carmen slowly sipping from her cup; "Whatever made you decide to come and consult *me*? You want to play the mystery man, I know. D'you know something, Signor Suckert? You made an instant impression on me. There's a light in your face, something celestial, it's like a magnetic force."

Now that Edda wasn't there to defend and leech off, Madame Carmen's manner had changed. She put down the little cup, rose from the table and flopped onto an enormous brown velvet sofa.

"Come, come here next to me, Signor Suckert. Today I'm simply too tired to remain sitting."

She brought the back of her hand to her forehead, as though to check her temperature. Madame Carmen's fingers were long, long, tapering, as white as marble and wonderfully manicured, but her nails were cut to a wedge shape and that gave her a vague touch of the vampire.

"You know, I'm not up to reading cards today. But if you come close to me here, I'll read your hand."

I sat on a stool before the clairvoyant and placed my fingers in her open palm. My hand was warm and rough, hers was icy and as smooth as polished marble.

"Now look into my eyes," she said. "That is how I receive information from the World of Shades."

We were wasting time, I was growing nervous.

The cartomancer stared intensely into my pupils, then closed her eyes. After about half a minute she opened them again. Her look was rapt now, as though she were receiving revelations from some bottomless abyss.

"You, Signor Suckert, have faced great dangers in your youth. You escaped something tremendous. A pistol shot, a bomb, something like that."

"That's true. I went to war, like everyone else in my generation. You've only to make an educated guess at my age, and you can see that at once."

"Eh? Ah yes, of course," said Madame Carmen, caught off balance. "Then I can see some danger in the future. Perhaps an infectious illness. But you'll recover. Yes, yes, you'll recover! But you must beware of heights and speed. Bear in mind that each one of us holds his destiny in his hands: if you can, avoid too much travel by air and don't speed too much in cars."

Madame Carmen's voice advanced by fits and starts, sometimes warm, sometimes as though she were absent, and she accompanied her words by vague, confused theatrical gestures. I'd been patient for quite long enough.

"Do you by any chance see blackmail in my future?"

"Is someone blackmailing you?"

"No, it's I who am on the point of using blackmail."

From my pocket I drew the anti-Fascist verses I'd obtained from Sirignano and pressed them into her hand. They were a satire on *Giovinezza, giovinezza, primavera di bellezza*, the famous Fascist anthem. From *"Youth, youth, Spring of Beauty"* it had been transformed into *"Youth, oh Youth, now it's Springtime for our Filth"*:

> Giovinezza, *youth, oh, youth,*
> *Now it's springtime for our filth,*
> *All the mob and all the mobsters*
> *Draped in our three-colored flag.*
> *Of the Huns the bastard spawn*
> *Join our home-grown hireling pawns,*
> *And the State protects them all.*
>
> *Depravity and Delinquenza,*
> *Of our Fascists the essenza,*
> *All that crime and thuggery*
> *Will never bring us liberty!*

They're all jailbirds, gallows-fodder,
They're a band of thieves and robbers,
Black Hand felons and brown-nosers
In the service of the Bosses.
Brigands all and desperadoes,
They're our Sect of the Assassins,
Red-scare scabs an' slimy snitches,
Work-shy finks an' bums an' butchers.

Delinquenza, Delinquenza,
Of our Fascists the essenza,
All that crime and thuggery
Can never bring us liberty!

"Have you read it all?" I asked afterwards.

"I've read it, Signor Suckert".

She took another look at the anti-Fascist song, leaved through it, and returned it to me.

"Very well, it was written by your husband, some fifteen years ago," I said.

"My husband? But that's not possible! My husband is an ardent Fascist!"

"D'you really think so? Have you perhaps checked through everything written by the *Onorevole* Buronzo? Can you really swear with absolute certainty that, before he met you, he may not have harbored sentiments hostile to the Duce? Besides, you know perfectly well how things work these days in Italy: to get rid of someone, to lose your job, there's absolutely no need for a formal sentence: the shadow of a doubt is quite sufficient. Fascism is like those great serpents in the Amazon jungle that feel threatened by every living thing, and attack it the moment it passes nearby. It doesn't matter if it's innocuous. Fascism doesn't seek out the guilty, just suspects."

As I spoke, the hieratic features of Madame Carmen turned, first yellow, then violet, and at length grey, revealing like a semaphore, moment after moment, the shock, rage and fear inflicted by my words.

"Why did you come here to tell me this tale?"

"To help you. I'd been wanting to do it for quite some time, but our meeting at the Charterhouse was a signal from Destiny."

"Speak clearly. What do you want of me?"

"That's simple: telephone the personal secretary of the Duce, with whom you'll certainly be very well acquainted, and plead my cause."

"And what cause is that, please?"

"That really doesn't matter. You have only to ask that Signor Suckert be left in peace. Failing which, there'll be a hex, a dreadful hex, it's written in the cards. Mussolini believes in you, in your prophecies and forecasts."

Madame Carmen fell silent, lowered her eyes and reflected briefly.

"You are a disgusting individual. An extortioner," she murmured in a very low voice.

"No, my only concern is to protect you. The wrath of Mussolini, if he were to discover these verses by the *Onorevole* Buronzo, would be terrible. Your husband's career would be over at once. I'm sure you know the Duce's Personal Private Secretary, Osvaldo Sebastiani, very well. Call him and ask that he cast a kind eye on Signor Suckert's predicament. Otherwise the Duce would risk grave reversals of fortune. The moment is grave, war could break out soon, and at war one needs luck, plenty of luck. That's all there is to it."

"Suckert, you lie. My husband's Fascist faith is perfect and immaculate. The *Onorevole* Buronzo is a Fascist of the first hour."

"I'm lying? All right then, let's put my word to the proof. Let's leave things just as they are. Then we'll see just what becomes of your husband's career. And his hopes of being appointed a Senator of the Kingdom."

The clairvoyant had thought about it for a few moments, making some curious grimaces and tormenting her lips with her teeth. At length, she announced in funereal tones:

"Very well, Suckert. Tomorrow I'll call Mussolini's Private Office."

"Not tomorrow, straight away. Here, in front of me."

We'd moved into another room, to telephone far from indiscreet ears. The message dictated on the telephone had been rapid, clear and effective: Madame Carmen had studied the cards and the cards said that Signor Suckert was entitled to special consideration, otherwise things would go badly for the Duce's affairs. The question was too complicated to be discussed over the telephone in greater detail, this was, however, what Madame Carmen had to communicate, and she requested a reply as soon as possible, at most within 24 hours.

At the other end of the line the voice of Osvaldo Sebastiani, the Duce's feared and powerful personal secretary, was rigid with stupor and consternation: that wretched Malaparte (Sebastiani knew perfectly well that Suckert was my old name) had managed to insinuate himself with the personal esoteric consultant of the Big Chief. Who was going to tell that to Mussolini, with his dreadful temper? A fine fix for him.

Just before ending the call, however, Sebastiani found the solution:

"D'you know what? I'll speak with Bocchini about this. Relax, Signora. Together we'll convince the boss."

Bocchini was the chief of police and, as Lucia had told me, it was he that Mussolini sometimes sent to consult Madame Carmen in his place. Bocchini, with his authority, was the only one in a position to convince the Duce to close the Suckert-Malaparte affair.

"Are you happy, Suckert? You've taken advantage of a poor, defenseless woman," said the clairvoyant before dismissing me. Then she pointed at the pamphlet containing the anti-Fascist verses.

"How many copies are there in circulation?"

"This is the only one I know of. As soon as you get a positive sign from the Duce's secretariat, and as soon as I see that no police officer is coming to lock me up, I'll hand it over to you. You have my word for that."

"Edda should be ashamed of herself to have a friend like you," said the clairvoyant before she closed the door on me.

"Edda is Mussolini's daughter," I replied, "she doesn't even know what shame is."

I left Madame Carmen almost dancing for joy, it was as though I'd taken a great weight off my stomach. I felt that the matter was almost closed, it would be enough for Sebastiani to take the time to talk to Bocchini, for Bocchini to talk to Manzi, and Manzi to his men in the police and the OVRA.

I knew too that the postcard that had belonged to Hitler was nothing to do with me. That had just been a silly, tragic coincidence; who knows why the Sturmbannführer had made off with the very book that contained the precious postcard signed by Doctor Forster? For some absurd reason, that foul Nazi business had crossed with my own destiny. But thank heavens none of that had anything to do with my person: neither the book, nor the postcard of the Saarburg crucifix, nor the heavy secret that lay behind it. It was an inexplicable coincidence, but still just a coincidence.

The infernal machine that had been grinding me down until that moment might at last begin to relent. I had only to hold out a little while longer, a very, very little while, until the reply from Mussolini's secretary reached Madame Carmen. I'd call the cartomancer from some public telephone and she'd give me the good news.

In the evening I'd go to Lucia's. I wanted to appoint her guardian of my moral and physical disorder. Schoolmaams make excellent guardians, don't they? I'd sleep at her place; that was possible now, things were calming down.

The Great Imbecile

"Oh, my love," said Lucia throwing herself round my neck, her eyes red and lined with crying, the moment I entered her room; "Pardon me," she said, freeing herself from my embrace, "I shouldn't have allowed myself..."

"Don't you worry, I adore passionate women, they're the ones I get the most pleasure from abandoning," I replied.

She forced a laugh, holding a silk scarf against her mouth to hold back her emotion.

I told her of the stratagem I'd thought up to get myself out of trouble: the blackmail against Madame Carmen and her husband and the clairvoyant's phone call to Osvaldo Sebastiani, the Duce's private secretary. Sebastiani's acid but resigned tone, then the promise that Madame Carmen's request on behalf of Signor Suckert would be fulfilled.

Lucia listened to me seriously, without commenting, clasping her hands. She seemed at once galvanized by the boldness of the undertaking and petrified by the risks I'd taken.

"Do you still have my present?" she said at length.

I pulled out the handkerchief with the imprint of her lips. She drew near and kissed me hard, in silence. Then she pulled away from me again, looking serious.

"You can't stay here. There have been police moving around here all day. They've even come into the pensione."

"How come? When I came, everything seemed peaceful. My problem's on the point of being resolved, have you or haven't you understood that?"

"Did you track down Carmine?" she asked.

"No. But I'm sure something's moving in Rome. The order to arrest me will be cancelled, I've already told you that. Well... that at least is what I hope."

Lucia looked at me with her eyes again clouded by tears. Moments later, there we were, clinging to each other half naked on her bed, caring nothing for the risk we ran, on the contrary, inflamed by our awareness that every instant together could be our last, a knock on the door and it would all be over.

"Malaparte, one day we'll not see each other any more. Don't say anything, I know that's the way it is," said Lucia as we rested next to one another, our legs and arms still entwined. "Tell me what you were like when you were a kid."

I closed my eyes and told her of my daydream at the house of Guglielmo Rulli, the dream of my weird, wild Tuscany, my barefoot childhood among the ears of corn, those naked peasant girls out in the fields, those madcap outings with my three ex-officer buddies, what were their names? ah yes: Paolo, Alcide and Moreno, the Feast of San Michele at Carmignano where you played chess, improvised poetry and, above all, got drunk, oh yes, and how! And then my outings with the ghosts, my two mamas, my old nurse Milziade who knew me better than anyone else, even better than my many, too many, women.

Lucia was listening to me, she too with her eyes closed. Then she gave a sort of start, opened her eyes wide and said:

"Malaparte, you're an imbecile."

"Come again?"

"How did that chessboard get to House like Me?"

"The chessboard with PAM written on it? Who knows?"

"I mean: are you quite sure it's not one of *your* things?"

For a moment, I could say nothing.

"No, I couldn't swear to that. I can't be quite sure. I had so much stuff brought from Prato and from Rome..."

"Then you really are an imbecile."

I stared at her open-mouthed, what could I say? So this was what my fans thought of me. Lucia was sitting on the bed, still naked, but as upright and severe as a Greek goddess. She was covering her breasts with one arm and with the other she was drying her cheeks still wet from weeping.

"Just listen to me, Malaparte. You've told me you played *chess* in that village, Carmignano, at a feast dedicated to *San Michele*. You've told me the meaning of San Michele – Saint Michael – it's he who is like God. Your three friends had names that began with *P, A* and *M*. Paolo, Alcide and Moreno, your three ex-officers. Now I'm asking you, just think!"

I burst out laughing, I sat on the edge of the bed and just kept on laughing. Then my laughter died on me. Staring into the void, I travelled back in time, back to the days of my youth in Tuscany, to the Feast at Carmignano, to those wild outings with my three crazy ex-officer buddies, Paolo, Alcide and Moreno, and how we'd get drunk together, ranting on about war, wine and women, about God and Hell, and my versifying to them under a tree and of how we'd roll on half-sozzled to the Carmignano chess tournament, moving the players' pieces to drive them crazy, while one of the trio, it's too long ago to remember whether it was Paolo, Alcide or Moreno, carved their three initials, PAM, all over the place: on a tree, a door, a chessboard, maybe even a chessboard I'd brought home with me...

My time-trip came to an end, and there I was again, sitting in front of Lucia as naked as a worm.

"You're dead right. I got it all wrong, all so wrong! The chessboard will have been packed at Prato along with a thousand other bits of garbage. The inscription *Who is like God?* refers to Saint Michael, the patron of the Feast at Carmignano. The three letters PAM have nothing to do with poor Pam or with a Russian word. And I'm an idiot. I'm an idiot because I got it all so wrong. But... but, my goodness, it's fantastic! So, all that fuss about a mysterious inscription was about nothing. Just a misunderstanding, blown up out of all proportion by the tales embroidered by Munthe, Cerio and Mona Williams... Munthe sold me the chessboard as a great historical souvenir, just like his fake coins, his fake statues and his fake vases... Paolo, Alcide or Moreno must have carved their three initials on the chessboard during the Feast of San Michele, when we'd been drinking, and the old chessboard must have stayed among my things. So that means no one was trying to tie me up in some strange game with that inscription. It's I who am an imbecile; but maybe it's another sign that soon everything's going to work out for me, don't you think so? At long last I'm going to be able to go out wandering like a stray dog tonight."

"Malaparte, Malaparte... I pity the woman who marries you, you'll give her a heart attack with that optimism of yours. With all those cops milling around here, I'd not have been so optimistic. Still, if you'd like to stay here..."

Her voice was overflowing with tenderness and apprehension. She hadn't the courage to send me away. She preferred to risk it and stay with me.

"Sure, you're quite right after all," I said in the end, "I'd better leave. But where to? Villa Lysis isn't a good idea. In the past few days I've almost put down roots at Sirignano's place."

We crept out furtively from the pensione into one of the neighboring alleyways. It all seemed so quiet in the dark, the air smelled of moon, of rosemary and a thousand nameless desires, that was the Capri night air for you. Maybe, I thought, maybe this is my last night out on the run.

"I've got the keys of a cellar near here," said Lucia, "a little underground room. An old friend gave me it to store some of my things, there's no space for them in my own room."

"An old friend, did you say?"

"A free single woman's entitled to have a past, isn't she?" said Lucia with a little wink.

"You're quite right, she's entitled to that," I said.

We moved furtively in the dark, constantly looking over our shoulders, and eventually turned into a little street.

"We're almost there, it's just a little further," said Lucia. "You'll see, it's not too bad. It'll suit you fine for tonight. There's light, running water, and two windows. It's a sort of clandestine hidey-hole."

"I suppose that your friend has nothing against lodging a fugitive."

"Don't be silly. He knows you well, but he'll never hear a word about your visit."

"He knows me well?" I asked, while Lucia stopped at a little door and tried to put a key into the keyhole.

"Sure, he's a lawyer and a journalist, a decent person. He was at Mona's party too, when you and I met."

In a flash I recalled how, at the Fortino, moments before she collided with me, Lucia had been talking rather animatedly with an individual whom I couldn't recognise in the dark. I'd sometimes wondered who he was, but kept forgetting to ask her.

The key wouldn't go into the lock. Lucia tried hard to push it in, then tried another one.

"He's called Arturo. Arturo Assante. `Nu bravo guaglione*, as they say in Naples, a good lad. But that's all water under the bridge, now he's just an old friend."

"Arturo Assante? I know him well. I saw him recently at Mona Williams' place, at the party where we met. And then at Baroness Uexküll's place."

Lucia didn't answer. She was having trouble with the second key too, and pushing it so violently into the lock you'd have said she wanted to force it.

"Can't you be a little gentler?" I said, "we're making too much noise."

"I'm trying. Unfortunately, this key doesn't work either, as you can see."

At that moment, I thought again of Baroness Uexküll's party, where I'd met Questore Manzi, the OVRA regional boss, and of the men who gathered around him when I arrived: *Commendatore* Freddi, flanked by the American actors in Italy, and the journalists Tavolato and Da Zara. I'd run into them again at the Villa Ferraro party, where I'd made an appointment with Lucia. These were OVRA operatives, I knew that from Winner. A phrase of Winner's came to my mind: *But there are others like them in the area. We know there are two of them. We'd like to know who they are*

Two other people. One of them must be Arturo Assante, who was standing near Freddi, Tavolato and Da Zara at the Villa Ferraro. And the other one...

Ah yes, at that moment everything at last fell into place in my mind. Now it was all quite clear. It wasn't pleasant, but at least it was clear.

"No!" screamed Lucia, while four hands grabbed me from behind and two others held the ether-soaked handkerchief to my nose.

That night, for the first time, someone knew where I'd be sleeping.

Don Chameleon

"Signor Malaparte! Did you kill the English girl?"
"Signor Malaparte, look this way so we can take your photo!"
"Signor Malaparte, have you picked a lawyer?"
"Signor Malaparte, a statement for *Il Mattino*!"

Two days had passed since my arrest. The sun had come out a few minutes earlier and it was just beginning to get warm. The water in the harbor was calm, barely troubled by the passing of some fishing boat returning to its moorings. The handcuffs cut into my wrists, sawing at my skin.

The cops were pushing me towards the coastguards' launch, under the greedy eyes of reporters and photographers.

In a few minutes we'd be speeding towards Naples, where I'd be welcomed by an army of crime reporters. The cops (twenty or more of them, I couldn't even keep count of them all) surrounded me like a phalanx. In actual fact, they were taking good care to ensure that the journalists could see me, talk to me, even touch me. I must drink of this cup right down to the dregs. I had struck with the pen, I must perish by the pen. My career as a writer, my economic wellbeing, my freedom, my very life, were all ending in this public crucifixion.

I and Sirignano had got the point from the very beginning: no one was to write a word about my going into hiding in the hills of Capri. They wanted to stalk me oh so discreetly: no manhunt, no raids on V.I.P. villas. But once they'd got me, the press was to tear me into small pieces.

Behind the newsmen and cops stood an inquisitive little crowd: women, youths, a few old men, fishermen. News of an important arrest had spread like wildfire. Suddenly, I recognized a face in the crowd: it was Ciro, surrounded by a group of *scugnizzi*, the ragged little hoodlums he used for his shady undertakings. The *camorrista* waved to me and I responded with a smile.

I caught glimpses of Sirignano and Tamburi, and, standing further off, even Chantecler who, being a nocturnal creature, must have made an incredible effort to get to the quayside at dawn. Judging by their expressions, you'd have said they were attending my funeral.

All this, take good note, did not bother me one bit: while the newsmen were bombarding me with questions and the handcuffs hurting my wrists, there I was, smiling and thinking of my books.

I was barely 41 years old, but what a lot of fine books I'd written! One of my best novels, even if the usual envious critics pretended they'd not noticed, was called *Don Camalèo*. The protagonist was a chameleon, which I and Mussolini came across by chance during a ride in a Roman park. The Duce said to me: Malaparte, as this animal has so many extraordinary qualities, turn him into a man. Under my guidance, the chameleon learns to speak, read and even write. He enters politics, gets on, is elected to Parliament and even becomes a rival to Mussolini. Before meeting a tragic death, he proves to be a good deal more valid than the Duce, despite the fact that the latter's no less of a quick-change artist than he.

Ah, my sweet Lucia! While the cops were shoving me along the quayside towards the launch, in the midst of a horde of newsmen and photographers, I thought to myself: why do we writers never learn from what we write? I'd written about the greatest of quick-change artists, the chameleon, yet I'd not realized that in Capri I'd had one by my side, I'd held her in my arms, I'd made room for her in my bed.

Two OVRA agents were missing from Winner's count: one was you, friend Assante. The other, my sweet Lucia, was you.

You'd never been able to foresee where I'd pass the night. But that evening you'd succeeded, because it was you who'd provided me with a hiding place. And it was you who'd set off the trap.

Straight after the arrest, as soon as the effect of the ether had worn off, locked up in a cell not much bigger than a toilet, I'd had time to think it all through. At Mona Williams' party it was no accident when you ran into me in the garden in the dark. You and Assante had thought out a splendid comedy. You'd deliberately collided with me, so that our meeting would seem to be purely a matter of chance. The rest was part of your repertory. Yet you'd taken a few days to entrap me. Every night I'd slept somewhere different, unknown to anyone, and I'd always come to see you without warning, taking you by surprise.

Ah, sweet Lucia! Wouldn't it have been better to arrange for a pair of cops to find me in your bedroom? I'd have believed you'd been followed, that you were a victim like me. I'd not have understood that the chameleon was you, that it was you who'd been double-crossing me.

But, it's true, you weren't properly organized. After my first surprise visit to your pensione, you thought I'd not run the risk of trying a second time. Instead, I'd surprised you by returning. So you had to improvise. You'd persuaded me to leave the pensione, offering to put me up in a place belonging to Arturo Assante and making me believe that he was a former lover of yours, while he was in fact an OVRA colleague. All that fussing with the keys at the cellar door (obviously, all a charade) was to make as much noise as possible and catch the attention of some nearby OVRA operative or cop. They were keeping watch, Villa Lysis was not far from there and they knew that, sooner or later, I might be passing that way. The moment your colleagues were pressing the drug onto my nose, you even yelled out "No!" – just to complete your scenario. Or maybe that came from the heart, maybe you really were sorry that you'd conned me. Anyway, what did that matter now?

Ah, sweet Lucia! What a waste of a wonderful opportunity. I'd never allowed a woman into my books. Never a love story, never a female protagonist. You could have been the first one. Instead you've chosen to send Malaparte himself to prison, though he could have given you eternal life among his characters. My only possible revenge will be to let you die unknown.

The newsmen's voices were like a spray of machine-gun fire in my ears.

"Signor Malaparte! Will you be selling your Capri house now?"

"Signor Malaparte! Is it true that you fought a duel with the SS officer who died at the Quisisana? Is it true that you had a row with the officer shortly before his death?"

"Signor Malaparte! Is it true that you've attended orgies here in Capri? Is it true that you use drugs?"

From their questions it was not difficult to guess at the next day's headlines. Malaparte had murdered a young English poetess, he'd had a part in the death of an SS officer who suspected him and who, note the coincidence, was a rival for the affections of the English girl. What's more, the slimy Malaparte, who had already been sent once into internal exile, took part in orgies in the grottoes of Capri.

Despite all this, I kept smiling, with my head held high. I'd always wanted to be buried near my beloved Prato, on the summit of Mount Spazzavento. Up there the wind blows like hell and if, like me, you like spitting hard and far into the cold air, you've got to stand straight and hold your head high.

A newsman sidled up to me:

"Signor Malaparte, have you telephoned Tuscany? Have you spoken with your family in Florence?"

I'd determined that I'd not respond to these stupid questions. But I couldn't resist this last one:

"I'm from Prato, idiot. One can be a Tuscan without coming from Florence."

"Prato? And where is Prato?" asked the journalist, bearing down on me with a stupid smile. The cops let him through, and we found ourselves facing one another.

"I'm a Tuscan from Prato, I'm proud to be from Prato. And if I weren't from Prato, I'd rather not have been born," I said, and spat in his face.

He was a journalistic slave, like so many of them, a worm, a lemur, a hack of the dictatorship, singing hosannas to Mussolini, but one day he'd be among those pissing on his body. Curzio Malaparte was one of the hard men of journalism, a pain in the ass, maybe even an opportunist. But never a slave, let no one say that of me. And if someone reading me doesn't agree, I'll spit in his face too.

The journalistic slave swore and wiped his face with his sleeve while his scandalized colleagues made a great hue and cry. To punish me, one of the cops punched me on the back of the neck, so that I stumbled. The other cops drove me forward towards the pierhead with kicks. There the boat lay waiting for me, a coastguard launch.

To get me aboard, five of them grabbed me, lifting me like a bundle. The moment my feet touched deck I raised my eyes on the lovely feminine forms of Capri, her rocky breasts, her armpits thick with rosemary and maidenhair ferns, her proudly pointing cypress nipples, her sumptuous Anacapri hips, clothed with vines and perfumed olive groves, and the white villas spread out everywhere, roasting in the sun. I smiled and bid it all a silent farewell. Farewell, House like Me, farewell Febo, farewell Prince Sirignano, farewell grottoes and cliffs jutting out over the sea, I thought. Farewell Kluck, farewell Chantecler, farewell to Capri's sweet folly. Your Malaparte will send you postcards from behind bars.

Then, with the newsmen swarming round the launch and frantically scribbling their slavish lies in their notepads, just as we were casting off and there was Malaparte, well and truly shafted at last, it all happened.

I saw the mass of newsmen and cops on the quayside split into two wings. Between them appeared two guys in grey pinstriped suits. They were elbowing their way through the throng waving some papers. They looked like two civil servants, perhaps from some ministry.

I caught sight of Ciro casting knowing, challenging glances to the left and to the right. He swelled up like a bullfrog, clenched his jaws, seemed to grow even taller, suddenly transformed from some wretched *guappo*, some third-class provincial mobster, into one of his Brooklyn buddies, a real New York or Chicago boss. Behind him, a rippling movement stirred through that strange bunch of *scugnizzi*,

418

ragged youths from the Naples slums, thugs with the feet of dirty apes and the lightning brains of tigers.

The two grey-suited officials showed their papers to some cops on the quayside, then approached the launch. They took me to the far side of the boat so that I should not hear what was being said. Still, I did manage to catch something of it. The tone could hardly have been more agitated. The crowd looked on, silent and shocked.

"...telegram from Naples... the *Questore*... no prior warning!"

"...order coming from Rome... His Excellency... no alternative... but you're crazy!"

"...take responsibility for this... set matters straight at once... where's the prisoner?"

Without warning, some cops approached and yet again lifted me by main force, dumping me on the quayside.

At that moment something incredible took place, and if the reader doesn't believe what I'm telling, well, so much the worse for him, because he'll be missing the best part of the story.

It all began when the onlookers burst out cheering, at first timidly, then with growing conviction. A wave movement swept through the crowd, then closed in on the journalists. It looked almost as though there was some secret string-puller, some clever claque behind it all. I'd got it. It was Ciro and his *scugnizzi*.

Ciro had at once grasped that for some mysterious reason my arrest had been called off, and that what's more, it should never even have happened, it was being wiped off the slate. So now the newsmen, menials to Fascist power, counted for nothing.

Three or four *scugnizzi* suddenly began to snatch cameras, fountain pens and notepads, throwing them all into the water. A splendid Leica housed in leather flew beyond the launch and sank in the blue green water with a great splash. Its owner, a tall, gangling young photographer, howled as though they'd killed his mother. I heard Ciro's voice yelling obscenities at the newsmen, panting victoriously and sighing with pleasure. At last his day of glory had come round, his personal vengeance against Mussolini and journalists: the people who were on the point of ruining me, and whom Ciro hated more than anything in the world. Hadn't he told me that a hundred times?

Spurred on by Ciro and his claque, the crowd completed the job (every revolution is the work of a claque, that I've explained in detail in *The Technique of Revolution*). A stout little reporter's notebook was grabbed and thrown to a flock of seagulls that were floating nearby and looking lazily on the scene. The gulls took it for something edible and began to tear the book to pieces, while the journalist cursed madly. Another scribbler did all he could to protect his little exercise book, stuffing it down his trousers. But that was a big mistake because he got thrown into the sea together with all his things, notebook included.

Ah, if only some film-maker, a Lubitsch, a Cecil B. de Mille, had been there to film that epic encounter! Ciro and his boys even went so far as to tear the spectacles off newsmen's noses and to throw them onto distant rocks, where the lenses shattered, or where they bounced off and joined the fishes. Some of the victims reacted, but Ciro and his band, hardened by years of robberies and street fighting, soon got the better of them. Slaps and punches flew, some well placed kicks were landed between the legs and a good few head butts broke fragile noses. The cops yelled at everyone and made a big noise, sometimes pushing the scuffling mass, but they didn't intervene: after the annulment of my arrest, they didn't know which side to take. They looked rather stunned, even scared.

"Come with us, Signor Malaparte."

Three cops again grasped me under my armpits and marched me at the double to the office of the port police, at the far end of the quay.

I glanced behind me, to see how the brawl would end. There were still blows and screams galore, but it was quite clear that Ciro's young thugs had won the day. Here and there, a journalist sat on the ground with a bloodied face and his jacket torn from his back.

The cameras and notebooks that had immortalized Malaparte's arrest now lay at the bottom of the sea. I was once more a free man, a great writer and the owner of the finest villa in Capri.

My last glimpse of the brawl between journalists, ordinary folk and *Camorristi* took in Ciro, jubilant, staring in my direction from far off and yelling in dialect, as he threw a fat notebook into the sea *Dreams always do come true!* or words to that effect.

Then the door of the police station closed behind me. We entered a little office. I took a seat, they offered me a cigarette and undid my handcuffs.

"Would you like a glass of wine, Signor Malaparte? Or perhaps a beer? Or a fresh orange juice? You must excuse the fact that we've no ice, but you know, the Duce is keen on making economies in public offices. Now we'll call you a taxi. But if you'll permit us, first we have something to deliver to you."

"Can you explain to me once and for all what's going on?" I asked.

"Orders changed," said one of the cops.

"Cancelled," corrected another one.

"Countermanded," said yet another.

"You must excuse us but, you know, these are things that happen. Anyway, you've nothing more to worry about. Everything's in order now and you can relax and go back home."

As they were sending me off, they placed a little wooden box in my hand. It was a walnut box, with a brass spring fastener.

"We were told to hand this to you, Signor Malaparte. It was left with us by one of the officials from the Presidency of the Council."

"D'you mean those two men in grey suits?"

"That's it."

The taxi came to fetch me a few moments later. The highest ranking officer gave me a small sum to pay the fare. Tamburi, Sirignano and Chantecler were probably still in the vicinity, but I wanted a moment on my own to enjoy my freedom. I suspected that the little box might contain something important. The moment I boarded the taxi, I opened it.

It contained a white linen handkerchief, folded several times. Inside was a tiny card, filled with a dense feminine handwriting:

Signorina L, a credible witness, reported as follows to M's P.S.: Madame C really is seriously concerned about the possible consequences for M in the event of failure to grant Signor S's wishes.

M, the moment he was informed of this, and contrary to the opinion of O.S., personally granted S an immediate pardon.

Signorina L has always appreciated S's writings, quite apart from anything else.

Under this came the stamp of the Presidency of the Council, dated the previous day. Under that, like a signature, a pencil drawing of a pair of woman's lips. To make quite sure I'd get the message.

I screwed up my eyes, holding back tears, then burst out laughing. The taxi driver glanced at me curiously but pretended he'd not noticed. Maybe he'd recognized me, I thought, but who cares?

The taxi, a fine white convertible, took the turnings calmly. All around was spread the panorama over the Bay of Naples, the coast at Sorrento, the hills of Capri, and the sun was beginning to beat down. My hands trembled slightly as I read and reread those few lines, replacing letters by names and surnames and coded expressions by complete sentences:

Signorina L(ucia), a credible witness (= OVRA spy), *reported as follows to M(ussolini's) P(rivate) S(ecretary): Madame C(armen) really is seriously concerned about the possible consequences for M(ussolini) in the event of failure to grant Signor S(uckert)'s wishes.*

M(ussolini), the moment he informed of this, and contrary to the opinion of O(svaldo) S(ebastiani, the Duce's Private Secretary) personally granted S(uckert) an immediate pardon.

Signorina L(ucia) has always appreciated S(uckert)'s writings, quite apart from anything else.

Yet again, I'd deluded myself. The blackmail I'd plotted, making use of Madame Carmen and her husband had not worked out. But Lucia had succeeded in getting it to work. Once she'd done her duty as a spy and got me arrested, she'd gone to Rome. And she'd saved me.

Osvaldo Sebastiani, the Duce's Private Secretary with whom Madame Carmen had spoken on the 'phone in my presence, had not backed up the clairvoyant's request. He'd not informed the Duce of the danger, so obviously neither had he spoken with Bocchini, the police chief. Thus, the arrest warrant issued against me had never been revoked. Lucia had in fact carried out orders, betrayed me and had me arrested.

But straight after that she'd gone to Rome, to the Duce's secretariat, where she'd placed Madame Carmen's dark forebodings on the record: if something happened to me, there'd be a dreadful hex for the Duce. Lucia was an OVRA agent and knew how to get her message across. Probably she'd have set down something in black and white, a note, a police report. This was more than a mere telephone call from Capri by a rather unbalanced cartomancer; it would have been a formal note from an OVRA agent, complete with file number. Faced with that, Sebastiani wouldn't have been able to keep the matter from the Big Chief.

Mussolini, superstitious as he was, had overruled his secretary and ordered that Madame Carmen's request was to be complied with, so that I was released as a matter of urgency. Maybe the old man was satisfied now that he'd turned me into a terrorized, humiliated fugitive, then freed me with a simple snap of the fingers. Once again, he'd have reminded that scoundrel Malaparte that Mussolini gave the orders.

Lucia had stitched me up, Lucia had saved me. And by saving me, she had taken a personal risk. She'd gone right to Rome, to the Duce's Private Office. Her bosses might have accused her of favoritism. She'd risked her head.

When she'd screamed "No!", that night when her OVRA colleagues had captured me, her cry really had come from the heart.

"Why, oh why?" I kept repeating to myself sobbing and laughing at the same time, my hair ruffled by the wind, while the white sports car climbed higher and higher, curve after curve, and the taxi driver kept staring at me in shock through the rear-view mirror.

"But of course, you've even put it in writing!" I said "It's the books. You liked my books."

That's why she'd done it: for the books. They were the truest, most authentic thing about that ordinary guy Curzio Malaparte. Whoever loved my books loved me, but I and the author of my books were absolutely not the same person. A writer's never himself: he's always only his books, those worn pages filled with black signs. An immense force calls on him, not to make him admired and famous, that's secondary, but to put himself into them, into those pages, to mount his book, saddling that strange creature, and fly... to Hell or to Heaven.

I reached into my pocket and drew out the other little handkerchief that Lucia had given me, that on which she'd imprinted her lipstick.

The two flaming red lips had already begun to fade.

La dracu friends, *la dracu* the lot of them, I wanted to be on my own. I got the taxi to drop me off near the Piazzetta, went straight into an alleyway and headed for the Villa Lysis. My hair was windblown, there were terrifying bags under my eyes, I was hirsute, my clothes were crumpled. Tired out, but happy.

Sirignano hadn't yet got back to Villa Lysis. I was received by a cleaning woman who was hard at work with other colleagues cleaning up the vast property. Everywhere it was covered with confetti, champagne corks, cigarette ends and food remnants. These were the remains of the party Sirignano had organized with Chantecler to enable me to get out of the villa masked and unrecognized.

I explained that I was a friend of the prince, and I'd only come to fetch my dog.

The woman hesitated, then she saw Febo rush joyfully towards me, with worry still painted in his eyes, and she decided to let me in.

Febo had understood perfectly: he'd been close to losing me for good. After the first effusions, he began to turn around me, as though he meant to tie me slowly up with a leash. I remained motionless, in silence, out of respect for his pain.

He'd have liked to chew my ass good and proper, and I'd have deserved it. He wanted to explain to me all I'd done wrong, all those times I'd lacked his wisdom. But I was so tired, and he knew this was no time for such things.

"I know, I know," I said at length, "you were worried for me. But it's all over now. No need to worry any more."

Before leaving, I saw something shining next to a cupboard. It was the Sturmbannführer's saber, which Sirignano had brought me at the Natural Arch, after which he'd kept it in the villa. I took it with me.

"That's the Prince's sword," said the woman.

"No, it's mine. I won it in a duel."

"In a duel? People don't duel any more," said the woman, eyeing me suspiciously, "that's all stuff from the past."

"You're quite right, it's stuff from the past. We're all of us stuff from the past, in this rotten old Europe. I, you, this villa, this saber: it's all rotten. But don't worry. It'll soon all be over, the problem will be cleared up."

The cleaning woman looked at me in perplexity. I headed for the exit. I went quickly down the grand staircase, with its banister in wrought iron replete with turgid penises. Febo trotted behind me.

"Everything will be put in order," I yelled again to the cleaning woman, before making my way across the garden. "In Europe we'll not be rotten inside any more. We'll be happy, every problem will be swept clean vertically."

"Vertically?" asked the woman.

"Yes. With bombs."

Before disappearing, I saw the cleaning woman turn to a colleague and tap her temple with her index finger: Prince Sirignano's friends are all a bit crazy.

It was a wonderful day. Febo and I made our way to House like Me, whistling in the shady lanes smelling of musk roses. Every now and then the perfume of some focaccia in the oven or a freshly brewed coffee would issue from a window, mixing with the air. It was almost like being reborn; in the next few days, I'd be thinking only of House like Me, of my work, of my next book. Febo, however, still looked ill-tempered. He kept sniffing at the saber, and seemed almost to be shaking his head.

"I know, it belonged to a Nazi. But I'll keep it as a trophy. I'll never use it," I said to him.

He was not convinced. As we walked, he kept looking around nervously. The hairs on his back were as straight and as stiff as a brush.

"Relax, they're not coming to arrest me any more. Don't you believe me?" I said to calm him down.

His only response was to growl at a bush we'd just passed I went up to the bush and shook its branches with the saber.

"Don't you see? There's no one. No police, no OVRA, no nothing. And stop making faces at me! It's not my fault if they framed me for Pam's death."

It made no difference: my friend kept looking all round worriedly and growling. In the end I understood: he was afraid they were *following* us. What a crazy idea! At times Febo disappointed me, he'd begun to think like any ordinary mutt. I explained that I'd been released, but if they wanted to put me back in jail, there'd surely be no need to follow me. Nothing doing, he was not convinced, he kept looking over his shoulder. When we drew near to House like me, he began barking like mad.

"So what is it now? We're home, aren't you glad?"

I tried to distract him, throwing sticks into the air for him to catch them. But he wasn't interested. He just kept baring his teeth and roaring.

"I get you, you don't want to come back to House like Me. But I've got to. Before we go back to Rome, we've got to find someone to take over the work. Poor Amitrano will still need time to recover after all that castor oil the OVRA guys stuffed him with."

Within minutes we were climbing the stairs to House like Me.

The improvised bed where I'd slept with Lucia was still there. We went up to it. Febo sniffed at the bed and began to growl again.

"No, Febo, don't do that. Lucia wasn't bad. She was just doing her job as a spy. What's more, she even saved me. No, she wasn't bad. Maybe I'd like to see her again, one day. But I don't think that'll happen."

From my pocket, I took out the handkerchief with its, by now, fading lipstick mark. Lucia had announced it as in an old fairy story: we'd be together only for so long as the lipstick was visible.

I looked all around me, caressing with my gaze the mighty cliffs of Cape Massullo, all set about with privet and myrtle bushes and maritime pines. Then I let my eyes wander over sea and sky, feeling my limbs invaded by all the fatigue accumulated during those days. I had to sleep, to sleep as a free man, not a beast in a cage.

We came down from the terrace and entered the great living room on the ground floor. It was still cluttered with all the boxes and cases I'd had brought from Rome and Tuscany. Suddenly I caught sight of the chessboard with PAM written on it. I picked it up and smiled. I turned towards Febo, who was looking at me in his turn, and feeling sorry for me: I've got a stupid master. I love him, but he's stupid. His eyes were big and wet, it was as though they were speaking to me. Emily Dickinson was right: "Dogs are better than human beings because they know but do not tell".

On the floor lay a pile of blankets, perhaps used by the removal men to avoid damaging the boxes. Up on the terrace I'd already been sweating, but in the living room it was lovely and cool. Through the great windows giving onto the Faraglioni there flooded a warm, pervasive light, a light so pure that it seemed almost like a sound, a distant tinkling. I took off my shoes and lay down on the blankets. Febo settled by my side, but keeping his eyes wide open, and growling from time to time.

For a few hours, I kept sleeping and awakening, quite incapable of getting up. Every now and then I'd lie there as though hypnotized, with my eyes glued to the wide picture window overlooking the Faraglioni. The pistol shots they'd aimed at me when I fled from House like Me at dawn kept ringing out in my head, then came the half-drunk crowd at Mona Williams' party, all those nights spent on the run avoiding arrest, Edda Mussolini leaping among the rooftops in the rain with her black make-up streaking her cheeks. And then one duel, ten duels, a hundred duels with the Sturmbannführer, every one of them ending badly for me, I'm falling from the Migliera viewpoint (and realizing as I fall that I'm going to crash to the foot of the Òrrico cliff), the Sturmbannführer looking triumphantly down on me from above and, as I fall into the abyss, Pam whispering "now it's your turn to die too".

And last of all, you, sweet Lucia, Woman like Me, your curly hair, your greyhound's, your filly's, your witch's body, your dark mystery made of lies, of phrases learned by heart, of meetings in an OVRA office with you explaining to your bosses how you planned to betray me.

And then I kept asking myself – why? Why had Mussolini had me framed by the OVRA? Why now? Munthe had said there was a denunciation, or at least some written document, accusing me. Who'd shopped me? And who had killed Pam?

I'd hoped it was all over, and yet in my guts I felt that the most important thing of all was missing: the reason why. No destiny is acceptable without that "why". I knew only why I'd got away with it: Lucia liked my books.

Her soul had proved to be more noble than mine: she'd loved my books more than I myself who had written them. I'd never have risked my skin to save anyone just because he'd written good books. She had done that. That's why she'd saved me, and for no other reason. She'd shown that readers (I'll never tire of repeating this) are nobler than writers. Readers believe in what they're reading while writers don't believe in what they write. Writers lie, they just know how to write their lies well.

I'd been saved by Lucia for my literary merits, by now that was quite clear to me. But all the rest escaped me: I didn't know why Pam had died, or why the OVRA had wanted to frame me.

I slept again. Again I was losing duels and falling into the Migliera abyss, into the Òrrico abyss. And the Greek chorus, the chorus of my women, Jane, Virginia, Flaminia, Bianca, Rebequita and Roberta, kept repeating: now it's your turn to die, Malaparte.

I awoke with a start many hours later. Already sundown, and I'd not drunk or eaten all day.

Febo was snarling, trembling with rage and fear. Someone was coming to House like Me.

"No, not another arrest," I murmured, "Lord help me!"

The footsteps were drawing near, light but assured. Whoever it was didn't expect to find me there. We heard him walking above our heads, climbing the steps that led to the terrace.

I had no firearms. I grabbed the Sturmbannführer's saber and went out.

For quite some time now, the sun had dived into the sea, like a tired body seeking solace in a warm bath. It was already twilight over House like Me, the Faraglioni, and all Capri. Febo and I climbed the steps to the terrace on tiptoe. When we at last got there, we saw the silhouette of the intruder standing there, at the far end of the terrace, looking out to sea.

I approached him slowly. Between us, nothing but the vast space of the terrace, surrounded only by sea and sky, and the unmade bed where I'd slept under the stars with Lucia.

At long last, the intruder became aware of my presence and gave a start. He turned round.

He had a long beard, he wore black trousers, a rather torn white shirt, and his hair was sticking to his forehead. He too looked worn down by a long period on the run.

Febo barked furiously, I had to grab him by the collar to stop him from going onto the attack. Then I drew nearer, still with the saber in my hand.

"Who are you?"

I observed him more closely: his was a waiter's shirt, the trousers belonged to some uniform. Now I'd got it.

"I... I didn't know you'd be back so soon. They meant to arrest you," said Carmine.

The Last Faun

"This is my house. Sooner or later, I'd be coming back here. How do you know they meant to arrest me, Carmine?"

"All Capri knew that."

"So you, when you learned that, got the idea you could hide here, isn't that so? No one knew you'd hidden at House like Me, nor would anyone ever have suspected that."

"I've stolen nothing. And I've spoiled none of your things, Signor Malaparte," said Carmine.

"How did you manage to eat and drink all this time?" I asked.

"How did you manage to eat and drink all this time?" I asked.

"The village kids kept me supplied. By day, I spent almost all my time in a little cave near here, where it's nice and cool, a perfect place for keeping provisions. But I came here to sleep. There was always some young couple coming to the grotto at night."

Only then did I lower my guard with the saber. I had nothing to fear from that scared, dirty waiter. I'd been looking for him everywhere, and all the while he'd been in my house. It was he whom I'd first glimpsed from Rulli's place, then from Winner's fishing boat. He'd made his lair in House like Me like some wild animal, like a mythological beast, like the last faun in Capri.

Febo too had understood that Carmine was harmless, and now he was yelping again in the direction of the cliff and the path that leads to House like Me. That evening my poor friend just couldn't find peace.

I sat on the bed in the middle of the terrace and laid the saber down next to me. Carmine, however, still wasn't at ease. He was still standing in the same place, just a footstep from the edge. As was once typical of lower class people in Italy, the waiter felt he'd been lacking in respect for someone more important than himself, and he just couldn't recover his normal demeanor. There he stood, as rigid as a pole at the end of the terrace, as though he were trying to keep as far from me as possible.

Meanwhile Febo left us, and went off to make one of his mysterious patrols on the cliff. He was moody and nervous. Just try understanding dogs, sometimes they're even weirder than men.

"Oh, Carmine, Carmine! I was looking for you everywhere. You were the only one who could save me. Why did you hide?"

"I didn't want to get involved in the death of that English girl, Signor Malaparte. It was dangerous."

"But it was me they were trying to frame! And they'd have succeeded if… if someone hadn't stepped in and saved me miraculously."

"Then you can see that I was right, Signor Malaparte. I did well to hide. All's well that ends well. Tomorrow I can go back to work. What's more, now that you've come home, I'll go and see my bosses this very evening."

"No, Carmine. You'll not leave here until you've told me how that English girl died."

"Signor Malaparte, that doesn't matter any more. You'd not believe me, what's more, no one would believe me. Please let me go."

It was just then that I heard Febo give the alarm. First I heard him bark, then yelp helplessly. He was somewhere on the clifftop, where the path led down to House like Me. It was hard to say where: by now the rocks were in the dark. Something was about to happen, I could feel that. Time was running out.

"Speak, Carmine. That SS officer killed her, isn't that so? You can say it now. He's dead too."

"No, it wasn't him."

"Did she kill herself? Pam was a very sad, unhappy girl."

"No, she didn't kill herself. If I said that I'd be lying."

"So what then? For God's sake speak!" I roared, instinctively grasping the saber.

At that moment Febo came rushing onto the terrace, barking wildly, as though he'd gone mad. But he was not alone. There was a presence behind him. I turned to Carmine, and when I saw his face, I knew that we'd been joined on the terrace by Pam's assassin.

To tell the truth, we knew him perfectly well. We'd simply forgotten about him.

His eyes were burning with hatred, with ferociousness, maybe even with envy. He'd followed us there out of pure hatred. He had no particular aim, he was just maddened by too much hatred, by that fierce impulse that can burst out in individuals of his breed, one that can be triggered by a provocation, an insult or more rarely, as in this case, great suffering.

Ever since he'd lost his dearest friend, he must have been brooding on a thousand dreams of revenge. Confused, crazy dreams, you couldn't ask too much of him. Dobermans are just dogs, even if they're high-class dogs.

He'd never have found us if it hadn't been for the smell of his master's saber. I can already hear those skeptics: it's impossible, the saber had fallen into the sea and spent years in another house. Poor fools. Don't they know that dogs on board a boat can smell whales and dolphins under the water and track them? Besides, if they didn't have extrasensory perception, how would they ever be able to guess half an hour in advance that their master was on his way, when he was still in a train or a car, miles away?

So Febo was right: on our way from Villa Lysis to House like Me we'd been followed. The Doberman had probably been freed by the Sturmbannführer shortly before he committed suicide and must have been wandering aimlessly for some time, shocked by the loss of his beloved master.

He must have been hiding not far from the Villa Lysis, which stood in a harsh, wild corner of Capri; and that morning, when we'd passed nearby with his master's saber, his mysterious perceptions must have awoken.

He'd lacked the courage to come out into the open. He must have followed us at a distance, like a thief, waiting for nightfall to approach. Dobermans are exceptional dogs, astute, wary and meticulous. Their real gifts are intellectual and spiritual, their ferocity is just an accessory, often due to a cruel training. He'd shadowed us silently all the way to House like Me, raising the alarm only with Febo, and on the clifftop he'd waited patiently for nightfall before joining us... what for?

"The dog... the German officer's dog..." stammered Carmine, catching sight of the Doberman's outline in the dark.

"Yes, yes, I've understood," I said, "He did it."

Febo was standing to one side, baring his teeth and growling proudly, but without making the slightest move to attack. He knew perfectly well he couldn't resist such a clash for more than a few seconds. This was no virtual skirmish, all facing down and threats, like the one Febo had kept up and won at the house of Richard Reynolds and Pam, four years earlier. This scrap could only be deadly.

Man has always succeeded in fighting almost all animals on equal terms. But a Doberman is no animal. A Doberman on the attack is a mortal weapon. Its bite does not merely rip through flesh, it doesn't just pulp muscles, it shatters bones. The bacteria in its drool make the wound unbearably painful. It lets go of its prey only for exceptional reasons, otherwise it grinds it to pieces. Only the bite of the hyena is more excruciating, and I still tremble, thinking of the wounded, abandoned at night in the middle of the desert, whom we'd hear screaming as they died in Eritrea, attacked by hyenas, and between the dunes you'd hear the snapping of femurs and elbows shattered in the jaws of those accursed beasts.

Three years later, during the war in Ukraine, I'd found an Albanian soldier hiding in the woods. He couldn't explain how he'd gotten there, war had driven him mad. He'd stolen the uniform from a dead Russian soldier and for months he'd survived hiding in the undergrowth, feeding only on dogs. He'd flay them, he'd butcher them and he'd eat them, cooked or raw. He was pock-marked all over with a devastating acne, he spoke in monosyllables, he couldn't bear the company of other men any more. He had no firearms, just a hunting knife. He was covered in scars. He explained his method of combat in a mixture or Russian, Albanian and Italian. He'd attract stray dogs with a few caresses, then he'd knife them. Sometimes it was they who attacked him and he'd defend himself, almost invariably ending up with a good dinner. When he was attacked, he'd hide a piece of tin piping up his left sleeve and try to get them to bite him there. The moment the dog bit there, he'd stab it in the neck, or he'd throw himself onto it with the whole weight of his body, crushing it to the ground until he'd strangled it. Other times, he'd get the better of the dog smashing its ribs or breaking its neck with a hard kick.

All this worked perfectly well with ordinary breeds, but was hopeless against a Doberman. Its reflexes are too rapid for any human being, the power of its bite homes in at two hundred kilos *a square centimeter*. No time to think: either it will go straight for the throat or with a great bound it will knock you to the ground and deal with you at leisure, ripping off your face and your head and tearing your chest to pieces. If it gets a leg in its jaws it's like being caught in a metal trap, it'll drag you around like a rag doll and won't let go until you've lost consciousness.

The Sturmbannführer's Doberman drew nearer in the dark. From him came a sort of rumbling sound, a deep guttural vibration.

Carmine would have been the first to die. First, because he was paralysed by terror, and that excites all dogs' aggressivity. Secondly, because he was on the edge of the terrace, with a deep chasm behind him.

I tried to drive off the Doberman, yelling in German: "*Weg! Geh´ weg!* Go away!"

I'd hoped to convince him that we weren't afraid, that we were still the dominant animals, but in vain. For an instant, the huge beast seemed to be thinking; then he began again to draw nearer. Carmine's terror was too obvious, he was like a red rag waved in front of a bull.

"Carmine, don't stay silent," I said in a stage whisper, "talk, for heaven's sake! Show the Doberman you're not scared!"

The poor waiter was trembling like a leaf. The Doberman moved a little further towards him, reaching the middle of the terrace. The attack would come in a matter of moments. Again I yelled at the great beast to go away, but without moving any closer. If he'd felt threatened, it was me he'd have attacked

The Dobermann again advanced on Carmine, growling louder and louder.

"Carmine, you must talk!" I said to him, "It's only by talking that you can save yourself, haven't you understood that? Tell me, how did Pam die?"

Carmine closed his eyes to work up the courage and at long last he spoke, while I too edged my way gingerly closer.

"I was near Òrrico, Signor Malaparte, where there's the sea cliff. It's a lonely spot. I'd go there sometimes to get a bit of peace, smoke a cigarette and read the paper…"

The Doberman took another couple of steps forward. It barked furiously two or three times to utter its hatred. Carmine broke off.

"Keep talking, for God's sake!" I screamed.

"…Yes, to read the paper. I was sitting on a bench a little to the side, where I couldn't be seen. The officer and the girl were quarreling and they'd not seen me. I couldn't understand a word of what they were saying. They were on the edge of the cliff path, just where there's no parapet. At some point he slapped her, and she returned the slap. Then he…"

Carmine broke off again. The Doberman had drawn even nearer, baring its teeth.

"Yes, Carmine, Keep talking!"

"… and then he yelled something at her in German and at that moment I saw the dog come up behind the officer and jump on the girl. Next thing, she was over the edge. It was an accident, of that I'm sure. The officer grasped his head in his hands, then he looked all round, to see if anyone had seen what had happened, and ran away.

He was scared stiff that he might have been seen by witnesses. But I'm sure he didn't mean to kill her."

Carmine panted, he'd said it. At long last I'd heard the truth with my own ears, that Malaparte was innocent. Only two dogs stood witness to this, but that was better than nothing.

"No, the German officer did mean to kill her," I said. "And he did in fact kill her. Dogs are a spiritual extension of ourselves. They do what we want to do, they are what we are. We are always responsible for their actions, even when we don't give them a specific order. The Doberman killed Pam because the officer wanted her dead. When the master hates someone, then the dog hates that person too. That's the truth."

At that very instant the Doberman went on the attack, shooting forward like an arrow.

The saber blow, unleashed with all the strength of both hands, caught it right on the muzzle, between the nostrils and the eyes. This was no straightforward saber cut, but a frontal clash between two projectiles. One metal, the other skin and bone. Black globs of dog's blood and pieces of cartilage went flying in all directions, spattering my face, my neck and my arms. The violence of the impact left the saber ringing like a bell, and I almost lost my grip on it.

Who knows whether the beast knew what abyss awaited it at the end of its rush; what was for certain was that the tremendous blow in its most sensitive place (the muzzle, centre of the sense of smell, the sense most highly developed in every dog) caused it to lose its balance and its reflexes. The dog skidded on its paws, fell, rolled over and stopped on the edge of the precipice.

Carmine had dodged to one side to avoid the Doberman's attack; in fact that wouldn't have saved him if it had not been for my saber.

I drew closer. The Doberman's muzzle was hanging half severed, attached to the rest of its head by a rag of flesh. One eye socket had been cut through, half of the eyeball and part of the skull had been sliced off. Blood was gushing out; the great beast had turned onto its back with its belly in the air, the posture that dogs hate most, except when they're trying to get petted by their master, because it lays open their belly and their throat.

Now I had to finish it off. At Bligny I'd put an end to the sufferings of Santoni, poor Santoni. By comparison, a dog was nothing. Again I grasped the sword in both hands to cut off its head. But just as I was about to strike, the Doberman stood up. It was staggering. It was blinded by the blood running down from its skull and flooding what remained of its forehead and muzzle. Suddenly, it sat. It was on the very edge of the terrace. A sort of tremor shook its body from end to end, it lost its balance and fell, swallowed up by the chasm, disappearing among the rocks and pines around the terrace of House like Me.

The first thing I did was to go to Febo, lean down and compliment him. He licked my face, to cleanse it of the black blood of the Doberman.

"D'you see what you've gone and done, Carmine?" I said, wiping my cheeks and forehead.

The waiter was again frozen in fear and horror.

"What have I done, Signor Malaparte?"

"If you'd not run away, if you'd gotten me off the hook at the right time, we'd not have come so close to getting torn to pieces."

"It's not like you think, Signor Malaparte. I didn't cause your problems. Don't you know what they're saying in Capri? Someone here shopped you. Here in Capri we always know everything about everyone, no one can keep secrets. You must excuse me if I tell you this Signor Malaparte, but it's like when a husband's being cuckolded. Everyone knows who his wife's lover is, except him. Everyone knows the truth, except him."

"And how about you, d'you know the truth?"

"I know it, Signor Malaparte."

On the next day, when Ciro had come to remove the Doberman's body from the cliff under House like Me, with the help of a pair of *scugnizzi*, I took a taxi with Febo and drove up to Anacapri.

I got myself put down at the beginning of the Migliera path. We walked fast, the walk took less than half an hour. But I didn't go to the viewpoint.

I'd got the taxi driver to explain everything to me in detail: the house Carmine had told me of was not easy to find. It was a sort of cube, with a door and one window, hidden behind a mass of bushes. A real hovel, it could only have suited a weird guy like its inhabitant. A misanthropist, one who leaves the house only once a week and lives on milk, eggs and weeds.

Febo and I came to the house. I knocked.

When he opened, he was bare-chested with a towel round his waist.

"Malaparte!" exclaimed Willy Kluck, blanching.

"Hi, Kluck. May I come in?"

He sat me down on an old broken-seated chair. All around, in the poorly furnished room, lay piles of great sheets of paper with sketches of sculptures that had probably never been completed. And then a number of wooden boxes filled with little strips of paper, all covered with tiny scrawled inscriptions. Kluck's famous philosophical treatises, which he'd use his apparatus to scatter from the Migliera, the Tragara, the Natural Arch and the lighthouse point.

For a moment we observed one another in silence. He offered me nothing to drink, he made no attempt at common courtesies. He'd understood at once what brought me there. I recalled that meeting at Zum with him and his friend Gratìs, the deaf-mute dancer: that time Kluck had been strangely fearful, he'd seemed scared of me. He'd thought I'd gone looking for him at Zum in the middle of the night, he was afraid of me.

I asked him the only question that came to me, without wasting words.

"Why, Kluck?"

He looked down. Then he looked up again, and found the courage to speak.

"They forced me to, Malaparte."

"They forced you. But why you and not someone else, Kluck? There were any number of people prepared to help the OVRA, whether for money, or for any other reason."

"Because I live here, Malaparte. A stone's throw from the viewpoint where you and that girl met, and where you fought a duel with the German officer. What's more, I could be blackmailed. And there's nothing the OVRA can't do."

"No, Kluck, it can't do everything. I managed to get away from the OVRA. I'm still free."

"You're Malaparte. I'm Willy Kluck, a poor bum, a failed sculptor, a nobody. Two gentlemen from Rome came to my place, they said they were officials of the Interior Ministry but it was obvious they were from the OVRA. They told me I'd better do what they said: you were unquestionably guilty, and I could make the decisive contribution. No need to lie, all I had to do was just to confirm what the police already knew. They came back a second time. They searched this house of mine and they found my little strips of paper, those we scattered with Miradois and Gratìs using our contraption. *Peace is the salvation of the Peoples... War and Arms are the enemies of the human race... Universal Brotherhood, come into our hearts and stop the hands of those who would kill...* You already know the words of wisdom I write on those strips, Malaparte. I love peace, that you know."

"Yes, I know, Kluck. You love peace."

"They told me it was ideologically compromising material. War might break out at any moment and Fascism could not tolerate defeatist and disloyal individuals. They said I was risking big trouble and they got me to sign a statement they'd written, after barely giving me time to read it. The statement said that I'd spied on the duel and later I'd seen you meet the English girl, then I'd tailed you all the way to Òrrico. There you'd quarreled, you'd tried to take advantage of her and she'd defended herself, kicking, punching and scratching. Then you'd pushed her."

"And you signed *that*."

"I signed. They came to see me several other times, to remind me of what I'd promised. The last time was just a few days ago."

"Now I understand," I said, "because I saw those two OVRA guys, Bianchi and Marelli, here in Anacapri when I was hiding to avoid arrest. So, they were coming to your place. Did you also promise to appear at the trial?"

"They said there was no need. Once they'd arrested you, you'd certainly confess."

"Confess? And why should I do that? An innocent man will always defend himself to the very last."

"They said it really was you who'd killed her, but the other witnesses couldn't be summoned to the trial. They're people with important public positions, they told me, they can't be involved in this. Mussolini doesn't want that, they said."

I rose to my feet and faced him.

"Kluck, why?"

"I've already told you: because I'm weak and I can be blackmailed. I'm not an Italian citizen, I'm out of work."

"That's no answer! Did they give you money?"

"No."

"Then why did you do it? Tell me why, damn you!"

I grabbed him by the collar and lifted him bodily from his chair. Rage had given me new strength.

"Kluck, I order you, tell me why!" I screamed, squeezing his neck.

Scrawny and thin as he was, Willy Kluck became as red in the face as a ripe tomato. He tried to break free, but my grip was too strong for his delicate little hands.

I wanted to strangle him, but I hadn't the courage to do that. I was sorry for poor old Kluck. Instead of killing him, I let him go. He collapsed onto the chair, as soft as a worm.

He stared at me in terror, shielding his face with one arm. I was panting, my eyeballs were almost bursting out from their sockets, but I didn't want to touch him anymore. I closed my eyes and clenched my fists by my sides in order to control myself.

"Why?" I asked, one last time, almost under my breath.

He coughed a couple of times; he couldn't even open his mouth, his neck must still be hurting. At length, he mumbled.

"If I'd not accepted, I'd have had to leave Capri for good. I'm a pacifist. And I can only find peace here in Capri. I can't live without Capri. You understand me, don't you?"

We both fell silent.

"Kluck, have you ever shot at anyone, in wartime?"

He looked at me in astonishment, unable to understand what I was getting at.

"No, I was behind the lines."

Kluck couldn't live without Capri. I moved slowly away and, as I drew back, I kept staring at him, screwing up my eyes in horror.

I'd have liked to slap him, but I felt that I no longer had the strength for that.

Kluck couldn't live without Capri. I ought to have told him: and what about me, could I live in prison? But he didn't deserve that, he didn't deserve my wasting words on him, he'd not get another syllable out of me. There's nothing meaner or more disgusting than a pacifist who's never fired a shot, an *Etappensau*, like Corporal Hitler. To become a real pacifist, you have to rot in the trenches, to hear the bullets whistling above your head and see your own men dying because they've been given the wrong orders, and to give the coup de grâce to one of them, a lad of the class of '99, with his guts spilling out from his belly. To be a pacifist, you must have shot at least once, damn it, only someone who's pulled a trigger is a real pacifist. How did Emily Dickinson put it? *Water, is taught by thirst. Land—by the Oceans passed. Peace—by its battles told...*

Febo looked at me; he'd understood everything, he could read in my heart, in my face. He too was making an immense effort to stay cool, and hold back his indignation.

I turned towards the door. Before leaving, with rage still twisting my face, I turned one last time towards Kluck. I wanted to block my ears, I didn't want to hear him any more, but I was too slow to avoid hearing his last words.

"Please, Malaparte, try to understand me, I'm a pacifist. And Capri's the most beautiful place in the world. Only here can you find peace. You do understand me, don't you?"

CAPRI, AUGUST 31ST, 1939

The Defense of Freedom Never Comes Free

"Malaparte, is that story about Mussolini going to the cinema on his own really true?" asked Count Marcellino del Drago.

"Of course it's true. I got it from the horse's mouth. Why d'you keep on asking me to tell it if you don't believe it?"

"Come on, come on! You made it all up, and I'll bet you don't dare repeat it," said Cyprienne Charles-Roux.

I was comfortably ensconced in one of Mona Williams' enormous flower-patterned divans, and the new party organized by Mona was a great success. There were at least forty people crowding around me, all utterly charming, all good Fascists, the best of the aristocracy in those years. Count Marcellino del Drago, who had a fine sense of humour, was trying as usual to make me pass off as an exhibitionist, with the help of Cyprienne Charles-Roux, his delicious French consort.

"Come on, Malaparte, tell us again," said Filippo Anfuso, my dear old friend Filippo Anfuso.

"All right, all right," I said, "I'll tell you again. One evening, Mussolini was feeling tired of his wife, of his daughter, of his mistresses, of all those women crowding in on him and causing him no end of problems. So he put on an overcoat, hid his face behind a broad-brimmed hat and went off to the cinema to see an American film full of those blonde beauties he literally adores. But then a voice announces: by order of the Duce the American film has been banned as contrary to Fascist morality. Instead they project a horribly boring propaganda film: Mussolini opening a fair, Mussolini making a speech in Parliament, Mussolini at the wheel of a ship, received by the Pope, patting a group of kids on the head, attending a military parade, in an airplane, in a car, in a submarine etc. etc. Instead of American actresses the poor Duce sees his own fat face bursting out from the screen. Bored stiff and depressed, forever hankering after feminine company, he stays sitting there motionless, hidden under his big hat. Suddenly, in the dark cinema, he realises that he's sitting next to an attractive unaccompanied blonde who seems to be smiling at him. The Duce's hands tremble with emotion. Gradually, he reaches out and puts his spindly fingers on the blonde's thigh. For a moment the girl lets him, he can see she likes it, but then she angrily tears the Duce's hand away from her leg and gets up to leave. Why? the Duce whispers desperately, trying to hold her back. The girl murmurs: You must excuse me but, you know, I'm afraid we might be seen. That moron Mussolini even sends his spies into cinemas."

The group around me roared with laughter, and that in turn attracted even more curious onlookers who came up and asked if the guy sitting on the flower-patterned sofa really was the famous Malaparte.

What a marvellous evening! No longer a walking cadaver, I was once again the great writer Malaparte, and they all wanted to talk with me, to touch me, then to be able to claim that they'd made my acquaintance. They were all over-excited and I too was in seventh heaven: the Sturmbannführer was dead, the Doberman was dead, Pam was dead, and – sucker that I was – I'd fallen for a spy. It really was a splendid evening, one of those you'll not forget.

No one asked me how I'd got off: they all pretended I'd never been a fugitive, never been arrested then released, never disappeared from circulation for days on end, as though nothing had ever happened at all. Greetings and smiles homed in on me from all sides. It was great! Willy Kluck was dead right, you can't live without Capri, only Capri can give you peace.

"What a story, that one of Mussolini at the movies," said the Marchese Blasco d'Ayeta. "But you, Malaparte, you're a reckless one."

"Why reckless?" I replied. "I just tell the truth. For Mussolini the cinema's a matter of great importance. When he's nothing better to do, he gets them to project pictures of Hitler, Roosevelt, Churchill, and all the great world leaders. He studies them *in slow motion*, to glean some good trick from them. For him, politics is all play-acting. And he's right. Just you wait and see, one day in America they'll elect an ex-Hollywood actor President, and in the Vatican we'll have a former stage actor for Pope."

"Malaparte isn't reckless, he's brave," said Princess Giulia Caracciolo di Leporano, broke now, but highly respected because every Tuesday she had Capri's English and American ladies for tea.

"It's easy for writers to be brave! They're above the powers that be..." said Marcellino del Drago.

"No, Marcello," I retorted, "We writers are not above power. We just think we are, but we aren't and never have been. We're the slaves of power like all the rest, like ordinary folks. We're whores. We lie like whores. We're whores like all the rest."

Del Drago didn't know what to say to that. He wasn't used to hearing me talk like that. There were a few seconds silence.

"But you writers defend free thinking..." he tried to riposte.

"Defending freedom never comes for free," I said, "and whores can't afford to make losses. At the end of every night we've got to go home with a full purse."

In the group, people looked somewhat stunned, someone moved away, others turned their backs on me, yet others murmured scandalized comments.

"Malaparte, you need to relax a little. Come and have a gin and tonic."

This time it was Chantecler, trying to let me off the hook. He was arm in arm with his new fiancée, a young Hungarian countess with an unpronounceable name.

"Yes, yes, Malaparte, come and drink something with us," said the girl, a beanpole over twenty centimeters taller than Chantecler. They took me by the elbows and dragged me out. But as soon as we were in the garden, I excused myself and went off on my own. I lit a cigarette, the twentieth that evening. *La dracu* mustard gas, *la dracu* my sick lungs, one's got to die of something, ain't that so?

Not far off was Mona Williams, besieged by such a mob that she couldn't attend properly to her distinguished guests. While she held out her arm for Alfonso XIII, the ex-King of Spain, to kiss her hand, she was already greeting the Maharajah of Rajasthan as he came up the drive. I extinguished my cigarette, crushing the butt on the priceless Majolica tiles of the garden and went back into the house.

"Oh, here comes Signor Massullo!" said Edwin Cerio, holding out his hand in an ironic pose.

We'd not met since I'd gone on the run. He too wanted to pretend that nothing untoward had happened, he too wanted to restore our former harmony. He was quite right: the sky was full of stars, the moon tasted of honey and pineapples, the band was playing Cole Porter, the magnolias and wisteria were drugging the air with mysterious effluvia, Capri was as wonderful as ever.

I looked all round: Cerio and I were somewhat isolated and no one was paying any attention to us; so I shook his hand and took advantage of the handshake to draw him into a little corridor that led to the bathroom, far from indiscreet eyes.

"What is it?" he said.

"Edwin, I just wanted to thank you for all the precious information you gave me about the Villa San Michele, Axel Munthe, Goering, the Fabian Society, esoteric Nazism and the hollow earth… It was all so useful to me. Thank you, thank you."

"Oh, think nothing of it…" said Cerio with a half- complacent, half worried smile. His white goatee was trembling slightly. He really was an old-fashioned gentleman, my dear old Edwin Cerio, and I really liked him, just as he too liked me.

I kept smiling; straight after, I dragged him into the WC and gave him a good backhander on his right cheek that turned his head 180 degrees. Then I gave him another slap on the left cheek that put his head straight again. Edwin Cerio slipped on the wet floor and landed up sitting on the ground next to the WC.

"I'll be seeing you, Edwin," I said, leaving him in front of the bathroom door with a rivulet of blood in the corner of his mouth.

Now I felt better. As I was looking for a drink, I saw Eddie von Bismarck playing host to Princess Soraya of Afghanistan. The moment he saw me, he advanced on me with open arms.

"Malaparte, what an honor to have you with us this evening!" he said, hugging me like a brother. There wasn't an ounce of hypocrisy in that embrace. For Eddie, all was again in order, for him too harmony had been restored. I was free again, Phli was in Rome, the Sturmbannführer was dead, the party was a great success, nothing could trouble us any more.

"Doctor Munthe hasn't turned up this evening," said Eddie.

"He's got eye trouble," I said.

"I know, he's blind."

"No, it's another problem. Someone made him a new pair of glasses."

"So what? For a blind man, all glasses are the same."

"No, Eddie, those he has now are special glasses," I said with a smile, as I moved off.

A pity I didn't have a pullover, I thought. For some time the evenings had been getting cooler; the sun too was going to bed earlier. The summer of 1939 was coming to an end; soon we'd regret it, like so many other things we'd grown accustomed to, things to which we thought we were entitled, and which we'd soon be stripped of forever.

Suddenly, a burst of applause. Those who were seated rose to their feet and everyone craned their necks to see. Edda had arrived with her husband, Count Galeazzo Ciano. They were coming up the main drive, followed by a host of friends and admirers.

Galeazzo was walking with his usual somewhat haughty gait distributing smiles to the right and to the left, above all to the ladies, but he had put on weight. A double chin bounced slightly as he moved; he must have gained that in Rome, at those long luncheons at the Acqua Santa Golf Club or those *après-midis dansants* at the home of the Princess Colonna, at which he'd make up his mind whether he'd be spending the night with Buby, Cicci or Lilly, afternoons when he'd brush off with an irritated movement of the hand all that reminded him of how Edda spent her nights in Capri jumping on roofs like a cat, while war was at the gates.

Edda was on her husband's arm, smiling at everybody with a glassy, absent smile. Her smile was that of a woman who loves death, who takes lunch with, sleeps with and goes to the movies with death.

The moment he saw me, Galeazzo broke away from his wife and came to greet me with exaggerated cordiality. He took me by the arm and led me to a corner of the garden. All around, the guests were eying me enviously: I was the only guest with whom the Duce's son-in-law was conversing man to man.

"Malaparte, you've offended me. You never came to see me."

"The OVRA was after me. They wanted to arrest me. I had to go into hiding."

"But what's this you're telling me? Nothing has come to my ears! Why didn't you ask me for help?"

"I asked Edda. She said you couldn't help me. You had plenty on your hands at the Ministry…"

"Are you joking? Hell, I'd have moved heaven and earth for you! Anyway, dear Malaparte, if anything disagreeable should ever befall you, I swear that…"

I saw Galeazzo's eyes wander away from mine and settle on a point some way behind me.

"…I swear that… Excuse me a moment, who's that girl?" he said, pointing out a splendid young beauty wiggling on the open-air dance floor.

"Princess Nadejda of Braganza."

"D'you know her? Could you introduce me?"

"I think so. But… Edda?"

"Oh, we've settled all the problems between me and Edda. We've learned to adjust to one another. We have the greatest respect for each other. So, will you introduce me to this friend of yours?"

As we approached the dance floor, I put one last question to him.

"Galeazzo, you're our Foreign Minister. How long have we till war breaks out?"

He looked at me with all the seriousness he was able to summon up. For a moment, his double chin stopped bouncing.

"There won't be any war, that I promise you. I'll manage to hold back the Germans, believe me. They're our allies. They'll listen to me."

"Beware of Mussolini. The old man detests you, you know."

"I'll be careful. It's a promise."

Galeazzo was a fine young fellow. He was sincere; he believed what he was saying. He wasn't to know that on the next day at dawn, Hitler's panzers would be on the move towards Danzig and Warsaw, or that little more than four years later Mussolini would have him shot. He was a fine lad, Count Galeazzo Ciano. He presented well, all he needed was to lose a bit of weight, then he'd have been perfect. He had a great future, so they all said.

I was just on the point of returning to the library when someone bumped into me by accident. I caught a whiff of a woman's perfume, it was *Shocking* by Schiaparelli, quite unmistakable. For a split second I thought of Lucia and our first meeting in the park of the Fortino, of an old record of Neapolitan songs crackling away on the terrace of House like Me, of an improvised bed under the stars, and of Febo howling a high B-Flat in unison with Enrico Caruso.

I turned. It was Mona. She was more attractive than ever, with a red Balenciaga dress and her dazzling Cartier sapphire.

"Malaparte, at long last I can greet you."

"If you'll allow me, I'll come and greet you rather better one of these evenings."

"Sorry, that's out of the question. I'm a married woman," she replied sharply.

"What are you drinking?" I asked, pointing to her glass.

"Orange blossom."

"I detest orange blossom," I said with a smile. I took the glass from her hand and gulped it down. Mona made an irritated gesture.

"Will you excuse me now?" she said, "Shum Samser Rana, the Prince of Nepal, is arriving and I must go out and receive him."

I remained alone. I could see the Marchese del Balzo, Prince Caracciolo and a whole band of importunate night-owls, out to extract from me some other anecdote about Mussolini. To get away from them, I fled in the direction of Mona's private apartments.

I opened a door and found myself in her private study. What harm is there in this? I said to myself. After all, Mona had once even let me into her bedroom.

In the middle of the study stood a fine table by Jean-Michel Frank, the famous homosexual Jewish designer, the lines of which were spare but exceedingly refined. Jean-Michel Frank was the great designer of the day, and no one could ever have imagined that, less than two years later, he would kill himself, jumping from a window in Manhattan.

I sat on that funny low, wide and wonderfully original table, as though it were a stool. How good to take a break! Malaparte you're growing old! I thought. Thus ensconced, I found myself facing a curious Empire-style bookcase, like a cylinder, with various quite deep compartments in which something had been placed. It was then that I found it staring me in the face, and recognized the title at once.

BESTIE DELINQUENTI

I could have told Mona. But that would only have attracted suspicion. No one would ever believe that I'd found it. Yet it was logical! The Sturmbannführer must have come here the same way. After taking the book from the library, in order to get away from the crowd he'd have gone towards Mona's private apartments. Then he'll have taken the same door into the study. There, he'll have left the book, slipping it into the little Empire bookcase, in a compartment visible only to someone sitting straight in front of it, on Jean-Michel Frank's table. He hadn't stolen the book, he'd just *moved* it. But why ever did he do that?

I picked up the book and leafed through it. As I hoped, Doctor Forster's postcard was still inside it. It was right inside the last pages, maybe that's why the Sturmbannführer hadn't noticed it.

The few words written in German were not too hard for me to decipher:

> *To the soldier Adolf Hitler*
> *Once an* Etappensau, *now a valiant warrior.*
> *With my best compliments on his cure,*
> *Dr. Forster*

There could be no doubt about it, this was the style of Dr. Forster, the military psychiatrist who cured hysterical soldiers by treating them as simulators. They were to be called what they were, said Forster, to give them a jolt and wake them up. And for Hitler there was just one name: *Etappensau*, "rearguard sow", the insult reserved for shirkers who skulked far from the front. Not even Eddie, when he'd described the card to me and Sirignano, had had the courage to reveal us its exact words. It was too much even for him, it was a ton of shit hanging over the head of the Führer and of all Nazi Germany.

On the other side of the card, the Saarburg Christ, in his unreal pose, suspended in the void as he falls with arms outstretched to Heaven and his torn face turned to the ground. I brought the card close to my lips and closed my eyes. How stupid the world could be! A few years earlier that postcard could have been the flag of truth. Of course, we'd not have stopped Hitler, but at least we'd have served justice. Surely someone had to tell the Germans how matters really stood. The Germans had never understood the first thing about Hitler, they'd not understood that Hitler was a cowardly little corporal, the great land of Germany had let itself be taken in by a wretch, a lying, hysterical Austrian corporal who'd usurped the warlike merits of a Jewish comrade, and I cursed Eddie von Bismarck for having told me those truths which were by now utterly useless.

I'd have liked to use that card to slap the Germans in the face, all the Germans, one by one, cooks and coachmen, whores and cops, ministers and generals, young and old, from the first to the last of them, sparing only the children, screaming at them down to the end of Eternity: how come you never heard the alarm? The Saarburg Crucifix had warned you of the coming of the Whore of Babylon! But you – instead of rejecting her, you welcomed her, you licked her boots, you raised her onto a great stage and you tickled her until she yelled her obscene proclamation, then you all cheered and told the whole world that the game was up.

I wished to God I could have told them this; then no German would have been able to whine that inhuman pretext to the war crimes tribunals: "We didn't know, we were carrying out orders".

But it was too late now. Within a matter of hours the German panzers would have crossed the Polish border. I put the card back into the book and closed it. I could have stolen it and sold it one day at Christie's, but that would not have been cricket.

I tried to think things through and set my ideas in some kind of order. The Sturmbannführer obviously knew nothing about Doctor Forster, Hitler's mental illness or the Pasewalk clinic, or he'd have taken the card. But then: why the hell had he hidden that book? What danger was he trying to avoid?

Delinquent Beasts... I picked my way through the index, then skimmed from chapter to chapter – and understood. Ah, you idiot Sturmbannführer, what a curse that nasty little mind of yours put on you! One should never be mean-spirited, it's the worst of sins, it's even worse than murder.

I slipped the book into my trousers, well covered by my jacket, and left Mona's study. So, what now? I hadn't the faintest idea what to do next.

Making my way through the crowd with some difficulty I returned to the library. I spotted Arturo Assante, who pretended he'd not seen me and left the room in the company of a pair of splendid ladies. I'll give your name to Percy Winner, I said, grinning inwardly, you'll not get away with it, you'll be on the Americans' list, the victors' list. Lucia's name no, but yours – you can be sure I'll give it to Winner.

"Signor Malaparte!"

The voice was that of Maria Anna Pignatelli Aragona Cortès, alias Manemà, the old princess with her face eternally plastered with ceruse who only slept between black sheets. I took it for a sign of destiny: it was with her I'd been talking days and days ago, just when the Sturmbannführer had taken the book from the library; and just there, in exactly the same place, I and Manemà were meeting again. The empty place for the book was right there in front of me.

"Signor Malaparte, did you hear about it? That German officer you quarreled with here at Mona's house... He's dead! A heart attack, in his room at the Quisisana."

"Really? Oh, that's terrible."

"Tell me the truth, Malaparte: it was you. You made that poor officer so furious that in the end his heart just gave out. Isn't that so?"

"Certainly, Princess. Just so."

It was then that heaven came to the rescue. Suddenly the whole Fortino was plunged into darkness; a salvo of whistles, screams and ironic comments followed. It was the usual blackout, the occasion when everyone found the courage to rail in the dark against the regime, against Mussolini, against the new electricity cable that was never completed. What a perfect opportunity! I had only to be swift and discreet.

"Signor Malaparte, please don't leave me, I'm afraid of the dark," said Manemà.

"I'm staying near you, Princess, don't you worry."

Instead I took a few steps, making my way through the dark and treading on a few feet, and did what I had to.

When the lights came back on, I took my leave of Mananà and went off looking for a drink. I'd put a bit of order into Mona's house, I was pleased with myself.

The moment I entered the garden, a tremendous explosion made me jump. The party was coming to an end with the usual fireworks display.

At last, I heard a friendly voice behind me.

"Malaparte, sorry I'm late! You know, that new girlfriend of mine from New York… I had to show her Capri from end to end. But I still managed to make it."

"Good thing you came, Sirignano. I was waiting for you. I'm off back to Rome tomorrow."

"Then we'll not be seeing each other for a hell of a long time".

"Don't worry, we'll meet again after the war."

"So it's for sure: there'll be war."

"No, there won't. I've just been told that by Galeazzo Ciano, our Foreign Minister. Don't you believe him?"

Sirignano smiled. "Malaparte, you're a rascal."

"Prince, I don't know why, but sooner or later everyone calls me a rascal, a show-off or foolhardy. They're already saying that the Sturmbannführer's death was my fault. The Fascists can't stand me because I'm not Fascist enough. I'm sure that when Mussolini falls the anti-Fascists will have it in for me because I wasn't anti-Fascist enough. And I'll take my destiny to the grave with me. And this evening, when Mona finds her famous book back where it belongs, she'll suspect me."

"Malaparte, are you serious? Mona's book back in its place? And the postcard? Was it there or not?"

"Sure, it was there. But calm down, Sirignano. Let's get ourselves a couple of orange blossoms and sit down. Orange blossom's disgusting but I adore it."

Among his many merits, Sirignano had one great gift: when I spoke, he didn't interrupt me. So I was able calmly to explain to him about the death of the Dobermann and my talks with Carmine and Willy Kluck. I told him of how scared the Sturmbannführer was of being accused of Pam's death, despite the fact that it had been his dog and not he that had caused the accident.

"You'll be wondering: what's all this got to do with Mona's book?" I said, "Well, that's right at the heart of it all. It's a rather rare book, and it deals with a really strange subject. The title *Delinquent Beasts* explains clearly enough what it's about. It's a treatise on the penal responsibility of animals. Since Antiquity, dear Sirignano, there have been arguments over whether animals can be punished for their misdeeds; for killing their master, damaging a crop, and so on. Well, that's what this strange book's all about: if a horse kills a child, can we condemn that horse to death or life imprisonment? In the Middle Ages, the answer was yes, and many, many animals were put on trial, condemned and sometimes even executed. When, for example, there was an infestation of animals that endangered the crops or public health, the first thing was for the judge to issue them a summons. If the animals failed to appear *in person*, they were tried *in absentia*, then condemned and excommunicated. There were proper trials with judges, lawyers, expert witnesses, judicial officers and so on. Thus, locusts, caterpillars, rats, leaches, and so many other swarms, herds, flocks, packs and schools of all manner of beasts were tried and excommunicated. They excommunicated ants, worms, locusts, caterpillars, moles, larvae, beetles and snails. In the year 824 in the Val d'Aosta a multitude of moles were excommunicated. In 1541 in Lausanne it was the turn of worms, mice and leaches. In 1596 they excommunicated the dolphins which had invaded the port of Marseille. In Canada in the 17th century, came the turn of some flocks of doves that were making a nuisance of themselves. Even at the end of the 19th century there was a trial in Leeds, England, at which a cockerel was tried and condemned."

But when it came to more serious crimes like the killing or wounding of a human being, I continued, if the accused was a domestic animal like a cow, a horse, a dog, a bull or a pig, it was arrested and brought before the judge in chains and, in the end, after counsel for the prosecution and the defense (obviously appointed *ex officio*) had put their respective cases, in the case of a capital crime, they were executed. Wolves and bears, being wild animals, could be killed without a trial. Household and farm animals, on the other hand, were tried and punished according to the most scrupulous rules, the same as those applying to human beings. In the course of centuries, sows were hanged, horses quartered and goats, cows, mules, sheep, roosters and any number of animals of all sorts were burned at the stake.

Obviously, no few death sentences were passed on killer dogs which had maimed or killed adults or children. Huge numbers of dogs have been tried and executed at all times and in all places.

"When the Sturmbahnführer saw that I was on the point of looking at that book," I said, "which he'd obviously just been leafing through, he became afraid that I might guess at the truth – that an animal was behind Pam's death, his dog."

But for Sturmbannführer Helmut Aichinger that beast was worth more than the truth, more than Pam's life, and it must be protected at all costs. This, I'd always known: every animal is only an extension of its master, his hidden nature, his real secret ego. The Doberman was the weapon with which the SS man wanted to sink his teeth into the world, the beast that made up for his own lack of courage, dignity and humanity, the delinquent beast that covered up his cowardice, his shame, his meanness, those shots at Santoni under the rain at Bligny, as he held his guts in his hands, and against me, unarmed.

"That's why the Sturmbannführer snatched the book from under my nose," I explained to Sirignano, "and then he went off to hide it in Mona's study. He must have been hoping that, at least for some time, I'd not be able to find it. But it was precisely that trick of his that was the end of him. If Doctor Forster hadn't disappeared together with the book, Phli wouldn't have summoned him and threatened him. The Sturmbannführer wouldn't have been panicked by Phli's tremendous rage, he'd not have killed himself, and today his Doberman would still be living too."

Sirignano shook his head and made no comment. I knew what he thought: why can't men think of enjoying life instead of getting themselves in the soup? But he said nothing, Prince Sirignano and I were too different to think in the same way. I was a loose cannon and he, an aristocrat who knew how to take life as it comes.

"Anyway, I have to thank you," I said, "for giving me that satire on *Giovinezza, giovinezza*. It almost worked."

"Almost? I was quite certain that it was your blackmailing Madame Carmen that had got you off!"

"No, that was something else. Someone else, to be quite precise."

Sirignano did not reply. I just noticed a shrewd, curious look flash across his eyes like an arrow.

"By the way," he said, "after you went to the Villa Lysis to pick up the saber, the cleaning women found something. I think it belongs to you."

He took something out of his pocket and handed it to me. Good heavens, it was true, I'd lost it at the Villa Lysis: the little message Lucia had got the police to pass me, explaining in coded language how and why she'd saved me.

Sirignano was too smart not to have noticed Lucia's absence from Capri after my arrest and, after I'd been freed, my silence about her. Reading the note, he'd have understood everything, or practically everything. But as he was a friend and not a butler, he wanted to be sure he'd understood properly.

"D'you think you'll be seeing her again?" he asked.

"Who?" I replied, smiling. And he knew he'd got the message.

We walked on in silence through the park of the Fortino, while the fireworks came to their grand finale, with the traditional three great bangs without rockets, in the dark.

It was late. People were beginning to drift away. Only Chantecler and his friends were still holding court with their schoolboy japes. A young Neapolitan aristocrat had surreptitiously undone the buttons on the back of a little Belgian countess, who'd been left half naked before a good thirty guests, and had fallen to the ground in a faint.

"How's the new girlfriend?" I asked.

"She's one of those hyper-anxious American girls: I can already see that when I leave her for another girl she'll start crying and imploring me, and that she'll give me no end of trouble... You know the type. Would you like to come and drink something with us?"

"No thanks. It's my last night before I leave, I'll sleep at House like Me."

"Pardon the question, but how do you manage to sleep in a building site?"

"I've a few old blankets for a bed, and for the calls of nature... there's the sea."

We were on the grand avenue, the tree-lined drive that led to the gate. We fumbled for something else to say to each other, for we knew we'd not be meeting again for a long time.

"Malaparte, there's something I don't understand. How come that Madame Carmen's visiting card which you took from Edda's house bears the same symbol as that inscribed on the Sturmbannführer's saber, and how come this was also among the papers in his room at the Quisisana with the name EDDA?"

"I discovered that only yesterday, Prince. Runes are a sort of pastime for the Nazis, and they come from an ancient poem called the Edda, that much we'd understood. But why was that rune also in Edda Ciano's house, what's more, on one of Madame Carmen's visiting cards? I really didn't know what to think. Then a doubt surfaced in my mind. What if that sign had nothing whatever to do with runes, what it it was a symbol for something totally different? After all, when I saw it, it was near a switch, wasn't it?"

"D'you mean the remote control switch operating those tremendous blinds. The ones Edda has in her villa, and which not even the Duce her father has in Rome."

"That's it, Prince. And then I thought: they use special symbols for electrical circuits. In the end I went out and got myself an electrician's manual. And there I found it. Take a look here," I said, tracing a few lines on the grass with my foot.

$$\bigtriangledown\!\!\!|$$

"See? That's the electrical symbol for an antenna, or even for a remote control device. On the visiting card, I couldn't see the difference between this symbol and the rune, because its upper, horizontal side, the top one, more or less coincided with the edge of the card. The symbol's almost identical: it's without the horizontal line, but facing downwards.

Edda had placed it near that switch, maybe acting on her architect's advice, to remind her that it was for opening and closing the blinds. When I met Edda at the monastery and explained to her how I'd found that card, she burst out laughing, but she wouldn't tell me what it meant. She must have thought I was a complete idiot and good for laughs."

"So now you can explain me the meaning of *bon bonad kind rabal mervu!*" said Sirignano, "Carmine must have told you."

"It's an international code in use in hotels. They use it for booking telegrams. *Bon* means "good", *bonad* means "double room", *kind* "child's bed" and *rabal* "Sunday evening". As for the famous *mervu*, that means "with sea view", from the French *vue*, meaning "view" and *mer*, which means "sea". It was just a booking at the Quisisana: "Reserve a good double room with sea view with twin beds and a child's bed." If you don't believe me, go take a look in the annual of the ENIT, the national tourist agency, and you'll find it on page 7 of this year's edition. The whole code is there. So the mysterious phrase had nothing to do with the rest of our story. It was nothing more than a booking that Carmine had brought home from the Quisisana together with some other things he had to deal with."

"That's crazy!" Sirignano exploded, "All those thousand questions we racked our brains on, poor Tamburi's research... I can just imagine his face when you explained him the *bon bonad* enigma ..."

"Explain to him? Are you crazy? He couldn't find the meaning of mervu or the mysterious phrase, so I can keep holding back his three months' pay. After all, even if I did pay him he'd soon waste it all drinking with his artist friends in some wretched dive. I've already sent him back to Rome post haste, to get on with his work! Dear Tamburi is a great artist, but he's also a great shirker. If I don't keep constantly threatening him, he'll soon be worth only half of what I pay him. Do you have any idea of how much it costs me to keep publishing *Prospettive*?"

"Malaparte, then what they say about you really is true: you're a skinflint," exclaimed Sirignano, laughing.

"You see, Prince? Even you are beginning to have it in for me. Like Mussolini."

"What's Mussolini got to do with it? Stop blaming the Duce for everything. Mussolini's a fathead. But you, with your provocations, forced him to teach you a lesson. That's why he had you framed by the OVRA."

The guests were swarming around us on their way out. I buttoned up my jacket and raised my collar, there was a nasty fresh breeze blowing, August was really over.

"No, Sirignano. It's not like you think. The reason, the real reason, is quite different. It's the war. Now war's on the point of breaking out, a war that'll seem endless, a war we'll lose – worse, a war we already lost a long time ago. Mussolini knows perfectly well how I badmouth him in Roman society, in Capri, wherever I go. He could have had me framed by the OVRA two or three years ago. But he did it only now. Why? Because war's coming. Because there's no more room now for unruly brats like Malaparte. Because dreamtime's over, now begins the hard slog, the nets are tightening. Vertical liberation will soon be on the way."

"Vertical?"

"Bombs, Sirignano. The American bombs that'll soon come raining down from on high to liberate us – vertically – and we'll have deserved them. All, all of us in rotten Europe, with our Mussolini, our OVRA, our Edda and Galeazzo Ciano, our Capri, our Chantecler."

Silently, unwillingly, we sipped at the last drops of our orange blossom. We didn't want to leave one another, not out of affection, but fear. For the first time, we were afraid. Now we'd have to get used to living with fear, fear was our future life. I put my glass down on a little wall.

"Farewell, Prince."

I turned on my heels and left, without giving him the time to answer, walking briskly down the driveway of the Fortino.

CAPRI, SEPTEMBER 1ST, 1939

Moussolini

Later, at four in the morning (but I wasn't yet to know that) the German 3rd army crossed the Polish frontier and went roaring on to Warsaw. It was the first day of September and the first day of the war, the one we'd already lost even before fighting it.

At that moment Febo and I were at House like Me, sitting on the edge of the terrace. We were barking at a distant dog, which was returning us fraternal greetings. The moon shone blinding white, like a silver dish under the anti-aircraft searchlights. Suddenly the dog stopped answering us. It had been shut up by its master, or maybe it had fallen asleep.

Silence fell like an axe. Now we could only hear the waves licking at Cape Massullo, and their blue-green breathing.

"So, what d'you say, shall I throw it into the sea or not?"

Febo looked at me wagging his tail. He too wasn't sure what to do. For about half an hour I'd been holding the Sturmbannführer's saber, and I still couldn't make my mind up.

I readied myself to fling it into the sea, far, far off, beyond Sicily, beyond Africa. But at the last moment, I stopped.

It was a fine sword, but something was telling me that I should throw it into the sea. I didn't know where that thought came from, it was irrational. Maybe it was just my desire to make an end of that whole story.

"But it's a lovely saber. It might come in useful again, sooner or later," I kept saying to myself.

It was then that I saw Mussolini.

He was dead, hanging head downwards, exactly like what did happen to him six years later, and he was talking to me. He was looking at me just as he'd looked when he was alive, with that rather jeering expression, a bit severe, yet with a soft spot for my harebrained youth. It was the look he'd always had, except that now he was upside down. In that brief flash of vision, the war was over and Fascism had lost, people were spitting at Mussolini's corpse hanging from a meat hook, they were pissing on him, they were insulting him, but he was talking to me.

"Malaparte, don't pity me," he said, "no one should pity me."

"That's not true, even dictators should be pitied. Even Mussolini, even Hitler," I said.

I emerged from my daydream; I was again on the terrace. I held the Sturmbannführer's sword in my hand. Again, I made ready to throw it, standing right on the edge of the terrace, as tensed up as a javelin thrower... but that second time too, I did not throw it.

"Did you see? I haven't the nerve," I said. Febo answered with a rather weak bark. He was lying stretched out, he was sleepy, his muzzle was weighing down on his paws.

"Malaparte, throw that saber into the sea."

Again Mussolini was speaking to me, hanging head down, with the blood from his throat running down his face.

"Throw away that saber, I tell you!" he repeated even louder, "It won't be any use to you, the times are changing. There'll be no more duelling. Throw away your tail-suit, your brilliantine, your fountain pen, your gaiters, all those old-fashioned things. Vertical liberation's on the way. D'you want to know how we'll all end up? After the autopsy, they'll remove my lungs, my liver, my kidneys and all my guts. They'll whip the lot up and make a fine mousse. I'll become *Moussolini*, and the rest of my body will be an empty bag. The Americans have booked my brain. They'll put it in a glass vase and take it home to the USA to study it in a laboratory. Pray for me. Farewell, Malaparte".

Mussolini vanished, again I was alone with Febo. I smiled. I'd been dreaming in broad daylight. How tired I was! I was getting old, I must stop beating myself up, I must try to limit my alcohol intake, all that smoking and getting myself arrested. I looked at Febo: he was asleep.

Yet again I grasped the sword. I took it with just three fingers to make it fly a long, long way, like a paper airplane. I readied myself again and started my run.

The sea was murmuring, gently.

ROME, SUMMER 1957
SANATRIX CLINIC, ROOM 32

Death like Me

"There. I've finished."

I'd hardly pronounced these words than I felt exhausted. I was sitting up in bed; my legs, which had seemed to recover while I began dictating, weighed a ton. In the mirror by my bedside I caught a glimpse of my face, again pallid, sweating and emaciated. I studied my hands: they were as yellow and cold as the feet of a plucked hen and covered in bluish stains. The blood clots had returned to their place, time was up.

The Angel of Death with the typewriter completed the final sentence with a sharp rattle of keys on the Remington keyboard. He ended as he'd begun, at impressive speed and effortlessly. His colleague stopped reading the paper and turned towards me.

Death too looked at me, with her kind, compassionate face, the face of Mona Williams, the world's most beautiful and elegant woman.

"Is there nothing else you want to add to your novel?" she asked.

"No. I've written what I had to. Don't you like it?"

"The narrative's fine, even if one did suspect that Lucia might be rather more than the little schoolmistress she seemed. But that's not the point..."

"I knew it!" I broke in. "I'd never wanted to have a female protagonist in my novels, and now that I've gone and done it for once, I've got myself in trouble. Never allow women too much."

"Forget it, Malaparte, that's not the problem. Rather... have you nothing else to tell me?"

"I'm tired, Death. I think I've written a good novel. It's a tale I've made up, these things never happened, but it reveals my most deeply hidden wounds. I've exposed for all to see my defeats and failings, my soul's poverty, my abjectness. What more do you want of me? My pain is coming back. Leave me in peace and let me die, once and for all."

"Then sign it, Curzio."

She opened her handbag and handed me her splendid gold fountain pen, a really high-class pen.

"Parker?" I asked.

"Wahl Eversharp," came her icy reply.

The Angels of Death drew near. They handed me the enormous mass of typescripts that had accumulated during dictation. This was the fruit of my last exertions, Curzio Malaparte's final novel.

Death and I remained a moment together in silence, looking each other in the eyes. God, how beautiful she was! I wished I could get closer to her before dying, tear that glass of orange blossom from her hands and kiss her, as I'd done with Mona Williams in my novel.

I took the last page, and under the last words "the sea was murmuring, gently" I wrote THE END, and signed.

"Is that really all, then? Is there nothing you want to add? Say, a postscript, some little note?" Death asked again.

"No. I'm tired, I've put into this novel all that I am. Frankly, I wouldn't know what more I could do or say."

I gave her back her pen. The Angels of Death took the heavy typescript from my arms.

Death seemed both disappointed and amused. I could not understand whether under her unbelievably fine *bisquit* features she was hiding an immense sadness or, on the contrary, a kind of snigger.

She rose from my bedside. She came towards me and stopped by my side, smiling. Then, delicately, solemnly, she placed a hand on my forehead.

"I'm sorry, Curzio, but now it's time for you to see and know," she said.

At that moment, the ceiling of Room 32 rose, like the lid of a shoe box.

Above the roof I saw, not the sky but earth, an endless expanse of earth, a waste stretching into the far distance. But it was not normal earth, it was ashes. It was a desert of ashes, plains and immense dunes of ashes, nothing but ashes. The light was dim, a light fraught with terror, the light of a dead star, like the blind sun I'd seen so many times at war, only a thousand times paler, cold and lifeless. This was because, above the wasteland was no sky, no sun, no moon or stars, only an enormous void, an immense, empty, dead sack.

The plain of ashes split, opening into a mass of crevasses that covered it like a huge cobweb, it was all cracked like a dried-up riverbed. The cracks grew wider and wider, in them something could be seen swarming, seething and trying to get out, something trying to be born. Then I heard a vast, dissonant chorus, as though five hundred singers were all intoning the same melody, but each a few seconds behind the next, so that all was lost in a deafening buzz.

From the furrows a swarming mass oozed slowly forth, and I saw that it was all bones. It was the skeletons of men and women, millions of them, all kinds of them. They were trying desperately to climb out into the open, as chaotic and quarrelsome as a swarm of insects. They wanted to flee the darkness of those deep cracks, and to emerge at last into the light, even if that light was dim, a light laden with terror.

Every one struggled to rise by climbing over the bones of others, mindlessly, pitilessly crushing them. The dissonant chorus was all-pervading, a music that was almost material, it seemed as though you could touch it – I was jostled, weighed down, crushed by it.

The hand of the woman with Mona Williams' face still lay on my forehead, and it seemed to me to have become a radio, a wireless set, with her palm acting as an aerial that enabled me to receive special waves and to see the desert of ashes.

An inner voice told me that the scene which lay before me was the Triumph of Death, the final apocalypse. It was the world in its last moments, after the final destruction, when every error had been committed, every evil perpetrated. It was we men who had reduced the Earth to this, and in the end Death had made it her dominion. Nothing was left: plants, animals and men, all had been consumed by fire, leaving first embers, then ashes. All the bodies had been reduced to ashes, only bones remained.

The furrows in the waste of ashes had left off growing wider but were still vomiting forth that swarming, frenetic mass of skeletons. It looked like a termites' nest, like those I'd seen so many times in Eritrea, a febrile whitish mass struggling to leave its gigantic nest and flee everlasting darkness. The moment they got out from the cracks in the terrain, the skeletons would venture forth onto the desert plain, but there they found the ashes unbearably hot, for under them was a layer of burning embers which they uncovered with their every movement. After taking a few steps, the skeletons would dive back into the cracks in the earth, other skeletons would crush them, and they'd be sucked back down, while their fellows clambered over them to escape in their turn, only to come to the same wretched end. The inner voice told me that the skeletons were those unwilling to repent their evil acts who, through the exercise of their own will, were obliged to suffer through all eternity.

I became aware of a new presence in the plain. I was not materially present in that desert, but it was as though my eyes were there, and they were looking at all that lay around them.

In the midst of that waste of ashes was the sovereign of that world of horror: Death. She stood tall and erect as a tower, and she was looking at me. She was dressed according to the most classical tradition, with a black shroud and a hood, and in her hand she grasped a great scythe. I could not see her face, I saw only her bony hands holding the scythe and the bones of her feet emerging from under the shroud. She was immensely tall, perhaps twice the height of a human being. Suddenly, she tore off her hood and remained bare-headed. Around her neck there hung a diamond necklace with an enormous sapphire pendant, and her face was that of Mona Williams, but already eaten away by putrefaction. Her cheeks were hollow, her eyes half shrouded by the eyelids, her nose grown thin and sharp, her complexion yellowish, while almost all her hair had fallen out. Under the skin of her face and scalp the bones of the skull were already visible, pressing forward, anxious to emerge.

"I am sorry, Curzio," she said. "I gave you a last chance. But you failed. You were to write the novel that would save you, the novel of your expiation. It was to be a novel written from the heart. Do you remember? I'd sent you Sandro, your dear brother, to remind you of all that you needed to repent: Matteotti, your women, the Spanish dead in the Balearics… Instead, all you could do was to give in to the eternal temptation of vanity, to your writer's gift. You wanted to write an intelligent, original, well-crafted novel, full of interesting characters, fine images, sometimes even a bit improbable, like all novels, but still a thing of beauty. A novel that would win you admiration. Bravo, you've succeeded. It's a fine, original novel, written in your unmistakable style, drawing on all your gifts. It does you honor. But, over-concerned with your fame as a writer, you neglected the fate of your soul and failed to attain the goal. You've wasted your life, you've lived in vain, and you have no regrets about it. A pity, because yours was a good heart, when all's said and done, and you could have saved your soul. But presumption and ambition got the better of you."

"No, one moment!" I cried, "You know I've confessed all my errors and failings. So, where have I gone wrong?"

Death fell briefly silent and her eyes narrowed, as though she meant to carve her words in the air:

"Pain. In your book there's not even a trace of your pain. That was what mattered most, and you've left it out. You've confessed to many things, but your heart was not pierced by what you'd done. You've never really renounced your ego. When the chorus of your dead women came, instead of feeling their pain and asking for pardon, you drove them angrily away. You felt no pain even when you looked back to the massacres in the Balearic Islands – you applauded them. Likewise Matteotti's murderers, whom you helped. But if there's no pain, if there's no self-renunciation, there can be no redemption, and you can never be free. This is true for everyone, even for the just. You, however, remain entrenched in your pride. Your soul is disfigured by the harm you've done and by the good you could have done but failed to. In signing your novel, you have signed your own death warrant; and wasted the good you've done in your life. That is the verdict, there's nothing more that can be done. I am sorry."

As she spoke, I felt an immense force drawing me upwards, through the uncovered roof and bearing me from Room 32 to the plain of ashes, sucking me up bit by bit, eating away at me from below like gangrene: first the feet, then the shins, the knees and the thighs... My terrestrial body would remain in my bed, the doctors would record my death, the undertakers would bury it with all due honors and the newsmen would celebrate the event with splash headlines. But I'd end up forever in that host of skeletons struggling desperately to escape through the fissures in the terrain, only to throw themselves back into them, roasted by the eternal embers under the ash desert.

"Nooooo!" I screamed, struggling vainly to hold onto the bed. But there was nothing doing, my spiritual body was coming apart, falling to pieces, drawn inexorably towards the plain of ashes. I could neither weep nor pray, nor could I call for help, I had become a little incandescent sphere of pure terror. Piece by piece, my spiritual body kept rising; after the thighs came the hips, the belly...

Just then, I felt a pressure on my shoulder. Someone had touched me, but it was not Death or her angels, nor was it one of the skeleton-termites.

I turned. I no longer knew where I was, I saw a familiar face before me: Sister Carmelita. She had woken up.

"Signor Malaparte, excuse me, I fell asleep. You know, I just can't take this heat."

I was at the height of agony, I felt close to collapse, and soon I'd be swallowed up by the desert of ashes, yet I smiled.

I looked around: I was still in my bed. From the moment when my verdict had been pronounced, everything in Room 32 had returned to normal: Death and her angels had disappeared, I was once again a terminal patient, Sister Carmelita was no longer in lethargo and she was glancing all round her. She had not, however, yet realized that I was on the point of dying and these were my last moments of life.

I must find some idea, I said to myself, I must try some subterfuge, there must be a way out. But what am I saying? There's nothing more I can do, it's too late, Death has told me that clearly enough, the verdict has fallen: I have lived for nothing, soon I shall die and be drawn back into the wasteland of ashes. I began to weep, slowly, silently. Sister Carmelita was observing me. I felt that already my arms had been sucked away, and now the force was beginning to pluck at my chest. Soon the sentence would be carried out in full, and I was crying.

"Oh, Signor Malaparte," said Sister Carmelita, "don't be sad! If you only knew how many sick people are suffering in this hospital! If you knew how many are suffering pain like yours, or even worse! Now listen: a moment ago, I had a dream. I dreamed of a man, a young gentleman, in the company of a girl, a foreign girl, I think she must have been English. I don't know where they were, I only know that they were on holiday, near the sea, maybe it was an island... The landscape was lovely and there were olive trees everywhere. Well, in the midst of these olive trees, these two fine youngsters were eating chocolate and holding hands."

"Yes, we were eating chocolate…" I stammered, hoping that Carmelita would keep talking and finish her tale. I couldn't say why, but I knew it was important.

"And then a little bird that couldn't yet fly fell from its nest. The young man picked it up and put it back in the nest. In my dream, I thought: when all's said and done, it takes only a single gesture of love, just one single small deed, to change a life. Here's the secret. Keep your mind fixed on that small gesture and say to yourself 'I've done everything wrong, except for this one small thing. My God, how I wish I could go back and start everything all over again! How I wish I'd not lived in vain.' What a lovely dream, don't you think so, Signor Malaparte? Strange, but lovely."

Carmelita could know nothing of my last novel, written in the presence of Death. She could know nothing of my meeting with Pam. She could not know how among the olive groves of Anacapri Pam and I had exchanged kisses tasting of olives and chocolate, or of how, together, we'd saved a little fledgling, while talking of Emily Dickinson.

> *…or help one fainting Robin*
> *Unto his Nest again,*
> *I shall not live in vain.*

Suddenly Carmelita sensed that something was amiss. Now my heart was being drawn away. She studied my face, realized my catatonic state, called the medical staff, called my relatives, who'd gone out to get a bite to eat.

They all came into my room and within a matter of minutes I was surrounded by an anxious little crowd.

On my lips I still had those ingenuous, almost childish verses, recited with Pam at Anacapri:

> *If I can stop one Heart from breaking*
> *I shall not live in vain;*
> *If I can ease one Life the Aching,*
> *Or cool one pain,*
> *Or help one fainting Robin*
> *Unto his nest again,*
> *I shall not live in vain.*

By now my voice was hardly more than a breath, no one heard a single syllable. I was murmuring the poem, and my thoughts were running so fast.

Yes, in my life I had performed one small, puerile, laughable gesture of pure generosity. Not in order to feel pleased with myself, as when I sent money to those unfortunates who wrote to me from prison or from hospital, but just for the good of another being.

No, I gasped, I couldn't end up among the skeleton-termites. Heck, I'd done something that really mattered, for once I'd made someone happy without a thought for myself!

Or had it happened only in my novel? It doesn't matter, I said to myself, it comes to the same thing – for me, writing it was living it. A writer lives in his novels, it's they that count for him.

That consideration, the consideration that everything I'd written in my life was true and alive, both the bad things and the good, gave me a kind of inner warmth. I've saved a life, I thought, brimming over with hope, I really have saved a life, the life of a little bird, and out of pure generosity. My God, I've done everything wrong, everything except for that one small thing!

At that moment an immense, stabbing, strangling pain smashed my spirit. Suddenly, I wanted to spew up my entire existence, save for that brief instant in which I had saved a life.

"*Ya napliwayu* Malaparte! I spit on Malaparte!" I roared from the depths of my soul. There, I'd said it! A vast sense of liberation flooded me through and through. Pain racked and shook me. I was broken. I was filled with joy.

At that instant, the force that was drawing me towards the desert of ashes slowed down, weakened, and ceased. The vision of the skeleton-termites dissolved into nothingness.

Relatives, doctors and friends were all around me, and I cried out.

AUTHORS' NOTE

Pamela Reynolds died in Capri falling from a cliff on 27 May 1935. Her remains rest in the island's cemetery for non-Catholics, beside her father's. Even today, the causes of the accident remain obscure.

The Reynolds family had a nanny who later baptized her own daughter Pamela in memory or the young poet whose life had been cut tragically short. This Pamela still lives on Capri and remembers her mother telling her how Pamela Reynolds died falling from the órrico cliff, in the far northwest of the Island. Richard Reynolds' third (and only surviving) daughter, Hermione, went to America after marrying, and had four children there, who are still living. Hermione died in Ithaca (New York) on July 6th, 2003.

Pamela's poems, some of which are quoted in this book, are kept in the library of the Centro Ignazio Cerio in Capri, together with other documents relating to her father (Fondo Edwin Cerio, cartelle 274 & 275).

Richard Reynolds, secretary of the Fabian Society, returned to Capri in 1947 and died there on December 22nd. His activity as a consultant and adviser has still to be studied, as has his influence on many writers like J.R.R. Tolkien (who sent him advance copies of several manuscripts, including the first draft of the *Silmarillion*), Norman Douglas, Compton Mackenzie, Francis Brett Young, Algernon Blackwood, Edith Nesbit and others. Reynolds taught Tolkien at King Edward's School, Birmingham and chaired meetings of the TCBS (Tea Club Barrovian Society) the literary circle run in his youth by the author of *The Lord of the Rings*. There was a strong friendship between the two: Reynolds drove Tolkien by car to his first university exam in 1911, at a time when cars were a novelty. On their relationship, see Michael C. Drout (ed.) *J.R.R. Tolkien Encyclopedia, Scholarship and Critical Assessment* (New York: Routledge, 2007, *ad vocem*).

Some information about the Reynolds family is contained, in the correspondence of D.H. Lawrence (*The Letters of D.H. Lawrence, edited by J.T. Boulton and L. Vasey*: Cambridge University Press, 1979), as well as in J. Briggs, *Edith Nesbit. A Woman of Passion* (London: Hutchinson Press, 1987), and L. Marks – D. Porter, *Seeking Life Whole. Willa Cather and the Brewsters* (Madison, NJ: Fairleigh Dickinson University Press, 2009).

Hitler's inglorious conduct during the First World War, his acts of cowardice and his relations with his comrades-in-arms have been investigated and well told by Thomas Weber, *Hitler's First War* (Oxford: Oxford University Press, 2010). Weber was the first historian to study the archives of the List Regiment in which Hitler served during the First World War.

An abundant literature exists on Hitler's hysterical blindness and on the Führer's stay at Pasewalk, some of it incorporating conspiracy theories. According to some authors, Doctor Forster, who had young Hitler as a patient at the Pasewalk clinic, used hypnosis to "program", or at least to influence the future dictator. This thesis was mentioned by J. Armbruster, *Die Behandlung Adolf Hitlers im Lazarett Pasewalk 1918: Historische Mythenbildung durch einseitige bzw. spekulative Pathographie*, in "Journal für Neurologie, Neurochirurgie und Psychiatrie", 2009, vol. 10 (4), pp. 18-23. Edmund Forster published his experiments with hysterical soldiers under the title *Hysterische Reaktion und Simulation*, in "Monatsschrift für Psychiatrie und Neurologie", LXII/1917, pp. 298-324 and 370-81.

As to Hitler's presumed homosexual frequentations (quoted by Malaparte in a talk with Eddie von Bismarck), it was the SS officer Eugen Dollmann, Himmler's personal representative in Rome and the Führer's interpreter in Italy, who told of the embarrassing file, used for blackmailing the Führer, kept in a safe by the Munich *Sittenpolizei* (Vice Squad). Dollman, himself openly homosexual, refers to this in his book *Roma Nazista* ("*Nazi Rome*"), written immediately after the war and published only in Italy (last edition: Rizzoli, Milan 2002).

Hitler had Prince Philipp von Hessen arrested during the Second World War, fearing possible treason. His wife, Mafalda of Savoy, was interned in Buchenwald where she died in 1944 during an Allied bombardment. After the war, "Phli" was arrested and put on trial, but acquitted and released by the Americans in 1947. His property, which had been confiscated, was returned to him. He died in 1980.

Mona Williams fled from Capri after the outbreak of war and returned to the island in the summer of 1945. Meanwhile, however, in America she was suspected of pro-Nazi leanings and lost some of her old friends. In 1953 she inherited the immense fortune of Harrison Williams and two years later she married her beloved Eddie, becoming the Countess Mona von Bismarck. After Eddie's death she had a fifth husband, an Italian aristocrat who died prematurely after showing very little interest in the elderly millionairess but plenty in her millions. Again widowed, Mona had his surname cancelled from her entry in the register.

The world's most elegant woman died in her Paris home in 1983, after spending a great part of her fortune. The Fortino was divided into various villas, then sold to private buyers, and these are now let out as vacation homes. Her furniture and works of art were dispersed in a 1987 Sotheby's sale, and those described in this book are taken from the sales catalogue.

Edda Ciano, after losing her husband Galeazzo, shot by Mussolini in 1944, and having all her property confiscated by the new government, returned to Capri after the war, getting involved in a new love affair late in life with Chantecler, who received her in his new house at Tragara Point. She died in Rome in 1995.

Madame Carmen, alias Carmela Buronzo née Capasso, after being esoteric consultant to Mussolini and Edda Ciano, was still active in Capri as a clairvoyant after the war. She was called "the doctor of souls". Her husband Vincenzo Buronzo succeeded in getting himself appointed Senator of the Kingdom of Italy but held office for little more than a year, between 1943 and 1944. He was purged after the fall of Fascism and lost all his property, including his Deputy's pension, so that he died in poverty. Anyone interested in reading the correspondence between Buronzo, Madame Carmen and Mussolini can consult the documents kept in the Archivio di Stato di Roma (Rome public records office), Segreteria particolare del Duce, carteggio ordinario 1922-1943, file 1317.

Willy Kluck, the sculptor from Berlin, continued to be part of Capri's artistic fauna until his death in 1978. His philosophical whimsy of scattering pacifist maxims to the winds was told by, among others, Prince Sirignano in his memoir *Capri. Immagini e personaggi*, Naples 1985. His tiny house near the Migliera belvedere, which he himself called the "cube of solitude" (*Einsamkeitswürfel*) was acquired and restored by a couple of Swedish artists and is still inhabited. The other itinerant German philosopher in Capri, Miradois (real name, Gustav Julius Otto Döbrich), left the island and continued his wanderer's life, living in caves and holes in the ground, until he was killed by a stray American bullet not long after the end of the Second World War. Julius Spiegel, the deaf and dumb dancer and freeloader known as Gratìs, was suspected of being an English spy on the outbreak of war, and imprisoned. He was freed thanks to the intervention of Edda Ciano and Axel Munthe, but again arrested by the Germans, then later by the Americans. His strange career as a dancer continued after the war, gaining him the amazed admiration of Joan Crawford, Lana Turner, Jennifer Jones, Liz Taylor, Clark Gable and Orson Welles. He died in Capri in the mid '70s.

Friend and confidant of Malaparte, who asked his opinion and advice on his work, the American journalist Percy Winner was until 1945 a senior official in US military intelligence. After the war Winner returned to America and got his Italian friend into difficulties by publishing the novel *Dario 1925-1945: A Fictitious Reminiscence*, an imaginary portrait featuring novelist Dario Duvolti, modeled on Malaparte, who collaborates with the Allied secret services. Winner published two more novels on the topic of espionage, betrayal and the sense of guilt: *Scene in the Ice-Blue Eyes*, the tale of a spy who "sells" Italian agents to the British, and lastly (in the same year as the other two books!) the novel *The Mote and the Beam*, another tale of secret agents, deception and immorality in pre-war Europe. He died in 1974.

The painter Orfeo Tamburi left an entertaining memoir of his friend and employer, *Malaparte à contre-jour* (Paris: Denoël, 1979). He died in 1994.

The poems of Emily Dickinson translated by Malaparte during his internal exile on Lipari are to be found in volume III of Malaparte's private papers published by E. Ronchi Suckert (the writer's sister), *Malaparte 1932-1936*, Ponte alle Grazie, Firenze 1992.

The description of Malaparte's last days (visions of his brother Sandro, cardiac arrests, the oxygen tent, visits by Professor Pozzi, etc.) are based on reports by the journalist sent by the magazine *Tempo*, who covered the deathbed scene to the very end, to the last cry (F. Vegliani, *Malaparte*, Edizioni Daria Guarnati, Venice 1957).

Casa Come Me (House like Me) is now the property of a foundation. It is closed to the public and accessible only for study purposes. After years of dereliction, Malaparte's creation found tenacious (and generous) defenders in the writer's heirs, who have done the necessary to maintain a house constantly lashed by wind and waves. Innumerable studies and testimonials exist concerning the villa, as well as films like Jean-Luc Godard's famous *Le Mépris* (1963) with Brigitte Bardot and Michel

Piccoli. A frame of Casa come Me from this film was, incidentally, selected as the image/symbol of the 69th Cannes Festival (from 11 to 22 May 2016).

The war scenes at Bligny are based on the letters Malaparte sent to his family from the front (published by Paolo Giacomel in *Tu col cannone, io col fucile, Alessandro Suckert e Curzio Malaparte nella Grande* Guerra, Gaspari, Udine 2003).

Historians are still arguing over the knotty question of whether Malaparte wrote his war reports from Capri or from the front line. Pending a conclusive answer, we preferred to imagine that he did both.

The Russian expression *Ya napliwayu* (meaning "I spit on") was used by Malaparte in *The Skin*. It is a special jargon used by the Ukrainian Jews whom the writer encountered.

As willed by the writer, Curzio Malaparte's grave is to be found on the peak of Mount Spazzavento, near Prato. To get there takes about two hours' walk on rough footpaths along the slopes of the Bisenzio valley.

After the failure of negotiations to sell the Villa San Michele to Goering, and disturbed by the dramatic events of the war, Axel Munthe left Capri in 1943 and returned to Sweden for good. A source of information for Britain's MI6, he died in Stockholm six years later. Today the Villa San Michele has become a museum, while the Torre Materita has been acquired by private owners.

Arturo Assante, lawyer and journalist, was active as an OVRA spy under the code name "Argus". After the war he escaped the anti-Fascist purges and continued his career becoming the editor of important newspapers. OVRA informers present in Capri include, as we have seen, the film producer Luigi Freddi, the writer Italo Tavolato (code name "Tiberio"), the journalist Leone Da Zara and Questore Giovanni Manzi, the OVRA regional boss (code name "Settimio Zona"). Manzi was in possession of a confidential report on the sexual preferences of the Prince of Hesse, drawn up by Tavolato, who – according to Manzi himself – had "special competence" in this area (M. Leone de Andreis, *Capri 1939*, Edizioni In-Edit-A, Roma 2002, p. 13).

The tragic assassination of Deputy Giacomo Matteotti (1924) was for decades attributed to Mussolini on the basis of broad political motives. Recent historical research has, however, shown up a more concrete motive: Mussolini's need to silence Matteotti in order to cover up corruption affecting the Duce himself, together with innumerable accomplices, in favor of American oil interests in Italy. Chief merit for identifying and developing this line of research goes to the historian Mauro Canali (*Il delitto Matteotti. Affarismo e politica nel primo governo Mussolini*, Bologna 1997). Thanks to research in the American archives, Canali ha salso brought to light Malaparte's relations with the American secret services, in particular with Percy Winner («Nuova storia contemporanea», XIV, n. 4 [2009], pp. 13-22).

A precious source of information about Capri on the eve of the Second World War is the excellent (although by now practically unobtainable) *Capri 1939* by Marcella Leone de Andreis (cit.), together with all the collection of essays and narratives published by Edizioni La Conchiglia, a series cultivated lovingly and intelligently by the Capri bookseller/publishers Riccardo Esposito and Ausilia Veneruso, whose catalog has over the decades become a veritable editorial monument dedicated to the island.

The treatise on the civil and penal responsibility of animals entitled *Bestie delinquenti* (Naples 1892), written by the jurist Carlo d'Addosio, long a rare collectors' book, was reprinted in 2012 by publisher Forni of Bologna (Italy) in an anastatic edition.

The Christ of Saarburg (today Sarrebourg, after its reincorporation into France at the end of the First World War) is still in place. A few years after that war, it was decided to place a wooden support behind the statue as a precaution, although there was no sign of any structural risk. There are still many postcards in circulation recording the extraordinary phenomenon of the statue of Jesus that remains standing despite being deprived of the cross. The postcard reproduced in the book is our property.

The Lenin-Bogdanov chess match took place in Capri in 1908 on the terrace of Villa Blaesus. Many would like to find the chessboard on which the match of all times was played, but all trace of it has been lost.

In 1909 or 1910, according to witness accounts, Stalin is reported to have visited Capri in Lenin's company.

His role as organizer of the Lenin-Bogdanov challenge and founder of the School of Capri did not play in Maxim Gorky's favor: according to some historians, the writer was killed by Stalin in 1936 using a bacteriological weapon developed by the secret services at the Lubyanka.

After the death of Benito Mussolini, his brain was removed and sent to the United States for the purposes of unknown laboratory experiments. Only in 1966 did the Duce's widow succeed in regaining possession of part of the tissue. It is not known where or whether the remaining part of the sample is to be found in the USA.

The style of this novel is inevitably colored by that of its protagonist, especially his musical taste for repetition and for lengthy discursive sentences. In America readers will have had a chance to get to know Malaparte's singular prose thanks to a recent anthology translated by Walter Murch, *The Bird that swallowed its Cage. Selected works by Malaparte*, Counterpoint Press, Berkeley, 2012.

The titles of the chapters of this book are inspired by (or quoted from) novels and tales by Curzio Malaparte, and are an invitation to read the works of this fine, once famous, author.

Fame is a fickle food
Upon a shifting plate
Whose table once a
Guest but not
The second time is set.
Whose crumbs the crows inspect
And with ironic caw
Flap past it to the Farmer's Corn –
Men eat of it and die.

      Emily Dickinson

PHOTOGALLERY

In the '30s

Percy Winner

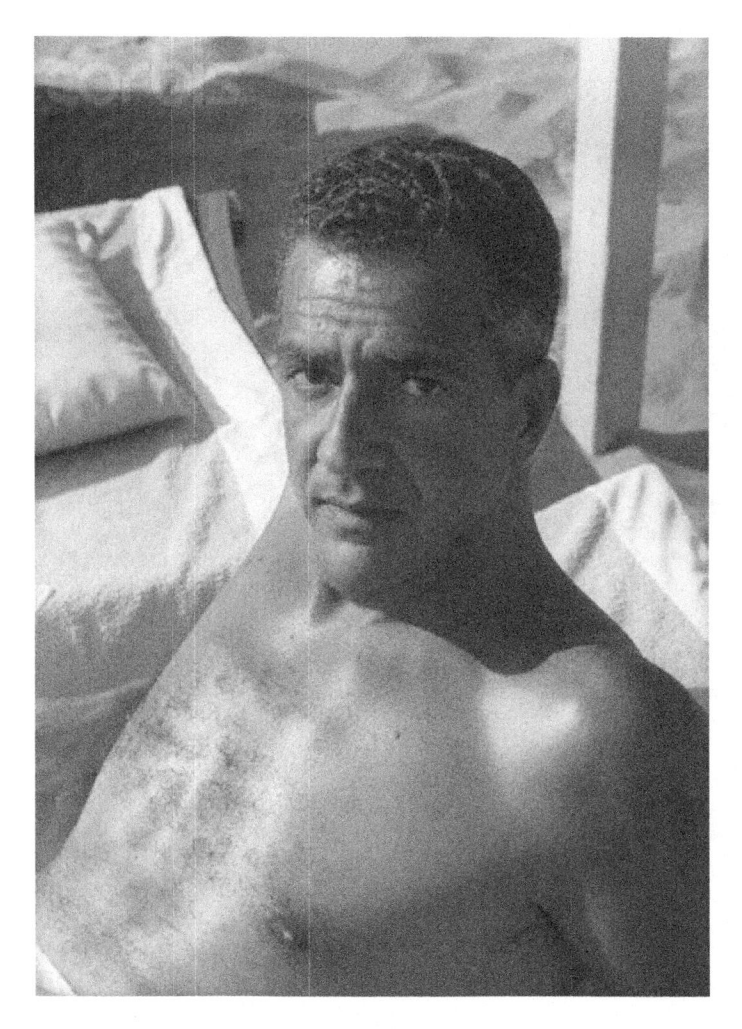

Prince of Sirignano

Mona Williams during one of her wild parties

Mona's Villa Il Fortino

Barbara Hutton

Gracie Fields

Gracie in 1935 at Capri…

…and with husband Monty Banks

Noel Coward in 1937

Princess Nadejda of Bragança

Febo with his beloved Malaparte, a few weeks after their first meeting

Chantecler at home

Chantecler with Ingrid Bergman…

…and with Jackie Onassis

Chantecler dressed as a woman in a party

Zum Kater Hiddigeigei in the early 20th century

The Hotel Quisisana in the '30s

Hermann Goering leaving the Quisisana after one of his visits

Edwin Cerio in his Capri home in the '60s

Cerio and his young wife Claretta

Maxim Gorky at Villa Blaesus, Capri

The chess match between Lenin (right) and Bogdanov (left). In the middle, Gorky

Gorky (first from left, standing) and a group of Russian revolutionaries at Capri

Axel Munthe in the '40s

Munthe's Torre Materita

Talking to his beloved dogs

Munthe with guests under the pergola of Villa San Michele

Villa San Michele

View from the Phoenician Steps towards Villa San Michele

The Òrrico cliff

Filippo Anfuso

Malaparte officer in WW I

Count Eddie von Bismarck

Richard W. Reynolds with his daughter Mynie at her wedding

Orfeo Tamburi

Malaparte at the Tiberio restaurant, smoothing back his well-greased hair

Pamela Reynolds

The grave of Pamela in Capri's non-catholic cemetery

The Reynolds sisters (from left to right Diana, Pam and Mynie)

Willy Kluck's carved stone portrait…

… and his house, the "cube of solitude", both on Via Migliera, Capri

Deaf-and-dumb dancer Julius Spiegel, aka Gratìs

Malaparte biking on the path that leads to his villa

The entrance as seen in the movie Contempt *(1963) by L.Godard*

House like Me, aka Villa Malaparte (© Alamy Stockfoto)

Brigitte Bardot and Michel Piccoli in Godard's Contempt

Villa Lysis, entrance and view from the front terrace

Villa Lysis, the living room and a panoramic terrace at the first floor

The owner of Villa Discopoli, baroness von Uexküll, and the entrance

A general view of Villa Discopoli

Edda Mussolini, husband Count Galeazzo Ciano and their children

Edda Mussolini in the '30s

Edda at Capri with Chantecler

Giacomo Matteotti

Harry Sinclair

Amerigo Dumini

Prince Philipp von Hessen, aka «Phli»

Princess Mafalda of Savoy between her children at Villa Mura, Capri

Dr. Edmund Forster, Hitler's military psychiatrist

Adolf Hitler aka «Ini» at WWI…

… and with his comrades of the List Regiment (first from right)

Spadaro the fisherman

Archeologist Amedeo Maiuri

In the '50s

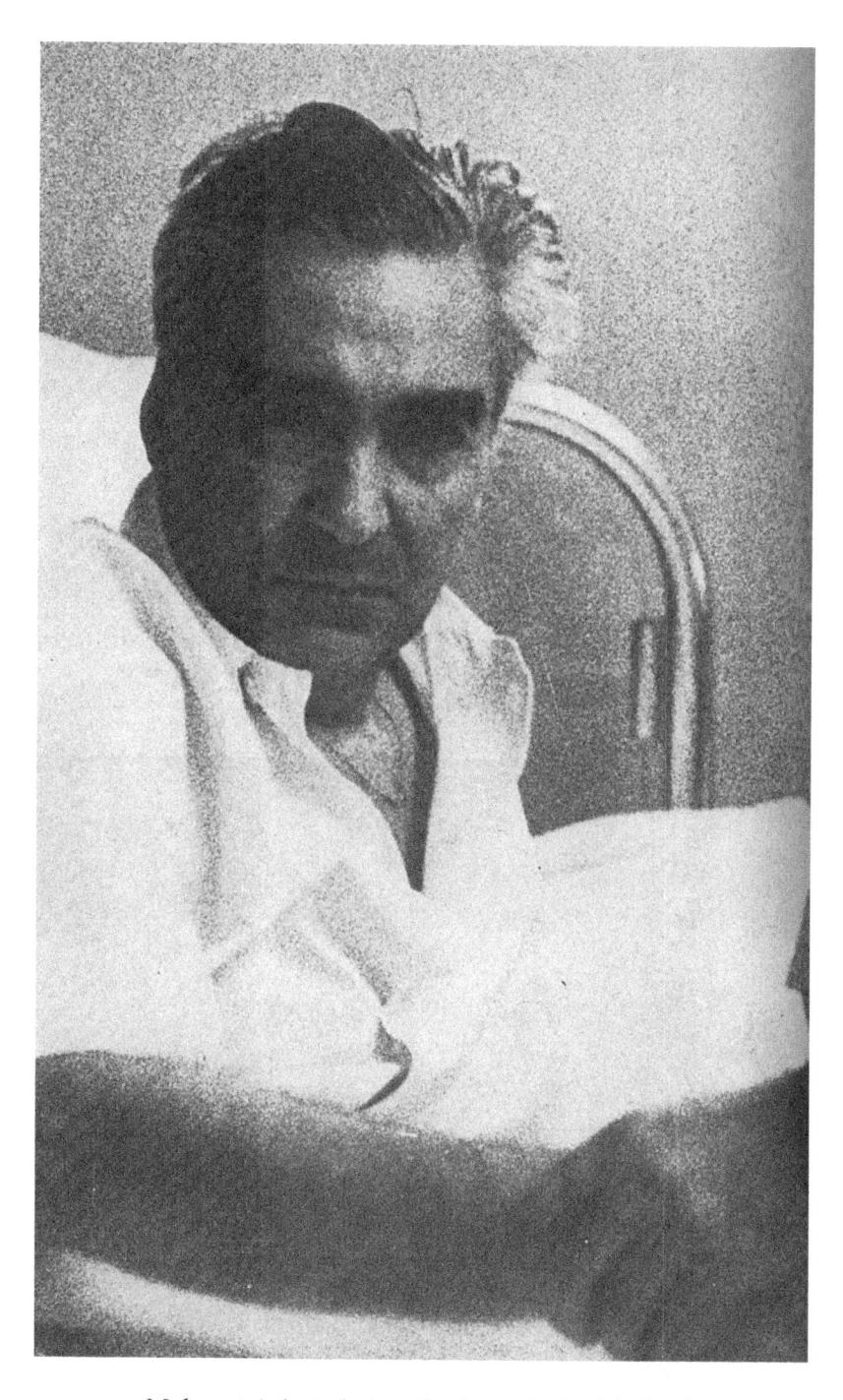

Malaparte's last photo, a few hours before his death

Made in the USA
Las Vegas, NV
15 August 2023

76145677R00308